No Rest for the Wicked

Mistress of None : Book One

Phoebe Darqueling

Black Rose Writing | Texas

ISBN: 978-1-68433-245-8
PUBLISHED BY BLACK ROSE WRITING
www.blackrosewriting.com

Printed in the United States of America
Suggested Retail Price (SRP) $19.95

No Rest for the Wicked is printed in Chaparral Pro

This book is dedicated to those who are brave enough to wander.
May you come to rest precisely when you wish it, and not a moment sooner.

Special thanks to the Sacramento History Museum.
Without my short tenure there and their excellent training,
Viola Thorne might never have been born.

No Rest for the Wicked

Mistress of None : Book One

Chapter 1

September 30, 1871
About two miles as the crow flies from Sacramento, California

Viola Thorne preferred to bathe by moonlight. Perhaps it was the quiet chirps of the crickets or the splash of stars above, but something about the nights here at the end of the world called out to her.

After weeks of aching muscles, she'd managed to reinforce the natural hot spring with stones from all over the ranch to build the perfect niche for soaking. Sulfurous steam rose off the water and eddied around her head and shoulders while the rest of her luxuriated in the gentle currents of heat.

A half-empty bottle of whiskey kept a waxed paper parcel company on the edge. Vi reached inside the package and pulled out a fragrant hunk of soap—the last of what she'd brought from back East four years earlier. No telling when she'd be able to get more, but she worked the bubbles through her hair and scalp with gusto. The smell of lilacs rose from the lather to combat the reek of rotten eggs emanating from the spring. Vi breathed it deep into her lungs as she closed her eyes against the tide of foam.

A sensation as light and dangerous as hornet wings fluttered on the back of her neck and slowed her hands. Miles away from anywhere anyone might possibly want to go, she should have been safe from prying eyes here in the pool, even in broad daylight.

All the same, someone was watching.

Unwilling to let the peeping Tom know she was on to him, Vi went back to washing her hair. She listened for the telltale crack of a twig or the whisper of cloth to indicate the direction of the infiltrator's approach. If it came down to it, she could always reach out with her other sense, but that was reserved for special occasions these days.

She leaned her head back to rinse, the lather floating around her tinged a dull red from the henna she used to muddy her identity. Though the chance of being recognized way out here remained remote, Vi favored distancing herself from her old life wherever she could. Her chestnut hair was a small sacrifice for obscurity.

The frontier night stretched out quiet and undisturbed before her, yet the prickling awareness spreading across her shoulders told her the invading presence somehow drew nearer. Beneath the water's surface, she brushed her fingers against her garter and the knife she always kept strapped to her calf. Having a jackrabbit for a stalker would be far more likely than encountering some poor soul wandering the prairie, but naked and alone (and if she was being honest, more than a little inebriated) out in a distant corner of her ranch, she couldn't take that risk.

With a deep breath, she reached into herself and quested for the feelings that always tickled at the edges of her consciousness. Reaching out with her mind, she washed through the waiting embers of her long-repressed senses. They flared to life, hot and sharp despite her years of denial. Vi allowed the unexpected feeling of satisfaction to curl the corner of her mouth before she returned to the task at hand.

Her audience stood behind her, his decidedly unrabbitlike outline burning vivid and blue inside her skull. In one fluid motion, her blade flashed moon-bright and hurtled toward the place he stood. A hollow "thunk" told her it had hit the tree behind him, just as she'd expected from the color of his aura.

"Are you crazy?" the ghost cried, patting his chest where the knife had passed straight through him. "You could kill someone like that!"

He took a few noiseless steps away from the offending blade, as if it intended to jump out of the tree and bite him.

"You're already dead," she mocked. "What are you so worried about?"

"What if I wasn't?"

With a shrug and a few splashes, Vi made her way over to the makeshift stone bench beneath the water's surface and settled upon it. "I knew what I was doing."

"Then what, pray tell, did you hope to accomplish with your little trick?" The insubstantial form crossed his arms and peered at her from under the brim of his transparent bowler hat. Even in death, the fine cut of his clothes marked him as an outsider the same way his accent marked him as a New Englander.

Vi twisted her hair into a coil at the top of her head before breathing out a contented sigh and resting against a pillow of moss. "I was hoping it would make you go away. So, if you don't mind?" Her fingers fluttered in a gesture of dismissal and she closed her eyes.

A few silent seconds ticked by, and she dared to hope he'd go before his curiosity shattered the quiet again. "Where did you even pull that knife from?"

He craned his neck as if he could see beneath the silver ripples of the pool. Vi's head snapped forward, face red from more than the heat of the spring. "It was strapped to my leg, you degenerate. Now go away. I want to finish my bath in peace."

The ghost removed his hat and simpered, "Please, I must speak with you."

"No. What you must do is move on and stop bothering the living. I'm out of the business of running errands for the dead, thank you very much." She traced shallow, annoyed furrows in the water with her fingers.

"But you don't even know what I want."

"No."

"It's my wife, you see—"

"Still no."

"There are these men and—"

"Definitely no."

"We owe them some money—"

"I can keep this up all night," she warned.

"But they're going to—"

"No."

"Please!"

Vi raised her hands above the water and moved them like a conductor as she sang to the tune of a new song that had been making the rounds. "I'm not interested in helping, all the live-long day." She let her hands drop back into the water with a splash.

If he could breathe, his chest would have been heaving in anger. In his current state, the ghost had to settle for pulling a sour face. "Well, I had to try. My wife is—was—my whole life." He donned his spectral hat and turned to leave, mumbling to himself, "He warned you that she wouldn't help."

"Yep, he was right," Vi called lazily. Then the water surged around her as she sat forward with sudden interest. "Wait. Who warned you I wouldn't help?" After the lengths she'd gone to to disappear, there shouldn't be anyone for hundreds of miles who knew about her "special talent."

"Will you help me if I tell you?" the ghost asked, hope written in the lines of his gently glowing face.

Vi squinted and sniffed. "I can guarantee I *won't* help you if you don't."

The spirit smiled and waved his hands in imitation of her earlier display. "I'm not interested in telling, all the live-long day."

She glared at the ripples on the pool. Not knowing the identity of her referrer was going to eat at her, but the information alone couldn't be worth the price of dealing with him.

Hat in hand, he tried again. "Forgive me. Please? I promise, I'll tell you the whole sorry tale of how I found out about you as soon as you agree to help me."

"No wonder you've gotten yourself into trouble," Vi spat. "You shouldn't offer to pay someone up front; you need to hold onto whatever it is for leverage."

"All right. Then I promise to tell you after you help me."

"Nope. Still not interested. It would take a lot more than that to get me involved."

His face fell for a moment before he brightened. "Well, there's always the gold."

Vi's smirk returned. "You didn't say anything about gold before."

"You didn't let me get that far!" The spirit took a few eager steps in her direction as he began, but his restlessness kept him pacing as he spoke. "I spent all I had getting out here. So, I owed money for my prospecting equipment, but I wasn't having any luck panning. When they came around to collect, I told them I'd go out again and try farther up the river. They gave me until noon tomorrow to pay my debt, but I don't think anyone really expected me to find anything."

"Of course they didn't. The big strike in these parts happened when I was a girl."

He stopped walking for a moment. Even in his insubstantial state, greed glinted in his eyes. "But I did. I found enough to pay them back and make up our losses from the trail."

"And then you died. That's a poor stretch of luck."

"I was jumped a few hours' walk from here by some bandits." He pointed out into the distance behind Vi and her hot spring. "They took my equipment and my mule, but they didn't take my gold."

She chuckled. "They must not have been very *good* bandits."

"No, you see, I buried it," he said with a hint of satisfaction. "I knew there might be people like them roaming around, so I dug a hole before I went to sleep and stashed it there."

"And we see how well that worked out for you."

"Well, yes, they were rather unhappy when they saw I was a prospector but wouldn't give them any gold." He allowed himself a gratified laugh, but the next memory sobered him again. "They beat on me for a spell, trying to get the information, but I knew if they took the gold, that was the end for me anyway. You see, ma'am, if I don't get that gold to Salty somehow, they said they'd kill her. They're going to kill my wife! I can't let her pay for my mistakes."

"Ugh, of course. Another man, another woman caught in the crossfire." Vi gave the water another contemplative splash. "That sounds like Salty all right."

"You know him?"

"He puts on airs like he's some sort of businessman, but there's a big difference between business and his way of doing things." She wrung the final drops of water out of her hair before letting it spill loose across her shoulders. "Even so, we have an understanding of sorts."

"So, you'll help me?"

"No." She stood, water streaming down her torso. "But I'll help your wife."

The ghost turned away in a flurry of embarrassed splutters. No surprise there—the frontier always ate up and spat out the honorable ones like tobacco. If he were an ordinary man, she'd have been more self-conscious about her nudity, but as ghosts are generally limited to looking and nothing more, she tended to treat them like furniture. The air was cool after her long soak in the spring, and she climbed onto the bank to retrieve her clothes.

"Well, if we're going to be working this job together, I suppose introductions are in order." The final button fastened, she grabbed her whiskey and took another swig. The world tilted and blurred pleasantly as she moved to retrieve her knife from the tree. "I suppose your mysterious informant told you I'm Vi, and you are...Oh, sorry. And you were...?"

He whirled back, a pained expression on his face. "I don't see what is so funny about all this."

"Sorry," she mumbled, making a show of shoving her foot into an oversized boot to avert her eyes. "This isn't my first time talking to a ghost, but I suppose this is the first time you've died."

"Obviously," he retorted, laughter bubbling up before receding into a weary sigh. An uncomfortable silence followed, and Vi cleared her throat. "Ah yes, my name. It's Tobias."

"Okay, Toby, this 'buried treasure' of yours, it's marked with an X or something?"

"Not exactly... I'll have to lead you there."

Vi pulled on her second boot and straightened. "When do we leave?

CHAPTER 2

October 1, 1871

The song of the prairie night disappeared, banished by the blush of morning.

Though picturesque, it was definitely not a time of day Vi usually considered possible. This went double for mornings after a late night full of whiskey and steam.

"Wake up, Vi!" Tobias called for what seemed like at least the thousandth time.

She dragged her stiff tongue around her sour mouth before groaning, "I heard you."

"It's about time," the ghost grumped. "We need to get moving if we are going to get to the gold and back before twelve."

"Is there time for coffee?" Vi pinched the bridge of her nose.

"Not really."

Her ability to glare remained unaffected by the hangover. "Let me rephrase that: There is time for coffee."

Tobias fussed while she lit a lamp and built the fire in the stove. As Vi poured the dark powder into the pot, she frowned; it was almost gone, too. Unlike her favorite soap, coffee was a cargo hauled by the regular steamboat traffic on the Sacramento, but the price varied depending on supply and demand, and she hated to haggle when she didn't have any power. After all, if she didn't buy it, someone else definitely would.

Vi took stock of her other supplies. With her spartan approach to existence on the ranch, it didn't take long. One cup, one plate, one fork—one person making an effort to make as small a dent in the world as possible didn't need much. Her place in town was nicer if she needed creature comforts, but sometimes whiling away the long nights, she had to admit a partner for cribbage wouldn't have gone amiss. Of course, it was safer for everyone this way.

When steam rolled off the water, she tipped the contents of one pot into the other and leaned into the fragrant plume. The smell of coffee helped clear away some of her whiskey-induced cobwebs, and she almost remembered how to smile again.

While her breakfast steeped, Vi gave yesterday's shirt a quick sniff and deemed it passable. On the other hand, the skirt she'd been wearing wouldn't be the best for horseback, so she pulled out one of the pairs of trousers she'd picked up after meeting some gauchos on her way around the horn. The *chiripá* over-layer may not be flattering, but it sure kept a body comfortable in the saddle.

She started toward the door, then remembered her uninvited guest. The poncho she pulled over her head made her voice come out porridge-thick. "I'm going to go get my horse ready while the coffee's brewing."

"I'll come with you. I could use a stroll."

"Suit yourself."

She grabbed the lamp and went outside, the ghost trailing behind. A barn slouched a few paces away, appearing as perturbed by the earliness of the hour as Vi. The only one happy to be awake was Smithy, who nickered a greeting when she pushed the barn door aside. He got a pat and a smile before she started checking the tack. Though no stranger to riding, she'd just learned how to take care of the equipment herself when she'd come out West. Now, the soft feel of the oiled leather and the clean glint of metal in the lamplight gave her a swell of pride.

"Any chance you've got two horses?"

"No, I've only got Smithy." Vi gave the black gelding's broad back a few strokes with a brush before grabbing a saddle blanket from the railing where she'd left it to air out. It cracked like a whip as she flapped it, sending a cascade of black hairs dancing. "But even if I had another horse, you can't ride."

"How would you know?" he whined. "I did fine on my mule."

She shook her head, sending the room into a momentary, bleary haze. It was hard to keep the annoyance out of her voice with last night's excesses pounding inside her skull, but she tried to treat his inane question with patience.

"It's not personal. It's spiritual, er, or scientific, or something. I don't actually know the specifics." Vi massaged the space between her brows and the pain receded a few paces. She smoothed the saddle blanket across her mount, then turned around to retrieve the saddle. "That is to say, I had someone try to tell me about it, but I'm a terrible listener. But you must have realized you can't touch things, right?"

A groan escaped her throat as she heaved the saddle onto Smithy. Despite the weight dropped unceremoniously onto his broad back, the horse remained still and obedient under her touch.

"Well, of course," Tobias chuckled. "If I could dig up the gold myself, I wouldn't need your help. I'm not completely incompetent."

Vi made her adjustments and looped the leather straps into place. Once she tested the cinch, she gestured between the ghost and the waiting saddle. "Okay. Hop on."

With a sniff, Tobias walked into the stall and reached for the pommel. Inevitably, his hand passed right through it. Next, he tried a stirrup, but his fancy, posthumous boot never made contact, sending him toppling through Smithy and onto the ground at Vi's feet.

The only thing stopping her laughter was the pounding between her eyes. "I'll keep the 'I told you so' to myself, shall I?"

The ghost got to his feet, his head sticking up through the saddle just enough to see the surprise in his eyes. The horse gave a twitch at the sensation of having a phantom pass through his midsection.

Tobias took a step backward to view Vi across Smithy's back rather than through it. "What about those stories?" he demanded, voice reedy with embarrassment. "The ones in the monthly. Ghosts knock on walls and move things. And people can see them."

She shrugged and took the bridle from its nail. "Sure, some ghosts can do plenty. The longer it takes you to cross over, the more likely you'll figure out how to move things. Not that it would be a good thing if you could, mind."

"Why not? That seems like a pretty fine consolation prize to me. I could at least write messages."

Vi sighed. "Honestly, it doesn't happen often. And it would mean it is harder to pass over when the time comes. Getting yourself seen by the living without some help is even rarer."

Tobias stroked a neat, semi-transparent mustache. "What kind of help?"

"Some ghosts learn how to crawl inside of objects," she evaded. "Heirlooms and the like. Though for some reason, there are certain materials they never touch."

"Could I do that? Haunt something and you carry me?"

Vi gave an exasperated, theatrical shrug. "Like I said, none of this is common. And believe it or not, I'm no expert. As far as I know, ghosts just sort of wander about, occasionally making demands of the living."

The bit clacked against Smithy's teeth as he took it. Vi rubbed his velvety, black snout with one hand as she drew the bridle over his ears with the other.

"Are you sure I have to walk all the way back out there?" the ghost bellyached.

"Well..." She smirked. "You could always run. It's not like you'll ever get tired."

"Nice to know death has *some* advantages."

"Absolutely. Think of all that pesky eating and belching you won't have to do anymore."

The dead man sulked while she finished getting ready to leave. With a broad-brimmed hat on her head and her supplies stowed in her saddlebags, Vi mounted up. Smithy had never gotten used to the slow pace out West, so he pulled at the reins, eager to be given his head. She kept him to a walk for the long miles to keep from leaving her guide behind.

The twitter of cardinals and towhees joined the horse's heavy footfalls as the morning progressed. Using her hand to shield her eyes, Vi squinted at the pale streak of the rising sun as it struggled over the Sierras and under her hat brim. The rainy season was due to return within a few weeks, but at the moment the rolling foothills were covered with parched grass and the occasional clump of stunted trees. The rain would be good for the prairie, but her body had been through too much to favor the cold. She planned to close the ranch house for the season any day now. There was less protection from gossips and prying eyes in town, but it was a small price to pay for the heat of a radiator during the damp winter months.

Tobias broke the silence. "So, what brought you all the way out here?"

"An annoying dead fellow, about yay high." She passed her hand through the top of his head and he lurched away. "Anybody you know?"

"No," he said with a laugh. "I mean what brought you to California?"

Vi returned her gaze to the horizon. "How far did you say we need to go? I've got things to do, you know."

"We're getting close… I think."

"You *think?*" The reluctant medium hit him with a glare before reaching into her saddlebag and retrieving her flask of coffee.

"Yes, we're getting close. But you didn't answer my question." Vi focused all her attention on unscrewing the top and taking a long swig of the gritty brew. "Come on," he prodded. "Why are you in California? Were you born here or…?"

She wiped her mouth with the back of her hand, savoring the freedom to behave so poorly. "My life story is both terribly interesting and something I have no intention of telling you."

The ghost stopped walking and crossed his arms in consternation. "And what's wrong with me?"

Vi pulled Smithy to a stop, twisting in her saddle to face him. "I like my privacy."

"Uh-huh. So, you're saying it has nothing to do with me being a spirit?"

She made a show of acting hurt and surprised. "How dare you? There are plenty of spirits I like. Whiskey, for instance. Rum…"

He grimaced. "You obviously don't like ghosts, though I can't really see—"

"Look," she snapped. "When I finish this errand of yours, you're going to pass over anyway. Why do you even care?"

His ethereal face didn't have any blood in it to start with, but he grew paler and stuttered, "Pass over?"

Despite her better judgment, Vi felt sorry for him. "Well, sure. That's the point of all this, isn't it? To finish your unfinished business?"

"I guess I hadn't thought that far ahead," Tobias said sheepishly. "I just wanted to help Bonnie."

Vi turned away from the longing in his voice and gave Smithy a squeeze to get them moving again. "That's your wife?"

"Yes," the ghost sighed, falling in step beside her. "She's an amazing woman. Dropped everything and came out here with me on this damn fool enterprise. Now, she's going to be all alone...."

The pause stretched on for too many footfalls. Vi finally blurted something to break it. "Malaeska."

"Um. Bless you?"

"It's a name," she chuckled. "*Malaeska; the Indian Wife of the White Hunter.* It's a dime novel I read as a kid."

"Okay...?"

"I'm answering your question. It's what inspired me to come to California."

"Really?"

"What, didn't think I could read?"

"No, that's not it." He thought for a moment. "It's, well, a rather *romantic* thing to do, following a book. You don't strike me as the sentimental type."

She snorted. "Ah well, *Malaeska* is why I chose California, but it has nothing to do with why I left in the first place. *That* wasn't sentiment, it was one-hundred-per-cent pragmatism. It was time to move on."

They crested the hill they'd been climbing. Tobias pointed to a clump of trees at the bottom of the trough and they meandered their way through the scrub. As they reached the edge of the copse, a huge snore ripped through the morning calm.

"Were you traveling with anyone else?" Vi hissed, tightening the reins and bringing them to a stop.

"No," Tobias whispered back. "And I didn't see a single house between my strike and town."

The sun was high enough now that a trickle of sweat ran from the edge of her hair and between her shoulder blades. "Well, shit. You know what that means?"

"It must be that gang. The ones who killed me."

"Yep," she drawled, leaning in to pat Smithy's neck. "Things just got a whole lot more complicated."

CHAPTER 3

Until they knew more, they agreed to go back to the top of the hill. Smithy snuffled and browsed while Vi lazed against a rock, soaking in the sun. She had her poncho balled behind her head and the brim of her hat pulled low to combat the glare. The coffee was long gone and fighting a losing battle against the effects of the previous night. If Tobias didn't come back soon, he'd have to wake her all over again.

Eventually, she caught the flicker of an approaching presence. She lay still as her companion crept along, his movements exaggerated and slow like a poor impression of a cat. With a flip of her wrist, she tossed a handful of pebbles right through his head.

"How do you do that?" the ghost cried. He gasped, and slapped his hands over his mouth.

Vi chuckled and sat up, her hat falling to the ground at her side. "They can't hear you. Remember?"

Tobias sighed in relief. "Oh, right."

"What did you find out?" She stood and beat her hat against her leg a few times to free it of grass.

"There's at least a dozen men."

"You could have mentioned this when you enlisted me," she said, scowling.

"Just a few men jumped me. I had no idea there'd be so many. Or that they'd be *here*."

"I guess that explains how they found you." Vi pulled her hat back on and peered at him with laughing eyes. "You camped right next door."

"I think we've established I fouled everything up, thank you. May I go on?" Hands on hips, he tapped his foot. She gave him a by-your-leave gesture and leaned against the boulder. "As I was saying, there are at least a dozen men. But there are also at least a dozen empty bottles around the camp as well. Kindred spirits, eh?"

"It's not like I was *expecting* anyone when you showed up," she said, grimacing. "But dead to the world. That's good."

"Unfortunately—"

"I was afraid there was going to be and 'unfortunately.'"

"—there's no fast way for you to go around. There's too many bushes and such on the hillsides. You're going to have to skirt right alongside the camp in order to get to the gold."

Vi pushed off from the rock and marched toward her horse. "I don't think you're paying me enough for this," she said.

"You don't know how much I'm paying you," Tobias reminded her. "And the only way to find out is to dig up the gold."

"You're getting better at this. But I could still walk away," she countered, a sly smile on her face. "I could forget this whole thing. Or maybe I come back later after they've moved on and keep all the gold for myself."

The glowing fog of Tobias' form darkened, and his edges became harder, his body something like a liquid rather than a vapor. "If you back out now," he replied, his voice an uncharacteristic growl, "and anything happens to Bonnie, I swear I will haunt you for the rest of your life."

The moments stretched as she met him glower for glower. Finally, she snarled, "Ask me again why I have a problem with ghosts."

Vi turned and closed the gap between her and Smithy. She undid the strap of the saddlebag and yanked the leather satchel open so Tobias could see the small shovel she'd been in the middle of retrieving.

He turned pale and misty again, his face awash with shame. "I'm sorry, really I am. I just love her so much."

"Yeah, I picked up on that." Vi threw the saddlebag over her shoulder and started walking down the hill. "But threaten me again and we're *done*."

The long, dry grasses rustled and cracked under her feet, but the noise couldn't be helped. When they reached the bottom, the blades gave way to tall trees that cast hazy shadows wherever the sunshine was high enough to touch them. They soon came upon the camp and proved the ghost true to his word. The bandits lay scattered around on blankets and sprawled over sacks of whatever they'd pilfered, last night's fires cold, black smudges iced with ash. The skeletons of covered wagons were piled off to the side along with a stack of wooden crates. She was tempted by the carton marked "coffee" but thought better of it.

"I think it's safe to say they aren't simply passing through," she whispered.

"They're dug in like ticks," Tobias agreed. They picked their way through the underbrush for a few hundred feet until the ghost swiveled around to face her. He pulled off his hat and fidgeted, eyes on his hands. "There's... something else I need to tell you."

"Now?" Vi gritted her teeth. "This probably isn't the best time."

"Yeah... I think now's the right time."

"Ugh, fine. Spit it out."

"The gold. It's... well. It's under my body."

Vi knuckled between her eyes in what was now becoming an all-too-habitual gesture in his presence. "What do you mean 'under' your body?"

"I thought that would be the safest way to do it."

"You've got to be kidding me," she hissed.

"When I filled in the hole, I put my blanket over it to cover the evidence. I suppose someone may have moved me and stolen the blanket, but the last time I saw the hole, I was still right on top of it."

With a sigh, she lowered the saddlebag to the ground. After a moment of quiet searching, she tugged out a worn, blue handkerchief. "And how long ago was that?"

"Why does it matter?" His voice became high with panic. "You're still going to go get my gold, right?"

Vi pulled the cloth across the lower half of her face and yanked the knot tight behind her head. Her hazel eyes flashed with mocking above the paisley. "I wanted to know how bad you're going to smell."

His mouth opened and closed a few times while she pressed on. The sounds of the camp faded as they rounded the trunk of a massive fallen tree. Even with her handkerchief in place, she smelled Tobias before she saw him about a hundred paces farther along.

He was lying with his back to her, knees curled, and spine bent in agony.

The sleeping roll was under him as promised; evidently, the bandits didn't know they'd left him for dead, or they'd have taken everything. As soon as the wind changed, the stench would reach the camp and they wouldn't be able to ignore him any longer.

Chubby, blue flies buzzed all around but scattered at the sound of her approach. She struggled not to cough as the smell of decay coated her throat and filled her lungs. He'd died at least three days ago, by her calculations. Only the presence of humans so close by had kept the animals from dragging him away, so there he lay between her and some shiny gold nuggets.

Despite the bile churning inside of her, she crept to the edge of his sleeping mat closest to his boots and gave it a heave. The ghost started to protest at her rough handling, but whether it was caused by the sight of his own head lolling in the dirt or his practical side taking over, he said nothing. Another hard pull and she'd moved him far enough to reveal the scarred earth beneath, his limbs lolling like jelly and maggots writhing in his wake.

She swallowed a throatful of vomit. "How deep do I need to go?"

"Just a foot or so."

Vi pulled out the trowel and a pair of gloves. The soil was loose from when Tobias had dug his hole, and she soon had a neat pile of dirt at her side and a filthy leather pouch in her hands. A low whistle escaped her lips as she hefted it in her palm. Maybe he *was* paying her enough after all. She brushed it off as best she could before putting it under her hat for safe-keeping. The stench, in combination with the remnants of last night's whiskey, made her dizzy. She was all too glad to get to her feet and put some distance between herself and the dead body at her side.

"Remember," the ghost said with a shake of his finger. "Most of that gold is going to Bonnie to pay my debts."

"Yes, yes. I remember." She tugged off her gloves and looked up to find the ghost staring wistfully at his body.

Hope made his eyes wide and childlike when he turned his gaze to her. "Do you think—"

"Don't get any ideas, Toby."

"You don't know what I was going to ask," he protested.

Vi put her hands on her hips. "Yes, I do. And I don't have time to bury you. We're on a tight schedule, remember? This whole thing has already taken longer than it should have."

"Of course," Tobias muttered.

"Oh yeah?" A gruff male voice spoke up behind them, sending them both spinning on their heels. "Where you got to be, darling?"

"Yeah," sniffed a second man. "What's your hurry?"

CHAPTER 4

Two grimy men were approaching from the direction of the camp, and Vi cursed under her breath. She should have felt them coming.

The one who'd spoken first appeared to be more beard than man. The other had the scars of some childhood ailment contorting his leer. The outlaws separated and paced to either side of her, the scarred man passing right through Tobias without realizing it.

"Vi," the ghost cried. "What should I do?"

"Gentlemen." She turned her face from one bandit to the other. "I've been looking for you."

Beard-face scratched his head. "You... huh?" Weariness pulled on the folds of his eyes; he'd barely had a chance to wake up.

"Us?" The other one squinted at her—sharp, awake, dangerous.

"What are you doing?" Tobias shouted. "You've got to run!"

"Well, not you specifically," she said cheerfully, ignoring the ghost. "But I heard there were some men out here with goods to buy, and I find myself with a powerful need for some coffee."

"Isn't that a stroke of luck?" The scarred man licked his lips. "Because we know all about *powerful needs*." His bearded companion made a lecherous grunt and took a step closer.

"I can pay you for it," she assured them. Vi took a step back and to her right, careful to keep both of them in view. "Don't you think your boss would like you to bring in a potential customer?"

"What's the boss got to do with our little party?" Beard-face reached out and tugged away her makeshift mask. "He don't even know about this place, or that fella."

Without the protection of the cloth, the odor of putrefaction redoubled, and Vi struggled not to choke. The scarred man jerked his chin toward Tobias's corpse. "I guess we got carried away with him. We'll make sure to be more careful with you."

He drew a step nearer, and Vi held up her hands. "I'm unarmed, so there's no reason to get excited."

The ghost slapped his palm against his forehead. "Idiot. Why would you tell them that?"

The scarred man snickered and took another step.

Vi's fist flashed out lightning quick and hit Beard-face in the throat. Despite the riot of coarse hairs protecting him, the blow caught his windpipe, and he fell spluttering to the ground. She jerked her thumb at the other would-be attacker as she grinned at Tobias. "Because I needed this one to come closer."

The scarred man stood with mouth hanging open. "What the f—"

The sharp heel of her boot came down on his ankle. Then he was on the ground with his companion and clutching his abdomen in pain.

The ghost stood blinking for a few seconds before he could collect himself enough to speak. "How do you *do* that?"

Her chest heaved more than she'd like, but it was satisfying to know that lack of practice hadn't made her slow. "Come on." Vi stooped to retrieve her saddlebag. "We've got to get moving. I can handle two, but we both know there are a lot more of them out there. And they're probably armed."

With her hand clamped onto her hat and saddlebag bouncing against her back, she crashed along through the underbrush in a line leading right to the heart of the camp. It wouldn't take long for the men writhing on the ground to regain their faculties and raise the alarm regardless, so no point being stealthy now.

She burst through a wall of grass, barely managing to stay on her feet as she hurtled forward. Someone had coaxed a fire to life since she'd passed by the first time, but for the most part the bandits still lay sleeping. A few men shifted toward the noise, their movements slow as basking lizards.

The scarred man's shrill voice called out as he and Beard-face stumbled toward camp behind her. A murmur rippled through the scattered bodies as man after man shook himself to wakefulness. Lungs burning, Vi urged her legs to carry her faster.

The ghost pulled ahead, unhindered by the threat of tripping or the need to breathe. The campfire glowed a few hundred feet away. Three men loafed against hay bales while a fourth used a spoon to poke at the contents of a pot suspended over the blaze.

"Look out!" Tobias shouted over his shoulder. "You've got some live ones."

If she could have spared the oxygen, Vi would have let loose some colorful language. Instead, she jumped over a sleeping bear of a man and pounded ahead.

The cook glanced from his porridge and caught sight of Vi's flailing limbs and long scarlet braid. He nudged the man closest to him. "Hey Boss?"

"Yep?" The bandana around his neck danced as he swallowed.

"We got any women in the gang?"

Jeb sat forward and wiped his nose on his sleeve. "What are you talking about, Hank?"

"Well, see, there's a wo—"

Vi dashed by and shoved over the wooden frame. Porridge flew through the air and onto the laps of the two men, sending them shrieking to their feet. They scrambled to free themselves from the sticky, boiling oats. She could hear their friends rouse themselves enough to laugh at their misfortune before she left the clearing and dodged through the trees.

By the time she reached the top of the hill, she could hear angry shouting coming from the camp. Smithy pawed at the ground and tossed his head in agitation. She collapsed against his solid, ebony flank and gasped for air, his earthy scent filling her nose and banishing the last of the smell of death from her nostrils.

"We're running out of time!" Tobias cried, pointing at the sun creeping across the mid-morning sky.

"I know," Vi puffed. "I'm going to have to leave you behind."

"That's all right. You go on ahead and I'll catch up."

"Where can I find your wife?"

"We're supposed to meet Salty at some saloon near the hotel. It had an instrument in the name. Fiddle, or maybe violin? No, *Vee-ola*."

She shook her head and reattached the saddlebag. "It's Vie-ola, actually."

"So, you know the place?"

Her laugh came out gruff and clipped. "I should be able to manage. That's *my* place. Salty likes to bring folks there because it makes him look good. Though, I thought I'd put a stop to him using it to make the sort of deals he made with you."

"Finally, some good luck." The ghost took in her knit brow and met her scowl for scowl. "What now?"

"I thought you should know... It's possible the moment I put that gold in Bonnie's hands you're going to pass over."

"I—what?" Tobias gaped at her.

"Unless we're wrong about what's holding you here, when I finish your unfinished business for you, you'll probably move on right then and there."

His voice broke her heart with every syllable. "I won't get to say goodbye to her?"

"I could be wrong," she replied, swinging herself onto Smithy's broad back with a chuckle. "Do you owe anyone else money?"

The angry sounds drifting from the camp grew louder, and Tobias smiled wanly. "So, I guess this is probably farewell."

"Yep, I suppose it is." Vi swallowed around an unexpected lump in her throat. "Wish I could say it's been fun."

"Thank you. For everything. This thing you can do. It's plenty strange, but it's also saved my Bonnie. I wish I could repay the debt."

Her loathing for farewells constricted her throat further, but she achieved a grunted, "You're welcome."

"Will it..." The ghost's eyes were trained on his boots, but several conflicting emotions played across his face. He mumbled, "Oh, never mind."

"What?" she coaxed.

"Will it hurt? Passing over?" He wagged a spectral finger at her. "And don't say you've never done it before so you can't tell me. You know more than you're saying."

"It might," she admitted. "But it's different for everyone."

"And what about you, Miss Vi? What does the hereafter hold for you?"

"Still a mystery, Toby." The thrashing and shouting got closer and Vi's uneasy gaze flicked to the hill and back to the ghost's face. "Speaking of mysteries. You owe me a name."

"The gent who told me where to find you? He didn't give me a name as such."

She smoldered. "You don't even have a name?"

"He said to tell you 'the boy is called Ignorance.' Whatever that means."

"What?" Her skin went cold, her voice soft. She must have heard him wrong. It couldn't be true.

"That's what he said. Seems like a stupid name for a child, if you ask me." The ghost shrugged.

Vi sat frozen except to murmur, "You're certain that's what he said?"

"Yes, I'm certain," Tobias replied. "Now get! Or I'll be forced to haunt you after all."

She kept the implications at bay with a cough, then managed a wan smile for the ghost. "And you still try to make it to town, you hear? You might get that goodbye yet."

In the camp, the bandits were still putting together the pieces. They stumbled about, groggy and disorganized. Some of them had taken off after the interloper on foot, their voices muffled by the swish and crackle of grass as they followed.

"Hank," Jeb growled, the hot stain cooling on his crotch. He shot a glare at the clump of horses standing unsaddled inside the slovenly collection of posts and crossbars they called a corral.

The other man tumbled back against a bale. He fanned himself with a rumpled hat; one of the many casualties of Vi's visit. "Yeah, Boss?"

"What was that about a woman?" he asked, stroking a cropped, black goatee.

Hank jerked his thumb over his shoulder and furrowed his brow. "Well, she just run by here y'see, and—"

"You get a gander at her face?" Jeb sniffed and sat back on the hay bale, his eyes boring into the hole Vi had left in the branches as she passed out of sight.

The lackey jammed his hat onto the bird's nest that passed for his hair. "I s'pose," he mumbled.

"I think we ought to go on into town and look her up," the outlaw replied, slapping Hank on the shoulder. "She owes us breakfast."

Chapter 5

Smithy fell into a steady rhythm, and Vi bent low against his neck as they galloped. The bandits wouldn't get a chance to get themselves pulled together and mounted up in time to catch her, but she wasn't racing other horses; she was racing the sun.

Tobias's words rolled over her in a distracted loop as she rode. It was impossible. No one knew where to find her, let alone any person who knew the significance of the line. Yet somehow the impossible had become possible.

"Peter." His name toppled from her lips for the first time since she'd left him and her old life behind. If anyone but her horse had witnessed the tears forming on her lashes, she would have blamed the breeze for putting grit in her eye. Instead, she was grateful the prairie wind dried the guilty tears before they could fall. No time for petty indulgences now.

He'd finally managed to find her, not to mention a way to use the dead to flush her out. Peter had always been the one interested in studying her "gift," so it shouldn't be all that surprising he found a way to tap into it himself.

It had been so long since she'd used their code that her recall was hazy, but the line from Dickens was a message. The question was, what was he trying to tell her? Given their past, it could just as easily be a threat as an invitation to dinner. The key to his meaning laid waiting on her bookshelf in town, and she silently urged her mount on to greater speed.

After a stretch of hard riding, Sacramento sprawled out along the river's edge before her. The smell of the water reached far beyond its shore, mingling with the billows from smokestacks along the pier. Stagecoaches and horses clogged the roadways, and pedestrians strolled along the raised wooden sidewalks as far as the eye could see. When she'd first arrived in California, this waterway and the steamers that traversed it were the easiest way to reach the capital, but the completion of the first rail line through the Rocky Mountains a few years prior had opened the city to unprecedented growth.

Smithy expertly nosed his way around the obstacles until they reached a loosely cobbled side street and slipped down the alley. His flanks heaved and nostrils flared as Vi dismounted. When she reached to slip off his bridle, he bumped her with his muzzle.

"You're welcome," she crooned and finished removing the jumble of leather straps and steel rings from his head. "You cool down a spell, and I'll send the kid out to tend to you."

She climbed the small set of stairs and pushed through the back door of the saloon. On the other side, a mantel clock reported it was ten minutes to noon.

Viola's catered to a certain class of clientele who rarely stumbled in before evening, so everything lay quiet. A passage on her left led to her second-story apartment and her carefully notated volume of *A Christmas Carol*, but finishing with Tobias's business had to take priority. Vi stowed her outer layers in a chest in the entryway, and with the pouch of gold weighing down her belt, she pushed through a door on her right.

An oil lamp by the door threw soft black shadows around the stockroom. A rustling in the corner grabbed Vi's attention, and she stood rooted to the spot. The occasional rat was to be expected, but this sounded much bigger. She reached out and turned the screw on the lamp, and it blazed to life. The rustling crescendoed, accompanied by a yelp and the unmistakable thud of a human skull meeting wood.

Vi's heartbeat dropped back to normal, and she kicked the crate nearest to her. "God dammit, you two. You scared me half to death."

A round face ringed with the mussed yellow curls of *Viola's* serving girl peeked out from behind a wooden carton. "It's Caroline, Miss Viola. Just… um… looking for some rum." She grabbed one of the bottles in front of her, trying to appear nonchalant and failing miserably.

"Uh-huh. So, what you're telling me is that when I go through that door, I'm going to find my bartender behind the bar, right where he belongs?"

"Well, see," the waitress sputtered, "Jimmy went out a couple of minutes ago to—"

Vi sighed. "Jimmy?"

"Yes, Miss Viola?" squeaked a young, male voice from somewhere behind the stack of boxes.

"I want you back behind that bar in five minutes."

"Yes'm."

Caroline had enough sense to look guilty when Vi shifted her gaze to include her. "I'm sorry, Vi. It's just, we went through the ceremony, but we still don't got our own place yet. We're with Jimmy's folks, and it's driving us crazy."

"I understand," she replied, then raised her voice so both of them could hear her. "Really, I do. But this *never* happens again during working hours. Understood?"

"Yes ma'am," the couple chimed in unison.

Vi reached to take the bottle from the blond. "Also, this is bourbon. I trust you can tell the difference when you're serving the customers." She winked and leaned in for a conspiratorial whisper. "Five minutes, Care. Make them count."

"Yes ma'am," Caroline giggled and disappeared behind the crates again.

With a shrug, Vi turned down the lamp before leaving the stockroom as she'd found it. "Newlyweds," she sighed, gazing at the whiskey in her hand. After the morning she was having, a little hair of the dog might be exactly what the doctor ordered.

The main room of the saloon turned out to be almost as empty as it sounded, except for a boy wiping tables. She squinted into the gloom and also found a woman sitting alone, a dark silhouette by the front window. Presumably, this was the famous Bonnie, early for her meeting with Salty and Tobias. She startled at the sound of Vi entering the room, then managed a polite bob of her head before turning her attention back out the window. One hand rested on a tarnished pocket watch, its delicate ticking filling the silent room.

Along one wall, rows of bottles stood guard from their shelves, waiting patiently for night to come and the real excitement to begin. Mirrored glass of every shape and size hung behind the bar, an attempt to bring more light into the dark room. Vi had made the mistake of accepting a mirror in lieu of payment once, so she'd gotten the reputation for liking them. If someone wanted to be on her good side, or wait another week before settling his tab, she added another mirror to the wall.

One exception was the painted wooden sign that read: House Rules. *Viola's* may not have been the largest or the most high-end establishment in town, but it was amazing what a few words scrawled on a sign could do for keeping the peace. That, and the knowledge that any fighting would lead to confiscation of the contents of the losers' pockets proved to be an effective deterrent.

As she sidled up behind the counter, not one, but dozens of reflected, sour-faced Vis made their way behind the bar and rifled around for a glass. The cork came out with a pop and took a bounce after she spat it onto the counter in front of her. The sweet-sharp smell of liquor burst out of the bottle and permeated the air as she poured two fingers, tossed it back, and poured a second glass. She added a splash of water and held it to the light to watch the liquids swirl, her free hand fondling the leather pouch. On top of the hill, she'd only been teasing Tobias when she'd talked about keeping the money for herself, but now it was there in her hands, the idea didn't sound half bad.

"George," Vi called.

The child put down his rag and ran over to where she stood. She smiled at his eager face.

"You go out back and give Smithy a nice brush down, all right?"

"Yes, Miss Viola."

He took off toward the stock room, but she remembered what was going on back there and she called out again. "Actually, first I need you to go down to Michaelson's."

The boy's eyes grew wide. "The candy store?"

"Yep," she said as she pulled out a tin behind the counter. "I hear they have those new bars of chocolate in now, and I've been dying to try one." She found a dime—enough to buy a dozen sweets—and sent it spinning through the air for George to catch. "Now, I'm going to want to see some coins come back with you, but I want you to take a long time choosing something for yourself. All right?"

"Yes ma'am!" He pocketed the coin and took off at a run out the front door. Vi chuckled; she could always count on Michaelson's when she needed the kid out of the way for a while.

The woman by the window fidgeted with her shawl. Her worry bubbled up and released in a weary sigh. Bonnie's body drooped against her chair, her anxiety no longer strong enough to keep her spine straight. Midday was marching closer and closer, and there she sat waiting for a Tobias who would never come.

Vi's breath caught in her throat; the tableau of defeat and sorrow was more familiar than she'd like to admit. She took a gulp of air before grabbing the bottle of bourbon and a second glass, then strode over to the table.

Bonnie took a moment to realize she wasn't alone and dragged herself to a sitting position. "Excuse me. That is to say, can I help you?"

Vi flicked her gaze to the front door, but there was no sign of Salty or his inevitable entourage yet. She clanked the bottle and glasses down. "I'm here to help *you*."

"What do you mean? Who are you?" The little brunette clutched at the other woman's hands. "Where's Tobias? Where's my husband?"

"We don't have time for questions," Vi twisted herself free of Bonnie's frantic grip. "Tobias can't be here right now, but he sent me to help." That was about as much truth as she seemed able to take.

"Why can't he be here?"

"That's another question." Vi wagged her finger and slipped into the other chair. "Now. It's almost noon. Salty's going to be here any minute, right?"

Bonnie went limp again. "Yes, but I don't have his money."

"I've dealt with him before." Vi pulled out the pouch and let it clunk to the table. "Leave him to me."

CHAPTER 6

The clock struck twelve.

Later, the glow of the footlights and the happy warmth of lanterns would light the room, but at the moment all was cool and calm inside its walls. The bottle of whiskey sat open and inviting in the center of the table, an empty glass waiting in front of an open stool.

Vi sat alone when the front door swung open to let in the scuffling sounds of the outside world. The murky stink of Salty's stubby cigar arrived at her table before his trim form. As he and his tailored gray suit stepped into the gloom, she could make out details of the neat, white beard that earned him his nickname. Two of his burly "business associates" darkened the door behind him. They didn't need fancy duds to make an entrance; their sheer size said everything a person needed to know about what their special role in the enterprise.

"Why, is that my friend Salty?" She motioned to the vacant seat. "Come, bend the old elbow and sit a spell. I'd love to have us a nice little chin wag."

"That's mighty kind of you, Miss Viola." He clenched the cigar in an oily grin. "But isn't it early for that?"

"Speaking of early, I'm surprised to see you here. I'm hardly ever here at this time myself. But I suppose you knew that."

"All the same," he replied tightly. "I'm afraid I have an appointment. So, if you'll excuse me?"

Vi held the bottle in his path when he tried to pass. "It isn't the sort of appointment I told you couldn't happen here anymore, is it?"

Salty glanced over his shoulder before straightening his tie; a nervous tic she'd noticed the first time they'd met. He took his cigar out of his mouth and jerked his chin at the bar. "Give us a moment, boys."

As the henchmen sidled up to the empty counter, a lanky man with sandy hair backed out of the storeroom, his fingers poised over his unfastened buttons. Jimmy gave a small yelp of surprise before rushing behind the bar and taking drink orders from the living mountains.

Salty undid the button on his jacket, then sat in the empty chair. His hostess splashed whiskey into the second glass and inched it toward him. Before she removed her hand, she caught his eye. "Don't lie to me."

He yanked the cigar from his mouth and used it to punctuate the end of his sentence. "I haven't said anything yet."

"I thought I'd save us the trouble of dancing around the subject." Vi lifted her hand from his glass. With a contented pull from her own drink, she relaxed back in her chair. "So, why do you keep doing this, Salty? I told you, you and yours are welcome to come in here, holler at some of my entertainers, and run up a tab that occasionally gets paid if it means keeping the peace. But I don't want you treating this like some type of headquarters. This is *my* place. I earned it."

"I swear, Miss Viola, I don't have any idea what you're talking about." Salty grabbed his glass and sniffed at the contents appreciatively.

"I met your friend Tobias."

"Oh, well, that wasn't a hustle. That was a business transaction." The chiseler drew out the final syllables. On a reflex, Vi noted that the suit had to be a new addition to his wardrobe; Salty's wandering accent told her he'd seen more hard living than the three-piece suggested. "He bought some equipment on credit, and he needs to pay me for it." His snowy beard bobbed as he swallowed a gulp of whiskey.

"I have no intention of getting in the way of business. Though you and I both know he had a better chance of being struck by lightning than striking gold out there after all these years."

Salty balanced the lit end of his cigar on the rim of his glass and held up his empty hands as if that would absolve him. "That's not up to me. He made the decision, I can't be responsible for his bad choices."

"But you have no problem profiting from one," she said levelly.

"Well sure, it's business." His guffaw boomed deeper than the laughter from a man of his size had any right to boom. He picked up the cigar and tapped the ash into a miniature snowstorm fluttering to the floor, then lifted his glass to toast her. When he took in her dark expression, he added a few confused crinkles to his sun-beaten brow. Hints of a coarse accent crept into his speech. "What's going on here? You've looked the other way on more'n this before. I suppose you're going to want a cut, now. Zat it?"

Before she could protest, the door burst open and all heads turned. Another one of Salty's regular entourage dragged Bonnie along by the elbow. She had a piece of paper clenched in her other fist, pressed firmly against her heart.

The henchman glowered. "This is her, right boss? I think she was planning to run."

"Let her go!" Vi snapped, getting to her feet. "She was on her way here, you idiot."

Bonnie wrenched her arm free and walked over to Salty. "Here you are. It's everything we owe you." She threw the banknote onto the table.

He reached out a perfumed hand and retrieved the paper. After a glance at the scrawl, he tossed it back down. "Where's the gold? And your husband? I made a deal with *Mr. Murphy* to get paid in *gold* for my investment."

"This spends even better than gold," she asserted.

"And what about the interest?"

Vi growled, "Don't push it, Salty."

Bonnie kept her bottom lip from quivering, but looked every inch the frightened eighteen-year-old she was. She shifted her concerned gaze to the other woman and back again. "What interest?"

"I gave you an extension, remember? This isn't enough anymore. The interest makes it, oh, let's see. Double."

The little brunette gasped and turned her worried face to Vi. The grifter gave a minute shake of her head. They both knew Tobias's strike could have paid Salty's demand four times over, but Salty didn't need to know it, too.

Bonnie added a convincing tremor to her voice as she implored the old man, "But, it's all I've got. You simply must accept it."

"I *mustn't* do much of anything, Mrs. Murphy," he said smugly. He sat forward and let his lecherous gaze wander. With a puff of smoke, he continued, "Except to think of a way for you to work off the other half of what you owe me." The henchman at his side chuckled.

"I'll play you for it." Vi slapped her hand onto the banknote and grinned. Bonnie had performed her role perfectly. "You and me. One hand of blackjack. I win, you take that banknote, and the deal is done. I lose, I'll make up the rest. You game?"

A thrill rippled through her body, and when she caught her own reflection on the mirrored wall, her hazel eyes sparkled even greener than usual. She hadn't picked up a deck of cards or bunkoed anybody since coming to California, but today appeared to be a day for reliving her past. And as with talking to the dead, the old compulsion came back with a vengeance. Her ears craved the familiar patter against a tabletop as the dealer bridged.

"I've got a deck right here." Jimmy pulled out a set of stained playing cards tied with a string.

Vi picked them out of the air when the bartender tossed them over. "If you're going to do business in my house, you've got to play by my rules, and I say we're playing for it."

Salty's men lost interest in their drinks and slid away from the bar. Their boss fiddled with the knot of his tie, reluctant to take her up on her challenge. Men like him didn't have the stones for gambling; they only liked to invest in things when they knew the outcome. She'd banked on the presence of witnesses to push him into accepting, but Vi now feared she'd overestimated his sense of pride. Of course, if he was comfortable with cowardice, then there were other means of persuasion. As the men approached, she whispered, but barely loud enough for Salty to hear her over the scuffle. "Playing cards together is something friends like to do, is it not? Friends also keep each other's secrets, such as certain threats made to Mrs. Murphy's safety. But I suppose if we are no longer friends...."

The grizzled man attempted a condescending laugh, but when he caught sight of her serious expression, it trailed off tight and worried. He made his face resolute by the time his lackeys finally stepped up beside him.

"All right, Miss Viola," he said a little too cheerily. "I'm in a generous mood. Let's see you put some money where that pretty mouth of yours is."

Vi shuffled and bridged a few times while everyone gathered around to watch. The notches she'd added to mark the cards caught on her callused fingers—her time out West had given her far more than peace of mind. Even through the thickened skin, she could still remember most of them by touch.

She dealt the cards with both of his, a ten and a six, facing up, but as the dealer, she got to keep one of her cards hidden. Salty chewed on the inside of his cheek as he pondered his next move and peered into Vi's inscrutable face. She lifted the corner of her second card, and though she already knew what she was going to find, her insides fluttered in anticipation.

He finally tapped his cards. "Hit me."

She kept the satisfaction from creeping onto her face as she flipped over a five, bringing his total to exactly twenty-one. His goons let out a whoop of triumph, and he gave his cigar a few smug puffs. Bonnie's mouth hung open, and she gawped at Vi in time to see her slight wink.

"I've got to hand it to you. You got me." She dipped her chin to underscore his prowess. "So how about you give me another chance? Double or nothing. If you win, I'll tear up your tab, and we'll be square."

Salty pulled the words like taffy. "All right, Miss Viola. Deal."

"Don't mind if I do." She chuckled and tossed out the next hand. To soften the inevitable, she made sure to give him a high hand of twenty this time, but couldn't resist twisting the knife and giving his goons a chance to slap him on the back and make their encouraging remarks before revealing her hand of twenty-one.

Vi raked the banknote toward her and stopped bothering to control her grin; a con well done. Just for fun, she twitched the twisted knife. "Always a pleasure doing *business* with you."

Her mark burst to his feet. "Wait… But, I—you must have done something."

"It was your choices that brought us here today, my friend. I can't be responsible for your bad decisions," she parroted with a goodly dose of mock sincerity, underscored by the hand placed oh-so-femininely on her collarbone.

His voice became low and dangerous. "I'm not going to forget this." Salty's goons had enough sense not to laugh, but they'd no doubt be telling this story in their cups that night.

She lazed back in her chair. "It was a *business* transaction, that's all." Twitch, twitch. "No use being sore over *business*, is there, Salty?"

He got in another dagger-laden glare, but had no choice but to grumble all the way to the door, his human mountain range in tow.

"I'll add those drinks to your tab, shall I?" Jimmy shouted.

The door swung closed behind the thugs, and Bonnie dared to exhale. "It worked. I mean, it did work, right? It's over?"

"He cannot very well go complain to the law now, can he?" Vi answered, handing the banknote back. "You'd better put this somewhere safe."

"You were so brave! I don't know how to thank you." The other woman collapsed into a chair and smoothed the wrinkled paper against the table top. "Tobias and me are lucky he met you. He'll be so happy when he finds out we got to keep it all."

"About that—"

"He had this grand plan," Bonnie prattled. "To come out here and get rich. Tobias always wanted to give me the world, but all I ever really needed was him. You know?"

Vi finished off her drink. "Bonnie, there's something I need to tell you. It's about Tobias."

"Yes?" She pulled her earnest brown eyes away from the note.

A male voice leaped from behind. "Did someone say my name?"

<h1 style="text-align:center">CHAPTER 7</h1>

"What about Tobias?" Bonnie asked, a slight tremor to her words. "Will he be here soon?"

Vi coughed, fighting the urge to spin around in her chair and glare at her unexpected acquaintance. As Bonnie couldn't see her dearly deceased husband, some subtlety would be in order. "We should go upstairs where we can be more comfortable and talk about it, okay?"

"It must be bad news."

"Did you do it?" Tobias ran around the table to look into Vi's face. "I saw Salty leaving, and he looked real angry."

"Yes," Vi answered both questions. "Jimmy, you've got the bar for a while." She stood and gestured to the back door. "Come on. I'm dying to change my clothes." Bonnie rose, and the ghost followed them past the empty stage and up the back stairway.

Her home in town couldn't be farther from the ranch in amenities and appearance, but despite the luxuries, she still had never come to feel like it was more than a dressing room. Rich colors and fine fabrics covered every inch that wasn't displaying cut crystal or artwork. Vi had met enough crooked bankers that she preferred to keep her rather substantial wealth nice and tangible.

The other woman let out a gasp of appreciation and ran her fingers over the gleaming woodwork. "I think this room might be the prettiest thing I've seen since we got to this terrible state. I wish we'd never come," she ended in a pained whisper.

Vi winced, all too aware Tobias could hear everything she said. He stood in the doorway, his relief at seeing her safe and the sorrow at their distance battling for possession of his features.

A satin couch smiled at them like a pair of crimson lips through the sitting room door. The Dickens books beckoned from a nearby bookshelf, but it would have to wait until Vi had finished with her guest. "Would you like some tea? Or something stronger?"

Bonnie passed right by the couch and lifted a lace curtain at the window. "He's dead. Isn't he?" she asked, her voice flat.

A memory cut through Vi like a stinging gash—back when it had been her turn to ask questions like that. She recoiled from her sorrow and pushed down the memory before replying to Bonnie's back. "I'm sorry."

"Oh honey. I'm so sorry!" Tobias cried, rushing to her side. "Vi, tell her how sorry I am."

"He wanted you to know…" she began, but her voice caught in her throat. Even after years of delivering the news of death, this part somehow never got any easier.

Bonnie turned away from the window, her face unexpectedly soft. "You lost someone, too. Didn't you?"

Vi did her best to swallow past the sour aftertaste of whiskey and keep her voice steady. "A long time ago."

The little brunette closed the gap between them in a few strides. Though she was the one with the fresh tragedy, she threw her arms around the other woman and crushed her into a bewildering embrace. Vi gave her a few awkward pats on the shoulder while Bonnie blubbered. "I knew it. Somehow, I knew he was gone. But I didn't want to believe it."

"Forgive my saying." Vi wriggled her way out of the hug but let Bonnie keep hold of her hands. "But it seems to me that in this day and age, the only purpose of a man is to die and leave behind the woman who loved him."

"Hey," Tobias objected from his place by the window. "It was an accident."

Bonnie looked over her shoulder to follow the sound and nearly burrowed through Vi to get away from the specter she could now see. She bolted away from the window, her face ashen and knees weak. "What was—what did I—where'd it go?"

Vi cursed her own stupidity; she never should have let herself be held.

"She heard me?" Tobias brightened and rushed to his wife's side. "Honey? Honey? I'm here, honey!"

Bonnie's lip quivered as her eyes darted all around the room in fear, but with the contact broken, the ghost was rendered invisible again. "Did you see it, too?"

"Yes," Vi replied apologetically. "I saw it."

"I'm not crazy?"

"Sorry," she sighed in frustration. "I'd planned to ease you into this."

Tobias peered intently into Bonnie's face, bursting with delight. "And she saw me, too. How is that possible?"

"What was that thing?" his wife's voice dripped with fear and disgust. "Is it dangerous?"

"No." Vi said firmly, then made an attempt to gentle her tone. "In fact, I know he would never hurt you."

"*He?*"

"It's me, Bonnie!" Tobias cried. "It's your sugar dumpling!"

"There's someone here who'd like to talk to you." Vi stepped over to where the other woman cowered and reached for her.

Bonnie gawked at her outstretched fingers and around the empty room before whimpering. "So, *you're* crazy, then?"

"She's not crazy, honey!" her husband shouted as if she were deaf or foreign rather than simply alive. "She's a clear-voy-ant."

Vi gritted her teeth and pressed on. "I promise you, Bonnie, this is really happening. And I'm here to help you."

"That's right!" Tobias called, just inches from Vi's head. Next, he added emphatic gesturing to the loud and elongated syllables. "Sheee iiiiz heeeeere tooooo helllllp yoooooooo!"

Vi could no longer contain her irritation and rounded on the ghost. "Could you shut your mouth for one goddamn minute, Tobias?"

"But I," he stammered and his whole body seemed to deflate. "I wanted to help."

"I'm trying to handle this, but I can't do it with you yammering."

"Sorry," he mumbled.

"Tobias?" a voice squeaked from the corner. Rage wash over Bonnie's face as she struggled to her feet. "What do you mean 'Tobias?' Is this some kind of sick joke?"

Vi wheeled back to face her. "I can explain—"

"What is wrong with you? This is cruel!"

She made a desperate grab for Bonnie's hand, but the other woman snatched it away before they could make the crucial contact. "Please, Tobias is—"

"Don't you dare say his name. Get away from me!"

"Bonnie, really! Tobias is—"

Vi's plea was cut off by a ringing slap across her face. The widow let out a peep of surprise as they touched and she saw the form of her husband appear and disappear again.

Bonnie had her hands clamped over her mouth, her eyes wide with shock. She took a few stuttering breaths through her fingers and managed to murmur, "Was that truly him?"

"As I was saying..." Vi stretched her jaw and touched the warmth gathering on her cheek. Apparently, some of her skills had gotten rusty after all. "Your husband is dead, *and* he'd like to say goodbye before he goes. But you need to touch me to do it."

One of Bonnie's shaking hands peeled away from her face. She reached out tentatively, whispering, "I'm sorry I slapped you."

"You can make it up to me later," Vi chuckled. "Right now, I need you to take my hand. I don't know how much time we've got."

The two women touched fingers and Bonnie gasped as her husband's pale form came into view.

Tobias gazed at his wife and let out a sad sigh. "Hello, my bonny lass."

"It really is you," Bonnie breathed, the tears welling in her eyes made him hard to see all over again. "What happened?"

Vi may have been the conduit, but she kept her eyes trained on a swirl in the carpet while the ghost brought his wife up to speed. She thought the less she was part of the conversation the better, but Tobias was making her out to be some breed of hero and Bonnie kept turning adoring eyes her way.

"...so, Vi had to leave me behind and ride like the devil himself was on her heels to get back to you. And evidently, she made it in time." Tobias smiled and tipped his hat at the reluctant medium in recognition.

"I'll say," Bonnie confirmed. "And in the end, that old snake didn't get any of the gold. I'll get to keep every cent."

The ghost turned from face to face. "He what? You're keeping it all?" His eyes fell on Vi, and she returned an embarrassed shrug. Bonnie didn't need to know she'd been offered a share and turned it down.

"Maybe that's why I didn't pass over," he said, smoothing his mustache as he pondered.

Bonnie's brow knitted in confusion. "What do you mean?"

"We thought as soon as Vi gave you the gold, I wouldn't be a ghost anymore. Something about finishing my unfinished business."

"So, what went wrong?"

"That's an excellent question, but one I don't know how to answer," Vi replied. "It's not always clear what's keeping a ghost here. Getting you out from under Salty's thumb seemed like a great candidate for the old 'unfinished business' approach, but it doesn't always work."

"It's my fault," Bonnie uttered. "I kept the gold and didn't give it to Salty."

Vi shook her head. "I doubt that's the issue. If it was really about the gold, then he could have passed over as soon as I dug it up."

"Good," the widow replied with relief. "Because I'm going to need it to get back home."

"Well, I guess this way I can stay and look after you," Tobias said.

"What, you, me, and Vi?" Bonnie barked out a bitter laugh. "One big, happy family?"

Her husband studied his ephemeral feet. "You aren't happy to see me?"

"I'd be a whole lot happier to see you alive!" she cried. "If you weren't already dead, I could kill you right now. I am so angry with you, Tobias Anthony Murphy!"

Pain radiated from the ghost and he hung his head in shame. "I'm sorry, honey. I know this whole scheme of mine hasn't exactly worked out—"

"That's an understatement."

"—but it seemed like such a good plan."

"Ha!" Bonnie's scoff rang out. "It might have been a good plan for someone *else*."

Tobias narrowed his eyes, and his voice became low and menacing. "What's that supposed to mean?"

"What do you think I mean?" she shrieked.

The mist of his body swirled faster and started to take on the same strange solidity as that morning on the hill. Vi let go of Bonnie's hand before the ghost could reply.

"Hey!" the unhappy couple cried out in unison.

"This isn't helping," she insisted. "Tobias needs to be *at peace* to cross over, and your bickering isn't going to help with that." The ghost mumbled an apology while his wife crossed her arms and dropped to the couch in a huff. "It's already been a long day for all of us, and it's barely lunchtime. Let's cool down a spell, and maybe have a little something to eat. All right?"

"Yes," the ghost agreed and gazed with adoration at his angry wife. "Excellent idea."

"Fine," Bonnie groused.

"Good." Vi motioned around her cluttered apartment with a chuckle. "That being said, I don't keep much in the way of food in this place, and the cook doesn't come in until dinner."

"Don't trouble yourself." The other woman burst to her feet. "I need to go for a walk anyway, to calm down. And lord knows I can afford it now, so I'll buy us something to eat."

"Are you sure?"

"Definitely." She spotted a mirror on the wall and checked the state of her face. "I need something useful to do."

"Thanks. I'll owe you one."

Bonnie sighed. "I think it's safe to say I already owed you. If not for the gold, certainly for losing my temper. I don't know what came over me. I've never struck anyone before in my whole life."

"I've had worse, believe me," Vi said. "You aren't the first person who didn't like what I had to say."

"Somehow, that doesn't surprise me," the widow joked. "Someone else found your honesty a bit too much to handle?"

One side of her mouth curled. "I don't believe anyone's ever accused me of being too honest before."

"Will you..." Tobias cut in, chagrined. "Will you ask her if it is okay if I go along? I know she's mad at me, but I never thought I was going to see her again. I don't want to let her out of my sight now."

Vi sighed. "Tobias is asking if he could accompany you. Not that he really would need permission, mind, you would not know where he is without me."

"You're not coming?"

"Nope. I'm a mess, remember?" Her eyes strayed to the bookshelf in the corner and her worn copy of *A Christmas Carol*. The meaning of Peter's cryptic message was just a few paces away. "Besides, I have some reading to do."

Chapter 8

Part of Vi longed to rush over to the bookshelf the moment the door clicked shut, but evidently that part wasn't in charge of her feet. Instead, she left the sitting room and set about making herself presentable enough for the public eye. People could tolerate a woman owning her own saloon as long as she made sure to be pretty about it. It was an old game and she knew it well, but a little rouge and a fancy dress were hardly the worst of her deceptions. Besides, bustles suited her.

The book in the other room whispered, begging her to find out what message was so important that Peter had employed a messenger only she could see to deliver it. Yet she dragged her brush through her hair and pinned it up in a tumble of coils at the back of her head. She straightened the seams of her emerald dress in the long mirror and touched up her eyeliner while the weight of dread and the burn of curiosity tore at her insides. A final spritz of perfume and there was nothing left to do; she couldn't stall anymore.

With a deep breath, she walked into the sitting room, her back straight and gait resolute. Even though she stood in the safety of her own home, Vi couldn't help but glance over her shoulder before reaching for the book.

The volume slid out, its weight familiar despite how well she'd managed to avoid touching it since the day she'd moved in. It had been surprisingly easy to shed the trappings of her old life, but for some reason she couldn't bring herself to leave this piece of it behind. Book in hand, she made her way to a wooden desk in the far corner. As she stroked the embossed letters of the title, a memory resolved before her eyes, the words and gestures barely muddied by time.

"It's perfect!" Peter had exclaimed as he held *A Christmas Carol* out before him.

"Perfect?" a younger version of Vi laughed. "Perfect for what?"

"For giving me cues. There's all sorts of mentions of ghosts and things in here that you can say in front of the marks, but I'll know you want me to pull a rope or flicker the lights or something."

"You want to add coded messages to our repertoire?" she'd asked. "I'm already worried I won't be able to sell this whole medium thing, and now you want to add something more I've got to think about?"

"It'll be easy, trust me." A wide grin split his face, his teeth a startling white against his dark lips. "You can even help me pick the lines and write the code. That will make it simple to remember."

"I see. You want to do this is as long as I do half the work," the Vi in her memory teased before snatching the book out of his hands and spinning toward a leather chair at the fireside. She slipped off her shoes and laid the book open on her lap. "You know I can't resist Dickens. Well played."

Her partner flopped into a matching chair and rubbed his hands together. "So, what sorts of things do you think we'll want to say?"

The pages were now worn and dog-eared, and Peter's crimped scribbles jumped out at her from the margins as she thumbed through the pages. The line about a child called Ignorance came from somewhere in the second half of the story, but that was the extent of her recollection. Her eyes flitted across the page while her lips took the shape of half-formed words as she read about the two children hidden in the robes of the ghost of Christmas present;

This boy is Ignorance. This girl is Want. Beware them both, and all of their degree, but most of all beware this boy, for on his brow I see that written which is Doom, unless the writing be erased.

"I see that written which is Doom." Vi's mouth went dry as she whispered the words, her heart doing acrobatics in her chest. The words "beware," "Doom," and "erased" leaped off the page and threatened to choke her. No doubt about it, Peter was sending her some type of warning, but a warning of what? He shouldn't even know where she was, let alone what might be threatening her. The churning bile in her gut tried to creep up her esophagus as a thought blossomed—maybe Peter *was* the threat.

Over the years, she'd pulled plenty of jobs and told too many lies to count, but she'd never wronged anyone the way she'd done him. Still, she'd always hoped he understood, that he realized her betrayal was out of a sort of survival instinct rather than malice. But she also knew too well how deeply the wounds of betrayal could cut.

She rotated the book to better make out the words in the margin. As she expected, she found the word "warning" scribbled there, at least twice as large as anything else. Despite her anxiety, she couldn't help but smile as she squinted to make out the rest of the words. They'd spent hours poring over that book, drinking and laughing as they added cryptic meanings to Dickens' words. To cut down on the amount of memorization, every line in their code had two different meanings. "Warning" was the obvious interpretation, but perhaps the secondary meaning would also apply.

The smaller words were smudged, but she managed to make out the phrase "for documents, letters, etc." in the jumble of ink. Of course, the word "written" was just as important as "Doom" in the line, and she allowed herself a small exhalation of relief. Perhaps Peter's message didn't carry a threat at all. She searched her memory and could recall one time they'd used the ignorance line during a job. Vi had used it to send Peter off to search for the mark's important papers, a practice that had never failed to yield interesting results. Illicit love letters, ship manifests, details about troop movements, evidence of dirty dealings—it was amazing what people kept in their desk drawers, and the uses they could be put to if the thief had half a brain.

Some of those documents were still locked in a trunk in her apartment, in case they ever came in handy. Abandoning it all would have been the cleanest, but she'd been in the game too long not to keep her options open. All the same, it had been years since she'd spared them any thought. They were a contingency plan, a security blanket, not anything she'd ever planned to use. Plus, Peter was the only one who even knew she had them.

Vi slammed the book closed and glared at it. She couldn't bring herself to believe he truly meant her harm, yet the documents seemed like a dead end. Most of them would be completely useless and outdated with the rebellion over, though the evidence of a cheating heart never went out of style. Her gaze wandered in the direction of the trunk, and she found herself smiling wistfully again. Dramatic readings of other people's love letters had been a favorite pastime for she and her partner, once upon a time.

A bolt of inspiration hit, and she sucked in a sharp breath. Not documents—*letters*. Peter could be warning her about something that had come in the post, or would be coming. When no one is supposed to know where you are, it's easy to get out of the habit of picking up mail. She often went months at a time without a visit to the Wells Fargo office and there was no telling what she'd missed.

With a final glance in the mirror, she grabbed her hat and rushed out the door in search of answers.

CHAPTER 9

The colorful storefronts of Sacramento spread their petals as she made her way to the office. Curious pedestrians fluttered and buzzed between shops, collecting the sights and sounds of the day. A few streets over, a train whistle squealed, but was soon swallowed by the general din of people going about their lives. Some women bobbed by wearing the full, flattering skirts and cinched waists of the newest fashions despite the dry heat of autumn. Others were content with simple blouses and straw hats. A few well-dressed men carrying suitcases cut off her path as they crossed the road to enter one of the dozens of hotels the waterfront boasted.

The long-time residents loved to talk about how the streets there along the river had been raised a few years back on account of frequent flooding. Now that both the Sacramento and the American Rivers had been tamed by levees and channels, there was an almost continuous influx of people both by river and by rail.

She stepped up to the desk and rang the bell. The voice of an old man hollered something unintelligible from the back room. Vi rested her forehead against the iron bars as she waited, the coolness of the metal a welcome respite from the afternoon heat. An elderly but spry man with a shock of gray hair eventually emerged, offering her an apology for his absence.

"You're here now," Vi replied. "So, let's get to business. Have you got anything waiting for Viola or "V" Thorne? With an 'e.'"

"Let me see what I can find." He hustled away into the back room, but when he emerged his hands were empty. "Sorry, ma'am. Don't see nothing for a Thorne no matter how you spell it. Anything else I can do for you?"

She chewed on her lip and grabbed a piece of paper and a pencil nib from the counter. The clerk craned his neck to watch her as she wrote out a list of a half-dozen names. After a quick count on her fingers, she nodded in satisfaction and slid the scrap of paper into his waiting grasp.

"How about these names? My friends asked me to check for them while I was here. Anything look familiar?" she asked, smiling sweetly. He glanced at the aliases and swayed dubiously as he considered her request. Vi hoped he wasn't being paid enough to care that she might be a mail thief and turned up the charm. When he felt the weight of her hand on his sleeve, he glanced at her face and found himself in the path of her fluttering eyelashes.

"It's a good thing you reminded me, or I would have forgotten altogether. Annabelle would be so cross if I forgot again." The fingers of her other hand came to rest on the lace of her collar as she forced a girlish giggle. "We all have our little jobs while we travel together you see, and I keep neglecting the post."

The clerk brightened. "Just a moment, ma'am. I'll be back in a jiffy."

"Thank you ever so much!" she called, employing her best damsel voice. As soon as he turned the corner, her impatient glower returned, and she leaned against the counter. Her stomach rumbled. Bonnie would be coming back to the saloon any minute, and Vi wanted to make it back first. Not that she needed to keep her errand a secret, but she didn't want to leave the other woman alone in her apartment. At least, not until she knew how to interpret her former ally's strange behavior.

"Never fear!" the clerk called. "Annabelle won't have cause for any complaints." He swept back into the room clutching a pair of envelopes in his wizened fingers.

She stared, momentarily dumbfounded at what he held in his hand. "Annabelle Sinclair" had been the last name on the list, the one she'd included even though she'd used it for one job—the biggest one, and the last.

Vi snatched the envelopes and checked the undisturbed seals. The smaller parcel bore Peter's name as the sender, but the larger one came from an address she didn't recognize. She caught a glimpse of the official-looking emblem in the glob of red wax as she turned it over.

"That small one came in with the load day afore yesterday. Filed it myself," he continued. "The other one's been here a while, maybe a few weeks? Got a batch going out t'morrow if your friend needs to send a reply.

Otherwise, it'll be a few more days afore we collect enough for another run."

"Day before yesterday, you say?" That would put the letter's arrival around the same time Tobias died, and she still didn't know the full story of the connection between Peter and the ghost. Time to ask good old Toby a few more questions.

"Pardon me, ma'am," the old man asked. "But you don't own a big, black horse, do you?"

She gave a murmur in the affirmative. The envelope from Peter felt oddly heavy, and her searching fingertips found a strange lump as she ran them along the bottom.

"Someone was looking for you."

Her head shot up. "What? Looking for me here?"

"Well, can't say for sure, mind," the postman replied. "He came in and asked about a lady customer with red hair and a black horse. You're the only copperhead I seen today, so I thought it might be you."

"Did he say what he wanted with this red-haired woman?"

"Yep. Wanted to know where he could find her."

Vi blanched, and her stomach progressed from its impression of a boiling soup pot to a volcano. "A dark man? A hair taller than me?"

"Nope. It was a real big fella."

Her brow furrowed. Nobody would ever have called a compact man like Peter 'big', so it couldn't be him. Vi wasn't sure if the insight made her feel better or worse.

"Well, who was it?" she asked. "Did he leave a name, or some way to get in contact?"

"It wasn't your Annabelle, that's for sure." The clerk chortled, but then his expression grew deadly serious. "He looked like someone who was looking for trouble. Didn't leave a name. And if you don't mind me sayin', I don't think you really want to be finding him."

"You're probably right." She exhaled wearily and pulled out her coin purse. "If he comes asking for me, or whatever unfortunate redhead, again, do you suppose I could persuade you to have lapse in your memory?"

"No need for that, ma'am." The old man waved her money away. "I won't say nothing. 'Sides, I already told him I didn't know you, so I don't expect he'll be coming back."

This gained the clerk a genuine smile as she put away her purse. "You're too kind."

"If I might be so bold, ma'am?"

"Yes?"

"Are you in some kind of trouble?" he asked, his face a caricature of grandfatherly concern.

Her expression curdled as she replied. "My friend, you have no idea."

"Well, I know it ain't my place, but it seems to me you should go and find the sheriff. Tell somebody what's going on. Whatever it is."

"Thanks, but I like to handle things my own way." Not to mention the last thing she needed was to get the law involved. "I'll be fine."

She slowed her racing mind enough to give a final nod of thanks and stepped back onto the busy afternoon promenade. The weight of the letter drew her attention to her hand, and she couldn't help but search the crowd to see if anyone watched her leaving. The people all around her continued to laugh and go along their merry way, but Vi slipped into the shade of a side street nonetheless before tearing into the envelope.

A single sheet of neatly folded paper slipped out, and she found herself gazing at Peter's handwriting for the second time that day. As with the outside of the letter, he addressed her by her alias. This may have been part of the game he was playing, or could be a sign of something far more worrying. In addition to the odd salutation, his note proved to be full of spelling mistakes. She'd seen him pull that trick and play dumb before. Even with the slaves freed back in '63, no one expected a negro to write, let alone write well—but he'd never pretended with her.

The note began with a relaxed and friendly tone, for all appearances simply an affable little missive between chums. He passed on greetings from imaginary well-wishers and begged to know when she would be coming home for a visit "because we all miss you so much." That part gave her a chuckle, but she stopped smiling when she reached the last paragraph.

The slope of the script and the size of the letters abruptly changed, and tiny splatters of ink dotted the page, the pen nib dragged along like an unwilling toddler. For the first and solitary time, he'd used a name that actually meant something.

"Curiouser and curiouser," she remarked, her voice breathy and uneven.

When she noticed her stiff fingers, she loosened her grip on the letter and hurriedly refolded it. Vi gave herself a shake and a scolding for getting so worked up over what was probably a ruse. This would all turn out to be a roundabout way for Peter to tell her he knew where she'd been hiding. The references to people who didn't exist certainly supported that theory, and it definitely felt like it could be one of his games. He loved to leave her riddles and cryptic notes even before they'd enlisted Charles Dickens in their schemes. Of course, if even some of what the letter said was true and the Colonel really had died, that would open a world of possibilities. She didn't dare to hope. Not yet.

Vi examined the inside of the envelope in case it would yield more information about its sender. The glint of metal caught her eye. As she tipped the envelope, a delicate tie pin slid into her open palm. It was made of gold, but it might as well have been a coffin nail for her theory that this was all a complicated prank. She forgot to breathe, her thumb gliding over the familiar onyx head of the lucky charm—something she had never known Peter to be without.

A dozen different moments shared with Peter crowded before her eyes and jostled for attention, and the black gem had been there for all of them. Her free hand flew to her brow as the world rocked; the presence of the pin said far more than any letter could. Darkness pulled at her vision, but she swallowed the urge to close her eyes against the truth. With a deep breath, she banished the bout of dizziness and slipped the pin back into the envelope.

No space left for doubt—despite the bizarre handwriting and the even stranger words, Peter had definitely sent her that letter. What she needed to know now was who had forced him to write it.

CHAPTER 10

Scenarios spun through Vi's mind as she made her way back to the saloon, the post tucked under her arm. She wouldn't know more until she could talk to Tobias about his dealings with Peter. The letter had come from a great distance only a couple days before, yet somehow, he'd been able to tell the ghost exactly where to find her to ask for help. Not to mention, he'd found a way to communicate with the dead.

The quest for answers had yielded more intrigue, but when her stomach settled enough to remind her how hungry she'd become, she pushed the letter and the vivid swirl of memories from her mind. With any luck, she'd sate her curiosity as well as her hunger during the impending luncheon.

The fact that a stranger had asked after her was harder to ignore. As she walked, she surreptitiously scanned her surroundings from under her lashes and schooled her features into a demure and compliant expression. The occasional reflection in a shop window or sudden movement in her vicinity gave her pause, but it wasn't the evidence of her eyes that made her feel jumpy. A tingling crept up her spine, as if an icy shadow had cut through the afternoon heat and was determined to follow her no matter what direction she turned.

Despite her serpentine route, the sensation continued to grow, the same way it had when Tobias approached her the night before. The temptation to reach out to taste the auras around her built as the feeling changed from a chilly tickle to an acidic burn. But this time she refused to give in. Experience had shown the more she employed those abilities, the stronger they'd grow, and she'd somehow already gotten herself committed to helping Bonnie and Tobias settle whatever it was they needed settling.

When she arrived at the half-darkness of the alley behind the saloon, she slipped around the corner and put her back to the wall, taking comfort in its solid bulk against her body. People came and went, and she watched them for a few minutes from the safety of the passage. No one approached her or even paused as they bustled along.

The sting of paranoia receded as she forced deep, steady breaths in and out of her lungs. The more she thought about her panic, the sillier she felt. The stranger's vague description didn't even necessarily apply to her; it wasn't as if she were the only woman with a black horse in all of Sacramento. In the face of something so trivial as a poor night's sleep and an empty stomach, she'd almost lost control and relapsed, almost taken that next fatal step. Falling back into the old ways would be so easy, but that path had no peace to offer.

She turned to go up the back stairs. Smithy was no longer tied where she'd left him, but often George took him around front where the light was better. Still, with everything that had transpired over the past several hours, she found herself with the acute desire for confirmation. There probably wasn't one, but if some stranger looking for black horse menaced from the shadows, no sense making Smithy easy to find.

Vi swept back out into the flow of traffic and around to the front of her bar. At first, she couldn't find the little boy and his large companion, but then she spotted the flick of the horse's ears above the gathered heads. George waved a brush around as he talked to a few local kids who had stopped to chat. She'd been here long enough to have watched those kids grow up and she felt a swell of loyalty for her adopted home. Vi dipped her chin to Jimmy as she passed the door to *Viola's*. Then she sidled up to the conversation, their jocular tones and the sheer normalcy of boys at play a balm to her frayed nerves.

"He could get there and back easy," George assured his comrades while Smithy enjoyed his feed bag.

"I don't know," said the son of a cobbler from the next street over. "I heard the best horses for long distances are them small ones."

The baker's middle child chimed in. "Yeah. They take less feed, see, so there's less to carry."

"But if you've got a big horse like mine, he can carry more feed," George insisted. His bony elbows jutted out as he put his fists on his hips. "That's just math."

"Oh, so he's *your* horse now?" the first boy teased.

"Aw, you just know I'm right," George replied with a laugh. "'Sides, he's as good as. I take care of him plenty, and someday Miss Viola's gonna let me ride him. I'll go all over the place, see the whole world. You'll see."

"By the time you're big enough for that, it'll be time to put this one out to pasture," the baker's boy added. He gave George a playful push and darted behind Smithy, giggling as he ran.

She idly tracked the kid into the hubbub of the streets and her gaze fell onto Bonnie's smiling face. The widow waved a bright handkerchief and made her way over to where the reluctant medium stood waiting. Tobias stomped along a few paces behind, his face screwed up in dismay. His wife stepped over to greet Vi on the raised walkway while he stayed sulking at street level.

Bonnie held a wicker basket and patted its round belly. "I've collected quite a feast for us."

"Vi, you've got to talk some sense into her!" Tobias cried. "At the rate she's going, that gold I found isn't going to last the month."

"You certainly did," she said to Bonnie, her stomach doing a happy but insistent jig now that it had confirmation that lunch had finally arrived.

"I probably shouldn't have gotten so much," Bonnie admitted. "But there are so many glorious things to buy. I haven't seen half of these foods since we left Chicago. And frankly, I thought we could both use a treat."

"You won't hear me complain," Vi replied, motioning to the saloon and offering her elbow. "Shall we?"

"Has anyone ever told you, you're a terrible influence?" Tobias scolded, though his manner was light.

Bonnie reached for the crook of Vi's arm but hesitated, her fingers hovering over the rich fabric of the sleeve. Uncertainty washed the happiness from her face.

Vi had seen that look before; it was how people always looked at her after they had an encounter with her "gifts." She let her elbow fall, coughing to cover her embarrassment. "It's OK," she mumbled. "I understand."

Bonnie appeared even more confused than before, her head cocked to the side like a curious pup until she gleaned Vi's meaning. "Oh no! It's not *that*."

Her voice dropped to an exaggerated whisper. "It's just, is *he* here?"

Panic washed over Vi, and her extra senses ached to be let out to find the threat. She tamped them down, glancing around them before she replied in a matching tone. "Is who here? Do you know something?"

"I know you said he wanted to come with me, but I thought maybe he'd gotten bored or something and wandered off. That's what does whenever we go shopping." Her words were colored by a pang of forlorn affection even though the content sounded like a complaint.

"Oh, for crying out loud," Tobias exclaimed and crossed his arms across the swirling fog of his chest. He bent low to scramble under the railing before remembering himself and simply passing through it. "That's because you take a year to make any decisions."

As she beckoned Vi closer, Bonnie's voice dropped back down to a whisper. "But if he is here, I'm not sure I'm ready to talk to him again."

"Tobias?"

"Sure," Bonnie replied earnestly. "Who else would I be talking about?"

Vi forced a smile. "Nobody. Sorry. I'm dull as dishwater when I skip breakfast. And yes, Tobias is here with us, but you wouldn't have to see him right now if you don't want."

The ghost's voice was small and childlike. "Why wouldn't she want to see me?"

"But I thought... if we touched?"

"That's just for skin to skin contact," Vi promised.

"Oh, thank goodness." Without any further hesitation, the widow took her arm and gave it a squeeze. "I'm sure you think I'm being a real ninny about all of this, that I need to face him. I just... I can't right now."

"You don't have to explain anything to me," Vi assured her. "There's no right or wrong way to grieve."

The remark was meant to comfort, but it landed heavier than she'd intended. Bonnie's expression became distant as they reached the doorway to the saloon. Vi was struggling to find something else to say, to lighten the mood, when George's angry cry pierced the air. At first, she thought the neighbor kids had simply come back for some more ribbing, but the figures that had now gathered near the boy and her horse were no children.

Vi swallowed hard. "Bonnie, I want you to get inside. Now."

"But I—"

"No arguments." She gave the other woman a polite but firm shove through the door. "I need you to go in the bar right now and stay there."

"What's going on?" the ghost interjected, as late to the party as ever.

"Just tell me," Bonnie pleaded. "Is it Salty? Did he come back for me?"

"No, it's not him," Vi hedged.

"Should I go get the police or—"

"No!" she said a little too loudly, then continued in a hushed tone. "There's no time for that. I'll handle it myself."

"Can't I help? Please, you have to let me help you after everything you've done for me." The little brunette tried to push past, but found her way blocked by Vi's arm as well as her iron resolve.

Tobias must have finally seen what she saw, because he started shouting. "Don't be stupid, honey! If Vi tells you to get out of here, you get out of here!"

"The best thing you can do for me is to get inside," Vi hissed and glanced back over her shoulder. The ruckus grew louder, and poor George was in the thick of it.

"Tell me who it is," Bonnie insisted.

A frustrated sound sprang from the ghost. "You know, she wasn't always this stubborn. I think you really *have* been a bad influence."

"I swear," the widow pledged, eyes shining with frightened tears, but the line of her mouth hard and resolute. "I'll go inside like a good little girl, but you have to tell me what's got you so spooked."

"It's them, Bonnie." Vi took her by the shoulders and looked her straight in the eye. "It's the men who murdered your husband."

CHAPTER 11

"Give it back, or you'll be sorry," George squawked, his outstretched arms barely reaching the shoulders of the man who'd stolen the horse brush. Smithy stopped munching, his ears flattened against his head.

"Oh yeah, what are you going to do about it? I could roll you like a tumbleweed," snarled Beard-face.

His counterpart tried his best to sound reasonable, but cordial speech didn't seem to be in his wheelhouse. His pocked face crinkled as he whined. "You tell us where we can find the owner of this horse. That's all we need from you, son."

"No way I'm gonna help you." The boy swept back his leg and landed a hard kick to the outlaw's tender ankle. He bellowed as George made a break for the raised walkway. He rolled under the bottom rung of the railing and found himself with a face full of Vi's hem.

She offered him a hand up, her heart swelling at his show of loyalty. "Thanks, kid. I'll take it care of it from here."

"You sure?" George stared up at her, eyes wide with fear. "They're real mean, Miss Viola. And there's a lot of them."

More men drifted out of the flow of pedestrians and coalesced around the angry shouting. "You got that chocolate I asked for?"

"Yes'm," he said, pulling something out of a pocket that had once been flat and rectangular but resembled a wagon tongue after his little bout of acrobatics. He held it out to her. "Oops."

"You hold onto it for me," she said with a wink. "Go on into the bar, and I'll be there in a minute to collect. I want to see my reflection in those tables, hear?"

He scrambled through the saloon door, but she knew that he'd be watching through the window right beside Bonnie and Tobias. Considering the ghost wasn't in any sort of danger, the least he could have done was to stay outside with her. But old habits like cowardice die hard.

On the street, the scarred man leaned against Beard-face while three more figures materialized out of the crowd. People stopped to watch the events unfold, clogging the busy thoroughfare and slowing traffic.

Vi did her best not to wince when she recognized some of the men from the cooking pot incident that morning. "Good afternoon, sirs. May I help you?"

A lanky man wearing a formerly red bandana raked his eyes from head to toe before jerking his goatee in Vi's direction. "That her, Hank?"

"Yeah. I think that's her, Boss."

She raised the pitch of her voice and said breathily, "Excuse me, but what is this about?"

"This yours?" he asked, running his hand over Smithy's sleek withers. The horse's head jolted toward the bandit, but he was stopped by his lead rope tied to the railing.

"Yes, this is my horse." She paced over to Smithy's head and scratched behind his ears to soothe him. "What has that got to do with anything?"

"You see, this morning my residence was invaded by a woman with red hair," he replied, his voice dripping with mock sincerity. "When I sent my friends to find out why she had so rudely decided to wake us, they told me she got away riding a black horse."

"I assure you, I don't know what you're talking about. I don't go around breaking into houses," she scoffed.

"I never said it was a house." A gold tooth flashed in the sun as he leered.

Vi raised her chin with as much imperiousness as she could muster and continued her bluff. "Well, there you are. I don't know what you're talking about. I've never seen these men before in my life."

"She's lying, Jeb," the scarred man panted. He limped over to his boss and flopped an arm around his shoulders for balance. "That's her awright."

Jeb glared at his lackey's arm pointedly until the scarred man noticed. He lurched straight and put all his weight on his uninjured foot with a mumbled apology. His boss jerked his chin at the bearded man. "What do you say?"

Beard-face hulked closer and took a long look at her, but eventually stepped back with a shake of his head. "I can't say. She was wearing a mask." The crowd whispered amongst themselves. She tried not to take it personally that several of them sounded disappointed.

His limping friend flailed a limb at Vi. "This is the one, boss. I'm sure of it."

"This is the woman who gave you that beating, Pox?" The head outlaw leaned his lanky frame against the railing and peered at her through the gap. He daintily lifted the hem of her dress and cocked his head at the scarred man. "I'd expected someone a little less frilly."

Laughter rippled through the impromptu audience, and the scarred man's face turned scarlet. Vi ripped her skirt out of his hand, but didn't retreat.

"What I do know," Beard-face interjected, "is that this definitely looks like the horse she used to get away."

"Yeah," Pox sniveled. "A whole bunch of the gang seen it."

"And what a fine animal he is." Jeb stepped back and surveyed Smithy again. "If he weren't so tired from your hasty retreat, I might even bet on him to beat my Clementine."

"He'd beat the tar out of your crowbait, Mister!" George's voice cut into the conversation from where he peeked around the doorframe.

Jeb sniggered. "He yours, too?"

She struggled to keep her voice level, but a rush of protectiveness added an edge of cold steel as she answered. "In a manner of speaking."

"You'd best teach him to show some respect for his betters."

Her true nature couldn't take it anymore, and a canary-eating smirk finally cracked through her façade of girlishness. "And who might they be?"

"You tell 'em, Miss Viola!" It looked like George was going to walk right over to Jeb and give him what for, but Bonnie caught him by the suspender and yanked his scrawny body back inside.

The bandit clucked his tongue. "It's one thing for a lady such as yourself to raise your voice to me. But you'd better teach that darky his place, or I reckon I'll have to be the one to show it to him."

Vi rested one elbow on the top of the fence and put her chin against her fist in a contemplative pose. "Didn't a lot of good men recently die and show that the color of your skin doesn't prove you're better than him?"

He shrugged, parroting, "In a manner of speaking."

"Where were you when all that fighting was going on, I wonder." She made a show of scrutinizing his torso as she stood back to her full height. "Or do I detect a hint of yellow on that belly?"

There were a few scattered gasps from the people gawping on the sidelines. Jeb glowered and grabbed the top railing to swing up and stand on the edge of the platform. His nose came within inches her face, but she held her ground and smirked. What showmanship—in another life, they probably would have been friends.

"Looks like he's not the only one who needs to learn a thing or two about how he addresses people." He hopped back to the street and addressed the crowd. "How's this for a lesson? I believe my friends and I should take this beautiful horse of yours to help you with that education."

"I didn't do anything to you," she retorted. "You don't have anything even in the same neighborhood as proof that I did."

His Adam's apple bobbed. "I don't see as that matters much anymore. The bottom line is that I like that horse and I don't see as I like your attitude."

Vi's fingers found the knot of Smithy's lead rope and tightened around it. "You can't do that."

"I can," Jeb replied and pulled out a shiny six-shooter. "And I will."

Several members of the audience took a step back and ducked out from the fringes, their errands suddenly much more important than they'd first thought. A few sympathetic folks met Vi's eye, but nobody seemed willing to do anything to help her. Not that she expected much in the way of help; prudence had made her work rigorously not to make much of an impression on anyone for some time.

An idea sprang to mind and before she could do anything about it, it sprang to mouth as well. "You want proof it wasn't me?"

The bandit turned back to face her with a wry smile. "Sure. Try me."

"You think my horse is too tired to race? Let's see if you're right." A thrill trembled through her as she made her way through the nearest break in the railing and over to Jeb's side. "I say I've been here all day and Smithy is fresh as a daisy. So, let's settle this. If you win, I won't even put up a fight when you take him, but you've got to give me a chance to show you that you've made a mistake."

The bandit nodded smugly and stowed his weapon. "I'm sure that can be arranged. But I've got to warn you, Clementine is the fastest horse I've ever seen. This probably isn't really a fair competition, even if your horse really were fresh."

"I guess that's a risk I'm willing to take."

As soon as folks heard about the challenge, they clambered to get onto the walkways and out of the way. Jeb's goons took up positions around the route to help keep bystanders from getting in the way. The legs of the race would be short, hardly long enough to get up a full head of steam. When racing in the middle of a state capitol one simply had to make do. Granted, it was a state capitol that was known for having the highest rate of alcohol consumption anywhere in the world, but there were certain standards of order that needed to be maintained. For instance, someone had the foresight to hide the lone bicycle shared by the handful of city police to ensure that by the time they even knew something had happened, the race would be over.

Vi strode out of her saloon in a fresh set of riding gear, careful to choose something with a full skirt and cinched waist to contrast with her garb that morning. Hopefully, her wardrobe could throw further doubt on their accusations. Her habit was a prim affair in a dusty gray and about as far as a person could get from the colorful billow of her usual poncho and sash. The skirt had hidden buttons in the front to hold up the fabric for easier mounting, and when hiked up, it exposed a pair of matching trousers tucked into her knee-high black boots to accommodate the Western style of riding. Sidesaddle was all well and good for a jaunt in the park, but too much depended on her winning to bother with the social niceties. Though she wasn't usually one for superstitions, she'd even affixed Peter's pin to her lapel in case it had any luck left to give.

"Here you go, Miss Viola," Jimmy said. Her saddle, blanket, and bridle hung over the bottom rung of the banister. "I brought out your tack like you asked."

"You going with George to cheer me on?" The bartender's neck and prominent ears flushed a delightful shade of pink. He mumbled something to a knothole in the sidewalk while he shifted uncomfortably. Vi put her hand to her ear. "What was that? I didn't catch it?"

"Caroline says I can't," he replied, eyes tight and ears turning a darker shade of crimson.

"Ah."

Jimmy stole a peek behind him, and when her eyes followed, she found his new bride standing in the smudged window of the saloon, concern marring her normal level of loveliness. Vi chuckled knowingly and set to work on getting Smithy saddled.

"Bonnie was talking, see?" he continued. "And she got Care all worked up and worried that something would happen. As if I couldn't stand on a sidewalk without getting into some sort of trouble. I got by fine for twenty-odd years before we even met, and now I can't be trusted to stand on my own two feet?"

"Don't fret it too much. It is simply her job now to worry about you."

"But I'm not made out of glass, for crying out loud."

"No," Vi said as she ran the leather straps through the cinch ring. "You're much more valuable than glass. I bet if you asked her, she'd say you were the most precious thing on the entire planet."

Jimmy stood with his mouth open for a few moments before he turned and scampered back to the saloon, and presumably into his wife's waiting arms.

George was too short to help with the tack, so he concentrated his efforts on standing on the walkway and whispering encouragement while he stroked Smithy. The horse stood placid, seemingly oblivious to all of the excitement now that the bandits weren't in his immediate vicinity. Jeb had retrieved his honey-colored mount, and several people milled between the two animals. A voice rose over the crowd to give the odds and collect bets. The sound awoke her competitive spirit all over again, and the familiar flutter of the excitement of the gamble made her giddy.

As she surveyed the scene, a pair of small but deceptively strong arms crushed Vi into a hug. After a few moments, Bonnie's distressed visage stared at her with teary eyes. "Oh, Vi. This is all our fault. If Tobias had left you out of it, then you wouldn't be in this position."

"You have no idea how sorry I am for this," the ghost piped up. He walked through Smithy. "I never thought I was even capable of causing this much trouble."

"It's fine," Vi replied, peeling off the little brunette. "I'm not worried."

"How can it be fine?" the widow cried. "Smithy must be exhausted."

"Nah, that stroll this morning was nothing. He's got plenty of pep." She gave her equine companion a pat. "In fact, you have any change left from getting that lunch I might someday get to enjoy?"

"Of course, she does," Tobias answered confidently and turned to his wife for confirmation. "You do, don't you?"

"Well, sure," Bonnie said. "You want me to go and offer them some money to call it all off?"

"No way. I want you to go place a bet. That palomino doesn't stand a chance." She made sure to say the last part loudly enough that Jeb heard her.

"We'll see about that!" he called back before placing a hand-rolled cigarette between his lips. The wide brim of his hat shaded his eyes, but the flare of his match revealed an expression every bit as confident as hers.

"Is there anything else you want me to do?" George asked. "Or could I go find a good spot to watch the race?"

"Go on," she replied. "I want you to make sure you yell really loudly once we start, to make sure Smithy can hear you."

"I sure will," he laughed, then scampered along the walkway.

"He's a sweet kid," Bonnie said wistfully. "Is he yours?"

"No, not as such. When his parents died he started hanging around the bar, so I'd give him odd jobs to do. Next thing I knew, he'd adopted me."

Bonnie watched George slip through the crowd and climb onto a post to get the best view, but her face soon creased with worry. "How can you be sure you're going to win?"

"I'd be surprised if there were a horse anywhere within a hundred miles that could beat Smithy in a race."

"But you can't know that. Not for sure."

Light, carefree laughter bubbled from Vi's throat. "That's what makes it gambling. You can't always know that you're going to win," she said to the world at large before she leaned close to the other woman's ear, her whole energy crackling with excitement. "Though, as you saw this afternoon with Salty, I try to make a point of having an ace up my sleeve."

"I fail to see how that applies here," Bonnie replied in an incredulous whisper. "There aren't any cards in horse racing."

"There aren't?" Vi made her sparkling eyes go wide in mock innocence.

"You're incorrigible!"

She replied with an impression of deep and abiding sincerity, "Thank you." Despite her exasperated scoff, Bonnie couldn't help but give in and eventually grin.

"Are we ever going to start?" Hank's whine cut through the quiet conversation. "It feels like we've been standing here forever."

"I guess that's what you get when you are dealing with women. Hassles, hassles, hassles," Jeb replied, his cigarette dangling from his full lips. His crew snickered in agreement.

"Does that explain why you're all single, then?" she yelled back. Several of the people ranged around the scene oohed appreciatively.

"If you're such a catch, where's *Mister* Viola, I wonder?" Hank cackled. Anyone who hadn't been paying attention before was now being elbowed by their neighbors.

"You've got me there. I do make a terrible wife," Vi admitted. As the crowd murmured, she milked the pause before finishing with, "but it seems I'm getting awful-good at being a widow." The gnarled man turned pale and didn't say any more. She jerked her thumb at him and called over to Jeb. "So, in the immortal words of this fine fellow, are we ever going to start?"

Jeb rocked up into his saddle. With a final scratch behind Smithy's ears, Vi hitched her skirt, dug her foot into the stirrup, and swung her leg over Smithy's wide back in a flourish of fabric. A few of the women let out scandalized gasps, one mother going so far as to turn her child away from Vi's unladylike display.

Her opponent leveled an approving stare at her as she and her mount approached. Smithy nearly pranced his way over as Jeb pointed down the street. "We're heading to the corner with the bank, then a hard left. At the next crossing, left again. Once you hit the boarding house, another left. We end at the line where we started. Understood?"

"No problem here," she sniffed. Except, she realized hollowly, that her horse had never raced around the sharp corners of a city street.

Smithy pulled against the reins and pawed at the sand in front of him, much more eager than his mistress for what lay ahead. The dash into town that morning had evidently fed his hunger for speed.

A helpful bystander drew a furrow in the dirt with a broom handle as the crowd looked on in hushed anticipation. Somewhere down the track, a voice still boomed the odds and took the final bets from the day drinkers at the saloons along the street. The riders lined up evenly, and Vi stole a diffident glance at the grinning bandit at her side. Jeb's blue eyes flashed in the afternoon sunlight as he gave her and her mount a lingering appraisal. She dipped her chin, favoring him with a coquettish curl at the corner of her mouth and filing away his wolfish smile in case she would need it for leverage.

The intimate moment exploded at the sound of the starting gun, and Smithy jerked forward without any regard to his rider. Despite all her experience in the saddle, her arms wind-milled, giving the bridle a violent tug. Smithy turned to his right before doing his best to stop under her direction. His obedience threw Vi against the pommel with a resounding, "Oof!"

Jeb didn't waste time laughing, but he did smile back over his shoulder as he and his brown mare took an early and decisive lead. Though people crowding the raised walkway were not so courteous, she hardly registered their snickers as she recovered the reins. Black and red spots swam in front of her vision, but she had no time for their nonsense. With a whoop, she squeezed her knees against the saddle, giving Smithy all the encouragement he needed to follow their opponents down the track. His hooves bit deep into the packed earth and threw up clods of dirt as they shot along the raceway. Within a few storefronts, Vi was on Jeb's heels and gaining ground. People started to hurl debasements and encouragement depending on what ticket they held.

Vi said a half-hearted prayer to anyone who would listen as they approached the first corner. The dirt road could offer plenty of purchase for the horses' hooves, or it could offer a chance to take a bad step and break a leg. Jeb took the inside lane, never giving Smithy a chance to nose ahead, but the big horse would never be able to cut off the corners; they'd have to rely on the straightaways. She directed him into a wider, gentler arc than their opponent, before kicking them into a burst of speed as they came out of the bend.

The dancing spots finally cleared from her vision in time to see the outlaw's gritted teeth as she took the lead. The next corner came a lot faster than the first, but with their rhythm established they took it with ease and entered the next straight path. News of the race appeared to have petered off on this side of the track, and the cheering crowd disappeared behind them. Much to her dismay, a cart rattled down the pitted street just a few yards ahead and they veered sharply to avoid a collision. The old man driving it sputtered and swore, as his mangy co-pilot barked his annoyance. The dog leaped to the ground, snapping and growling around the frightened horse's ankles. Smithy veered and narrowly missed hitting Jeb as he snaked through the chaos and slipped back into the lead.

There would be no amnesty nor second chances, so no reason to try asking Jeb for it. With a few choice words for the irritated hound and his master, Vi tugged her horse's attention back to the matters at hand. The lane stretched out straight and clear for a few hundred feet, the sunshine winking off the river in the distance. As they neared the third corner, she let out a gleeful guffaw. Smithy tore up the distance, leaving Jeb to watch her pass him for a second time. The spectators let out a cheer as they approached, and Smithy sailed across the finish several horse-lengths ahead.

She took her time slowing them before wheeling back to the sight of an astonished Jeb reaching the end of the course at a trot. The bandits grumbled their way over from the walkways and from inside *Viola's*, scratching their heads and shrugging bemusedly.

"That's one special horse you've got there," Jeb quipped as he dismounted. He sauntered over to Vi, who accepted his hand when he offered to help her down.

"He doesn't appear all that tired, in my opinion. It seems that I am not the ne'er-do-well you think I am."

"No, I suppose you're right. You did beat me across that finish line." He laid a kiss on her knuckle and sniggered. "But that don't mean I didn't already promise that horse of yours to the men you walloped."

Half a dozen firearms found their way into sweaty, calloused palms as his men fanned out around her. The happy crowd evaporated in the face of danger, all signs of the race erased in a matter of moments as they scattered back to business as usual. Vi never turned her head, but imagined Tobias, Bonnie, and her staff huddled at the windows of the saloon. She couldn't really blame them; a lifetime of experience had taught her how to face things on her own.

Vi jerked away her hand. "We had a deal, Jeb," she said darkly.

"Yes, we did," the ringleader replied. "And I do hate to break a deal, especially when a woman's honor is at stake." He leaned in close, but she didn't give him the satisfaction of flinching away from the smell of horse. His sarcastically apologetic whisper tickled her cheek. "But, you see, the boys got it into their heads already that a horse is coming back with us and they're pretty stubborn."

Rage boiled up her neck as he leaned away. "That may be the case," she spat. "Though I'm sure a man like you could do an awful lot to persuade them if he had a mind to."

"If I had a mind to," he replied smoothly, amusement tugging at his eyebrows as he mistook the flush of her skin for arousal.

"But Boss," Hank cried. "We can't let her get off that easy. She busted my hat, and she made me soil my britches."

Vi gasped dramatically, stealing focus back before Jeb's minion made too much sense. "What you do with your unmentionables is between you and your god," she admonished in mock-horror. "I certainly don't want anything to do with your laundry."

"She'll play you for it!" Bonnie's shrill cry broke over the display of effrontery. The little brunette elbowed her way inside the ring of men and rushed to her side, repeating, "She'll play you for it." Everyone traded confused glances until she clarified. "Not the laundry, the horse. Let her play you for the horse."

Vi hissed through her teeth. "What are you doing?"

The circle of men mumbled together until Jeb hushed them. "Play? Play what?"

"Cards," Bonnie said brightly. "If she wins, she gets to keep Smithy, and if you win, you can have...um..."

"You have to play to find out," Vi blurted, then lowered her voice and infused it with velvet. "It's a surprise." Jeb's face crinkled with intrigue as she favored him with calculating, bashful smile and a few bats of her lashes. "What have you got to lose?"

"What are you doing, Boss?" Hank interjected. "Why don't we take the flea bait now and call it a day?"

"We can have our game in my bar," she pushed, swallowing her ire over the flea bait remark. Jeb stroked his chin thoughtfully, and she decided in for a dime, in for a dollar. "That means drinks and a show during the game. Should be quite a shindig."

The ring of men exchanged hopeful glances, and a few holstered their weapons as their leader smirked at her artful manipulation. "All right, ma'am," Jeb acquiesced. "On account of you asking so nice, me and the boys'll come to your little 'shindig' tonight. But if that horse ain't tied outside when we get here, there's gonna be hell to pay."

Vi gave him a decorous bob of her head. "Fair enough."

The bandit turned to his cronies. "Okay boys, let's go find ourselves some grub and make ourselves presentable-like. We're having ourselves a night." They hooted and hollered as the remaining weapons were stowed. The threat dissolved as they broke off in clumps and pairs to await nightfall.

Once they were gone, the block let out the breath it had been holding. The first people took tentative steps onto the street.

Bonnie clapped her hands in delight. "There, problem solved."

Vi spun on her. "You call that solving a problem? I'd call it digging me a deeper pit to crawl out of." She stalked off toward the saloon.

"But... I was helping." The widow pouted as she trailed a few steps behind. "I thought you could beat 'em like you did earlier, and maybe we could get some justice for Tobias."

"I appreciate the sentiment," she sighed, slowing to allow the other woman to catch up. "And you're right. There was a time when I could have done it easily."

"No ace up your sleeve this time?" Bonnie asked.

"I can manage one, but a job like that would take more aces than I can hold on my own. It's going to be me versus all of them." They came to the gap in the railing, and she stepped up onto the walkway. "I used to have a partner. It takes two to do a job like that."

"What about me? I could be your partner." Bonnie stopped short, her face open and delighted like a child informed there'd be cake after dinner.

Vi hated to disappoint her, but there was no way around it. "The system we used was complicated. It's not something I could teach you in a couple of hours. No, actually I was thinking more along the lines of getting out of town for a while." Her suitcases called to her from her apartment. Vi passed through the bar, ignoring the questions that came at her from anyone who'd been watching from inside.

When she reached the foot of the stairs, she found Tobias blocking her way and shaking his shimmering head. "That won't help!" The fresh memory of the pain he'd experienced at the hand of Jeb's goons made his voice crack. "They'd find you at the ranch right quick. The ones you clocked this morning are useless human beings, but that Jeb is no slouch."

She sighed and walked through the ghost to mount the stairs, his wife right behind her. When they got to the landing and Vi's front door, Bonnie reached out and squeezed her arm. "Where will you go?"

"I got an extremely interesting letter from an old friend today, in fact, and he invited me for a visit. It's only a matter of time until they blow out of the area, so it's sounding more and more like the best thing to do is take my friend up on his offer and lay low down South for a while."

"I wouldn't recommend that." The honeyed baritone voice came from somewhere at Vi's back, but she found empty space when she turned.

Bonnie took in her furrowed brow as she stepped back. "What is it?"

"You didn't hear that?"

They stood together in silence for a few moments, but the only sound that came was a muffled laugh from the saloon downstairs.

"No. I mean, I don't think so," whispered Bonnie. "But I don't know what 'that' I was supposed to be hearing, do I?"

"Never mind," Vi replied, raking her hand across her face. "Just forget I said anything."

The disembodied voice snickered. "It really is that easy for you to forget me, isn't it?" A pale figure stepped through her solid oak door as the voice rose behind her. His fashionable clothing was marred by slashes and burns, but his face wore a cocky grin. In life, his eyes had been a deep and penetrating brown. Now, as it was with all ghosts, death had turned them a bright, unbroken blue. The effect was so jarring it took Vi several heartbeats to believe the truth before her.

Bonnie regained her balance after her friend's sudden turn and scuttled around to face her again. She placed a hand on her shoulder. "Vi, seriously. What's happening? What do you see?"

Shock rendered her voice soft. "Peter?"

CHAPTER 13

The spirit of her former partner dipped his head at Vi from over Bonnie's shoulder. Oblivious to the weight of the name, her friend tried to follow her gaze and asked in bafflement, "Who's Peter?"

"Hello, stranger," the ghost said silkily. He gestured at her companions. "Is this a bad time?"

"That's him!" cried Tobias, his outburst unnecessary in both content and volume. "That's the man who told me where to find you."

A long-suffering sigh escaped the reluctant medium's lips. "Thank you, Tobias."

"Did you say 'Tobias'?" Bonnie muttered.

"No. I mean, well I did. He forgot to mention there was another ghost in town." Vi raised her voice from a whisper and pulled out her key. "We're going to go inside before I'll say anything else. To *anyone*."

In a show of ghostly prowess, Peter passed through the door before Vi could finish opening it. She huffed her way into the house and stomped into the sitting room in a white-hot rage.

"I am totally lost. Again." Bonnie pulled at her bonnet strings and threw herself onto the couch. The wicker basket full of food grinned from the floor near her feet. "Please. You've got to be honest with me about what is going on. Obviously, there is more on your mind than merely your horse."

"You didn't go out looking for us, and right now you probably wish you'd never found us," Tobias interjected as he settled in next to his wife. "But now that you've got us, you've got to let us help." He directed his next words at the other ghost, who lounged in the doorway. "You hear that? Whatever you think you're doing, you have to go through me first."

"That's sweet, but not necessary," Vi said by way of answering both husband and wife. The second unexpected show of support in as many hours made her feel both grateful and as if her insides were squirming. She yanked at the buttons constricting her throat and looked in any direction but Peter's. Her stomach added a flip-flop in case she'd forgotten she still hadn't eaten.

"I'll decide what's necessary for my own self," Bonnie scolded. "And I say I need to do what I can to help you. Especially now that I fouled things up with the cards."

Tobias had reverted back to his devoted gazing at his wife, but his words were meant for Vi. "I told you she was something, didn't I? You might as well give in now. Once my girl decides you're one of hers, you don't stop being one of hers."

"All right. You win," Vi replied. Despite her best attempt to sound relaxed, her voice came out tight and her laughter thin when she finally addressed the other woman in earnest. "Right now, I'd sell my soul for something to eat, so getting by with only a story is a bargain. You unpack the feast and give me a moment with my friend Peter, then I'll tell you all about it. Agreed?"

"Agreed." her friend picked up the basket and immediately set to work unloading its contents onto the low table in the center of the room.

The pleasing sound of Bonnie's humming accompanied Vi's weary footfalls. She dragged her eyes over to her former partner long enough to jerk her head at the door. Peter moved out of the doorframe, dipping his chin at a surly Tobias as he followed her down the hall and into her bedroom. An ornate wooden screen stood at attention near her closet, and a canopy bed dripping with brocade kept company with a mahogany side table before them. She stepped through the door and rested her back against it once it clicked closed. With a deep breath, she funneled her flash of blind anger into a low-simmering fury; easier to control who would got burned that way.

"You've certainly been enjoying yourself with all your little games," she seethed. "You nearly scared me to death."

"That's a poor choice of words," Peter replied wryly.

Vi narrowed her eyes. "And sending me a ghost-a-gram like that? Now, that was low."

"I admit, I have been... deliberate in how I have handled myself since I arrived. Honestly, I didn't expect you to speak to me if I showed up like this.

Or if you even could anymore. But I wanted you to see my letter, and to make sure you understood what I was trying to do."

"Looks like you're going to have to spell it out for me because I have no idea what you are trying to get at."

He sighed. "Did you even open the other one yet?"

She'd completely forgotten her second parcel. It rested on her bureau a few paces away, strewn aside and pushed out of her mind in the wake of the race.

"I haven't had the chance," she admitted. The scarlet seal stared at her like an ominous bloody eye, but when her gaze fell on Peter her wrath returned. "You may not have noticed, but I've had a busy day thanks, in no small part, to you."

"The thing with the horse? You can't possibly hold me responsible for any of that. I couldn't know how this would all turn out," he cried, then his voice became a jocular scold. "Don't think I don't recognize that horse, mind. I always suspected that was you."

"Never mind that. You couldn't know about Jeb, but you *knew* that I wanted ghosts to leave me alone," she snarled. "Now who's being forgetful?"

They boiled at one another for a few moments before Vi's face relaxed into a shrewd smile. "You got me into this mess, and you're going to help get me out of it."

"Oh no. You weren't the only one who retired."

"Peter, it's one more job. Please. We can do it together. It'll be simple." She raised her hand to touch his arm before her brain could remind her that it'd pass right through. The sudden chill made her jerk back, and she failed to mask her discomfort with an embarrassed throat-clearing and anemic murmur of, "Like old times."

The ghost's voice was low and earnest. "Those old times were in the well-mannered nightclubs of a real city. We're nearly as far from civilization as you can get and still call it the same country. If they find out you're cheating, these men won't politely ask you never to patronize their establishment again. They'll shoot you and leave you for dead."

Vi's incredulity defeated her awkwardness, and she squared off against him. "How would they possibly be able to figure out I was cheating? By my thinking, this job would be even safer than any other time because no one would even know you were there."

"I suppose that's true."

"Plus, Bonnie's right. Those men are so crooked, they could swallow nails and spit out corkscrews. They deserve some payback for what they did to Tobias." Her expression darkened even as the corners of her mouth curled upwards. "I'll make their wallets bleed a little, and use the proceeds to buy a ticket on the next train East to dole out some punishment to whoever did this to you."

"That's exactly why I don't want you to go back. The people who killed me were brutal. They took their time with it."

She winced when he used the word 'killed' but pressed on. "But why? What did you do to them?"

"I didn't do anything." He sniggered. "I expect that's what got them so angry."

"You'd better start making some kind of sense." Vi sighed, her fingers returning to their crusade against the buttons of her jacket.

"Forget I said anything. That's in the past. What matters now is that you think about your future. And now that they know you're here, the faster you should be anywhere else."

"It was because of me, wasn't it?" she said, her hands dropping to her sides. "That letter. They made you write it and—"

"I said to let it go. I'm finished talking about it."

The remorse that had begun to assert itself scattered as her resentment clawed its way back to the surface. "If you won't talk about it, then what are you even doing here?" she sizzled. "You went to all that trouble and now you won't even tell me what happened to you?" The ghost mimed locking his mouth with a key and Vi narrowed her eyes. "Fine. If you won't tell me more about your death, at least it sounds like this letter is going to shed some light on the rest of it."

"By all means, open it," he insisted. "But promise me you'll do the *opposite* of whatever it says."

Vi plucked the official-looking envelope from the bureau and revealed Peter's note below. The out-going New Orleans stamp showed it was less than a fortnight old, and she wrinkled her forehead. "How did you even get here so fast?"

When she spun back to face the ghost, he stood right in front of her. He extended a spectral hand to her lapel, and her eyes were drawn to the gold pin. "With a little luck."

"You possessed it?"

"That I did."

She laughed in appreciation. "Leave it to you to think of a way to outsmart even the art of correspondence. And right after you were made. That's pretty high-level haunting for a new ghost."

"I had a first-rate education when it came to haunting." Despite taking on a new color, the way his eyes danced at her was utterly familiar.

She realized how close they stood and took a step back. "I suppose you did."

"Those were good times. While they lasted."

Under the weight of his regard, her insides felt like a pressure cooker; the only way to dispel the heat was to let it out at whoever stood nearest. She snarled, "This is a touching reunion, but you gave me your warning and you don't seem to be going anywhere. So, why are you really here, Peter?" She eyed him suspiciously, the embers of her fear still glowing as she clutched the sealed envelope in one hand and waved his letter with the other. "This sage advice you're offering me wouldn't have anything to do with revenge, would it?"

"No, of course not."

"Then what?" she retorted.

His voice dropped to a pained whisper. "We both know you don't want me to say it."

The words caught her off-guard, but they shouldn't have. Ghosts were made from strong feelings—anger and fear, but most often, love. It didn't matter that she'd put a thousand miles between them, he was keeping the promise he'd made the night she'd married someone else.

She wielded the haughty tilt of her chin like a shield before quietly replying, "No. I don't." Her fingertips rested on the cool metal of the knob but did not close around it. "It appears I am in the market for a partner. You've already turned me down, so let's see if my *loyal* friends can help me make any sense of this mess."

"You don't really mean it?" he scoffed.

"I really do." A flick of her wrist and she was out the door.

CHAPTER 14

Bonnie daintily nibbled at a chunk of maple sugar as Vi re-entered the sitting room. "I wasn't sure how long you'd be, so I started without you," she tittered. "These are my favorites. I hope you don't mind."

"No, of course not," Vi said cheerfully and passed the letter to her friend as she sat down for lunch. "But be a dear and open this for me, will you? I am finally going to fill my belly."

Bonnie rose to retrieve a letter opener, and the grateful con woman started picking over the spread with her fingers. Salted meats peeked out of their paper jackets among jars of spicy relishes and fragrant mustards. A metal tin lay open, begging to be divested of the candied nuts and dried fruits. The sound of Bonnie sliding the silver knife through the paper accompanied Vi's murmured appreciation over the selection of food.

Tobias looked over his wife's shoulder as she pulled the single sheet of paper from the confines of the envelope. "Would you like me to read it to you?"

"Yes, please," Vi said, her words garbled by the pastry in her mouth.

"It's from someone named 'Edgar Marsh' in New Orleans. He's part of a law firm, Marsh and Devine. Oh, wait. There's been a mistake."

"Hm?"

"It's not for you. It's addressed to 'Annabelle Sinclair.'"

"Oh that. Yes, that's me. It's sort of a nickname."

"You should be honest with her," Peter said. He loomed at the doorway, still unwilling to fully enter the sitting room.

"She's hasn't been honest so far?" Tobias asked, disappointment pulling at the tilt of his shoulders.

"It's a name I'm known by in New Orleans," Vi clarified, glaring at Peter. "Happy?"

Bonnie began reading, no longer surprised when her friend spoke to what appeared to be the empty corner of the room. "Dear Mrs. Sinclair, I regret to inform you that your husband Edward recently fell victim to a fever and we were unable to reach you before he passed away—Oh Vi!" The little brunette let the letter fall to the ground as she dashed to the couch and threw her arms around the other woman. A fat tear fell from her eye as she squeezed all the oxygen out of Vi. "You mean to say you've just found out? But I thought you said that your husband died a long time ago. And here I got you in that pickle with the poker game and—"

"It's not like that," Vi gasped as she struggled out of Bonnie's iron embrace.

Her friend sat back, perplexed. "What are you saying? This Edward person wasn't your husband?"

She braced herself—ready to fall from the top of the pedestal Bonnie had built for her. When they finally came, the dreaded words toppled out in a rush. "He was my husband, but the whole thing was a con."

Bonnie's look of confusion deepened. "A what?"

"A bunco? Or I suppose you could say… a trick?" Vi hastened on before the other woman could react. "And I did know before now, but only since this morning. I was sent a sort of warning. See? The 'Peter' who is here now as a ghost is the one who wrote it." She passed the envelope to Bonnie's waiting hands before standing to retrieve the letter that lay abandoned on the floor. "It's in a sort of code, to tell me to do the opposite of what *this* has to say," she continued, waving the paper vaguely as she returned to her place on the sofa. "But so far they say the same thing; old man Sinclair is dead."

Bonnie wrinkled her nose at Vi's callousness. She reached for a sweet and read Peter's strange missive. When she finished, she handed the letter back. "So, what does this all mean?"

"It could mean trouble, or it could mean I inherited the Colonel's whole estate," Vi exclaimed, greed making her eyes nearly glow with excitement.

"What sort of trouble?"

"Keep reading," Peter said dryly.

Vi turned from her former partner in favor of her new ally and began unbuttoning her cuff. "I think it's time we brought everyone into the conversation. You want to help, and Peter says he's here to do the same thing. So, touch my arm, and you two can get acquainted. If it gets to be too much, you can always let go."

"I'm not sure..."

"I'd also completely understand if you wanted to walk out the door right now," Vi said reasonably. "I've been trying to leave all this ghost nonsense behind and it keeps finding me." She finished with the fasteners and exposed her wrist. "But this—talking to the dead, seeing what I see. This is what being let in means."

"That's not the problem really," Bonnie dithered. "It's that... Tobias is here, too, isn't he?"

"Yes. He's here. He's *always* here." Vi deflated in disgust as domestic drama once again reared its ugly head. "You should talk to your husband," she groused. Tobias watched the exchange in silence, sorrow deepening the haze of his form from white to gray.

Bonnie sighed. "Yes, I probably should. It's just... Oh, it's selfish. I shouldn't even think such a thing."

"Well, now I'm curious," Vi replied, sitting forward with interest. "Though frankly, I doubt anything you have to admit will be much of a scandal after my little confession."

The widow hesitated, chewing over her words with her next serving of brie. "If it's wrong to speak ill of the dead, it must also be wrong to be feel cross with him."

"Must and mustn't? Right and wrong? That sounds an awful lot like religion." Vi pulled a face. "I don't really think in those terms, myself. As you can imagine, my line of work didn't exactly lend itself to a godly state of mind," she said with a shrug. "What I do know is that if it were me, I'd rather stop being angry. Not for my soul, but for my own peace of mind."

Peter's mumble broke into the conversation. "You're one to talk."

"I came all the way out here to escape my demons," she reminded him pointedly. "They simply found their way to my doorstep again."

"I'm not ready," Bonnie insisted. "I need more time."

"And they say time heals all wounds," she replied sympathetically. "But in my experience, wounds left too long just fester."

Tobias looked on expectantly as his wife finally agreed. Bonnie clasped Vi's wrist and let out a gasp as the forms of both ghosts appeared before her. Even though this was her second encounter with the dead, her face was awash with wonder as she took them in.

"Bonnie, this was my partner, Peter Freeman."

"Charmed." He dipped into a shallow bow and stepped across the threshold.

"He's the one who told me to find Vi, honey," Tobias added eagerly.

"I see," she replied, acknowledging her husband with a sheepish bob of her head, then shifted her attention to the other ghost. "I suppose I owe you some thanks."

Peter smiled and jerked his thumb at the woman he was trying to rescue. "Vi doesn't see it that way."

"Now that we're all acquainted," she broke in. "What does the rest of the letter say?"

Bonnie traded the small page for the large one and continued reading aloud:

"I have been made executor of the estate in your absence, as dictated by Edward Sinclair's last will and testament. I understand you have been out managing properties on the edges of the estate for some time, but I must request that you return to New Orleans at the earliest possible convenience.

"Reginald Sinclair has recently returned from France to escape the escalation of hostilities with Germany. He informs me that the two of you have never met, and he is anxious to finally put a face to the name in his father's letters. The sooner matters of the estate may be put to rest, the sooner Edward may rest easy with the Lord."

"Please inform us by telegram when you plan to arrive and any special arrangements you will require. The house on St. Charles Street has been made ready for your stay, and we all eagerly await your return."

"Best Wishes, Edgar Marsh, Esquire," Bonnie finished.

Silence hung for a few moments, but Vi's chuckle eventually shattered it. "As death threats go, I've certainly heard worse." She plucked up the letter and examined it again, her eyes jumping rapidly from line to line as she searched for hidden meanings. The return of the wayward son and the letters from his father were troubling, but she'd need more information to know if he was a threat.

"It wouldn't be effective at luring you out of hiding if it was obvious, would it?" Peter shook his finger at her. "They told me they sent dozens of these to properties all over the estate holdings trying to find you."

Tobias's Adam's apple did a dance before he was able to mutter, "D-did you say *dozens* of holdings?"

"Hm?" Vi lifted her eyes from the page. "Oh yes, my late husband was quite wealthy. Ergo, the appeal." When she reached the end of the letter, she waved it at Peter. "I can't believe the old fool never admitted what had happened to anyone."

"Would you go around bragging about how you'd been jilted by your bride?" her former partner replied. "He stayed quiet to save face. At least, publicly."

"Is that what happened?" Bonnie asked the other woman, crestfallen. A tinge of anger entered her voice as she glanced from her own husband and back to Vi. "You married a man, and then you just left him? But this afternoon, I thought—"

The ghost cut in before she could answer. "It's not like he was a particularly *good* man, mind. In fact, that's exactly why we targeted him."

Vi held up the letter for emphasis. "*This* was always a job, Bonnie, but I didn't mislead you." Her voice grew quiet in the face of the painful memories. "Old man—Edward—was my husband, but he wasn't my first."

"And he never changed the will," Peter interrupted a little too loudly. "So, they need you to come back for the reading."

Vi smirked. "I thought this was over the moment I left, but it seems to me that you aren't the only one with unfinished business."

Despite the lightness in her voice, panic made Peter's come out shrill. "You can't. Don't you see? When the first letters didn't work, they hunted down your known associates, such as yours truly, to find out if we knew where you'd gone."

"But I didn't tell you where to find me, so that shouldn't have worked."

"No, but I did figure it out. You weren't the only one to rifle through the Colonel's papers, and I put a few facts together. I do know you pretty well, Thorne," he admonished. Her throat grew tight, and he continued. "All the same, I wouldn't tell them what they wanted to know."

For the first time, Vi connected the tatters of Peter's shirt to his state when he died. If every slash to the insubstantial fabric represented another cut to his flesh, he would have had gashes all over his body. Mercifully, blood stains seemed to be too earth-bound to be part of a spirit manifestation, but her imagination did a fine job of filling in the blanks.

Anger made her voice hushed, but acidic. "They tortured you. Those animals have to pay."

"This is why I didn't want to tell you more. You've got bloodlust in your eyes, and that's not going to get you anywhere. Besides, we don't know exactly how they are connected to the estate and the Colonel's death. I gathered a few bits and pieces over the days they held me."

"It took days?" Vi asked darkly, then realization made her soften. "And you never said anything?"

"No, I didn't. But I—"

"What about the second letter?" Tobias interrupted. "They sent it *here*, so someone must have known."

The last pieces of Peter's tale were drawn from him by the weight of many eyes. "Eventually, they got so tired of waiting they brought in a ghost to help with the questioning."

"What would that do?" Bonnie twisted in her seat to read Peter's face as he paced. "I thought only Vi could see them."

"How did you even know?" the reluctant medium asked.

"I wasn't sure *what* had happened until afterward. I'm still not completely sure, but I'm used to watching Vi talk to empty air so that is my best guess. All that aside," he said airily, "There was this rush of cold inside my head, and it felt like something rummaged around until she found the answer she needed."

Bonnie's voice quivered with fear. "Ghosts can do that?"

"Not any I've ever heard of," Vi replied skeptically. "But I suppose it could be possible."

"Not only possible, it's happening." His voice grew quiet. "I wasn't the first." Righteous indignation bloomed on her face, but he pressed on before she could question him further. "They told me they wouldn't kill me if I wrote a letter to entice you to come home, but when I refused to finish it the way they wanted..."

"What did they do?" Bonnie asked, sounding every bit like a small child around the Christmas fire.

"The ghost, she passed all the way inside of me somehow. She moved my hands. I've never even heard of such a thing. I fought her as hard as I could, then everything went blank. Next thing I know, I'm standing next to my own body and watching her go, but she didn't spot me."

"That is… troubling." Vi leaned forward and rested her chin on her fist, mind racing through all of the accounts of hauntings she knew and coming up blank. They certainly possessed objects sometimes, but to step into a body was wholly new to her.

Peter pressed on. "There's something powerful rising back home, and the safest place for you to be is far, far away from it."

Tobias's happy tenor cut through the tension building between them. "Can't argue with that."

Peter ignored him, his stare penetrating, his voice soft and insistent. "Promise me you won't go back. Now, or after I…."

The unspoken ending to the sentence hung in the air between them for a few heartbeats. "That's a question for tomorrow," Vi finally said, tamping down the unwelcome grief and averting her gaze as she diverted the conversation into safer waters. "But I'd like to discuss the here and now for a second. About my horse—"

"Not this again." He threw his arms up in exasperation. "I already told you, I'm staying out if it."

"I heard you, but that doesn't change the fact that I need help to do this poker job."

"I could do it," Bonnie piped up.

Vi slid her attention from wife to husband. Desperate times called for desperate measures. "I actually had someone else in mind."

"Who, me?" Tobias squeaked. "I can't do it. I don't know anything about gambling."

"There's nothing to it, really," she said. "Besides, I believe you owe me one. If you hadn't burst in on me in the bath—"

"The what?" Bonnie interjected, giving her husband a glare so hot it would melt steel.

"—I could've spent today sleeping off my hangover in peace," Vi concluded.

"And I'm grateful," the ghost said. "But I also offered to pay you for your trouble. No one forced you to help."

"Didn't you? Or was that some other ghost who threatened to haunt me the rest of my life?" She wanted to get to her feet, but her friend's grip kept her grounded. Tobias sputtered half a reply, but he didn't squirm long.

Bonnie's voice sliced through his rambling. "You really did that? For me?"

"Well... A little."

Peter leaned close to his old partner, whispering, "Given the circumstances, that might be the most romantic thing I've ever heard."

Whether Vi's words or the way his wife looked at him made him change his mind, Tobias said, "I don't know anything about playing poker. Is there time to teach me?"

"All you have to do is tell me what they've got," she assured him. "But could you stop acting like you expect me to answer you in public? I don't want to look like a complete imbecile in front of people." The ghost returned a chagrined glance that she hoped constituted acquiescence.

"I can't make myself invisible, but I'll do what I can," Bonnie added. "I could stake you. Or give me a job to do. Any job."

"You can keep your money. Tobias went to a lot of trouble to get it for you. No, the most important thing you can do for me is to make sure that the drinks keep coming and they're happy. Caroline will take care of everyone else, but you make sure the poker table gets roostered up. Only give me the 'oh-be-joyful' every other glass or so, but make it look like I'm drinking as much as them. Got it?"

"No!" Tobias exclaimed. "Nothing doing. I don't want her anywhere near those men."

"I appreciate that you want to protect me, darling," Bonnie cooed. "But that's not really your decision."

"I won't allow it," her late husband quavered, stamping his foot ineffectually.

"Oh yeah? What do you think you're going to do about it?" she shot back, tearing her hand away from the contact that made him visible to her.

Peter cradled his forehead in his palm, murmuring, "This is a very bad idea."

"Without you, they're the best chance I've got," Vi replied.

"I'm going to be frank with you, Thorne. It's obvious that you *need* my help, and the only way you're going to get my help is if you give up on solving my murder."

"Vi-ie!" the other ghost whined. "Make her talk to me."

"I've thought about all the angles here," Peter continued. "Admit it. You might as well save everyone the trouble and give in." He pointed at Vi's co-conspirators. To her embarrassment, Tobias chose that exact moment to stomp over and slouch in the corner, leaving Bonnie to make rude gestures at the empty air. "Because without me, you're going to need a lot more than those two. You're going to need an army."

She glowered harder and hoped he couldn't see how close she was to agreeing with him. Times like these, she wished she'd made more of an effort to meet the neighbors. Sure, not having friends kept everything tidier, but now that the former swindler found herself backed into a corner, it would be nice to have a gang of her own.

Rather than admit it, she said, "I've gotten by just fine without you before and I'll do it again."

He clucked his tongue and shook his head. "If you are too stubborn to cooperate, I suppose I cannot stop you. Honestly, it's sort of nice to see some things haven't changed," Peter said with a chuckle before beginning to sink through the floorboards. "I think I'll go find myself a ringside seat." The last part of him to disappear was a playful wink and his curls.

"He's right, you know," Tobias piped up. "You shouldn't count on me. What if I can't do this? What if we try and we fail? Then I've put my wife in danger all over again."

Vi wheeled on him, but swapped her flare of anger for a persuasive nonchalance before she responded. "You heard Peter, he's going to be right there, watching over us."

The ghost scratched his head, "I don't think that's what he m—"

"Bonnie's only going serve a couple of drinks to a few people, she's going to be fine. You have my word." The little brunette didn't know where Tobias stood, so she nodded her assurance to the room at large. "I want you to focus on learning about the cards. And I'll take care of the next step in the plan— recruiting that army."

CHAPTER 15

Darkness fell early that time of year, but thanks to the mirrored glass that covered the walls, the inside of *Viola's* glowed bright as day. The woman who sang on Thursdays always attracted a nice crowd of regulars, but an ample table in the back remained off-limits, cordoned off until the poker game could begin. With a crack of his knuckles, the piano man started the next number, and the chanteuse waited patiently for the introduction to end so she could start a funny little ditty featuring a man and his mule.

Caroline had pouted when she had first heard Bonnie would be joining her that evening. Her surliness in no small part hung on the fact that Vi had loaned what appeared to be a brand-new employee a gorgeous dress from her employer's own bountiful selection. Eventually, the head waitress had been reassured by her employer's promise that the situation was both necessary and entirely temporary. Given the type of crowd they were expecting, Vi had even offered to give her the night off. But Jimmy had already agreed to work the bar, and that meant Caroline wouldn't dream of being anywhere else. After an hour, the two waitresses now exchanged smiles as they flitted from table to table.

Peter lounged against the far end of the bar, and some part of Vi's brain noted the fact he could lean at all was not a good sign. It was bad enough that both ghosts mounted the stairs with no problems, but the more her former partner could touch, the stronger his ties were to the living. If he really would be staying around for a while, she'd need to watch for other indications he was getting too comfortable in limbo, but one thing at a time. He looked up to find her staring and wiggled his fingers in greeting. Whether or not he was willing to help her, he seemed tickled to watch whatever happened to unfold.

The other half of Vi's undead entourage paced back and forth at Peter's feet. Tobias' eyes never left his wife as she moved around the room distributing mugs of beer and tumblers of spirit. He rubbed his agitated face with his evanescent hands and muttered. "I was afraid something like this would happen."

"Really?" Peter drawled. "You were afraid you and your wife would become embroiled in an elaborate con job several days *post*-post-mortem?"

"No. Not that." Tobias peered out the saloon window at the darkening sky. "Those men who are coming tonight. They killed me."

"So I gathered. But what does that have to do with the soft shoe you're doing now?"

"Huh?"

Peter pointed at the floor. "If you could touch the floorboards, you'd be wearing a hole in them."

"Oh, sorry." The other ghost chuckled. "I suppose you're right, I shouldn't be so nervous."

Once Vi freed herself of customers, she made her way to where the ghosts stood talking. The stage show and the men who hollered at it kept her words from reaching beyond their small stretch of counter. "How are you doing, Toby? Feeling ready? Because they should be here soon."

"Yes. I think so." His glowing blue eyes rolled to the ceiling as he struggled to remember. "The one with two of one card and three of another has something to with a house, and the cards with faces are better than the ones with numbers. Is that right?"

Keeping her features schooled around Tobias turned out to be a great way to prepare for holding a poker face for the next three hours. She smiled tightly. "You'll do great."

Peter's repressed snicker finally hissed out through his teeth. "Nothing to worry about here."

She glowered at him before turning an encouraging look to the other ghost. "We'll get through it, okay, Toby? Remember, we don't have to win big, we just have to make sure not to lose." Her nervous hands found a stray glass to polish, but she was careful to keep grit away from her gloves—the expanse of silken fabric a reliable barrier between her abilities and the world at large. "Jeb seemed almost sorry for living up to his promise to his gang, so maybe if I give him enough excuses, he'll forget the whole thing."

"Has that ever happened before? Ever?" Peter asked, one eyebrow creeping skyward.

"No, but they say there's a first time for everything."

The song ended, and the audience erupted into another round of approving hollers. The crowd was both larger and rowdier than usual. Evidently, news of the game had already been spreading.

George tumbled into the room, his head swinging wildly from side to side. When Vi flagged him, he mouthed the words "They're coming."

The grifter returned a silent, "Good boy," and shooed him away. She draped herself against the bar and waited to see the scope of the enemy forces. Sure, she'd doubled her meager numbers by enlisting her staff, but she had the sinking suspicion the most reliable lieutenant in her army was too short to see over the counter.

A line of bodies passed by the windows, dimming the room as they made their way to the door. Jeb entered first, trailed by at least a dozen men who pooled around the entryway like the contents of a giant upturned ink pot. A few people on the fringe of the audience shifted uncomfortably as the cause of the artificial nightfall took in its surroundings with appreciation. Their leader spied the table meant for them and sauntered over. The gang had grown since that afternoon, and they wouldn't all be able to fit around it. A handful approached a full table, and a few snarls later, they claimed it as their own.

Bonnie nattered with a couple of regulars across the room, unaware their marks had entered the bar. Her late husband wasn't the only one watching her as she moved from person to person, which was more than likely the point. Nothing like a little petty jealousy to make your man squirm, dead or alive. As far as Vi was concerned, the widow could play whatever games she wanted, as long as it didn't interfere with the real stakes.

Vi finally caught the other woman's attention, and Bonnie's eyes went wide at the sight of so many new people slinking across the floor. After a moment's hesitation, she gave a thumbs-up and snaked her way over to where Jimmy stood behind the bar. He dipped his chin at his boss before loading a tray with a bottle of top-shelf whiskey and stacks of clean tumblers as they'd discussed.

Despite her anxiety, the thrill of the gambit tugged at the corner of Vi's mouth. She pushed away from the bar, rubbing her hands together. "Time to get to work."

Others proved less enthused. "I hate this!" Tobias cried, motioning to his wife. "She shouldn't be wasting her time as a barmaid. She should be sitting by a cozy fire in the cabin I should have built for her, a stew happily bubbling away on the stove while the kids play—"

The other dead man smirked. "You've given this a lot of thought."

"I give everything a lot of thought!" Tobias nearly bellowed. "I'm an accountant, it's who I am."

"Was," the other ghost corrected. "And no matter your feelings, the work certainly seems to agree with her."

"That's exactly what I hate about it."

"Relax," Peter clapped Tobias on the arm. "It's not permanent. It'll all be over tonight."

"*This* may be for only one night, but what about the rest of her life? I've left her all alone. The last thing I want her to do is wind up a barmaid."

"You've got to work on letting that go." All hint of amusement drained from Peter's voice as he twitched his chin at Vi's receding back. "She told me the ones who stay too long get sort of tattered. It isn't pretty. Haven't seen many, but I'm sure it's only a matter of time."

The two ephemeral gentlemen finally stopped their yammering to watch their subject perfectly time her approach with Bonnie's retreat. "Good evening. It was Mister...? I'm sorry, I don't believe you ever did introduce yourself."

She leaned forward to serve the whiskey, and the goateed outlaw, as well as every other man in the room, took in the delicate play of lace across her décolletage. The decoration did little to hide way lay beneath, ensuring no man at that table would be focused on cards when the game started. At the same time, when paired with her gloves, it meant it would be difficult to touch her and get an eye-full of the ghosts by mistake.

"You can call me Jeb." He tilted his head, openly appreciating the view.

She ignored his rudeness, taking it for a good sign. "Well, then. Good evening, Jeb," she crooned. Her smile almost slipped when Peter's derisive snort interrupted the moment.

The other ghost snickered. "What was that about letting go?"

Vi could actually feel a weight lift as her former partner dragged his eyes away from her. An unexpected heat crept into her face.

Peter steered his conversation with the other ghost in another direction. "She's going to take care of her, you know."

"What?"

"Vi. She's going to take care of your wife," he explained. "She's got a soft spot for widows."

"And is this an example of that care?" Tobias said hotly. "Because I can't say that makes me feel any better. She's making us both accessories to a crime."

The accusation sent a tremor through Vi's hand, almost spilling whiskey.

"Well, you know my position. I don't think any of you should be doing any of this. Especially not over some dumb animal." Peter sniffed. Ever the gallant. "But I guess that's what you all get for having an inflated sense of honor."

A fiddle player stepped onto the stage and received a smattering of applause. Vi said a silent thank you to him when he began the next song; with the chatter from the undead peanut gallery silenced, she could pay attention to the job at hand.

She finished passing out the glasses and gestured at the saloon. "What do you think, gentlemen? Doesn't really seem like a place that belongs to someone who goes traipsing around bothering people at all hours, does it?"

"I'd say we're way past what did or did not happen this morning," Jeb said jovially. "But this is right fine establishment you've got here, Miss Viola." His eyes wandered over the tucks and folds of her gown appreciatively as he spoke.

She smirked, feeding into the flirtation by adding a slight huskiness to her voice. "Thank you, I've worked hard to make it that way."

A voice across the room exploded—one of the bandits at the other table making his dislike of the song selection clear to all. The singer did her best to continue, but the heckling made it difficult to keep the beat. Vi frowned and indicated the rowdy table of thugs near the stage. "And I wish to keep it a fine establishment, if you catch my drift."

"Don't worry, the boys'll behave," Jeb said lazily. The henchmen who were within earshot exchanged a few significant glances and menacing snickers.

"Oh, I'm not concerned," Vi said sweetly, leaning against the back of an empty chair. "Especially after you tell all those fine friends of yours the House Rules."

"Rules?" Hank whined from his place at the table. "I thought this was a poker game."

His boss snickered. "Well, I suppose even poker has rules." He turned back to Vi with a by-your-leave gesture, his tone surprisingly respectful. "Go on ma'am, tell us your rules."

"In honor of your visit, I've told my staff to keep the drinks flowing." She allowed the happy, grateful susurrus to ebb before going on, her eyes moving from face to face as she spoke to each man in turn. "Now, I know how that can make a man's blood hot, but any brawling—just one of you lot starts something—and the house takes the whole pot." The table let out a few groans and scoffs, but she flashed them her most charming smile. "Have you seen you boys? I'm sure if you got going you'd do a whole mess of damage." A few other henchmen puffed up in pride, sitting up straighter after her compliment. Even the man she'd clobbered the worst that morning treated her to a scar-crinkled smile.

Other were less impressed. "Boss, this is ridiculous—" Hank began.

"No," Vi snapped. "What's ridiculous is how often I have to buy new chairs. You think replacing everything that gets broken during a fight is cheap? I've got a business to run," she finished mulishly.

The protestations rose up, but Jeb's amused voice cut through them. "And that's a mighty smart way to run your business, ma'am. I admit, it's been a long while since me and the boys have gotten an invitation to such a fine establishment." The men quieted as he took them in with a flinty glare. With a wave of his hand, one of his cronies dashed off to relay the message to the other table. Jeb rose and pulled out the chair he'd reserved for Vi at his side. He gave her what would have been a charming smile if it hadn't included quite so many teeth. "We won't start nothing. You have my word."

"That's all I needed to hear," she purred back, the deep amethyst silk of her dress swishing as she took her seat. She perched on the edge of her chair, back painfully straight to keep her structured bodice from pushing her flesh all the way up to her chin. The ensemble was best for standing or dancing, but when she'd chosen it, she had a mind that Jeb would like her best in something dark and rich, and based on the way his eyes followed her every move, her instincts appeared to be right. Of course, Tobias would try his best, but if he wasn't up to the task, she needed to deploy every weapon in her arsenal. That included a cinched waist and practiced disregard for breathing.

Despite her lack of oxygen, the butterflies in her stomach did happy somersaults as she took up the cards.

Once more into the fray.

CHAPTER 16

Seconds stretched into moments, and moments piled into a minute.

The corner of Jeb's mouth twitched, and he slid some of cards facedown toward the dealer. They had been playing for more than an hour.

"Three."

The surly young man to his left groaned, "Same."

The players took turns trading in their cards until the bidding circled around to Vi. She tilted her head as if looking at her cards, but peered through her lashes as Tobias moved from man to man clucking and tutting. Somehow, he managed a continuous string of words without giving her much in the way of useful information.

"Well, er... this fellow took two cards, and it looks like... let's see. Yes, it appears he has two of the ones with the man on it..." he stuttered.

To make matters worse, Peter had changed seats to get a better view. He slouched in the corner, the same smug grin on his face whenever she glanced his way. Occasionally, he'd rise and walk around the table, nodding and murmuring to himself, but giving nothing away.

Vi regretted her decision to monitor her alcohol intake. If she believed in hell, it would probably look much like this poker game.

"Well, do you want cards, or don't you?" the dealer sneered. His boss's frown made him change his tone, and he added a well-mannered, "Ma'am."

"I fold," she declared. The men around her groaned and muttered.

"This ain't your night, is it Miss Viola?" Jeb said with a mix of sympathy and glee. His fingers walked their way from the top of her chair to rest on her shoulder.

"Really, Vi?" Peter shuddered. "You're resorting to letting *that* touch you?"

"It sure looks that way," she pouted and fluttered her lashes prettily at Jeb as she spoke, though she mostly intended to needle Peter. Jeb actually wasn't too terrible on the eyes, but she'd never resorted to the world's oldest profession before and didn't intend to start that night. All the same, she added coquettishly, "You can call me Vi, you know."

"I'll remember that," the bandit said, eyes alight with possibilities.

Bonnie sauntered up to the game and put another bottle of whiskey on the table. Hank leered at her. "You sure know how to show a feller a good time, Miss Viola."

"Yeah, awful considerate of you to share your money so freely." Beardface's hoarse guffaw rose over a sudden burst of applause from the people ringed around the stage.

The little brunette hovered over Vi's shoulder, wringing her hands. "Excuse me sirs, but may I borrow her for a moment?"

"This isn't a great time, sugar," Jeb answered for Vi as his fingers slithered over a lacy seam. Despite Bonnie's best efforts at keeping their glasses full, his words came out with only a slight slur. "Your boss is very... comfortable right now."

No matter how much Vi would have loved an excuse to leave, she had to tread lightly. She turned her grimace into a forced but delighted smile as she turned to Bonnie. "We're still in the middle of the game. Can it wait?"

"I know, Vi," the other woman bubbled, then remembered who she was supposed to be. "I mean, Miss Viola, but there's something I need you to show me. In the back room. Now?"

"What's wrong, honey?" Tobias asked.

To sell what came next, Vi let loose a long-suffering sigh—aided in no small part by the ghost. "If you'll excuse me gentlemen, I had a new girl start today, and she still needs some breaking in. I'll be but a few minutes."

She gently returned Jeb's hand to his side, but as she rose, his rough grip crushed the delicate fabric on her arm. "Hurry back, Miss Viola."

"Of course," she replied, getting to her feet. "Please, feel free to refresh your drinks and enjoy the entertainment while I'm away."

"I surely will, ma'am," he replied as he rose beside her. He caught her fingers in his grasp, murmuring, "But just so we're clear, a coupla my boys'll go wait outside and make sure that new horse of mine doesn't wander off while you're gone."

"As you wish." She rolled her eyes and dismissed the room with the flap of her hand before setting off for the storeroom.

Bonnie fell in step beside her, whispering. "I don't know anything about poker, but even I can see that you're losing."

Her husband's ghost squeaked. Tobias ran through the table and bumbled over to her side.

Vi cringed. "Thank you for your support."

"Am I wrong?"

"No," she admitted, pushing through the door. They passed into the darkness of the back room. "I am definitely open to suggestions."

"I want to talk to Tobias."

The ghost gawped between the two faces, stunned. "You do?"

"Now?" Vi scoffed. "What's that got to do with the game?"

"I've been terrible to him all day, and it's eating me up inside," Bonnie replied, turning the lantern key to give them more light.

"I'm sure it has," she said, pinching the bridge of her nose to keep her tone civil—like husband, like wife, it seemed. "And I'm sorry for that, truly I am. But we're in the middle of something right now and as you recently pointed out, we're losing."

"Exactly," the other woman insisted. "This bad blood between Tobias and me is probably ruining his concentration. It seems he couldn't have been much help to you so far. And we owe you after how you handled Salty."

"Well, I didn't really 'handle' him. Not in a way that will last," Vi sighed dejectedly. "I'm actually sort of surprised he and his lot haven't come back in here to make trouble for me already."

And when they did come back, there would definitely be trouble. Though, perhaps just the kind of trouble she needed. Of course, more people would mean splitting the pot. Splitting the pot meant splitting the losses…

"Fiddlesticks, you're a hero," Bonnie declared. "You got good and even with him. I'd be surprised if he set foot in here again. At least, not without an invitation."

The gears in Vi's brain turned. The idea clicked into place.

The widow mistook her contemplative silence for encouragement. "So, let me talk to Tobias for a minute. I'm sure if I can clear the air between us the game will turn around."

"Though he might think I was setting him up..." Vi murmured absently.

The ghost misinterpreted and answered her remark. "I wouldn't feel set up. Really, Vi. I want to talk to her. And it's true," he added somberly. "I have been awful distracted."

The grifter's eyes snapped into focus, and she dashed to the door. She peered into the main room of the saloon and crooked a finger at George, who immediately scrambled from his seat and took off across the room.

"It would only take a moment," the widow assured her. "I know I've been avoiding him, but honestly now I'm dying to see him."

Vi controlled the urge to point out her pun, replying, "Yes, all right. Give me a minute."

George arrived, beaming. "Got a job for me, Miss Viola?"

She delivered a few quiet instructions into his ear, then the boy took off through the back door and into the night. With a satisfied brush of her hands, she perched on the edge of a wooden crate and turned to the mismatched couple. "What have we really got to lose? But it'll have to be quick. Jeb won't wait long before he sends someone looking for me. You know, I believe he expects me to try to steal my own horse."

"You told me earlier today how you tricked a man into marrying you in order to steal his money. But someone *hinting* you *might* be a thief upsets you?"

"Only because I didn't think of it myself," she said drolly. "I'm going to face away this time. No buts. I may have to be here to facilitate this chat, but I'm staying out of it. This is bound to get... emotional." Vi pulled a face and got herself situated with her back to the couple and tilted her head to give Bonnie access to the skin of her neck. "Ready?"

"Ready." Bonnie took a deep breath before placing her hand on the medium's flesh. She let out another appreciative gasp as his spirit body materialized before her.

"Hi, darling," he said shyly and doffed his spectral bowler hat.

"I've got something to say to you."

"That's fine, honey." His voice was quiet and dejected. "And I'm sure I deserve every word of it."

"In fact," his wife said affectionately. "I'd hoped to make you feel better."

He returned his hat to its rightful place and stood taller. "All right. I think I can handle that."

"Coming out here was a mistake," she said plainly. "It was a silly, romantic notion that has changed our lives forever, and not for the best."

"So far that doesn't make me feel better."

Her voice quivered as she pressed on. "But what those men did to you? That wasn't your fault."

"That's sweet, honey, but we both know I never had any business being out there in the first place. I don't even have enough common sense to check the area before I make camp." The ghosts' words swung from one side of the room to the other as he paced.

"It wasn't your fault," she promised, but her assurances were no match for his guilt.

"I was never even a good *accountant*, what on God's green earth made me I could be a prospector?" he yelped.

Bonnie's grip tightened as she repeated herself, her words falling heavy as lead. "It. Wasn't. Your. Fault."

"And the worst part is now you're all alone!"

"But I'm not!" she declared, then checked her volume with a glance at the barroom door. "I've got Vi, and I have you to thank for that. And the gold, darling. You were so clever that you hid the gold, and you loved me so much you came back from the dead to make sure I got it."

"Of course, I did," he said with pride and confusion in equal measure. Vi sensed the motion of his aura as he rushed over to her. "I didn't even think about it. It was the right thing to do."

Vi felt the tremor pass through Bonnie as she let out a sob. "And I love you for that, Tobias Anthony Murphy."

"Oh, honey! I'm so sorry."

The medium turned her head just enough to watch the last hint of anger evaporate from Bonnie's being as she reached out automatically to try to comfort him, but the mist of his body swirled in the wake of her hand. The widow's tears glittered on her lashes. "I know it was an accident, and you don't deserve the way I've been treating you. That's why I dragged Vi out of her game, I couldn't wait any longer to tell you."

The fog that made up his spirit body began to swirl, but instead of darkening and growing solid, it glowed a soft blue. The light crept to every corner of the room as it grew and cast eerie shadows on the walls.

If he could have seen himself, Tobias would have been dazzled, but his eyes never left his wife. "Oh honey, do you think you can ever forgive me? Truly?"

"I already have, darling." Despite the tear trailing down her cheek, Bonnie smiled at him. "I already have."

The eddying blue of his form whirled faster, and at its brightest points, tiny fissures furrowed through his insubstantial body. A wind kicked up from nowhere, blowing around their hair and clothes but leaving the rest of the objects in the room completely untouched.

"Brace yourself," Vi advised.

Bonnie trilled, "What's happening to him?"

The white light spilling from the spreading cracks almost blinded the living, but the ghost's face was serene as he whispered his final farewell. His eyes closed and his face drifted up toward the ceiling, a peaceful smile on his lips.

"You've finished it."

CHAPTER 17

Vi knew what to expect, but she clapped her free hand over Bonnie's mouth to keep her from screaming. No one in the saloon knew what was happening in the stockroom, and most importantly, no one would believe them even if they were told.

The blaze poured out of Tobias with the force of an explosion, but the fireball made no sound. Its percussive force punched the air, pulsing through the pair of onlookers and dissipating through the walls. The room plunged into gloom.

"I only wanted to make things right between us." Bonnie sobbed, collapsing against the other woman like a puppet without its strings.

Vi stroked her hair as she cried. "You did."

"But... the way he... that must have been so painful!"

"No. You saw his face. That didn't hurt him." She pulled back to look at her friend directly. "I had a teacher of sorts, once. She told me her own theory."

"Really?" Bonnie snuffled. "What did she say?"

"She said it feels like love," Vi answered with a smile. "And this was a woman who didn't hardly know the word."

The widow wiped her eyes with the back of her hand, the gesture and her voice childlike in their purity. "I don't understand one thing."

"Only one?" Vi pulled a lace-trimmed handkerchief from her bodice and passed it over.

Bonnie regained control of her spine and dabbed at her face. "When I came back here to talk to him, I had no idea that would happen. It certainly wasn't what I was trying to do."

"Really? You weren't planning to blow up Tobias? Because, I tell you, there were times…"

She was rewarded for her tasteless joke with an eruption of giggles. "No, I suppose I wasn't. But I wasn't trying to help him cross over either. I thought we'd have more time, what with his unfinished business. There's still the gold and whatever comes next—"

"It was forgiveness, Bonnie," Vi blurted. An embarrassed squelching inside of guts kept her from meeting the other woman's eye, but she continued. "Recruiting me to get you the gold, that was a small part of him trying to make things right between you. He wanted to let you know how sorry he was."

"You mean to say, all I had to do was accept his apology?"

The reluctant medium flexed her empty hands a few times thoughtfully. "I'm not sure *you* were the one who needed to forgive him."

Peter's face and shoulders burst through the solid wood of the stockroom door. "What the hell was that? It felt like I got socked in the gut, but I shouldn't be feeling much of anything right now."

"Could you excuse us for a minute, Bonnie?"

With their contact broken, the widow could no longer hear the ghost, and she looked at Vi in concern. "Everything okay?"

"Yes, but I need the room a minute. Peter's here."

"Oh."

The ghost grumbled, "Are you going to tell me what happened, or not?"

"Tobias passed over," she snapped over her shoulder before returning her attention to Bonnie. "It'll just a be minute, then I'll be out to finish the game."

"Ah, I see." Peter's eyes lit up with intrigue as he passed the rest of the way through the door and into the room. "I never knew that other ghosts could feel it when it happened. Fascinating."

"Oh no," Bonnie gasped. "I ruined your game. Tobias can't help you win anymore."

Vi smirked at the knowledge of her secret gamble. "He wasn't doing much to help me win anyway, and this needed to be done. Plus, I could've interrupted if I'd wanted. If Tobias was a better card player, I may even have considered it," she joked, then her voice grew somber. "Nah, I wasn't going to take that from the two of you for a few hands of cards." She infused her next words with as much enthusiasm as she could muster. "Speaking of which, Jeb and the boys probably need a refill," she hinted.

"Right." The young widow grabbed a new bottle from a waiting crate and made a beeline for the main room. "I'm on it."

The door clicked shut behind Bonnie. Peter examined Vi's face expectantly. She cracked her neck as she gathered her thoughts, an old boxer's habit she'd picked up in her twenties. The silence stretched between them until the ghost broke it.

"Game's not going well, is it?" he said, searching for a solid footing for conversation. "I told you this was a bad idea—"

"I'm going back to New Orleans," she interrupted, her words clipped.

"No, you are not," he vowed. "I'm not going to let your greed—"

She shook her head and took a step toward him. "It is not about the money."

"—or your pride get you into trouble. Not again. Look where it has gotten you just *today*." He indicated the poker game with a broad sweep of his arms.

Her voice was quiet, but her eyes spoke volumes. "That's not why I have to go." She paused to take a deep breath, and the words tripped over each other as she exhaled. "I have to make this all right, Peter. With you, with these things I can do."

"You of all people know you do not *have* to do anything. Everything is a choice."

"I may not have always welcomed my abilities, so I will not claim to be an expert," she replied. "But I don't believe you will be able to rest until you get to the bottom of who killed you and why. And frankly, neither will I. Who is in a better position than me to find out for both of us?"

"You are just saying all of this because you are losing," he accused, crossing his arms and turning away from her earnest face. "You want me to help you win a pile of money off them. This has nothing to do with me." The fog inside his body began to swirl in agitation, but his voice was soft. "It never has."

The allegation stung, but it wasn't more than she deserved. Vi pointed at the ceiling. "You've seen my place. You know I do not need anything I might win tonight to buy passage back to New Orleans. It might take me a few days to sell what I need and pack my things, but after that, win or lose, help me or don't, I'm going home to solve your murder. And I'm going to *make* you forgive me." She stabbed her finger into his chest—the effect of the gesture only slightly lessened when it passed right through his sternum.

"What? No! You don't have to do that," he protested.

Her skirts rustled across the floor as she left him and made her way to the door, voice colored by a hint of laughter. "I will make you forgive me, even if it kills me."

Peter would have protested, but the sharp bang of the saloon door rebounded through the room on the other side of the door. The happy babble of the crowd in the bar hushed, but even through the stockroom door, Vi could hear Jimmy's voice calling, "We're closing soon, fellas."

"No, you're not," Salty's familiar wheeze replied. "Looks like you're having yourself a grand ol' time. And I've just decided, we're invited."

Chapter 18

Vi burst out of the storeroom. Too soon, it was happening too soon. She hadn't had time to let everyone in on the plan before her unwitting cavalry had arrived. All around her, she could hear the subtle click of guns being freed from their bondage.

Bonnie and Caroline cowered at the far end of the room, completely cut off from the exits by the wall of flesh. Jimmy stood behind the bar, hands raised and eyes flicking from thug to thug. One of the men held a struggling George by his collar. "Let him go," Vi gasped, but instead of complying he shifted his grip, pulling the boy onto his toes.

This was very little like the scenario she'd pictured when she'd sent George to tip off Salty. Clearly, she'd underestimated how much she'd bruised his pride that afternoon.

The only person who remained unmoved by the turn of events was Jeb. He finished shuffling as Salty sauntered over, careful to make sure the Colt at his waist was visible to all. He spoke to the whole room, turning in a circle and gesturing widely. "My, my, Miss Viola. I must say, I'm disappointed. You know, it's rude to start before everyone arrives to the game. Now that we're all present and accounted for, I say 'Let the fun continue.' Where's that music?"

He swung around and glared at the musicians. The piano man peeked out from behind his instrument. When he caught sight of the gun Salty was stroking, he hesitantly took his place. Once the music began, the sharply dressed gunslinger called, "You keep that up now. No matter what you hear." He faced Vi and beckoned her to assume an empty seat at the table. "So, who's got the blind?"

She kept her hands up and crossed to the chair, but remained standing next to Jeb. He scrutinized his cards and growled, "Friend of yours?"

Her reply squeezed out through her grimace. "That is not precisely the word I would use."

The bandit raised his head slowly and deliberately, sneering at the older man like he was prey that wasn't worth hunting. Jeb snaked his arm around her waist possessively. "This here's a private game."

"No reason to get excited, friend," Salty replied. "But a man deserves a chance to win his money back. When I heard her urchin shooting his mouth off about this here gathering, I thought the boys and I would avail ourselves of the hospitality."

Jeb leaned in and refilled his glass with his free hand. When he finally responded, his voice was as steady as a ship on a windless day. "That's quite a liberty to take."

"I think you need to get out of there, Vi," Peter said nervously. "I don't like this."

"Now, now. It don't have to be like that, friend." Salty held up his hands in conciliation, but his goons took a step or two nearer to the poker table.

"You ain't my friend. I couldn't stand to be friends with someone with a face like yours."

Nobody moved much, but every hired gun and piece of criminal scum in the room moved slightly toward the action, while all the innocent bystanders winced away minutely. The air was thin and hot with so many bodies crushed together. Salty gave Jeb a yellow-toothed smile. "I'm going to let that slide. In fact, I'll even go so far as to do you a favor."

"My, isn't that kind of you?" Vi said sarcastically, then remembered her precarious position and kept her snark in check. She needed the situation to calm down, not escalate. All she'd wanted was to add some more competition to the mix, but Salty seemed bent on winning the outlaws to his cause. Jeb leaned in protectively, and she took a moment out from her terror to reflect how she may have been a smidge too good at playing with his heart. Though it sure was proving to be useful.

Salty continued addressing the bandit as if she weren't even there. "You see, I've got reason to believe that this here woman is a dirty cheat."

"Don't be such a sore loser," Bonnie piped up. "She beat you fair and square." One of Salty's men leaned in at her menacingly and she let out a squeak. Caroline waited until his back was turned and made a rude gesture.

"Well, if'n she is, she's got to be the worst cheat I ever saw," the bandit said with a smirk, leaning back and opening his jacket to reveal his own pair of side-arms. "Honestly, I'd started to feel sorry for her. She hasn't got any luck at all."

"Are you sure about that?" the 'businessman' asked silkily.

"Vi!" Peter yelled. "Get out of here. Just make a run for it."

As much as she would have liked to heed his advice, Vi couldn't tear her eyes from George struggling against the giant's grip. Sure, she could run. But what about everyone else?

Jeb slowly rose to his feet. "You saying I'm too stupid to know when I'm being taken?" he asked darkly.

The world held its breath.

"He ain't saying you *ain't* too stupid," someone hollered.

Later, no one would likely admit to being the one who said it. But once it was said, the entire saloon surged into action. The poker table tipped over as men on all sides rushed to their feet and an assortment of money, cards, and glasses flew into the air. Vi ducked behind the table to avoid the first onslaught of fists and sweaty bodies tangling together all around her. It would be so easy to simply slink out through the back door, but Caroline's piercing shriek pushed the idea out of her mind.

Humans didn't blaze the way ghosts did, but pearly ripplings somewhere in her awareness told her the direction of the threats presented by the living. Unfortunately, it didn't tell her whose side they were on. Vi peered out from behind the table, but she couldn't tell where one gang stopped and another began. Dirty, angry men clashed with other dirty, angry men on all sides.

Amidst the disarrayed tables, she finally recognized one of Salty's colossuses. He battered at a group of bandits and shielded his boss from actually putting himself at risk. The other half of the titanic pair still held George in a headlock near the front door. He rumbled a laugh as the little boy swatted ineffectually at his thick arm, toes scrabbling for purchase as he struggled for breath.

Vi bellowed loud enough to put a mama grizzly to shame, before catapulting herself from behind the safety of the table and into the melee.

With a show of agility no bear could ever hope to possess, she leaped over a man who fell in her path. Two men grappled before her, and she ducked under a wild haymaker to roll across a table. By the time she had landed on her feet on the other side, the thug holding George was no longer laughing.

She approached slowly, tugging at the fingertips of her gloves. "I said, 'let him go.'"

The giant recovered from his shock. "Oh yeah?" he drawled. "What are you going to do about it, lady?"

The silky fabric slid soundlessly from one hand, then the other, as she replied. "I'm not sure you want to find out."

"Try me."

She balled the gloves in one hand, ready to throw them into his face and act as a diversion. "You asked for it."

Before she had the opportunity, a new threat whooshed into life in the swirl of action at her back. Something small and fast sailed through the air above her head. It smashed into her opponent's prominent brow. The aetheric forewarning gave her enough time to throw her arms up and protect her face as it rebounded. When it landed on the floor, the glass burst into shards at her feet.

Jimmy's voice rose over the chaos. "Oops! Awful sorry, Miss Viola. Didn't mean to get you there." When she twisted to see, she found the bartender standing with next glass he'd planned to launch resting forgotten in his slack grip.

"No apology needed," she sighed, turning back to the big man as he rubbed his forehead. "As I was saying—"

"Yeah," her well-meaning employee interjected. "She told you once, er, twice. Don't make her say it again."

The thug sneered. "I guess I don't hear so good. Maybe you should come over here and tell me, boy."

"No thanks," Jimmy squeaked and hurled the second glass.

It soared through the air and hit the other man square in the nose. After a sickening crunch, he roared and clutched at his face, releasing George. The boy stumbled and coughed as he regained his footing. Vi reached out to steady him, but before she could drag him out of harm's way, he spun back to his captor. George pummeled his solar plexus and liver with tiny but determined fists. The hulk doubled over, blood from his squashed nose seeping through his fingers as he sputtered to the floor.

Her tiny defender crowed triumphantly, and wound up to kick the fallen man. Vi pulled him away, and he wriggled in her grip. "Let me at 'im, Miss Viola!"

She knelt so she could look him in the eye. "No, not right now. I have an important job for you to do."

"You just want me outta the way again."

"Not this time, kid. I need you. Smithy needs you." The boy chewed on his cheek for a moment, but otherwise remained still. "You must go outside and get him out of here. Don't take him far, but take him and yourself somewhere safe and out of sight."

"Yes ma'am! I can do that."

He turned to go, and she caught his arm. "Safe and out of sight, you hear? I'm going to need you again soon, and I want you to be in one piece." George gave her a salute with a solemnness reserved for the armed forces and little boys with big hearts. He waited for an opening, then bolted for the door.

CHAPTER 19

"Good boy." Vi rose awkwardly, limbs made clumsy by the unexpected swell of affection. A flicker in her extra sense sent her ducking once more as a chair careened through the space over her head and into the wall behind the bar. It missed Jimmy by several feet, but the collection of mirrors shuddered. A few of them lost their purchase and came crashing onto the counter.

She let loose a string of language so colorful it would give a rainbow a run for its money. It was one thing to destroy her furniture, but some of those mirrors were antiques. Her eyes narrowed as she searched for the culprit. While distracted by the further threat to her collection, two grappling figures rudely collided with her.

"Botheration." Her fingers clenched into fists, adrenaline coursing through her body. She swung into a fighting stance to face the men who had dared run into her. In theory, at least one of them was an enemy.

"Begging your pardon, ma'am," a stubbly man cried before dealing his opponent a jab to the teeth. "I'll take care of him for you."

Vi turned on the other man, glad to finally have someone to hit. But blood gushed from his face, his voice thick and pathetic as he groaned, "He's the one who did it. I wouldn't hurt a lady."

"Liar!" the first man replied incredulously.

"It wasn't my fault!"

"Was so!"

She blinked dumbly as the two men resumed punching one another. The scruffy one tripped toward the stage, and the other followed, flashing his gap-toothed grin. She clucked in disgust, then resumed the search for a foe, and a chance to wreak some destruction of her own.

Hank and his battered Stetson had flopped on the bar earlier that evening. Having refrained from joining his comrades, she spied him in the same place. In a few steps, she closed in and had a fistful of his faded flannel shirt. "Face me like a man!" she shouted and yanked at his shoulder. A potent miasma of alcohol nearly knocked her over as his head lolled at her. He favored her with a vague stare and a crooked, drunkard's smile before slumping against her grip.

"Tarnation," she gritted, releasing his shoulder and allowing him to sag all the way to the floor. He left behind two fingers of some dark liquor in his forgotten glass. Vi eyed the poor orphan drink, feeling altogether too sober for this turn of events.

As her fingertips grazed the rim, a tremor to her left pulled her attention. Vi spun toward the threat with her knuckles raised defensively. Pox and Beard-face stopped dead in their tracks, their outstretched arms frozen, as if she would somehow fail to see them if they could hold still enough.

She chuckled. "You boys have very short memories, don't you? Not that I mind, really. I find myself in the mood for a good row."

The two injured men melted enough to exchange a look. They spluttered a few apologetic syllables as they elbowed at each other all the way out of the exit. As they flailed through the door, there was no sign of George, but she caught sight of Smithy's ample hindquarters outside. The doors rebounded and swung inward in time for her to see the horse kick out at the limping pair of bandits. His hooves thudded into the men, sending them flying them through the air to darken her windows one more time.

Jeb materialized at her side, shaking his head. "That was a shameful display of cowardice. I do believe I will be firing them."

"Either the dime novels got it terribly wrong, or they simply don't make outlaws like they used to," she agreed, then turned back to Hank's abandoned glass.

"I'm no coward, ma'am. I wouldn't abandon a lady to this fight. I'll protect you."

Vi kicked back the rum, savoring the way it burned all the way down. "That's kind of you, truly. But what no one seems to realize is that I don't *need* anyone's protection." She leaned this way and that, trying to see past Jeb to the last place she'd seen Bonnie and Caroline. All she could make out over his shoulders was a flash of blond hair and red fabric near the piano. The musician had taken Salty's warning to heart, and kept on plunking out the honky-tonk as the barfight raged.

"I'm sure you don't," Jeb replied, his eyebrows dancing.

She scowled, giving him a hard push to the breastbone. "Not now."

"Oh, you gonna hurt me?"

"Only if you make me," Vi spat, raising one fist.

"That can be arra—Ah!" The outlaw's flirtation was cut off by the Christmas hams that grabbed him by the collar. Salty's immense bodyguard wrenched him out of her sightline and into a fistfight.

"Thank you," she exhaled.

"Don't mention it," Salty growled as he stepped up to her. He clutched her arm with one hand and pushed the muzzle of his pistol against her temple. "How's this for doing business, eh? I want what you owe me." The pressure from the gun eased from her skin, and her captor pointed it at the wall of mirrors. He squeezed off a pair of shots, sending two sheets of silvered glass crashing to the ground. "*Plus*, interest."

The giant who wasn't busy taking shots to Jeb's kidneys shook the last of the broken tumbler from his clothes. The bartender's missile had opened an angry gash across the bridge of his nose, but the sound of gunfire brought him back to his senses. With a grunt, he pushed himself onto his hands and knees, then stumbled in the direction of the bar.

Jimmy cowered behind the bar, and Salty's white beard parted to reveal a maniacal, butter-colored grin. Yes, she had definitely underestimated how much of a sore loser he was. On the other hand, she had a powerful urge to paint that smile red. Her mind leapt from angle to angle, racing through a calculation that had very little to do with mathematics, and much to do with causing damage to the right people. Just as she settled on the right course, Caroline's shriek ripped through the chaos.

All eyes turned to the corner, and a blur of scarlet and gold dispatched one of the thugs with a lacquered tray. Her curls bounced as she sashayed around the prone figure, shouting, "Don't you hurt my Jimmy!"

Salty fired the gun at another unfortunate mirror, and the thunder stopped the waitress short. Bonnie rushed to the blond woman's side, tugging her away from the well-dressed man and his shiny weapon.

"There's no need to shoot up the place," Jeb shouted. He ducked below a wild swing from the bodyguard and moved in to hit him with a punch to the liver. "There won't be anything left to collect."

After the reverberation of the gunshot died, a mirror as tall as a man came loose from its fitting. It dropped a few inches to the back countertop, then begin to tip under its own weight. The bartender swung around and caught it with his upturned palms.

His body buckled and Vi jerked in his direction. The barrel pressed into her temple again, the tip warm from its recent firing. The bartender managed to hold his ground, for the moment.

The twang crept back into Salty's voice as he addressed the angry waitress. "Your sweetheart don't need to get hurt, little lady. This is between me and your boss. So, you leave her to me, and you can all go peaceable-like." He dug his fingernails into Vi's arm, drawing a yelp.

"Peace?" Peter shouted, his azure form burning behind her. "I left peace behind a few states ago." The old man startled at the new voice, and Vi's gaze trailed down her arm to where his hand touched her bare skin. With her gloves gone, her partner was now a piece in play.

Unaware of the drama unfolding on the main floor, Jimmy teetered, moaning, "This is really heavy...."

Salty sputtered in terror as he stared slack-jawed at the ghost, but didn't loosen his grip. "You're doing this. Aren't you?" he rasped in Vi's ear. "You're trying to trick me again."

Peter continued, bolstered by the living man's fear. "You're not going to hurt her."

"Stop this right now!" he yowled. His panicked breathing made the gun shake.

Vi spoke as calmly as her captor's erratic behavior allowed. "Hey, Pete? Not certain, but I don't think you're actually improving my situation right now."

"I'm warning you. Stop or I'll sh—"

Salty's threat was cut off by a resounding thud, followed by a shower of brown glass. A tide of whiskey sloshed across his collar and seeped into his expensive tie. The swindler's eyes rolled into his head, and he followed the last drops of liquor to the floorboards.

CHAPTER 20

The neck of the bottle tumbled from Bonnie's dainty hand, her mouth a perfect zero. Vi was evidently not the only one surprised she had it in her.

Jimmy had his back turned to the room, but his looking-glass doppelganger watched the action as he wavered beneath the giant mirror. "I could really use some help here."

"I'm coming," his wife chirped, tip-toeing around the array of limbs and broken glass in her path. But when she reached the bleeding hulk near the door, Caroline stopped to deliver a sharp kick to the face. His head lurched sideways, and he fell into a heap. She scampered out of the way just as the second bodyguard collapsed at his side.

Jeb spat on the fallen ogre and ripped off his bandana to mop his brow. He spotted Vi and slung his arm around her waist, giving her a squeeze and letting out a whoop. When she tried to wiggle away, he nuzzled into her neck. Peter rolled his eyes.

"Oh, for crying out loud," she muttered, but couldn't help but smile. "Don't you ever give up?"

"Nope. I don't," the outlaw agreed. "Which is exactly why I am still standing, and the other man is not."

"I think you've earned yourself a drink."

"As I see it, I've at least earned myself a kiss."

Caroline came to the far end of the bar and swung open the false top. She rushed to Jimmy's side, adding her support to the expanse of silver and gilt. "Vi, Bonnie, anybody! I don't think we can hold this," she shrilled.

Vi made another attempt to dodge past Jeb, but he stepped into her path. Once again, something was standing between her and her chance to prove

Bonnie right. At least, she finally had someone she could hit.

The outlaw smiled at her, then winced. Her eyes traveled over the swell of his blackening eye and the small cuts on his rather attractive cheekbones. She couldn't bring herself to make a fist. He had gone through all of that on account of her, even if he didn't know it.

"You know what, you're right," she said, throwing her arms around the bandit's neck. He didn't resist as she gently eased him backward until his back rested against the bar.

"Vi, you can't be serious," Peter grumped.

She pushed onto her toes to plant a kiss onto Jeb's waiting lips. His arms tightened around her back, stealing her breath and sending a happy tingle down her spine that had nothing to do with danger. The moment lingered until a grunt from the distressed bartender brought her focus back to the matter at hand.

As she leaned away, the outlaw left his eyes closed, savoring the moment and murmuring, "You sure know how to throw a shindig, Miss Viola."

"You can call me 'Vi,'" she reminded him, and took two steps to the side. She admired the view for one last moment, then wiggled her fingers in farewell. After all, he did try to steal her horse. "Goodnight, Jeb."

Once her employees saw she was clear, they let the mirror topple backward over their heads. Jimmy cradled Caroline's mop of yellow curls and turned them both away from the danger.

Jeb opened his eyes dreamily. "So soon?"

The mirror came crashing onto the back of his head, erupting into a surge of silver.

The saloon's double doors swooped open. George stood panting at the threshold, taking in the scene. When the outlaw slumped to the ground, the kid gave a shout of triumph. He edged his way around the unconscious men clogging the doorway.

Vi leaned over and pressed her fingers against Jeb's neck. As she'd hoped, he appeared to be unconscious, but otherwise unharmed.

The boy rushed to her side. She pushed him behind her, spinning to stand between him and the ensuing bar fight, only to find that the brawl had rudely neglected to tell her it was over.

Men in various states of consciousness lolled on every surface. One of the chandeliers had been set swinging and still oscillated on the far end of the room. Money and other detritus lay strewn among the legs, and occasionally backs, of smashed and overturned chairs. First Jimmy's hair, then his disbelieving gray eyes appeared over the top of the bar. Caroline's flushed face followed.

"You got him good." George grinned.

Vi's lungs heaved with unused energy. "I thought I told you to wait until it was safe."

"It looks plenty safe to me, wouldn't you say?"

She winced as a single, round mirror on the far corner of the bar dropped to the floor. "Safe is relative."

The couple behind the bar picked their way through the glass, feet crunching all the way. "What a mess!" Jimmy cried.

Vi surveyed the damage and sighed. "Well, kid, as long as you're here, do you remember the House Rules? Good. Well, right over there is money, George. Fistfuls of it. I want you to go out there and grab whatever you can for me. Watch yourself on the glass, mind, but be quick about it. Pretty soon, Care's going to bring back the police, and I want you and the money cleared out of here and upstairs before she does."

"I am?" Caroline gasped. "But you never want them coming in. You said so."

"That's when this was my place," Vi replied, waving them to follow her into the back room. "But as of right this moment, I am turning over the reins of *Viola's* to the two of you."

"Really?"

"Just until I get back, mind," she added hurriedly. "I need to go away for a while, and I can't think of two more capable, responsible newlyweds I'd rather leave in charge."

The bartender and his wife looked to each other in delight, then Jimmy's eyebrows drew together. "You sure this isn't only about getting out of the clean-up, is it?"

"Nope, the saloon and all the profits you collect are yours until I get back. But I have some conditions." Vi held up a hand and ticked off the items on her fingers. "First, George'll tell you where to pick up my horse, and Jimmy, you'll take him out to the ranch for me and close it up. I don't think Jeb'll give you any trouble, but let's get Smithy out of the way for a day or two all the same."

The waitress whimpered. "But he'll be gone all night. Maybe more."

"Second," Vi continued, turning to her other employee. "When Jeb wakes up, you tell him he's got a man to bury out near his camp, and I'd consider it a personal favor if he'd give him a good burial. Also, tell him if he does the right thing by Tobias and brings him to the cemetery, you'll leave him out of condition number three."

"What's that?" Jimmy asked.

"Once I am out of Sacramento, you are both going to the police. You tell them some version of what happened here. Leave me out of it, but ask for them to watch over the place after the violence. I doubt anyone will do anything here in the middle of town, but better to have Salty see the police see *him* if he comes sniffing around."

Caroline grimaced. "I'm not sure this is such a good plan anymore."

"And last, but not least," Vi said, raising the fourth and final finger. "When that's settled, I need you to pack your things, because you're moving into my place upstairs."

The waitress's mouth hung slack for a moment, then she said, "Do you really mean it?"

"I'm going to need someone to keep an eye on Smithy, not to mention all those beautiful dresses I'll be leaving behind while I take care of some... unfinished business. You think you can handle that for me?"

Caroline had let out a squeal at the mention of clothes, and now bounced up and down next her husband. He scratched his head and contemplated her smiling face. "Yes, Miss Viola. I think we'll be able to do that for you. But where are you going?"

"I think it would be better if I don't say. I'll let you know more when I can, but for now, let's get going on this before they all come-to."

A disheveled Bonnie leaned on Vi's shoulder. She directed a puff of air at the stray hairs falling over her face. "Now what?"

"Now, we pack." The grifter turned the corner and darted up the stairs, the widow following close behind.

Once they were safely through the door of her apartment, her friend wheezed, "What? We're running away?"

Peter walked out of the wall and into the conversation. "Are you sure there isn't any way I can talk you out of this?"

"Not running away, my friend." Vi waved at the younger woman to follow her into the bedroom. The steamer trunk at the foot of the bed beckoned. The stray bit of clothes and papers were shoved aside, and she threw it open. "For the first time in my life, I think I'm running *toward* something."

"I understand," Bonnie sighed and put on a brave face. "You need to go. I want you to know, I meant everything I said. I think you could do a lot of good, but no matter what happens, I wish you all the luck in the world."

When her lips began to quiver, Vi glanced away to rifle through the trunk. "What are you talking about?"

"Oh, Vi." The other woman crossed to her side and hauled her into a boa constrictor embrace. "I'm going to miss you so much."

"Good. It's settled," Vi replied, squirming an arm free to pat her friend on the shoulder. "You'll just have to come with me. Won't you?"

"Really?" Bonnie sniffed. "I mean, are you sure about this?"

Vi dumped an armload of linens onto the bedroom floor, chuckling. "You have something keeping you here?"

"No," Bonnie said, her eyes nearly doubling in size as realization struck. "I suppose I don't."

Vi dashed to the closet. "So, come with me to New Orleans. Or get off the train anywhere you want. It's up to you."

"My things, they're over at the hotel…"

Vi's mouth twisted into a lop-sided smile as she returned to dump an armload of clothes into the trunk. "Then I suggest you go there right now and start getting ready. I'll meet you there and stay the night. Hopefully, we can clear out of town on the morning train."

"I can't believe I'm doing this." Bonnie shook her head and disappeared into the hall at the same moment George rushed into the room, pockets bulging. Peter followed the boy as far as the threshold, but regarded the open trunk in stony silence.

When George spied the lacy contents of Vi's luggage, he averted his gaze and giggled. "I got the money, Miss Viola. Some of them are starting to wake up, but I got it."

"Excellent. Put it on the table, and take a five-dollar bill for yourself."

"Yes ma'am!" he yelped gleefully. Once he unburdened himself of his spoils, he waved a crumpled bill at her before tucking it into his shoe. "You say you got something else for me to do, ma'am?"

"How would you like a promotion, George?"

"I think I'd like that a lot."

"You've been hanging around here going on two years now. I realized you been working here, but we never did get around to making you an official member of the staff."

He waved away her concern. "Aw, that's okay, ma'am. I eat awful good here, and I like working for you."

"No, it's not okay. You may not be all grown yet, but you deserve to say you've got a job and to earn yourself a salary. So, from now on, you're going to be my valet. That sounds good to you?"

His grin widened. "I don't know what a 'valley' does, but you can count on me."

"Valet," she gently corrected and gave his shoulder a squeeze. "And your first task will be to head over bright and early tomorrow morning to take a telegram over to the station."

"Yes'm. I can do that."

"Good boy." Vi gestured to the mouth of the trunk and its many tongues of fabric and folds. "But, most of what a valet does is handles a lady's luggage."

His face wrinkled in confusion. "You going somewhere?"

"No, sir. *We're* going on an adventure."

CHAPTER 21

October 2, 1871
New Orleans, Louisiana

To the untrained eye, the silver platter simply floated across the room. No strings held it aloft, and nothing supported it from below, yet it made slow and steady progress, hovering across the polished wooden floor. A seated figure watched from the other end of the well-appointed room, patiently awaiting whatever lay at its center and smiling at the strange parody of King Solomon and his magic carpet.

"Very good," he said. "You get stronger every day, Mary."

The ghost held her mouth in a firm line as she took another deliberate step. "Thank you, sir." A tremor traveled through the tray as she spoke, and she puffed out her cheeks as she focused her energy on her hand. The mirrored surface of the tray flashed as she crossed into the pool of candlelight and it crashed to the floor. Mary made a sound of disgust at her inadequacy.

"One thing at a time," the man scolded as he rose from his leather chair. "Remember, throwing something in a burst of energy is much easier than being steady enough to carry things. But you are making excellent progress. You should be very proud. You died less than a year ago, and you've already come so far."

"I want to be ready," she simpered. "When the time comes."

"And I'm sure you will be," the man replied before stooping to retrieve both the platter and the folded slip of paper. "Now, what is this you've brought me?"

Mary shrugged. "A boy brought it around for you a few minutes ago."

He reached into his smoking jacket to pull out a pair of glasses before settling back into his chair to read the note. At first, his eyes moved slowly across the page, then he sat forward in excitement and hastily finished.

"Sir, what is it?"

"I've just received word that there's been a new development. My idea worked perfectly, and we've managed to flush out Annabelle."

The ghost clapped her hands in delight, but they made no sound. "You were able to use the information I got?"

"Indeed," he confirmed, pride over his pupil adding a swell of affection to his words. "You are mastering all of the arts of the dead, it seems."

"I'm ready," Mary declared. "Let me finish this for you. If we know where she is going to be, I could go meet her along the way and—"

"I don't want there to be even a hint of foul play, not outside of the city where we can't control the situation. It could make things complicated for our endeavor." He wagged his finger. "I can't have any mistakes, not so close to success."

The ghost twisted a strand of her misty hair. "But I know I can do it," Mary insisted. "You have to give me a chance. I don't understand why—"

"I said 'no' once already," the man barked. "I don't suggest you make me say it again."

Even as her spirit-flesh churned, the ghost bowed her head and returned a resigned, "Yes, sir."

"Now, go and practice some more on your own," he continued, his tone patronizing. "She's coming to us in a few weeks, and that will give you enough time to get stronger." With a wave of his hand, he dismissed the ghost to start making the necessary preparations.

With an effort, she kept the anger off her face until she could seethe alone in the hallway. She'd made such progress; proven herself to be the best of the recruits.

"You don't think I can do it?" she snarled at the man behind the door. "I'll be the judge of that."

CHAPTER 22

October 2, 1871
Sacramento, California

If the average person found herself in the middle of a blank, eternal void, she'd probably give panic at least a few moments of her time. But the relapsed grifter simply put fists to hips, and painted on her best surly glare.

"I know I wanted to get a clean start, but this is ridiculous."

A light breeze kicked up, kissing her cheek and gently tugging at her clothes. The force of the wind redoubled, the darkness rippling in its wake as the nothing began the process of becoming something.

The wisps gave way to elegant ball gowns and silk cravats, candlelight and champagne. Though dancers reeled across the shining floor, time robbed the scene of its colors. She blinked and opened her eyes on a different scene, but music still wafted through the crack beneath the door and swirled through the giddy evening air.

As she surveyed the room, her eyes fell on Peter, his face creased with joy rather than worry. He gazed at a woman with dark hair and an elegant dress, her feet scandalously bare and tucked beneath the skirt. Vi stifled a gasp as she recognized the moment, but the memory continued to unfold.

"I believe we need a toast," the Peter of the past slurred, dark eyes dancing.

The younger Vi screwed up her face and gazed into her empty glass. "Didn't we just have a toast?" she asked.

He replied with the kind of gusto reserved for the small hours of the morning. "A partnership of this magnitude deserves to be celebrated!"

"Keep your voice down," she hissed. "And there's a whole ballroom full of people celebrating right now." The shadow-Vi pulled off her long silk gloves. With so many people wanting to dance with the bride, she'd had to take precautions against revealing anything. They'd worked too hard on fitting in here for it to unravel because of carelessness.

"They're celebrating you and this sham of a marriage. I'm talking about celebrating you and *me*, Thorne."

"That's technically 'Annabelle Sinclair' now."

"Nah, you'll always be the 'Thorne in my side.' The 'Sinclair in my side' wouldn't have the same ring to it."

Vi chuckled and held out her glass for more champagne. Peter grabbed the bottle from its place on the low table, sending a stack of papers tumbling to the floor. Her packed luggage hulked nearby, ready to depart with her on her honeymoon to Chicago the next morning.

He laughed and handed her the champagne bottle before kneeling beside her to retrieve the papers. She'd always loved that laugh, so full and completely uninhibited. That was the last time she'd heard it. The dead weren't known for their sense of humor; she'd likely never hear it again.

After he retrieved the loose pages, the sepia-colored Peter blew out a low, appreciative whistle. Awe knocked the slur out of his voice as he surveyed the stack of deeds, titles, and other important papers he held in his hands. "This has to be one of the biggest scores of all time."

"Big enough to get out of here and never look back, that's for certain," Vi confirmed, carefully tipping the heavy bottle over the narrow opening of her champagne flute. "To my new husband, and his extremely deep pockets," she said with mock seriousness and raised her glass. Some of the golden liquid bubbled over the brim, and she giggled as it sloshed and dribbled over her fingers.

Peter captured the woman's hand in his. His lips caught the ribbon of champagne the instant before it dripped onto her dress, and for several heartbeats Vi's shadow-self locked eyes with him.

The flesh and blood Vi knew what came next, and couldn't drag her eyes away.

Her counterpart drew back her hand and cleared her throat, shattering the tension building between them. "Thank you... for the champagne. I should really go back to the party. And stow all of that." She slipped her feet out of the fold of her dress and looked around for her shoes.

Peter rose gracefully, mumbling to the stack of papers. "Yes, you should probably go." He put them into the shadow-Vi's outstretched hands.

"So, I shall see you in Chicago," she said, too cheerful by half. "I may have some trouble slipping away, mind. I am not certain I'll be on time."

"I've only got to get a few more things together for our little disappearing act, but I'll wait for you at the station, and we'll go wherever you want." He gazed into her troubled eyes and misread what he saw there as lack of faith in him rather than a glimmer of a guilty conscience. "I promise, I'll wait as long as it takes. We're partners, and that means I'm going to take care of you." The young Vi opened her mouth to protest, but he raised his hand to stop her, adding softly, "I'll see you in Chicago."

"Yes," she said, a tear clinging to her lashes, but not for the reason Peter thought. "I'll see you there."

The real Vi's eyes were dry, but the knowledge that even in that moment she'd already plotted to leave him behind clawed at her throat. His rapt expression broke her heart all over again.

The shade of herself smiled at him one last time. With the spoils of their job under her arm, she swept out of the room, and so she'd thought, out of his life forever.

Vi blinked her true eyes, sending her head swimming with the shock of so many colors after the gray-brown of the memory. The heady aromas of food and perfume told her she'd returned, though the question of if she'd actually left still remained.

"Well," she muttered. "That was new."

As she came back to herself, she could feel the sharp jab of her fingernails digging into her palm. When she relaxed her grip, Peter's pin greeted her from the cradle of her hand—an artifact of the life she'd tried to leave behind but couldn't seem to shake. The point winked at her from the four-inch shaft as she glared at the carved, black rose on the head accusingly.

"Is everything alright?" asked a female voice beside her.

Vi cleared the last of the strange scene from her mind. "Yes, I'm fine. Just daydreaming, it seems."

"Do you want help with that?" Bonnie didn't bother to wait for a response before taking the pin from her loose grasp. "If you're having second thoughts, it's understandable."

"No, nothing has changed," Vi replied with conviction. "I took myself out of the picture, and someone I care about got hurt. It's time to try something different."

"I happen to agree with you." The little brunette scrunched her brow as she affixed the pin to Vi's jacket.

She snorted. "And your attitude is not being affected by the prospect of a luxurious train ride to a far-off, exotic locale, is it?"

"Of course not. I'm thinking of all the poor souls you could help if you try," her friend cried. When the seasoned liar quirked an eyebrow, Bonnie continued sheepishly. "But a chance to get away from here has its appeal." The widow's unspoken pain hung in the air until Bonnie came back to herself and eyed her companion suspiciously. Her voice dropped to a whisper. "Are you sure you're alright? If you were anyone else, I'd say you look like you've seen a ghost. But of course, we both know you've gotten awfully good at hiding that trick."

The reluctant medium chuckled. "No, ghosts I can handle." Her eyes flicked to Peter's lucky charm and back to the other woman's face. Worry gnawed at her insides, but she hadn't mastered cheating at cards without learning to keep it off her face. "Everything's fine. I promise."

CHAPTER 23

The day of their departure had dawned bright and clear, but most of all, hot. The only hint of moisture lay on the brows of the people who shuffled around the train station, their movements sluggish and heavy. Bonnie went in search of something cool to drink, leaving Vi alone on the platform with those few items the ladies preferred to carry personally.

The station sprawled long and narrow beside a wide brown ribbon of water. Giant paddleboats shared the Sacramento River shoreline, moored and ready to take passengers down to San Francisco or beyond. Though still an early hour, sweat plastered Vi's hair to her forehead, and she swiped at it with a fresh handkerchief. She'd never expected to have any cause to make a journey like this again, and she wasn't looking forward to it. The opening of the railroad a couple years earlier would make it go a lot faster than the ship she'd taken out to California. Five days of cramped quarters surrounded by strangers would be bad at any temperature, but in the smothering heat, the notion bordered on unbearable. They could have taken their time, transferring trains and staying in hotels. That would also mean Peter's ghost would have that much longer to become accustomed to his new state, which was not a good thing for anyone involved.

Vi craned her neck in search of her friend and the promised refreshment. An elegantly dressed woman and a nervous porter stepped into her eyeline instead.

"I find that completely unacceptable," the woman said, her prominent nose held high. Despite the swelter, she wore a heavy, tailored traveling suit, which couldn't have done anything to help her mood. The feathers on her hat bobbed as she tapped her foot in irritation.

"I assure you, your belongings will be safe," placated the porter. He forgot his edginess for a moment and beamed with pride. "We've never had a theft on board, ma'am, and I don't intend to let the first one be on my watch."

She clucked her tongue. "The path to hell is paved with good intentions. I've ridden this line before, and the standards of decorum have fallen significantly. They'll let anyone on the train these days." In case he didn't catch her meaning, the odious woman measured the negro porter with her eyes and made it clear by her frown she found him wanting.

"Anyone who can buy a ticket can ride the train, ma'am," he replied calmly. Vi admired the way he managed to keep his voice level even as her own hackles rose. "But your quarters are far away from all but the first-class passengers, and we won't let anyone who doesn't belong near your private car."

"See to it you don't!" the woman huffed and pounded her way down the platform toward the back of the train.

As her great green bulk and many-feathered hat scuttled out of view, Vi caught sight of both Bonnie and George. Even at a distance, she had to admire how sharp he looked in the clothes they'd found for him on the way to the station. He closed the final yards at a run, then stopped at attention, struggling to keep an expression on his face that befit his new job.

Bonnie followed and handed Vi a bottle of lemonade dripping with its own perspiration. "Look what I found. This should offer some relief from the heat."

"That sounds perfect," she replied. Vi popped the cork and slurped a third of the bottle in one go. The other woman sipped delicately, careful not to spill a drop. Vi bowed to their impending return to civilization enough to use her handkerchief to wipe her mouth rather than using her sleeve. "Is everything ready, George?"

"Yes'm. I oversaw the porters myself, just like you said. They've got your bags tied down tight." His voice lost its serious, grown-up tone and he became ten and excitable again. "Did you know the porters is all named George, too? And that you and Miss Bonnie will be sleeping on beds that come right out of the wall? I've never seen anything like it before."

"I imagine you'll be seeing quite a few new things on this journey."

"Speakin' of which, if you don't got nothing else for me to do right now, can I go look at the locomotive for a minute? I never been so close to one before."

"Yes, but make sure you're on the train when it leaves," Vi replied with the hint of remonstration employed by nannies and mothers everywhere. George's little chin bobbed so fast, he could have been a woodpecker. After doing so much traveling herself, she'd forgotten how much fun a long journey could be with the right company. Seeing it all through his young eyes would be refreshing.

"You've got your ticket?" She leaned in gave him a conspiratorial wink.

"Yes ma'am! And I'll guard it with my life," he said, patting his breast pocket.

Vi straightened, sighing. "I'm sorry I couldn't find a way for you to sleep up in first class with us. But on such short notice, it was a miracle I could get a sleeping berth for Bonnie and me." She left out the fracas it could have caused with people like the rude aristocrat. The war had been over for six years already, but old prejudices were harder to kill than young men.

"Aw, that's okay ma'am," George replied brightly. "I'm small, so I don't really need a bed like you folks to be comfortable. And I'll be there every morning bright and early to see if you need me."

"Let's say bright but not too early, shall we? Now, go on and enjoy the station." She shooed him off with a smirk as he broke into a run, forgetting all decorum in his glee. His slight form dodged between the passengers clogging the platform.

A figure burst out of the crowd in George's path, but the boy could neither see nor feel him as he passed through. The ghost walked in a straight line with no mind to any would-be obstacle, the foggy material of his body swirling in response to the contact without hindering his speed. When she took in her former partner's furrowed brow, she had a fleeting fear he was another flash of memory that would walk right by. Her concern was short-lived; the ghost's annoyed voice cutting through the crowd told her *this* Peter could see her.

"Why did you insist on bringing the kid? You know they only complicate matters," the ghost harrumphed, coming to a stop and crossing his insubstantial arms across his chest. Vi blinked away the memory of the living Peter's lips brushing against her fingers as he continued. "Not to mention, he doesn't know anything about your abilities, so you'll have to be on guard all the time again."

"He doesn't have anyone else," she murmured, allowing the sound of the busy station to cover her hushed words. "I couldn't leave him behind."

"Of course not," Bonnie assured her, unaware of the ghost's presence. Vi moved her free hand so the back of it touched the other woman's skin, and Bonnie let out a knowing "ah" as the ghost came into view. It was hard to believe this was the same woman who'd slapped Vi across the face for even implying she could talk to the dead when they'd first met.

Vi took a lingering gulp of her lemonade before answering her dead companion, careful to appear deep in conversation with Bonnie to the passersby. "George is the whole reason Salty and his gang showed up to the saloon last night. If that weasel got any idea about how I set him up, it would paint a giant bull's eye on the kid's back. And if I'm not there to protect him, who knows what will happen? Besides, I need a valet. I don't have you to carry my bags for me anymore," she teased.

The ghost made a disgusted sound. "Don't remind me. I'd gladly carry all your luggage, plus Bonnie's, with George thrown on top for good measure, if it meant I could touch things again," he groused. "I've been practicing some, but—"

"You've what?" she blurted.

"Been practicing. I cannot be much use to you on this ill-conceived adventure if all I can do is watch, so I've been trying to get a hang of moving things while you lazy living people slept. Just small stuff, mind, but I swear I got some water in a glass to ripple. So, it's only a matter of time."

"How does that work exactly? Moving things," Bonnie chimed in.

Peter startled, unaccustomed to including a third partner in their conversations. "As far as I can tell, it has a lot to do with concentration, and a ghost's emotional state. One named Ruth told us a story about an accident, where a great big roof beam fell from a building site and was going to crush a child. Ruth put herself in the path and stopped it."

Bonnie was the best sort of audience, steadily leaning in as he spoke before gasping at the appropriate moment. "That's amazing!"

"In addition, it was heavier than anything she could have lifted when she had a body, but she did it with her spirit energy. Or force of will? I don't know for certain, but there are theories…"

Vi rolled her eyes. "This again?"

"*You* will find it interesting to know, no doubt," he continued pointedly to Bonnie. "That when I am around Vi, I feel much stronger." He chuckled and brought her under his gaze again. "There is definitely some sort of energy exchange that occurs. I suppose that explains why spirits like you so much."

"Perhaps," Vi replied, filing the fact away for further investigation. If she knew what attracted the ghosts, she'd be that much closer to figuring out how to keep them away.

"Maybe, if you help me practice, you could have the world's first invisible valet."

Bonnie tittered, but Vi fixed him with a stony glare. "No."

"Oh, I know, it would call a lot of attention to you," he replied. "But it sure would be funny."

"I'm not joking. You have to stop trying to touch things."

"But why?" the ghost whined. "I'm finally starting to make progress!"

"You know very well why," she spat back.

"Well, I don't," interjected Bonnie. "Why would it be a bad thing? It sounds like we are going to need all the help we can get." Peter gestured at his unexpected ally to punctuate her point.

"The strongest ghosts have the hardest time passing over," Vi replied wearily. "The more he can manipulate solid things, the more solidly he is tied to… the earth." It was his tie to Vi that really had her worried, but she wasn't going to voice it now.

"Starting to doubt your brilliant plan?" Peter snickered. "It's not too late…"

"Oh no," she assured him. "I'm certain that when I get to the bottom of your murder that will be enough to finish your unfinished business. The best way out is through. But only if you don't get too good at being not entirely deceased."

"You're going to need my help," he insisted.

"No, I won't. Not that kind of help anyway."

"How can you say that?" Peter's hands balled into fists at his side. The fog that made up his spectral body swirled and darkened. "You already begged me to help you once, or have you already forgotten?"

"I have never begged anyone for anything in my life." Vi's tone was so harsh she actually felt the other woman wince, but Bonnie had the good sense to stay out of the conflict. "And I don't really anticipate any more poker in my near future. Besides, in the end, I got out of that jam myself."

"If you call inciting a riot and nearly destroying your business getting out of it," he replied smugly.

"That was all according to plan," she blustered. "And I wouldn't have had to resort to it if you had simply helped me in the first place."

"So, you do want me to help, or you don't? Because my head is spinning here with all your female logic."

"That's it." She broke her contact with Bonnie and narrowed her eyes at the ghost. "You say my powers help you feel stronger? Let's see how you do without them for a while."

His jaw went slack. "You wouldn't."

"Watch me." She closed her eyes, breathing deeply and calling on every ounce of will she could muster to push the vision of Peter away. The darkest places inside her were reserved for keeping the dead at bay, and with each measured breath, she tamped all of the extra sensations down into the blackness. After letting them out, however briefly, she now struggled against a surge of resistance from deep inside her. Sweat that had nothing to do with the unseasonable heat sprang forth as she struggled, her stomach churning with her efforts. When she opened her eyes again, all hints of the ghost were gone.

Bonnie allowed her friend's ragged breathing to quiet before she spoke. "I didn't know you could do that—make them disappear."

"It's not easy," Vi conceded. The inside of her skull howled like a tempest, but she refused to sway along with the rush of blood to her head. It certainly wasn't getting any easier.

"Where did he go?"

"He's not really gone. We are simply not *looking* at him." Vi hooked her arm through the other woman's elbow and tugged her toward the train door. "Come on, I'm dying to get to this little enterprise underway."

CHAPTER 24

The bustle of the platform receded as the pair of women made their way up the steps and into the train car. Vi led, eager to turn the corner into the sumptuous sleeping car. This route wasn't finished when she had come to California, and she'd read marvelous things about the progress of train travel. She only had a moment to take in the rich fabrics and elaborate carvings of the Pullman before the world became on incoherent white blur. A male voice squealed a late warning as she put her arms up to shield herself from the unexpected flash of light.

"What was that?" Bonnie cried, rounding the corner behind her.

Footsteps pattered toward Vi as she rubbed her eyes. They brought the man attached to the voice with them. "My fault entirely, ladies. I was trying to get a tintype of the interior before anyone boarded."

The harsh burst lasted but a moment, leaving the car once again bathed in the soft light of gas lamps. Dark spots bobbed merrily between Vi and the rest of the world as she scowled at the culprit. Between the splotches, she could make out a man in his twenties with tawny hair giving her a chagrined smile. He gestured at a contraption on the other side of the car, a brown accordion perched on its stilt legs and watching her with it's single, shining eye.

"I am still getting used to the magnesium flash. It makes for brighter photographs, but it packs a big punch," the man babbled. "I am here on assignment to report about the experience on the new sleepers. Going all the way to New York from California. I wasn't sure if I would get another chance at taking a photograph of the inside without other passengers. I apologize, ma'am."

The little brunette peered around Vi as the sight of the man and his camera chased away the dancing black spots. "You're a reporter?" Bonnie asked. "What's your name? Maybe we've heard of you."

"Arthur Sands, New York Star," he replied, chest rising as he claimed his pedigree. He looked at her, finally registering her presence. Vi smirked as she became invisible, and the young man turned all of his attention to the other woman. His fingers fumbled in his pocket for his card case.

"That must be exciting. Do you travel for the paper often?" Bonnie stepped around her friend, eyes shining with curiosity. With a slight tremor to his hand, he passed her his calling card.

"I love the railroad! It is a hobby of mine. There is a private car right behind us I would *love* to get inside. Though, to be honest, this is my first assignment of this sort." He dropped his voice and beckoned her to lean closer. She obliged, and he stage-whispered, "I'm a little nervous."

Bonnie frowned and trailed a few fingertips over the seatback. "It is so beautiful in here. I'm sorry we ruined your photograph." Vi rolled her eyes—nearly clear of all remnants of the assault by the flash—but the other woman continued cheerfully, "I cannot imagine that helps with your nerves."

"It isn't ruined at all. Please, do not spare it another thought. I'm sure there will be another opportunity. I've been reading all the brochures. In theory, I know what I'm doing. In fact, would you ladies care for a tour?" Sands moved to the center of the car without waiting for an affirmation, like a diva taking the stage for her aria. He motioned at a pair of seats beside him. "Unlike British sleepers, our car has entrances on the far ends of the car. This model has been in use on the East coast for some time, but it is new to the Central Pacific line. Because it is sometimes inhospitable to move between cars while we are in motion, it comes equipped with everything we could need. During the day, we have this configuration with two seats facing one another to ease conversation. Each seating area has a window for light, though ventilation occurs through those gaps you can see up above. Originally, this type of car used candles, but it was recently upgraded. The Pullman company thought of every detail..."

Vi let her mind wander as he went into the minutiae of who carved what and how far away the fabric had traveled from. Though she tried to keep them from her mind, snatches of her strange, gray daydream replayed. Peter's joy, the bubbles as they trickled over her fingers, and then—

Something made a slight tug between her shoulder blades, and Vi froze. An irritating sensation niggled at her, questing for a reaction. Of course, Peter would be following her around, assaulting her walls.

She was concentrating on swallowing her spirit sense once again when another passenger materialized at her back and sniffed at her to step aside. Vi startled, then pressed against a seat to let him past, careful not to make any contact with his skin. A gentle probing of energy around her told her the thread pulling at her had snapped, leaving her momentarily robbed of breath but free of any ghostly presence. As she steadied herself, she poured her attention into Sands' monolog; anything was worth keeping Peter from her thoughts at that moment. She could not allow him to win this tug-of-war.

Vi re-entered the conversation in time for Sands' explanation of how the space would transform from day to night. The beautifully adorned panels near the ceiling were not decorative as she'd first thought, but folded down to create plank beds. Sands assured them the pamphlets promised comfortable beds and ample bedding, which the porters stowed during the day. Both women were relieved to learn they would have access to a powder room on either end of the car even though they would have to get their sustenance along the rails.

As Sands spoke, passengers began to fill the car and a knot of listeners formed to clog the passage between seats. Soon, the newcomers began bombarding him with questions about subjects he'd already covered. Like the railroad employee they mistook him for, he happily obliged, but as Vi and Bonnie tried to slip by and take their seats, he excused himself from his newest conversation.

"I've enjoyed meeting you. Both of you," he corrected himself, dipping his chin slightly at Vi before gazing at her companion. "And I hope to spend some more time with you during the journey." His hand twitched as if he would reach out and touch Bonnie's hand, but propriety stilled it. He could not, however, control the wash of infatuation brightening his face.

Vi chuckled knowingly, but the young woman at her side was either completely clueless or a much better actress than Vi had taken her for. Given the evidence, the former seemed far more likely.

"It was nice to make your acquaintance," Bonnie replied. "Given the circumstances, I believe time is something we shall have in abundance. I would love to hear about all the interesting things you've written about. And sorry again about your... what was it called?"

"My tintype? It's a new type of photographic process. They develop in a trice. Another hobby of mine." He beamed. "And as I said, there is no need for you to apologize. Any photograph with you in it is vastly improved, I assure you. Miss...?"

The ex-con woman held in her derisive snort at the obvious flirtation, though when she turned her eyes to Bonnie, the widow was anything but amused. Shock drained her pretty face of all its color, and it appeared as if Sands had somehow absorbed it.

He dipped his head, ears burning bright enough to help ships find safe harbor. The journalist backed away, mumbling, "I am too forward. Please, accept my apology. And I do hope you have a pleasant journey." Before either of them could collect themselves enough to reply, he turned and maneuvered his way back to the people who still clamored for his assistance.

Bonnie stood frozen a few more seconds before abruptly taking her seat and staring out the window. Vi moved hesitantly as she settled in across from her, unsure if her presence was welcome. The other woman kept her eyes trained on the world outside the window. Despite how much had happened in the past day, it was still mere hours since Bonnie had truly lost Tobias.

The sounds of the people settling in around them filled the strained silence for a time, then Vi cleared her throat. Her companion didn't turn, so she leaned closer. "You were just being curious. And friendly. No one did anything wrong."

"Remind me, how long will we be on this train?"

"We go East until Chicago," Vi replied, ignoring the obvious evasion. "Then we change lines for one that goes South to New Orleans."

The young widow sighed, but still did not meet her eye. "He was all alone."

"Not when it mattered," Vi corrected. "You were there for him in the most important way anyone could be there."

Bonnie tilted her face toward her friend, her expression pained. "I didn't mean for that to happen back there, with that reporter."

"I know you didn't. But what do you expect? You are young, pretty. I would be rather surprised if it doesn't happen again." Vi had expected her words to be a compliment, but they made Bonnie sag. She thought for a moment. "When we stop tomorrow, perhaps you want to visit a dress shop. If you were in widow's weeds, I am sure Mr. Sands would not have said what he did."

The train began to creep forward. Bonnie returned her gaze to the window as the people slid away. Her eyes were surprisingly dry as she murmured her reply. "Not yet."

"Are you sure?"

"Tobias hated black. So, it wouldn't be for him." She smiled wanly. "Besides, *you* are supposed to be the one in mourning, Mrs. Sinclair. I am simply acting as your chaperone as you return. Remember? If anyone should be wearing a black dress, it's you."

Vi pulled a face. "Widows draw too much attention, and attention is the last thing I want. Besides, it is hard to relax when everyone is feeling sorry for you." Her friend flicked her eyes to her face and back out the window. "Ah, I see. Well, as you say, you don't have to do it yet. Or ever. Take your time," she stammered, self-conscious in the face of such familiar decisions. Though of course in her case, war widows had been so prevalent no one had really paid much attention. In those precious years of peace since then, death and its trappings had become oddities that reminded people of what they had already lost. And she would be the last person to tell Bonnie she had to bow to any particular fashion.

Vi leaned her elbow against the armrest and followed Bonnie's gaze out the window. She watched as the last of Sacramento's outline melted into the horizon. Despite her efforts to stay detached, places and people have a way of getting under a person's skin, and she certainly had some of California's grit in her. Hopefully, it would be enough to help her find her way back again.

<h1 style="text-align:center">CHAPTER 25</h1>

Some people reported the gentle rocking of trains acted like a tonic, sending passengers straight to sleep. If one was not sharing the Pullman with two dozen people and their various snores and snuffles, it might even be true. Vi's bunkmate was courteous enough to limit herself to a few soft coos, but their neighbor could have been wrestling a wild boar.

Hours after she'd extinguished her lamp, Vi lay filling the blank canvas of the ceiling with the memory she'd faced that afternoon. She had worked very hard not to think about that scene since it happened the first time. Then she had to go and open that envelope, and find Peter's pin inside. The ground beneath the wall she'd built up around her old life had begun to shift, leaving cracks and vulnerabilities for the guilt and doubt to slither in. Now, her own memories threatened to burst through from the inside.

Vi had to believe leaving was the right thing to do then, the same way going back was the right thing to do now. There was time, there had to be time. She could still make it up to him, return to her life out West, and with a little luck, she could also walk away with the other half of the colonel's ill-begotten fortune.

Thinking about luck brought her back to the pin, and she sat up in her cot. With one curtain pulled aside, she could make out her jacket hanging on its hook and a glint of gold. She stretched forward until she could slide it free from her lapel.

Vi rolled back into the safety of her bed, her heart pounding as if she'd just committed some heinous crime. As much as she wanted to forget it all, she wanted to hold some small piece of her past in her hand. Her thumb traced the smooth, stone curves of the rose, a point of pure black in the muddy darkness. The sound and motion of the train melted away, pushed by an invisible wave to the far corners of her mind. The heavy air receded, leaving goosebumps in its wake.

Figures composed of dark, billowing clouds melted out of the void behind her eyelids. They darted erratically through the space around her, sometimes winking in and out of existence between locations without traversing the distance. Others had to strive to make progress through air turned to honey. A handful of the humanoid shadows zipped through the scene, their legs nothing but a sooty blur as they passed. As the blackness ebbed, the frantic boiling of the shadow-people's bodies burned away, leaving behind defined human shapes void of color. The wall of gloom retreated to the corners of her eyes, almost gone but impossible to forget as it bristled at the edges of her vision.

The washed-out people got their chaotic movements under control, and she could make out more about them. They were too solid to be ghosts, and lacked the telltale blue glow. Yet they weren't really there in the room with her either.

An ash-colored child tugged at an annoyed older sibling while their mother tutted at them to be careful. Men in drab hats and lead-hued overcoats shook hands as they made their farewells, and a janitor emptied the contents of a trash can attached to one of the massive supports of the station. Though the pace of the shadow figures evened out, they jolted and changed if she closed her eyes, losing several moments with every blink.

An old woman heaped in shawls warmed her hands with a packet of roasted chestnuts as she shuffled along the platform, but no hint of their aroma lingered. Vi turned her attention to the massive steam engine groaning and hissing in front of her with the same result.

Her eyes traveled over the iron beams and brick walls as her brain struggled to decipher her whereabouts. Trains scurried along the tracks, their cranks rising and falling like the legs of massive centipedes. Young stewards hauled steamer trunks and carpet bags on and off the trains while a white-haired man in a tailored uniform consulted a tiny notebook and directed their movements. She'd stood in plenty of train stations in her lifetime, but the interior of the cavernous room did not strike her as familiar, no matter how long she squinted at it.

The figures lurched along with their lives, unaware of her presence or choosing to ignore her. As she turned, her gaze fell on one of them, his utter stillness completely at odds with the fitful movements of his comrades. He sat on cast iron bench, his head bowed and eyes downcast.

She took a few hesitant steps toward the strange man. When she reached out to touch the bench, she'd half-expected her hand to pass right through it, but her fingers found a smooth, solid surface. He didn't lift his head as she approached. Now that she stood closer, Vi could peer around the brim of his hat to see his nostrils flared in agitation, the taut skin around his unblinking eyes. Serenity had not made a statue of the man; a deep anxiety rendered his flesh to stone.

As she leaned toward his stern profile, she realized she knew the face. Deep furrows of concern and the murky gray light had morphed it into a pained mask, but the longer she looked at the square chin and slant of his shoulders, the easier it was to find her former partner buried within the still figure. It seemed impossible that Peter's laughing eyes were even capable of carrying so much turmoil, yet here he sat before her in a stoical, anticipatory silence.

"Peter?" she asked, swinging around the bench and into the space beside him. "Is that really you?" He didn't acknowledge her, even after she called his name a few more times. She tried shaking him by the shoulder, but no matter how hard she pushed against him she could not make him move. Peter was every bit as solid and unyielding as the statue he resembled.

"What is this place?" she grumped, turning away and searching for an exit. To one side, the maw of the station gaped wide enough to accommodate rows upon rows of tracks. The main body of the station lay in the other direction. She gave the shadow-Peter a moment of contemplation, but as he didn't seem to be going anywhere, she left the bench to explore.

Vi's full skirt whispered across the stone floor as she wandered through the station desperate for any hint of her location or how she'd arrived. The ticket windows displayed signs marked 'CLOSED,' and the crowd of gray figures began to disperse for the night. She followed the tide of humanity to the main door of the station, the traveling cloaks and bustled dresses around her lackluster in the muted light of the vision.

They passed through the entryway, and she stomped several yards onto the flat expanse of lawn before she turned around to look at the building. For a moment, she thought the void had returned to swallow the station, but when she gazed into the black dome, stars winked down at her. Their march across the sky may have been slower than the heave and stagger of the shade people, but she could still sense their motion as she stood blinking. A clock tower came to a peak several stories above her, and the moonlight cast its long shadow across a rippling lake at her left. When she swept her eyes over the façade, a large, rectangular sign above the main entryway reported she was looking at the Central Station.

"I'm in *Chicago*?" she scoffed. "What the blazes am I doing in some nightmare version of Chicago?"

The shades had all dispersed, save for a lone man struggling with the gate at the base of the tower. She rushed over, waving her arms, terrified at the idea of being locked out of the station and unable to return. The steward's head shot up, but he turned to listen to something behind him rather than noticing the flailing woman on the lawn. Vi's eyes closed and opened on two more uniformed men dragging a layperson roughly between them. When they got to the threshold, they dumped his body unceremoniously onto the pavement.

Peter let out a groan as he tumbled to the ground. "Please, I can't leave yet."

"Well that's too bad," replied a sandy-haired youth with a flippant wave of his hand. "The last train pulled out, and we're locking up for the night."

"Yeah," said the man with the keys. "I'm ready to get myself a well-deserved quaff. Any of you gents with me?" The gate creaked closed with the stewards inside, and the tumbler clicked into the latch.

"No!" the shadowy copy yelled and threw himself at the bars, wild-eyed and desperate. He clutched the gate with one hand and grabbed the shoulder of the man with the keys. "She told me to wait for her. I have to be here."

The man scrambled away from her ex-partner's clawing hands and raised a fist in warning. "You just get, now. I don't want to have to make you leave, boy, but we will if we have to."

"Come back and look for your friend in the morning," added the third man, age and experience at the station gentling his tone.

Rage glowed in Peter's eyes for a moment before he sagged against the bars. "Sure," he sighed. "Tomorrow."

The stewards disappeared into the dark interior of the train station mumbling about drunks and crazies. Peter looked out over the lawn and the wide expanse of the lake. He turned wistfully to the row of hotels and the inviting light that poured out of their windows. Instead of crossing the street as she'd expected, he slowly slid to the pavement and settled against the curve of the cold, stone archway for the night. His breath came out in puffs of steam as he pulled his coat tighter around his body.

"What are you doing? Don't just sit there," she cried. He didn't react, but she could see his lips moving and bent close to hear his whispered words.

"She'll come," he assured himself. "Vi won't let you down. She'll be here."

As she let out of a gasp of recognition, the infinite depth of the void swirled between her and the scene, blocking her view of the man she'd abandoned four years ago and thrusting her back into the present. The vision closed and spat the Vi of the present back into herself. The sounds of the train's steady progress crashed into her ears. She dragged hot air in and out of her lungs, banishing the last of the frigid Chicago night from her body and nearly choking. Though the scene had the same colorless people and vivid reality as her experience in Sacramento, this couldn't be a simply a dream, or even a memory. At least, not a memory that belonged to her.

The room gently spun like the first moments of a hangover. As her hands reflexively rose to massage the pounding in her skull, she remembered the token she held in one. Peter's pin. Peter's memory.

Despite the dizziness, Vi flung the curtain aside. Inside the vision, it was impossible to know how much time had passed, but some snatches of light outside the window below her illuminated the interior now and then. She glared at the pin for a few breaths before lunging for her jacket. Angry tears gathered on her lashes as she stabbed the pin into the fabric and recoiled to the safety of her bed linens. Even with her eyes squeezed shut, the image of Peter, broken and betrayed on the pavement, flashed against her eyelids. She knew it couldn't have been easy to be left behind, but she never dreamed it had been so hard.

When she tried to swallow, the dry walls of her throat begged for water. Bonnie snoozed peacefully, blissfully unaware of Vi's movements. Vi stumbled down the aisle to the powder room. A porcelain pitcher and basin waited on a shelf that could fold into the wall. Without thinking, her extra sense made a sweep of the cabin, but thankfully Peter was nowhere to be found.

She splashed tepid water into the bowl. It sloshed over the side, and she used the hem of her shift to mop it up, then dragged the damp cloth across her eyes. The tears couldn't be allowed to fall. No one could know—*he* couldn't know.

After scooping a few palms full of water from basin to slake her thirst, Vi leaned against the wall of the train compartment. Her ragged breathing filled the true darkness until the train rocked to the right, rounding a corner. Outside, the wall of black trees broke, and she flinched at the sudden expanse of golden sunrise painted across the horizon.

Ready or not, the time had come to face another day.

CHAPTER 26

October 3, Somewhere in Nevada

"I figured it out," Bonnie declared.

Vi leaned closer to the mirror, checking to see how much damage her sleepless night had done to her face. She gave her cheekbones a pinch to add color, then met the other woman's eyes hovering over her reflection's shoulder. "What did you figure out?"

"Your secret," she whispered mischievously.

"You'll have to be a bit more specific than that. I'm a woman with many secrets," Vi replied. She tried for a chuckle, but it came out strained. The scheming, selfish part of her had to admit the appeal of a window into her partner's life. Of course, she'd have never expected to experience it in three dimensions, or to stumble onto such an intimate and painful moment.

They made their way out of the powder room and waited behind the other passengers filing out in search of breakfast. In the night, the parched California grassland had given way to the rugged crags and scrublands of northern Nevada. Tiny yellow flowers dusted the terrain in the distance, clinging to the dry earth and squeezing every ounce of moisture out of the beautiful but unforgiving landscape.

Once they were both on the platform, Bonnie said, "I know why you're looking so grouchy."

"Really? And why is that?"

"Well, you keep trying to hide it, but I know the truth...." the little brunette trailed off suggestively, eyes shining. "Trains make you sick to your stomach." Relief flooded Vi's body, and she let out the breath she didn't realize she'd been holding. Bonnie mistook it for admission of guilt. "Aha!"

"Yes. You've found me out," Vi replied, applying just the right amount of remorse to her voice to sell it. Feigning motion-sickness was far more appealing than trying to explain the true source of her restlessness. Bonnie may have proved more resilient than she first appeared, but everyone had to have a limit. Vi couldn't bring herself to test this one yet. And Peter could be anywhere.

"You don't have to act so perfect and controlled all the time, dear. Not around me," her friend gently scolded. "If you need something to settle your stomach, you should simply say so. Now look at you, you tossed and turned all night. I insist you get yourself something with ginger for breakfast."

A familiar voice broke through the din. "Did I hear someone say they are having trouble sleeping?" asked Sands. He stood a few paces away, camera tucked under his arm. Bonnie let out a peep, then turned her attention to the other end of the platform as if searching for George. A hint of magenta returned to the reporter's ears.

George emerged from the crowd at the front of the train. Bonnie raised her arm and hurried toward him, leaving Vi alone with the newspaper man. He fidgeted and muttered as the stream of people ebbed and flowed around them, admonishing himself for repeating his mistake of being too forward.

Vi pinched the bridge of her nose, then took pity on him. "Missus," she said.

"Excuse me?"

"My friend. She's not a Miss. She's a Missus." It was close enough to the truth to do the job.

"Oh, I see. Thank you. Though I do still apologize about before. And now, for intruding." Sands shifted the camera to the other arm, but the nervous tremor left his voice. "Normally, I wouldn't inquire about a lady's sleep. I just, for the story, you see? About the Pullman cars?"

She sighed. "The bed was excellent. The problem was me."

He made an exaggerated sound of commiseration, rife with wisdom Vi doubted he had put in the time to earn himself. Likely, he'd picked it up from listening to actual worldly men. "I've learned that I need to do at least an hour of reading every night to calm my mind. I have several books with me if you'd care to borrow one."

"What sorts of books?"

"What sorts do you like?"

Vi thought for a moment before replying with a smirk. "Ghost stories."

A grin nearly split his face in half. "Really? I don't know that I'd recommend them as a sleep aid, but I have do have a collection of sorts. The Star prints them sometimes, but it's always been a—"

"Hobby?" she finished with him.

George materialized at her side and stood at attention. "Do you have any instructions for me before breakfast, ma'am?"

"Please," Sands interrupted, "don't let me keep you. I'm waiting here in hopes I can talk to the owner of the private car and ask for that tour. But if you decide you are ready for some chilling tales, I am happy to loan you some from my personal collection. Good day."

Vi and her valet joined the wave of hungry passengers descending on the Elko station neighborhood. Once the trains arrived in Omaha, some of them had dining cars, but anyone traveling West of there had to rely on the stops along the way.

George told her he'd found a cafe with a thirty-cent breakfast special and led the way. When Bonnie saw them, she started to rise, but Vi waved at her to stay seated. "I'll see to coffee and breakfast."

"And ginger!" Bonnie tutted.

"Yes, mother."

Vi headed over to the small yet well-appointed bar with something a little stronger than ginger on her mind. Peter had remained blissfully silent since her dismissal, though she couldn't be certain how long it would last. Every fiber of her body buzzed, begging her to reach out to the invisible world of ghosts and memories.

A drink or two would help her keep her abilities—all of them—under control. As she approached the counter, something in her periphery told her a spirit loomed somewhere nearby, but she swallowed the throb and refused to turn her head. Peter could follow her around all he liked, but she had no intention of letting him get to her no matter how much everything conspired to deepen their connection.

She got a server's attention, and he hurried over. "It's breakfast time, ma'am. The bar doesn't open until later."

"The bottles are just sitting there, begging to be opened. Surely you can make an exception?" Vi batted her eyes and the young man's resolve toppled.

"Of course, ma'am," he said, his gaze landing on the fine fabric of her dress. He ducked behind the counter, and when he reappeared behind the bar, he was all smiles. "Would you care for some champagne?"

"Definitely not." She pulled a sour face at the reminder, before adding sweetly, "I'd like a ginger beer, please."

"One ginger beer, coming right up," he replied. "Anything else?"

Her eyes traveled over the wooden shelves full of bottles. "I'd like two coffees with sugar, but make one with a goodly dash of whiskey. One hot chocolate. And three breakfast specials."

He disappeared in search of a coffee decanter at the same time a tall, blond woman in an impeccable tweed traveling ensemble walked up to the bar. "Typical," she snarled.

Vi instantly recognized her as the abhorrent woman who terrorized the porter in Sacramento. "He'll be right back," she assured her, but bit back any further words.

"Please do excuse my manners," the woman replied wearily. "It has already been a long and tiring journey."

"I feel the same way, believe me," Vi replied and indicated the bar. "And I see we have the same approach for getting through it."

The well-dressed woman laughed and held out her hand. "I'm Mrs. Bella Harrison."

Vi stared at it numbly for a moment, afraid the brush of skin would reveal the presence she felt in the room, but clasped lady's fingers for a moment without consequence. "Viola Thorne," she replied.

"I can't wait to make it back home to Chicago," Bella said, leaning against the bar and craning her neck in search of the bartender. "Are you going there, too?"

"Yes, but it's only a stop along the way." The server came back with a pair of steaming coffee cups on a tray and set them before Vi. He took the other woman's curt order for a tonic and gin before turning away to retrieve the bottles of liquor.

The smartly dressed woman's tone swung wildly back to completely pleasant as she addressed her fellow first-class passenger. "Have you ever been to Chicago before? It's a wonderful place."

"I've got family there," Vi admitted. "But I don't plan to let them know I'm coming into town."

"Ah, that sort of family. I know all about *that* sort of family," Bella said sagely.

Vi's shoulders rose and fell awkwardly as she counted the years between visits. "My aunt isn't so bad…"

Bella took a sip of her drink and sighed contentedly. She looked around the crowded cafe. "I think I'll go and enjoy this at a table. Would you care to join me?"

"No, thank you, I'm here with a friend."

"Oh, I'm glad to hear that," she replied and pointed at something behind Vi. "I'd hate to think of rubbing elbows with a stranger. They'll let just about anyone on the train these days."

Vi turned to follow her meaning and realized her companions lay in the path of the accusing finger. Compared to the other diners, Bonnie's clothes were well-worn around the edges, but she certainly didn't deserve the disdain dripping from Bella's voice. George alerted Bonnie to something exciting outside the window, and she laughed.

Bella made an ugly sound in her throat. "I swear, it gets worse and worse every year."

Vi swung her head back around and repressed a glare for the other woman, her voice innocent. "Whatever do you mean?"

"Well, that negro of course." The overstuffed woman didn't even bother to lower her voice. She fanned herself dramatically and took another sip of her drink. "He came from the first-class area of the train, no less! This is why I have a private car, mind, but still. It's appalling to think of him creeping around so close to where we sleep."

Vi gritted her teeth, her fingers flexing and begging to be turned into a fist. Her body almost shook with the effort to keep her rage in check, but her extra sense asserted itself through her distraction and sent another warning of a spirit. Without her gloves she couldn't risk contact, no matter how much she wanted to sock the other woman in the jaw. Instead, she picked up the tray the bartender set down.

"Have a nice morning," she said with a wide smile to the bartender, then walked straight to where her friends sat waiting. Once she set down the tray, she gave Bella a wave. She and her ample bosom huffed out of the cafe.

"What was that about?" Bonnie asked as she retrieved a cup of coffee.

"Some people have no class," Vi replied, stopping her friend's hands before she brought the whiskey-laced concoction to her lips. "That one's mine."

The trio enjoyed their beans and eggs, and under Bonnie's careful scrutiny, Vi drank her whole bottle of ginger beer. Once they paid their tab, they headed back across the platform in hopes of getting seats in one of the comfortable parlor cars for the next leg of their journey.

"You're a pretty lucky valet," Bonnie teased. "Not everybody gets spoiled like you."

Vi chuckled. "Let's call it hazard pay. I really don't know what to expect once we reach N'awlins," she drawled. Then, she added in her normal Yankee accent, "Or Chicago for that matter. It's been a long time since I've been back to either place."

"Because of your... work?" Bonnie asked, her gaze flicking to George and back again, unsure of what he knew or what Vi wanted him to know.

"You could say that, but not the job you're thinking of," Vi replied. "Leaving the south had to do with an issue of a more... *spiritual* nature."

Bonnie caught her reference to ghosts and crinkled her brow. "Anything I need to be concerned about?"

"No." The reluctant medium smirked, pausing at the foot of the stairs leading to the parlor. "Let's just say my services were in demand and I got tired of trying to fill all the orders. You know, like how I met your husband."

"I see," the young widow replied, stepping onto the metal stair. "That's a relief. You had me worried for a second."

Bolstered by Bonnie's sincere concern, Vi made a decision. She took a deep breath, and said, "Wait a moment, please. There *is* something strange happening, but I didn't know how—"

A shout cracked over the comings and goings of the stations as loud as gunfire. Mrs. Bella Harrison stomped off across the platform, trailed by a pair of hesitant porters. She barreled her way toward George, her finger held in front of her like a lance. "There he is! Just like I said he would be."

"Me?" He pressed against Bonnie and looked to Vi in his confusion.

"What did I do?"

"I demand you search him at once," Bella screeched. "He's a thief, and I want him arrested."

Vi stepped between the fury and her prey. "What's all this about?"

"I saw him. He was coming from the direction of my car, and now I return to find I've been robbed. And it was him. I know it!"

"That's your proof?" Vi asked in disbelief. "It's a train. It only has two directions."

The woman shot a revolted glare at the petrified stewards and dove to grab at George herself. From her place inside the train car, Bonnie held him with one arm and batted ineffectually at the incensed aristocrat.

"Stop it!" Vi cried, her rage propelling her to grab Bella's wrist before she remembered to be cautious. In her anger, her repressed energy surged forward and poured into the other woman, coursing like an electric shock through her arm and into George. The jolt momentarily stopped his flailing, but it redoubled as he spotted something and started to scream in terror.

Vi turned to find a shimmering blue shape glowing through a train window, it's form in ragged tatters and a low moan emanating from its slack jaw. It drifted through the car, a dazed and forlorn expression covered what was left of its mangled face. The ghost reached out its shriveled arm and drifted nearer as the sorrowful groan gave way to a piercing wail.

Bella recoiled from the boy's shriek and let go of his arm, and Vi's grip went slack in her surprise. With the contact broken, the ghost disappeared, and panicked tears welled in his eyes. For a moment, Bonnie stood in shocked silence at the top of the stair, then hugged George against her.

"He's not only a thief. He's insane," Bella declared.

"He's neither, you harpy," Vi sizzled, trying to ignore the very un-Peterlike ghost that continued to wail nearby. "Don't you dare touch him again."

"Or what?" the other woman sneered. "I could have the whole lot of you left here if I wanted to, and over what? Some little coon using his newfound freedom to rob people."

"How about you bring me some proof besides the color of his skin, and I *might* let you ask him some questions," she replied. Vi waved at Bonnie and George to get onto the train, and she squared her shoulders. "He's my employee, which means he's my responsibility, and so is his punishment. When, and more importantly, *if* the situation calls for it."

Somehow, Bella's face flushed an even deeper shade of scarlet as she gritted her teeth. "I don't want to catch him anywhere me or my things ever again. Is that clear?"

"I assure you, staying away from you would be our pleasure."

<h1 style="text-align:center">CHAPTER 27</h1>

As Bonnie helped George up the stairs, Vi steered them away from the tattered ghost and into the other parlor car to catch their breath. She did not hear it shriek so much as felt its sorrow vibrate across her skin, sending every hair standing on end.

"I think I might be cracked, Miss Viola," George squawked. "I saw something. Something terrible! Or at least, I thought I did." The boy ahead of her moved like he was in a trance as they made their way back to their seats. Most of the other passengers were still out enjoying the fresh air, giving them some degree of privacy. Bonnie supported George as he walked, trying to calm his terror with an arm around his narrow shoulders.

"There is nothing wrong with you. I promise," Vi assured him, then added in a whisper, "Let's get you sitting down and I'll tell you more."

His eyes didn't retract from their rictus of surprise as he continued to stumble along the narrow passage and between cars. As they approached their berth, a different ghost paced along the aisle. Peter's face lit up in a moment of relief before settling again into a frown. "You may not be listening, Thorne, but that doesn't mean I'm not here," he called to her. "You're being childish."

Vi dragged her hand over her face in frustration and disgust; of course, he wanted to talk right that moment. "Not now, Peter."

"Oh! I guess you are listening."

She passed through him and into their cabin. During breakfast, the porters had stowed the linens and converted the beds back into seating for the day to come. Vi glanced around for a panicked moment, but soon spied the pouch where she had put Peter's pin safely stowed beneath one of the spacious seats.

Bonnie hissed, "What happened? Was it of a 'spiritual nature'?"

"Something happened? Are you alright?" Peter interjected.

She waved the ghost away. "Five minutes, Peter. Can you not give me five goddamn minutes? I've got a different fire to put out right now." Any response he might have had was cut off as she turned her back. With her power awakened, she clearly felt him stomp away to the other end of the car to sulk.

George huddled on the opposite bench, hugging his bony knees to his chest. Though his tears stopped falling, he regarded her warily. Bonnie stood at his side, rubbing his shoulder.

Once seated, Vi took a few breaths and softened her expression. "Do you believe in ghosts?"

"Is *that* what I saw?" he asked as gravely as his childish face would allow.

"Yes. And I know this because I saw it, too."

"Really?"

She risked a sideways glance, but the nearest neighbor had his eyes fixed on a newspaper. "Absolutely. I've been seeing them for some time now. And when I touch someone, or they touch someone touching me, then they can see them, too."

His eyes grew wide again, but this time in admiration. "But it was so awful Miss Viola. You seen a lot of 'em?"

"Yes. A great many, in fact," Vi replied, turning to meet his gaze and seeing no hint of disgust over her confession. She chuckled, adding, "And they aren't all so horrible as that one."

At the sound of the whistle, other passengers began wending their way to their seats, but the more people who came, the more secure Vi actually felt. The scuffle kept their conversation private.

Bonnie murmured. "What did you see? Are you talking about Peter?"

"No, this was another spirit, a really old one. Or perhaps it was never strong to begin with. They sort of... wear out." She pulled a face and turned back to George. "As far as I understand it, ghosts are made from big feelings that a person can't let go. The one in the parlor car just now, it's so old that the feeling is all that's left. It doesn't have the strength to hold its shape very well, and it can no longer speak."

"Where do you see them?" George asked. Some of the earlier fear crept back into his voice. "They can't just be on trains, right?"

She gave a noncommittal shrug. "You can find ghosts just about anywhere, I suppose. There really is not anything to stop them from going wherever they want—" George's whimper of fear stopped her, and she cleared her throat. "That is to say, not all ghosts are scary like the one you saw."

"They're not?" Hope loosened his features and his hold on his knees.

"No. Most of them look like regular people, but made of smoke," she said, the shift in his mood buoying her. "In fact, I have a friend who is a ghost. He's been around for a few days now, and he hasn't hurt anyone."

"He has? But I never saw nothing."

"I have," Bonnie piped up. "I've seen them, too." The boy grinned at her gratefully. The train crept forward as the final whistle blasted.

Vi sighed. "Back there was my fault. I wasn't being careful and you got caught in the middle. But you need not see ghosts ever again. Not if you don't want to."

Peter chose that moment to storm over, shouting, "You've had plenty of time to ignore me. You don't need five more minutes."

Vi seized on an idea and continued talking to the child at her side. "Or, you could meet my friend, and you could see for yourself that he's not so scary."

"Wait, what?" the ghost asked, his befuddlement robbing him of his pique. "What's happening?"

"He's here?" George asked with a mixture of anxiety and delight.

She crooked her finger to bring the boy closer and whispered. "He's standing right here."

"What are you doing, Vi?" Peter groused. "You know I hate kids!"

"What do you think? You want to meet him?" The little boy nibbled on a thumbnail thoughtfully, then agreed. Relief washed over her, and she rested her hand on the table between them. His acceptance meant more to her than she would like to admit. "All you've got to do is touch me."

"Damnation. I know what you're doing," the ghost grumbled. "And this won't get you out of talking to me. Not forever."

George squeaked as he took hold and Peter came into focus before him, but after the initial shock, all signs of fear melted away. Despite his earlier declaration, the spirit pasted a bright and congenial smile on his face and greeted the boy.

"She was right, you're not so scary," George said happily. His voice dropped into a conspiratorial whisper. "Have you seen the other one?"

"Ugh, the wailer? Yes, I ran into it once already." Peter chuckled. "Quite literally in fact. I'd never realized how solid one ghost felt to another until I became one. Really, Vi, we should be writing all of this down."

She patted herself theatrically. "Damn. No pen."

He glared at her complete lack of scientific procedure, then turned back to the kid. "Anyway, I've been avoiding the wailer and the parlor car ever since. Which is a real shame, because there was a ghost we helped once who told me about the joys of haunting a cocktail and I'd love to curl up inside a glass of something for a while. I tried to warn your employer here about the wailer, but she decided she didn't want to hear my opinion for a while."

"I already admitted that what happened was my fault," Vi replied. Her extra senses crackled across her skin, buzzing like angry wasps the closer Peter stepped. She tried to push it down again, and her next words came through a tight-lipped grimace. "You don't need to make a criminal case out of it."

Bonnie interjected. "And speaking of criminals, what do you suppose that nonsense about George being a thief was all about?"

"Ignorance, mostly," Vi seethed.

The ghost smiled down at the boy. "Got yourself some light fingers, eh kid?"

"I didn't do it!" George cried. "I swear."

"We know you didn't," Vi assured him, then favored the ghost with another glower.

"I was always getting blamed for things when I was your age, too. And you know what I did?" Peter whispered.

George leaned forward with rapt attention. "What?"

"I proved them right," he said with a chuckle.

Vi let out an exasperated sigh. "Oh, excellent advice."

"It's true."

"And see where it got you?" she spat.

"I thought I had you to thank for that." His quiet words stunned her to silence even as he blazed clearer and darker before her, his pain manifesting in his spectral body. His sharp edges dissolved as he turned to the boy. "Anyway, George. I figured as long as people were going to think the worst of me, I might as well live down to their expectations."

Bonnie settled beside George, outside of the conversation but looking to change the subject after her friend's angry shout. "I think we'd better stay out of that awful woman's way for the rest of the trip."

"I second that motion," Vi said. "Especially if there's a screaming ghost haunting the parlor cars. I won't be able to go near them without going insane."

"Can't you shut it out again?" the other woman asked.

Peter interjected bitterly. "Or is that a privilege you only reserve for me?"

"Let's just lay low for a few days," Vi hedged. "Then I won't have to."

"You started to say something before, about something strange happening," Bonnie said with concern. "Is this what you wanted to tell me? That you're having trouble keeping the ghosts out?"

As much as Vi longed to tell her friend about the flashes of memory, she couldn't bring herself to admit to what she'd seen with Peter staring daggers at her. Even though the first experience had been every bit her own memory as much as it was his, there was no denying her role as voyeur stealing a glance at something she never should have seen. Rather than dissipating, their tie seemed to deepen the longer he was dead.

"Yes," she replied, both a truth and a lie at the same time. "Ever since I started to use my abilities again, I'm having more and more trouble shutting them back off. I thought that keeping them under wraps for four years would have been good practice."

"Or your powers are too strong to ignore," Peter said. "I always told you I thought pushing them away was a mistake, even dangerous. You're right. You aren't an expert. You've never really learned where it comes from, or what any of it means."

"I know where you are going with this, but don't," she said darkly.

"We'll be passing right through town, no reason we couldn't—"

Vi glared. "I don't want to see her."

"But why not?"

"See who?" Bonnie asked with exasperation. "I can't hear anything you're talking about right now."

"Sorry. Peter is suggesting we stop by to see my aunt while we are in Chicago."

"You've got family in town? How delightful. I'd love to meet another member of the Thorne clan," Bonnie bubbled.

"We haven't exactly been in touch..."

"All the more reason to visit," she declared. "It will be so nice to be in a home after this journey, especially if we are going to be cooped up in this tiny space for the rest of the trip."

"All the more reason," the ghost agreed.

Her friend clapped her hands in delight and continued. "We can send her a telegram at the next station, so she knows to expect us."

"It's complicated." Vi pinched the bridge of her nose. "You don't understand."

"Evidently, neither do you," Peter mocked. "The best way to get answers would be to talk to Prudence."

Bonnie pouted, but relented to show her friend a face open and willing to listen. "Then explain it to me."

"Fine," she sighed. "I spent several years of my youth in Chicago. My father would come and go, but he left me in that house with his sister, Pru. She's a complete tyrant and more than a little touched. As soon as I could, I got out, and I never wanted to go back."

"But that's only half the story!" the ghost cried.

Bonnie's reply was soft and sad. "So, she's all alone?"

"I wouldn't exactly call it alone," Vi mumbled. "She has August, the butler. And some... visitors from time to time. But mostly she works on her weird experiments."

"Really? What does she study?"

Vi let the question hang in the air before her mouth curled into an enigmatic smile. "Death."

Chapter 28

October 5, 1871
Somewhere in Wyoming

"I don't think that's a scarf."

"Then what would you call it?" Vi asked, holding up the crooked rows of yarn. She could make out the pearly blue of Bonnie's dress through the gaps. The other woman shifted and one dark eye peered through an especially haggard loop.

Bonnie giggled. "I'm fairly certain I'd call it a mess."

"Ha, ha. Laugh all you want," Vi huffed, tossing the gnarled yellow mass onto the table. "We cannot all excel at the womanly arts."

A trickle of sweat gathered on her neck and slithered along her spine. She arched her back against her seat back to scratch away the irritation of its path. Even with the windows open, the heat inside the train car had lain heavy as a wool blanket for the past two days. The only reprieve was when they took turns buying meals at the stations while the other stayed behind to keep George company. If it wasn't for the Harrison woman, they'd have been able to take full advantage of amenities. Instead, they had to worry if George got off, he'd never get on again. By unspoken agreement, even Peter stayed close.

Bonnie's knitting needles clicked together, her scarf already two feet long and growing. "It's nice to know you aren't good at everything."

"It's like I told Hank. I make a terrible wife. Though I'm not too shabby at sewing."

"Something you learned from your mother?"

Vi pulled a sour face. "Hardly. Mother didn't really do things with her hands. But one of the costumers showed me, and I'd help mend things while Mother rehearsed." A teasing grin replaced her grimace. "Personally, I believe that I did my best work sewing soldiers back together during the rebellion. I could handle mending people while the guns fired on the other side of the hill, but I tell you, knitting is totally beyond my capabilities."

Bonnie tried to give her the glower of an exasperated governess, but she didn't have enough frown lines yet to really sell it. Vi fluttered her eyelashes pointedly, and her friend laughed. "All right, have it your way. You do not have to knit anymore. I thought though, on account of you spending yesterday teaching George and me poker, the least I could do is teach you something in return." She sighed and held the tangle up to the light to get a better angle.

At the mention of her valet, she glanced at the door. He had gone to find a porter to order them supper some time ago. Peter may be shadowing the kid, but she still felt uneasy with George out of her sight. Bonnie's frustrated tutting caught her attention, and Vi turned back to the conversation.

"The difference is, teaching you poker was *fun*. Learning to knit is a bit like torture," she teased.

The young widow picked at the furry glob with a knitting needle, carefully undoing everything Vi had done. "No, taking out all these knots is torture," she fussed before sighing wistfully. The sorry excuse for a scarf rested in her lap, momentarily forgotten as tears came to her eyes. "Tobias used to do that part for me."

Vi smirked. "I never pegged him for a knitter."

"He was actually really good at it. With all his older brothers off fighting for the Union and his father gone, it was only Tobias and his ma. They were close. I think it just about killed her when we left for California...." The last shreds of levity drained out of the room as the reality of Tobias's death settled in all over again.

While uncomfortable seconds ticked by, Vi kept her gaze directed out the window. They'd already traded the painted, rocky outcroppings of Nevada for the white plains of Utah and forged on to the rolling plains of Wyoming. Smudgy clouds seemed to be following their route, bringing down the sky to make their captivity feel even closer and more stifling.

"I suppose I'll have to let her know what happened." Bonnie wiped her eyes discreetly and resumed her work with the needle.

"If you need to go home, you know I'd understand," Vi murmured. "I dragged you along with me, but that doesn't mean you have to stay."

"Trust me," Bonnie replied with an uncharacteristic, derisive snort. "I would much rather be here than looking Mama Murphy in the face."

Vi chuckled. "So, I take it you're close?"

"With his mother? Lord, no," the widow laughed, running a piece of yarn through her deft fingers. "You think anything I could do was going to be good enough for her?"

Before she could respond, Peter slipped through the door and down the aisle. "Dinner is on its way, madams! Our young friend is right behind me." Vi dipped her chin in recognition.

"What about yours?" Bonnie asked idly, her eyes glued to the knots.

"My what?"

"Mother-in-law. Or laws, I suppose."

Vi shrugged. "Never had the pleasure, in fact. Already dead when I entered the scene, on both counts."

The other woman smiled. "Lucky you."

"According to Patrick, it was lucky for her, too. She wouldn't have been able to bear the war. Nor his part in it."

From over Vi's shoulder, Peter's brittle voice announced, "I'm bored."

Vi twisted in her seat to face him, but he'd already stormed past her to the far end of the car. With his back to her, the ghost bent over an old man's shoulder to read his newspaper. She turned to the other woman, mulling over the last things they'd said.

"What happened?" Bonnie asked, still looking at the place where Vi had first glanced.

She let out a muttered curse, then replied, "I think I may have upset Peter. He just left in a bit of a huff."

"But, why? We weren't even talking about him. Or New Orleans."

"He doesn't like it when I talk about Patrick." Vi knuckled between her eyes, silently berating herself at her lack of care. She hadn't said his name outside her head for years, so of course, she mentioned him in front of the only person who felt worse about his death than she did.

Bonnie pouted. "That doesn't make any sense."

"It doesn't have to," she snapped.

The little brunette opened her mouth to say more, but a basket appeared, followed by George's smiling face. "I'm sorry that took so long. But I've got supper."

Vi rubbed her hands together greedily. "And not a moment too soon."

The smell of fresh, crusty rolls filled the air, momentarily chasing out all of the scents of their prolonged captivity. Bonnie cleared away the knitting to make a space for their meal. "How is it sleeping in the front, George?"

"I'm fine, Miss Bonnie." He cracked open his roll to stuff it with cheese and pickles. He stood at the head of their small fold out table, blocking the aisle, but most of the passengers were out enjoying the evening air.

"Are you sure?" Bonnie said. "You're awfully brave riding up there all alone."

"Well... it would be nice if I wasn't so far away. It can be a little scary." An anxious giggle escaped, then George cajoled his features into a brave expression. "That is to say, in case you need assistance."

"You're much safer from that Harrison woman in steerage than back here with us," Vi interjected. "You don't have to be frightened."

"It's not that—"

"Then what's wrong?"

He heaved a dejected sigh. "I know you said it couldn't hurt me, but I'm still afraid of that ghost. Not Peter. The screaming one," George said sheepishly. "You'd tell me if it was here, Miss Viola. Wouldn't you?"

"Of course," she lied. The less he knew about what he couldn't see, the better. So far, she hadn't seen any trace of the tattered ghost outside of its occasional restless pacing in the parlor car. But even it was standing right beside him, it didn't do him any good to know about it. The troubled look on his face told her he was still a few cars behind her on that particular train of thought. As she groped for something more reassuring than the word of a con artist, Peter wandered to another group passengers in search of distraction and gave her an idea.

"And I suppose you didn't know this, kid, but Peter would be able to help protect us if that scary one did bother us."

"He would?" George and Bonnie chorused.

At the sound his name, the ghost took a few steps closer. "I would what?"

"Yes, he's in much better condition than the other one," she continued to the boy, but pitched her voice at an exaggerated whisper to ensure Peter would hear her. "*We* can't touch spirits, but *they* can touch each other. He could push it away if it got too close."

"Like a guardian angel," Bonnie said.

The ghost blustered his way to Vi's side. "Hey, now wait a minute!"

George beamed. "Do you think he'd come and make sure it isn't by my seat? Just 'til I fell asleep?"

"I'm sure he would, but let's ask him just to make sure, all right?" Vi met Peter's gaze, and let the exaggerated flutter of her lashes ask the question for her.

"Fine," he groaned.

"He says he'd be glad to," she assured her valet.

They talked about what there would be to do and see the next day of the journey as they finished their late supper. With the promise that Peter followed, George returned to his seat to make sure he had a place to sleep for the overnight haul. This left the ladies with time for a few hands of stud to continue Bonnie's tutelage. The porters came a while later and converted the space for sleeping, the daily rhythm of life on the train folding them all into its embrace.

Soft blankets and thick pillows notwithstanding, Vi still found herself staring once more into the blackness of night long after the other passengers were asleep. The darkness appeared to be of the regular variety that evening, and not the sort that was going to whisk her away into a vision. She'd stowed the purse full of trinkets to make sure she couldn't touch the pin by mistake. All the same, she found it difficult to trust it would stay that way if she closed her eyes.

Inside her head, Vi walked from car to car, picturing the space and trying to remember every detail in turn. Her mind touched it all—the decoration on the lamps, the curve of a butter-smooth railing, the red swirls on the thick carpet—nothing was safe from her careful scrutiny as she tiptoed through the setting on imaginary feet.

Her extra sense quivered to life and quested outward, eager to pinpoint an unexpected danger. The curtains that had felt like a shield now left her feeling blind. An energy approached, and for a moment she hoped it was simply Peter coming by to check on them.

A wave of malice rippled through the air and probed with greedy tendrils. Vi touched it, and her senses recoiled, scurrying back to the safety of her skull like a whipped pup. If this was her former partner, something had changed him in the intervening hours. Her awareness lightly tasted the thing moving through the car and came back with the barest hint of familiarity. Without giving in and engaging fully, she wouldn't be able to make out its real form, but it must be the wailer out for a stroll. It was too much to hope it would have disembarked somewhere in the desert simply to improve the quality of her journey.

The ghost drew nearer and Vi turned toward the wall, as if this would somehow hide her. The longing and sorrow she'd first felt that day in Nevada had been replaced by something far more sinister. Based on her own experience, Vi wouldn't have said it was possible for a ghost to change so quickly, but there was plenty about the spirit world she didn't know.

The presence moved along the passage, the thunder of Vi's heart quickening with each pulse of rage. Despite the knowledge that the tattered spirit-thing likely would not have the coherency to touch her, every fiber of Vi's body grew taut, and she struggled to keep her breathing steady. This strange ghost didn't know she could sense it yet, and she'd like to keep it that way. She felt the blue aura draw nearer, its energy gently probing for something. Pins and needles spread down Vi's spine that deepened to an acid burn. It singed deeper when the presence was still a few steps away. It paused and drew on the energy in the room, as if scenting the air, and the temperature dropped a few degrees.

The rest of Vi's mind scrambled away from her awareness of the spirit world. Invisible teeth tore at her sense of the ghost until the pieces were small enough to swallow into the void. The acid boiling across her flesh lost some of its heat as the strength of the presence grew fainter and a wave of nausea broke. She could no longer sense the blue flame or its progress through the train car, but that should mean it couldn't feel her either.

Minutes, hours—Vi didn't know how long she lay inside her curtained cage before she finally allowed herself to relax. Chicago was still over two days' journey, and with the unexplained visions fraying her nerves and working so closely with Peter, she wouldn't be able to keep pushing the spirit sense away. The wailer would be drawn again, and the next time she'd likely have to confront it. The only way to keep from going mad would be to somehow find peace for the wailer, if there was any peace to be found.

And as she knew too well, not everyone was granted the luxury of peace.

CHAPTER 29

October 5, Bryan, Wyoming

Vi fell asleep sometime after she had finally tamed the angry swarm that nested in her brain. When she opened her eyes, she flinched away from the late morning sunshine streaming across her face. The duplicitous world outside her window had conspired with the sun to become a dazzling blur while she had slept.

With a groan, she rubbed her eyes and squinted into the room. None of her traveling companions, living or dead, could be found. The siren scent of coffee coiled into her nose, and she realized the scene outside the window, though painfully bright, also stood still.

Vi swung her legs over the side of the bed and stepped to the floor. The stations were few and far between in this stretch of the journey, and she didn't know how long they had already been there. Any chance to get off the train, and away from the wailer, was a welcome one.

She rushed to the powder room to change into fresh clothes and tried to put her scattered thoughts in order. Struggling for control over the spirit world was familiar, but the pain was a new and unwelcome development. Finishing Peter's business under the noses of whoever pursued her would have been difficult before. The key was to take back control of the situation before it got any farther out of hand.

To ward against repeating the incident with George and the wailer, she finished off her ensemble with a pair of short gloves. Vi smoothed out the wrinkles in her skirt, then yanked open the compartment door and sped to the exit. When she swung down to the platform, she nearly bowled over

Arthur Sands as he stood lighting a match. He cursed as the cigarette flew out of his mouth and through a gap in the decking, but when he saw who it was, he smiled at her. Though he told her he hadn't seen Bonnie, he offered to help her with her search, and they strolled to the edge of the cafes.

Sands held out his cigarette case as they exchanged a few pleasantries about the city of Bryan, and the progress of his article. He asked, "And where's our young man today? Off enjoying the sweet shop, I expect. The one on Main here quite good."

Her brows knit together. "Mrs. Harrison asked you to keep tabs on my valet, did she?"

"Well, she did, ma'am," he admitted, his ears turning a delightful shade of magenta. "But I didn't mean anything by it, honest. Just being polite."

"I see," she said, pursing her lips. "And would you happen to know where Mrs. Harrison is at the moment? We've been trying to make sure 'our young man' doesn't cross her path."

"That's not likely," the reporter assured her with a snort that almost knocked his cigarette free all over again. "Strictly speaking, the powers that be don't want anyone talking about it because they don't want the line to get a reputation. I found out strictly off the record." He swung his head, nervously gazing up and down the length of the train. After finding only a few distracted patrons going about their business, he deemed it safe to go on. "They don't think your valet had anything to do with any of the thefts, but they can't simply come out and say it without calling her a liar. She's a cousin or something to one of the owners, so they've been humoring her."

"Thefts, did you say?" Vi leaned into the 's.' "As in, more than one?"

"Yes ma'am. First, she claimed a letter opener went missing. That's what she made a fuss about there in Nevada."

Vi flapped her hand dismissively. "Piffle. What would George have wanted with that?"

"It's made of silver, I suppose."

"You said she 'claimed' it went missing. Did it or didn't it?"

The thrill of conspiracy lit his eyes and hushed his tone. "That's just it. The company searched her car for her, and they found it. She swears it wasn't there before, but who knows? Then this morning, she reported a *necklace* went missing. She's completely beside herself because of it. They've searched this morning, but no sign of it, and it looks like everyone has reached the end of their rope." They had continued to stroll, so no one could have heard all they'd been saying, but he still glanced around before he spoke again. "Some of the staff are saying there never was any necklace in the first place. That she's having some sort of episode. And you know, the Star did run an editorial about the effects of traveling at such high speeds can have on women."

Vi resisted the urge to point out that she and the other female passengers remained completely sane despite traveling at those same high speeds. "Is this going to become part of your big story?"

"I suppose that will depend on whether something more interesting happens to take up the ink." He winked one of his walnut-dark eyes. "Speaking of my story, though, I realized that I never got the name of yourself and your traveling companion."

She stopped short and dropped his elbow. "This is certainly the first I've heard about a necklace. And that goes for George, as well. We didn't have anything do with any of it."

"You mistake my meaning. The society pages will want to know who else was enjoying the Pullmans with me. We'll be picking up a French ambassador in Chicago, in fact," he said, eyes twinkling with the promise of an interview. "I simply wanted to add your name to my inventory for the society pages."

"In that case, I'm Mrs. Annabelle Sinclair of New Orleans, traveling with Mrs. Bonnie Murphy of Boston." Vi doubted anyone reading the society column would recognize either name, but she might as well get used to living in her alias's skin again. "And what about Mrs. Harrison and her claims? Is she going to make trouble for me?"

Sands chuckled. "No need to worry, ma'am. She has decided to take her business elsewhere. They are unhitching her car as we speak." He gazed wistfully at the custom train car and its freshly painted window trimming, the regret over losing it as palpable as when he'd been staring after Bonnie.

His longing reminded Vi of his many hobbies. "I'm actually glad I ran into you, Mr. Sands."

"How can I be of service?" he asked earnestly, careful to flick his ash away from them.

"You told me about your collection of ghost stories, and I was curious, do you have any about haunted trains?"

His glee returned despite the morbid turn in the conversation. "Workers and engineers are lost, sometimes, when boilers burst, that sort of thing." The reporter's Adam's apple bobbed and stilled, as if uncertain if it should proceed.

Vi prompted him with a few bats of her lashes. "And?"

"I don't want you to get frightened, ma'am."

"I'll do my best."

Sands beckoned Vi away from a knot of people. "Okay. There *is* one story I know, and it is about a car I believe is attached to this train. Back in the early days, before they had all the railroads connected, some of these cars were already running. I tracked a story about a murder on a stretch West of Omaha. A group of men robbed the train at gunpoint. Most people cooperated, but this one young lady refused to hand over her valuables. They shot her right there in front of her father."

The reporter paused, searching her face for a reaction. "No," Vi whispered, playing the part of the willing audience. "That's terrible."

Sands seemed to grow taller under her attention and continued. "And can you believe it? The father still works for the line. A Mister...." The reporter held up his finger and retrieved a small notebook from his pocket. He leafed through the pages until he found what he sought. "Miller. I've been asking around with the staff, but Miller wouldn't give me a comment. The others told me people report hearing weird things on the line, especially when they pass through that same stretch of open country where she died. We'll be coming up on it tonight." His finger crooked and Vi leaned in to hear his excited whisper. "I'm going to wait in there all night and try to get a photograph. This new flash could be just the ticket."

She quirked an eyebrow. "You really think you're going to see something?"

"I think there's no harm in trying to show people the truth."

"Tell that to Darwin," she muttered. As much as she'd like to stop hiding her supernatural abilities in the shadows, she didn't believe the world was quite ready to come into the light when it came to ghosts, either. There were a few photographers who claimed to capture the dead, but so far there hadn't been anything that looked enough like proof to call attention from the general public. And better for Vi if it stayed that way.

"If you still can't sleep tonight, perhaps you'd like to join me. I would love the company."

Vi chuckled and released his arm. "Bring a bottle of something strong and a couple of glasses, and I might take you up on that offer. But no promises. Now, I really must go and see where my friends have gone off to."

"I'm sorry I couldn't have been of more assistance." He slipped the notebook back in place, shaking his head.

"Not to worry, my good man," Vi replied. "I think you gave me exactly what I needed."

CHAPTER 30

Vi gave up on finding her companions among the small collection of shops and eateries and strolled to the Pullman, hoping to find them already back on the train. When she arrived, she found Bonnie making another attempt at taming the failed scarf. George shared her seat and dealt himself a hand of solitaire. Peter was nowhere to be seen, but Vi could hardly ask the others about his whereabouts.

"Good morning, Miss Viola!" George crowed.

"When we stopped, we thought it better to leave you sleeping," Bonnie said. She picked at a particularly stubborn knot with her teeth. "But you had a chance to stretch your legs?"

"I took a nice stroll with our friend Mister Sands. He had some interesting gossip to share."

Bonnie glanced up briefly but returned her attention to the knots. "Do tell."

"Firstly, I think I know who our wailer used to be," Vi replied, removing her gloves. "Which means, I may be able to figure out what it wants. And that means I may be able to get rid of it." The widow's head shot up, recrimination pinching the youth from her features. Vi faltered under her regard, then corrected herself. "I mean, I can ease her passage."

"That's better," Bonnie said and bent over her knitting again. "Anything else interesting?"

"Ah, yes. I have some wonderful news. There's been another theft."

George's eyes grew wide. "That doesn't sound like great news to me."

"It was not great news for Mrs. Harrison, either. The important thing is that no one is blaming *you*. The old cow is leaving the train, and we no longer have to give her another thought."

The boy let out a relieved sigh, but Bonnie frowned. "What was stolen?"

"A necklace. And it could not have happened to a kinder, gentler woman," Vi replied, but winking at George. She could feel her spirits lifting along with the corners of his mouth. "The next stop, you and I will celebrate with a something sweet."

George dug into the folds of his trousers and pulled out a tiny fist clutching a few coins. "I've still got most of my money."

"Piffle, it will be my treat," she declared. Bonnie glanced from her work with a distracted smile, then her gaze snagged on something near the boy's hip. Vi followed her gaze. "What's that?"

The boy's eyes flicked to the glint of metal sticking out of his pocket. "Nothing," he said a little too forcefully, then tried to nonchalantly push it back down. "Just a sweet wrapper."

"George," Vi said. "What have you got there?"

He turned his frightened face from one woman to the other, and promptly burst into tears. Bonnie gathered him into her arms, her dumbfounded expression showing she hadn't put the pieces together yet.

But the ex-grifter had. "Oh, George," Vi sighed.

"What is it?" Bonnie asked as he burrowed his face even farther into the crook of her neck. His repeated apologies came out thick and frantic. An old man with the newspaper shifted in his seat, the rustle of the paper reminding them all they weren't alone.

Fury rendered Vi's voice a quiet simmer that cut through his sobbing. "I'd put even money on that being Mrs. Harrison's missing necklace."

"Oh, George! You didn't," Bonnie gasped, leaning away to try to look into his eyes.

"Will you both please calm down?" Vi gritted. "We are drawing attention."

"I'm sorry," he whimpered. "She was just so mean. And she thought I done it anyway."

Bonnie held him by the shoulders. "When did you even have a chance? We've all been looking after you. Even Peter—oh." She turned to Vi. "He didn't say anything to you?"

"I'm going to kill him. Again," Vi growled. "Now, spill it George."

"When I went to get our supper last night," he snuffled. "I put in an order like you asked, and I saw her there, the mean lady, on the platform. I was going to come back to wait her out, but then I realized that meant she wasn't in her car, so...."

Vi filled in the end of his sentence. "So, you decided to make a liar out of me."

"No. I mean, I didn't mean to!" he squealed in terror. "Please, don't be mad."

"How long has this been going on?" she sizzled. "Did you take the letter opener, too?"

George's face screwed up in confusion. "Letter opener? I never took no letter opener." His employer scoffed, and he untangled himself from Bonnie. "Honest, Miss Viola. I only took the necklace, and I'm awful sorry about that. I knew I shouldna' done it the moment I did."

"How am I supposed to trust you?" Vi spat. "You're not just supposed to be my valet, kid. I thought you were my friend."

Bonnie rose from her place at the table, her voice maternal. "Now, Vi, don't be hasty—"

She ignored the other woman, her eyes boring holes into the slight figure before her. "Answer me."

George stuttered for a few moments, a fresh bout of tears springing to his eyes. "You can trust me. I never took nothing from you, and I'll never take nothing ever again. I swear!"

"See? No real harm done," Bonnie interjected.

Vi held out her hand, nostrils flaring. "Give it to me. We'll have to figure out what to do with it now that we've got it."

The tiny thief wiped his face with his sleeve, and his whole body sank into the bench seat, his fear no longer enough to keep his spine straight. He smiled sheepishly and handed over a silver chain dripping with cut, green stones— a small fortune a child could hold in his hand. Vi let out a low, appreciative whistle as she reached for it. When her outstretched fingers met the necklace, the sound in the room hushed as a now-familiar swirl of darkness cut through her vision. The last vestige of reality she saw was George's brown eyes widening with concern before the vision blotted out her sight.

The gentle breeze from the earlier memories had vanished, replaced by gusts that slicked the smoky darkness into gnarled claws around her. Vi covered her face as the torrent surged and twisted for several labored breaths. As suddenly as it flowed, it ebbed, dragging away the fog and leaving the shapes of two people. A woman in her twilight years and wearing the green necklace glared at the girl with long blond hair.

"Isabella, you're filthy," snarled the shadow-woman.

"I'm sorry, grandmother." The girl gazed at her soiled clothes and brushed ineffectually at the twigs that clung to them. "I was playing with Annie in the yard."

"And what have I told you about that?" the old woman bellowed. Her next words dripped with malice. "No wonder you are so dirty. Disgraceful! What if someone had seen you?"

The child gawked on in bewilderment. "It's just mud. Why are you so cross, grandmother?"

"Yeah, lady. Lighten up," Vi interjected.

"I'm not talking about the mud. I'm talking about Annie!" the inky lady shouted. "You can't go around playing with that colored girl. And out where people could see."

"But why?" the child took a step forward, her pale hair spilling across her back like moon-spun silk. "She's my friend."

"She is nothing of the sort. You cannot be *friends* with animals." The old woman pulled at the lace of her collar. "No, they are even worse than animals because a cow can't beguile you with smiles and lies; a chicken won't lull you into a false sense of security. Believe me, my dear Isabella, Annie is not capable of being your friend."

"But—"

Vi let out a gasp as the little girl's head whipped to the side in the wake of the back-handed blow from the apparition. When the young Bella put her hand to her cheek, her fingertip came back with a trickle of blood from where the stone on her grandmother's ring had cut her.

"Do not contradict me, girl," the old woman snarled. "Or maybe I'll decide you're just a filthy animal, too."

The darkness poured into the vision and swept Vi back into herself. Her head pounded and stung, as if the dark, polluting cloud was crowding out her gray matter. The room swayed, and she teetered on uncertain feet in the middle of the cabin, clutching her head.

In a flash, Bonnie stood at her side, but a sharp ringing in Vi's ears obliterated whatever she was trying to say. The pain tunneled deeper, leaving her gasping as her vision swam with red spots. Then she went limp as the comforting, true darkness of unconsciousness claimed her.

Chapter 31

Nebraska state line

When Vi's eyes opened next, it was twilight. Whether because of the force of the vision or the string of restless nights, she'd snoozed away the day after her collapse.

The world outside the window was unusually still. The small outpost only had a handful of buildings, and most importantly, a water tower some men were using to refill the boiler. Railroad employees scurried around making their inspections in the dwindling light.

Now that she'd regained consciousness, Bonnie entreated her to see a doctor. Vi made an effort to stretch out the kinks in her spine from being slumped in the same position for hours. She rubbed her sore neck as she shook her head. "I'm fine. Where's George?"

"He's confined himself to quarters," Bonnie replied, her voice tinged with amusement. "He's worried he'll upset you so much you'll faint again."

"That's not what happened."

"It isn't?"

"No, of course not. I was just... over-tired. That wailer kept me up all night, and I needed to rest."

Bonnie eyed her suspiciously. "So, you mean to tell me you feel fine?"

"Sure do."

"And I spent the entire day worried sick about you for no reason?"

"Uh-huh. I feel better than fine, really. Everything is under control," Vi deflected. "In fact, I feel so well-rested, I think I shall take a stroll." When she rose, she wobbled some, but more or less seemed to feel as good as she claimed. She teetered for a moment, unsure where it was she intended to go except for somewhere to think. When she had the visions before, they were memories connected to her. But she had no business wandering around a stranger's skull and stumbling on such painful moments.

Bonnie's voice broke through her reverie. "Shouldn't we talk about what happened with George? And what you're going to do about it?"

Vi balled her fists at her waist. "It sounds to me as if he punishing himself pretty well, so far. And Mrs. Harrison is long gone by now. It'll keep."

At the mention of Bella, the fear and confusion from the pilfered memory washed over her. Her senses felt chafed, raw, as if she'd tumbled down a mountainside with only her spirit sense to break her fall. She shivered it away, but as she looked around at the bodies pressing in around her, her breath caught in her throat.

"So, you're going to go off and leave me here?" Bonnie scolded. "You know you'll be stuck out all night if you aren't careful."

"I don't mind, really." The room pressed in, sending her head swimming. She willed it to stay steady, which brought on a pounding at the base of skull. With a deep breath, she kept her next words calm. "Besides, I'm tired of sitting still and everyone here is going to sleep soon."

As if on cue, Bonnie's delicate features scrunched with a yawn. "Too bad you can't go to the parlor cars. You could be pretty comfortable there all night if it weren't for you-know-who."

Vi snorted, then remembered Arthur Sands' invitation to stake out the wailer together with his camera. A quick scan of the room told her he was already gone. He wouldn't have been her first choice for company, but if he was right about the ghost making an appearance, it would be the perfect opportunity to root it out. And there was always the chance he'd taken her suggestion of liquor seriously.

"Actually," she said. "That's a great idea. I'll go to the parlor car for the evening and perhaps I can take care of two birds with one stone."

Bonnie stood to her full, but diminutive, height. "Oh no. You're not going there all alone. Someone needs to keep an eye on your health, even if you won't."

"Mr. Sands will be there," Vi warned.

"Whatever for?"

"He's helping me. With my *work*." She raised her eyebrows to help convey the additional layer of meaning.

Bonnie chewed her bottom lip, weighing her options. Her face became resolute. "Well, I also said I would help you with your work. I want to help you help them. I owe you, and it is a debt I plan to pay in *full*." She patted her friend on the shoulder before slipping past her. "We'll have to get moving. We could pull out at any moment."

Too mentally battered to protest, Vi stood gawking after her for a few seconds. At some point in her life, she'd stopped believing kind people like Bonnie even existed.

The younger woman waited for her outside, and they made their way two cars down to the lit windows of the parlor car. The fresh evening air helped to banish some of her headache and lighten her step.

"I'm not interrupting some sort of lover's tryst, am I?" Bonnie teased.

"Hardly." She snorted. "We made a tentative appointment to investigate a ghost story. One that may mean I can get the rest you are advising me to get, I might add. The last thing I want is complication."

"Are you certain you're up for it? After this morning?"

When she had first suggested the parlor car, she'd been looking for an excuse. Now, she'd have to actually deal with the wailer. They were still a few feet from the entrance to the car, and she pushed outward with her spirit sense. She'd expected it to hurt more the harder she pushed, but the soreness receded slightly as she flexed. A weak, sorrowful energy was gathering in the center of the car, but it didn't feel dangerous.

"Yes, I don't think the ghost will be a problem," Vi replied, surprising herself. "I'm better rested now than I've been since leaving California. Mr. Sands, on the other hand? There is no such thing as being ready for all those 'interesting' facts."

As they re-entered the warmth of the car, Vi spotted the reporter. He had his back to them, but the camera was easy to recognize. His head rested against his palm as he gazed out the window into the night. Though the women took turns making slight coughs and "ahems," he wouldn't turn.

Vi stalked over to stand before him. As requested, a glass bottle full of something amber-colored and a pair of glasses rested on the tablecloth. The one closest to Sands had the dregs of liquor at the bottom. Evidently, he'd grown impatient. She was about to beg his pardon when she saw his eyelids drooped. When a soft snore escaped, she motioned to Bonnie to stay quiet and join her at the other end.

Bonnie held in a giggle when she caught sight of the snoozing man. Vi was going to follow, when she turned back to the bottle. He'd gotten it for her; it would be rude not to accept his gift.

A distinct Peter-ness trickled across her shoulders. It wasn't an unpleasant sensation and invited her to reach for it. He stepped through the wall of the parlor car and to her side. "You're awake. Thank god."

"I appreciate your concern," she murmured, picking up the bottle for closer examination. She pulled out the cork and sniffed appreciatively at the harsh sweetness of the liquor. The scent stung her eyes, but the pain in her head receded as it coiled through her sinuses.

"Concern? What is there to be concerned about. I've been *bored*."

She pulled a disgusted face, then poured some of the whiskey into the clean glass. The intense flavor gave her somewhere to focus as it burned its way down her throat and into her uneasy stomach.

"Rough day?" he asked, all hint of his whine disappearing as he took in her expression.

She whispered, "Go away, Peter."

"Oh, don't be so stubborn. We could get stewed like old times, and you could tell me all about it."

"What are you doing?" Bonnie hissed from her place at another table, careful not to disturb the sleeping reporter.

"This really is not a good time." Vi put the cork into the bottle. She added with a derisive chuckle, "Besides, you can't drink."

"I still want to try haunting myself a tipple. I figure I already got the hang of the old 'haunted object routine,' so no harm in doing it again."

"I don't know," she sighed. Despite her trepidation, her fingers lingered on the bottle's neck.

The ghost lit up when he didn't get a definite denial. He pressed on, widening the crack that weariness had left in her convictions. "I know, you don't want me getting too attached to being a ghost. But don't forget, I want to know who killed me just as badly as you do, so we're on the same side. Let me be on the same side." His strange, opalescent flesh crinkled at the edges of his eyes. "Now, are you going to get me that glass, or aren't you? I'd do it myself, but somebody told me I'm not allowed."

She smirked in spite of herself, then gathered the bottle and glasses. They made their way to Bonnie's table, and Vi poured the ghost a couple fingers of whiskey into each glass.

"Oh no," Bonnie fluttered, "I don't drink."

"It's for Peter." Vi slid the glass across the table to an empty chair. Without hesitation, Peter passed through the seat back before settling in. Vi grimaced at seeing him so comfortable. It wasn't the same as moving things, but he could keep himself in a chair, and that was still a step away from crossing over. "To the joys of fine spirits," she held up her glass, eyebrows wiggling to point out her bad joke before she took a sip.

Peter groaned at the pun and dipped his face forward to swirl with the path of his own drink's vapors. He sighed appreciatively. "Fascinating. Maybe when we are back home, you can go to my rooms and retrieve my notes. This is an unprecedented opportunity to document these phenomena."

She tilted another gulp down her throat. A pleasant numbness crept in to replace the last of the stinging rawness of her spirit-sense. "You know, Bonnie? Peter and my aunt Pru would make quite a team."

"Is that a promise of an introduction?" he asked. "I'd love to meet her."

Vi snorted, then remembered to keep her volume low. "I wouldn't be so sure of that. Her tastes run along the lines of summoning and *expelling* spirits."

"The way you do? Finishing unfinished business, I mean." The other woman placed her hand on top of Vi's. "Hello, Peter."

"What Pru studies and what I get wrapped up in is nothing alike. She is not so tender-hearted as yours truly," Vi replied. "And don't forget. Pru seeks all of this out. If I could, I would wake up tomorrow and pretend this is all a bad dream."

Peter leaned away, but he appeared more puzzled than hurt as he examined her face. She regretted saying the words as soon as she finished saying them, but they were also true. No point apologizing. She poured another drink.

"What happened? You are even more surly than usual." The ghost rested his insubstantial elbows on the table and propped his chin against his fists.

"Same side, remember?"

As she peered at him over the top of her glass, the gap in her resolve widened further. Even though death stripped his features of their color, it was still a face she could trust.

"Please, Vi," Bonnie prompted.

With one more gulp to fortify her, Vi confessed, "I seem to have developed a new… talent. I am seeing more than ghosts now—visions. At first, I thought it was linked to objects that ghosts had touched, but I'm beginning to think I must be seeing memories."

Peter scoffed. "*Seeing* memories?"

"That's unusual?" Bonnie asked, but took in Vi's annoyance and backpedaled. "What? How should I know what is normal for someone like you?"

Vi glowered at her glass. "It's difficult to explain, but I got an unsettling and intimate glimpse into the early life of Mrs. Isabella Harrison this morning." She recounted the scene between the little girl and her grandmother, but stayed clear of any mention of the other memories she'd seen. The train trundled along, drowning out Sand's snores. The wailer continued to gather itself in the middle of the room, but it remained a low-level tingle and nothing more. Bonnie listened intently, her pretty brow furrowed.

Peter pulled himself out of the path of the alcoholic vapors, his expression dreamy. "I checked in on you earlier and I saw you were sleeping, but I never would have guessed why. How would that even happen?"

"In order to follow your brilliant teachings, my valet took up burglary," Vi said, heat creeping into her tone. "And thank you ever so much for the warning on that, by the by."

Peter flashed her his most endearing smile. "You found out about that little escapade, did you? Don't be too hard on him."

"George's life of crime isn't the real issue." Vi gestured vaguely toward the front end of the train where the boy slept, her drink sloshing over the brim in her carelessness. "He stole that necklace, and when I touched it, I got a nightmare of a scene dumped into my head. It appears that any object can bring on a vision. Nothing is safe."

"What made you think it had anything to do with ghosts?" Bonnie asked.

Vi answered with a noncommittal sound, but Peter pushed her for more. "Unless I am mistaken, the only haunted object you have been in contact with is the pin I rode in on." His voice grew husky with accusation. "Which one?"

"Just a party or something," she lied. "Everything was a big jumble, really. I didn't see anything specific."

He eyed her suspiciously. "And where is my lucky pin now?"

"Why does that matter?" Vi concentrated the swirling liquid in her glass rather than the indictment in his eyes.

"If there was something lying around with your whole life story stored inside, wouldn't you be curious about its whereabouts?" he asked.

"I haven't touched it again, if that's what you mean. Don't you think for a second any of this has been fun for me. All of the things I've seen so far have been rather more bitter than sweet."

Bonnie interrupted. "Have you heard of anything like this before? Maybe in Pru's research?"

When Vi shook her head, the room shook with it. But at least the headache was finally gone. "I was doing my best not to listen to her back then, remember?"

"Perhaps we should pay her a visit before we reach New Orleans," Peter said.

"Out of the question."

The ghost held Vi in an unblinking stare. "Whatever is happening down there, you're going to need to be at your best."

"I know," she sulked.

Though he was at no risk of waking Sands, Peter dropped his voice to a whisper. "And I don't only mean ghosts and murderers, either. There's something even worse."

"Excellent," Vi said, voice dripping with insincere cheeriness. "Please, tell me, what else will I be facing?"

He beckoned her to lean closer and she rolled her eyes. Peter put his face within inches of hers, the cool swirl of his spirit body chilling her cheek as he whispered. "Lawyers."

A guffaw leapt from her throat and cut through the quiet parlor car. Sands shifted, but did not wake as Vi clapped her free hand over her mouth. Bonnie struggled between giggling and shushing. With effort, the grifter brought her unexpected laughter down to a quiet snickering.

Once she finally had herself under control, Peter murmured, "I *am* sorry. About George. I didn't think he would take my advice quite so literally."

"That poor kid will never be the same after his time with me, and not for the better." Vi wiped away the tear the laughter had forced from the corner of her eye. "First, I expose him to even more death and danger. Now, I find out he's turning into a criminal. He'd be far better off if we'd never met."

"I bet if you asked him, he wouldn't agree," Bonnie said.

Vi harrumphed, and Peter wagged a spectral finger. "You're avoiding him, aren't you? That's the real reason you're here."

"Certainly not," Vi declared with far more fervor than she felt. "I told you, I am on a case." He glanced to the bottle and back again with a grin. "I am. I happen to be hunting the wailer right this moment. It is simply my good fortune that she chooses to haunt a place where I have such excellent whiskey to keep me company while I wait."

"I guess Bonnie, me, and the whiskey makes three," the ghost replied, eyes dancing.

She'd come clean, exposed her weakness, and... nothing. Peter the unrelenting, Bonnie the unflappable caretaker—there they sat. Vi didn't deserve her; she didn't deserve any of them. George's sojourn into crime was proof of that. Even so, for that moment, she was sure she'd succeed in her quest for answers.

Vi topped off her glass and clinked it against Peter's untouched tumbler.

"A fine spirit, indeed."

They laughed together at her terrible joke, and the last of the tension in Vi's shoulders drained away.

<h1 style="text-align:center">CHAPTER 32</h1>

As the train hurtled towards its destination, the chilly tingle emanating from the middle of the room grew and spread. The wailer pulled the heat out of the air, but underneath it Vi felt a distinct and hungry tug.

The entire contents of Vi's glass disappeared down her gullet. "It's coming."

"How can you tell?" Bonnie asked, a puff of steam escaping from her mouth. "Oh."

A few feet above the floor, the presence coalesced into a shining ball. The low, sorrowful moan fought its way through the crackle of energy.

"What do you plan to do, exactly?" Peter asked.

Vi pushed away from the table. "See what it wants."

"That?" Bonnie shouted.

The ball abruptly expanded like a gigantic soap bubble, its edges reaching every corner of the parlor car. The shriek dissipated as the presence expanded, but as the meniscus touched the furniture, grey-brown figures populated the chairs and aisles. They came and went, their movements made jerky by the ravages of time.

Vi stood, her hand flying to her hairline as the headache tried to reassert itself. The presence pulsed and pulled at her, drawing power to bring the memory figures to life. When she turned to Bonnie, she would have told her everything she saw. She owed her the truth. But the little brunette already stared, knocked dumbfounded by the vision. The reluctant medium traced the line of the other woman's arm and found her hands clenched in the tablecloth.

They weren't touching.

And she could see it.

Vi turned next to Peter, who took a slow step toward one of the restless figures. "What is happening?"

"I told you it was difficult to explain," Vi replied, breath labored from the nagging pull of the wailer. "This is a memory, not a ghost. Or both? Either way, I seem to be feeding it."

"I feel it, too," he said, his glow paling. "Maybe this wasn't such a good idea?"

The sepia figures slowed their movements. Two tables away, the shapes had edges sharper, more distinct than the others. A girl with dark hair and pale eyes threw her head back and laughed, as happy and at ease as Vi had been a moment before. Her voice rang out clearer than any other sound; she had to be the one at the center of the memory.

The man across the table reached out to touch her fingers. His hair held the first hints of gray at the temples, and the lines in his face told the tale of many happy years. "Cassandra, I'm so proud of you."

"Ah, Daddy. It is just confirmation. Everyone does it." She returned a shy but dimpled smile.

"That don't mean it isn't an achievement," he replied, reaching into his pants pocket. When he pulled his hand free, he held out a box no bigger than his palm.

Cassandra opened it and displayed the contents. A tiny silver cross dangled from a delicate chain.

The door on the far end of the parlor car burst open, except that it didn't. Bonnie squeaked as the memory door banged against the spectral wall. The real door remained exactly where it was, though for the first time Vi became aware of a soft, insistent thudding from the other side.

The armed men of the vision passed into the car and trained their guns on the passengers. They huddled against each other as the trio of robbers stalked down the aisle. The hulking men had smudged scarves to cover their faces and broad-brimmed hats to shade their eyes. The two in the back fidgeted, sweat rolling down their temples. The man in front, on the other hand—time may have robbed the scene of its color, but it did nothing the quench the deadly fire in his eyes.

"This, as they say, is a stick-up," he declared, bass voice barely obscured by the mask. "We want all of your valuables. All of them. And we don't want any fuss about it. Nobody knows we are here, and we want to keep it that way. Are we clear?"

"Sands was right," Vi mumbled.

The flunkies each pulled a burlap sack from their coats, snapping them wide to make enough room for all of their spoils. They moved from table to table, one hand on the sacs and the other with a finger on the trigger. When they got to where Cassandra huddled against the wall, Vi stepped forward.

"You can't do anything, can you?" asked Peter.

"No."

"No," the shadow-girl echoed, necklace clutched against her chest. "It's hardly worth a thing to you."

Vi sighed, "But I can witness."

"We have a problem?" the leader asked, sauntering over.

The flunky whined, "She's got something in her hand."

Her father had been frozen, but he loosened his jaw enough to plead. "Honey, give it to him."

"See, darling?" The big man threw his hands up, his gun dangling casually and dangerously from his loose grip. "Ain't nothing to make a fuss about. Trust me, if I wanted you to make a fuss, or any other sound for that matter, you would. Now, I'm going to give you five seconds to hand it over. Five." The gun snapped into his palm. "Four." He leveled it at her.

She turned unblinking eyes to her father, shock robbing her of comprehension. "Daddy?"

He quavered. "Cassandra, what are you doing? Give it to him."

"But I—"

"Three."

"Please," she gasped, reaching out one trembling hand to the robber.

"Two."

Cassandra shrieked, her death knell an all-too-familiar sound.

The gun discharged, a clap of thunder in the enclosed space. No one, real or made of memory, dared to move, except for Cassandra's limp body slumping over the table. A charcoal pool spread over the white linen.

The shooter chuckled into the ringing silence. "One."

"What the hell?" the flunky spluttered. "Now they'll know we're here."

The leader stowed his gun, then took up the dead girl's hand. The man across the table sobbed, but checked his movement when the masked man turned his glower at him.

"We've got what we came for," he replied, prying open Cassandra's fingers.

As if attached by a thread, a flaming blue aura followed the path of the necklace as it came free. An insubstantial, skeletal form draped in tatters of malformed spirit flesh pulled against the atmosphere, and became itself for the first time that night. Unlike Peter, she had no clear end to her legs, no feet to rest on the floorboards. She floated a few inches above the ground, her eyes nothing but deep sockets interrupted by a pinprick of luminescent blue.

The robber couldn't see the form Cassandra took after death, but when she slammed into him, he did stumble backward. The necklace flew from his hand as he hit into a stack of chairs. He drew his gun, pointing it from face to a frightened face, trying to find his attacker.

The train heaved and began to slow.

"Let's get out of here," called the other henchman, a sack of loot slung over his shoulder.

The leader staggered to his feet. "Nobody get any ideas, y'hear? And you won't end up like her." He followed the other men out of the false door, still swinging from its broken hinge. The people from the memory dissolved as the gunman disappeared, the parlor losing its sheen of the past.

Vi turned her attention back to Cassandra. The ghost's half-formed body was hunched over a baseboard, her insubstantial fingers digging away at the wood without ever making contact. Her edges were more distinct, her spirit body denser than any other time Vi had encountered her, but she was a pale comparison to free-moving spirits like Peter, hardly more than an echo.

The tide of energy continued to eddy to the figure as she cried out in frustration, but Cassandra hadn't worked herself up to the incoherent rage Vi had felt the night before. At least, not yet.

"Cassandra?" Vi whispered. The spirit stopped its fitful burrowing, so she continued, "Can I help you?"

"Vi!" Bonnie cried.

"Not now. I think I'm getting through to her."

The world became a dazzling sheet of white. For a moment, Vi thought the ghost had somehow started the vision over again, but as the wash of light receded, black spots danced in her vision. She knuckled against her eyes in a vain attempt to rid herself of the camera flare. When she opened them again, she could make out the horror painted all over Arthur Sands' face. His lips moved, but no words came out.

Vi couldn't help but take some satisfaction at seeing the reporter rendered speechless. "You," she snapped, stabbing her finger in his direction. "I will deal with later."

At the same time, she became aware of the protestations of the brakes. It wasn't just the train from Cassandra's memory that was slowing, the real parlor car was also coming to a halt. An insistent pounding sound rose louder, and it took Vi a moment to realize it was not the return of her headache. Someone outside the car was trying desperately to come in, but no matter how the knob rattled or the frame shook, the door would not open.

The wail rose from the spirit on the floor, calling Vi back to the task at hand. She examined the spot where the spirit fixated, but it seemed like a stretch of carpet like any other.

"What do you want?" she asked. Cassandra screeched and went back to digging.

"Check underneath," Peter suggested. "I don't think there was carpet before."

Bonnie rushed to Vi's side and helped her clear away the table and chair. The two of them worked at the edge of the carpet with their fingernails until it came away from the baseboard with a loud tearing sound.

"Hey, what are you doing?" Sands stammered. "That came all the way from Vienna."

Once they had the floorboards exposed, the silver cross glowed dully in the gaslight from the place where the wall met the floor.

Cassandra's lopsided, tattered body rose, buoyed by Vi's understanding. The ghost exhaled the extra energy it had gathered, her edges becoming blurred and the light ebbing away.

"What did you do? Where'd it go?" Sands blustered.

Vi pulled a bobby pin from her hair and wedged it into the crack. She wiggled the chain free. Vi held the necklace up so the frayed spirit-thing could still clearly see. "Look! We found it, all right. You can go now." The ghost, visible now only to Vi, shook her head, and the discordant cry cut through the air.

The train ground to a halt, sending the reporter teetering back into his chair. Cassandra lifted her arm, one bony finger pointing outside. As Vi stood to follow, the dead woman drifted through the door.

CHAPTER 33

Sands scrambled as far away as he could from the medium as she passed, but Vi had no time just then for his fear or the damage he could do if that photograph worked. The door opened before she could even put her hand on the knob. The brakeman's face was flushed and worried. "You all right in there, ma'am? I been trying the door but it wouldn't budge. When I heard screaming, I pulled the emergency break."

"I'm fine," Vi assured him. "Everyone is fine."

Cassandra drifted to the grass. With deliverance at hand, she waited patiently.

"As she said, nothing to see here." Bonnie's head appeared from around the doorframe. "Would this be a convenient time to return to the sleeping car?"

"Er, yes, ma'am. It will take us a few minutes to make our checks and get underway again," the brakeman stammered, stepping to the ground to make way for Vi. "But what should I tell my boss? I'm only supposed to pull the brake if it is an *emergency*. I could lose my job."

He stood in a trough between the tracks and a berm, leaving anyone walking near the train cast in shadow. A shout rose from somewhere near the locomotive, but they couldn't see to whom it belonged. Cassandra drifted to the edge of her invisible tether to the necklace and leaned against the barrier holding her to Vi. The shout came again, closer now, and a figure crested the rise, stepping into the moonlight. A stout man in a gray uniform waved at them.

"Uh-oh. That's Miller," the brakeman said. "I'd better go tell him I made a mistake."

"What my friend meant is there's nothing to see *now*," Vi said, the idea crystalizing as she made her way down the steps. She beckoned to the young man, and he followed to the pool of golden light cast through the window of the car. Arthur Sands was slumped against the glass where she'd left him. "You see that man there in the window? A little while ago he was hysterical. It was shocking. He was screaming about who knows what!"

The brakeman stroked his chin. "I see. Well, that is another kettle of fish, ain't it?"

"Indeed," she replied. "And you know? I think it may have been something about the camera that set him off. Those bright flashes are detrimental to one's health. Believe me."

Bonnie picked up the thread, saying, "I think you should probably take it from him immediately. For his health."

Cassandra heaved against her constraints, towing Vi's hand in the direction of the shouting. "Will you excuse us?" she asked the brakeman. "After all the excitement, I need some fresh air, and then straight off to bed."

"I could escort you. The slope is steep."

"You could help my companion, yes. But I am going to walk the length of the train first. And don't worry about your boss, I will tell him the whole story." Bonnie met her eyes, but acquiesced to whatever it was she had in mind by taking the brakeman's arm. As soon as their backs were turned, Vi wheeled on the spirit and gritted, "Hold your horses. I'm coming."

The ghost drifted up the short hillside, so Vi hitched her skirts and scrambled up behind her. The climb would have been easier if she didn't have the necklace clenched in her fist, but eventually, if not gracefully, she found herself at the top. The man who had shouted drew nearer, and Cassandra's relentless tugging redoubled.

They'd stopped somewhere within a wide expanse of cornfields. The night was so clear, she could make out the pale strands of silk bursting from the ears. On the other side of the berm, another set of tracks cut parallel through the gently rolling plains; the lines straight and regular, a pair of seams sewn by a giant hand to hold the landscape together. Somewhere in the distance, another train rumbled toward them, but the sound was too low to cover the song of night insects that populated the fields at night.

"We have everything under control, ma'am," the man called. "No need for you to be out and about."

His voice hadn't changed much in the intervening years. The shadow from his cap obscured most of his face, and he'd put on several pounds, but there was no doubting that the same Miller approached. Once her father was in range, Cassandra swirled around his feet before coiling around his back to regard Vi over his shoulder. The medium startled when she found fully formed, radiant blue eyes gazing back at her from the spirit's face.

"Ma'am?" Miller asked, slipping his cap off his head. "Are you all right?"

"I have something for you." Vi turned over her hand and opened her palm. The porter stared at her face quizzically, then at the necklace in her hand. Cassandra draped her translucent arms over his shoulders, but he could not feel the brush of her lips against his cheek as anything more than a cool breeze. As he took the narrow chain from Vi's hand, the spirit glowed brighter. Miller stared at her, but Vi watched as Cassandra's spirit flesh gently flaked and floated like flower petals on the breeze. Though she'd never gathered enough of herself together for pyrotechnics, her end held a somber dignity the reluctant medium had never seen. The wisps of her spirit flesh dissipated to a shimmering nothingness before they reached the ground.

"How? Where?" Miller stammered.

Vi blew out a relieved sigh as the last of Cassandra disappeared. "Does it matter?

"No, I suppose not. But thank you, all the same." A tear trickled from the corner of his eye, but he didn't seem to feel it.

His gratitude hit her like a hammer. She had been so consumed with finding a distraction, she'd forgotten her visit to the parlor car could also affect the living. Vi mumbled a reply, her gaze diverted over the landscape. The trainman offered to help her down the hill, but she waved him off with a promise to be back on board in a moment or two.

The moon painted the rooftops of the approaching train with a silver sheen. Stars crowded one another for real estate in the great expanse of blue-black above her head. In the train cars behind her, people were packed together like sardines. In two days, they'd arrive in Chicago and the press of buildings. But there on that narrow hilltop, Vi could breathe. Hopefully, Mr. Miller could breathe easier now, too.

Vi had acted out of selfishness; she was big enough to admit it. She may not have set out to do him a kindness, but she had to concede there was something to Bonnie's point of view. Though her headache had begun to creep back up the back of her neck, and she felt dull and depleted after the unexplained power exchange with the spirit, Vi also felt lighter. She may not deserve the loyalty of her comrades yet, but perhaps if she stayed on this path, she would someday.

The second train kicked up a cool wind and whistled a mournful hello as it approached. Her fingertips tingled as the whiskey reasserted itself. With a sigh, she tilted her face to bask in the moon for a few heartbeats before she had to return to the confines of the Pullman.

The temperature dropped another fraction, and Vi's eyes shot open. The train shouldn't make the air cooler like that; she was out in the open. The trill she'd thought was coming from the other train morphed into her spirit-sense and its urgent warning. The whiskey and exertion made her dull, the figure behind her barely registering as she turned. Something struck her in the chest, catching her mid-twist and sending her teetering backward.

She sailed through the still night for an impossibly long moment before slamming into the bank. Her body rolled, and as she came to rest, her ribcage collided with a rail, pushing all the air from her lungs. Vi craned her neck, but found no sign of an attacker or other cause for her swan dive.

Some part of her brain heard the shout of someone, but the sound that occupied most of her brain was the steady, inexorable approach of the second locomotive. Her body shook with a bout of coughing, and she tried to drag herself upright.

Vi struggled against the snarled layers of fabric, her bruised ribs aching as her body was wracked by more coughing. The brakes squealed with fury as the engineer caught sight of the body on the tracks, but there was no way it would stop in time. She managed to get to her hands and knees, but when she tried to stand, her right ankle revealed it had been wrenched during the fall with a bright flash of pain. She yelped and toppled onto her elbow. The rail hit her square in the gut, pushing out any air she'd managed to drag into her lungs.

Peter's voice broke through her panic. "Vi, I'm here." His misty form jumped onto the tracks and knelt by her side. "We've got to get you up."

He reached out to comfort her, but his hand passed through her body.

When he pulled it back, his arm glowed from fingertips to forearm. Anywhere he had tried to touch her swirled excitedly before the glow sunk into his spirit flesh.

"I've got to do something," the ghost roared, rising to his full height. The fog of his body swirled and darkened as he gathered his impotent rage to him. Tiny, golden bolts of electricity crackled across the storm clouds of his body. "And sometimes the biggest things are the easiest, remember?"

"Don't," she managed to choke, her breath now visible as Peter drew extra energy from the air around them.

"Let me try," he growled, then ran toward the train engine. The dazzling flashes of lightning coursed over his form as he flew at the locomotive. He raced away from her and down the tracks. When he was a few dozen strides from where she lay, he threw his hands up before him, planted his feet and let loose a furious cry.

The huge black machine barreled mercilessly through the ghost, who burst into a plume of sparks.

The shriek of the train whistle brought Vi far enough out of the moment of shocked immobility to get her feet underneath her. In a few desperate lurches, she pulled herself off the tracks as the locomotive trundled over the spot where she'd been lying a moment before. Pain shot through her torso as oxygen clawed its way in and out of her battered rib cage. She lay there for some time catching her breath before the train was stopped and someone came to retrieve her. Miller helped Vi to her feet and supported her as they went back over the top of the berm. He tried to question her, but she simply shook her head. Eager faces stared at her from the windows. Every light in both trains was lit, capturing her between the machines and bathed in a golden light for all to see.

Vi chuckled ruefully and muttered. "So much for not drawing too much attention to myself."

CHAPTER 34

October 6, 1871
Omaha, Nebraska

Vi may have been able to talk her way around Bonnie's concern a second time, but after all of the excitement the night before, there was no way to escape a doctor's visit the next morning when they arrived. Even before breakfast, she found herself flanked by Bonnie, George, an Omaha police officer, and two representatives from the rail line in the well-appointed office. She had the feeling that Peter was somewhere in the room as well, but his essence remained depleted and his aura insubstantial. She would have liked to try to talk to him, but she couldn't shake the hovering concern of the railway staff all night.

Now, she watched the physician as he stroked his salt and pepper muttonchop whiskers, and willed the visit to be over.

"So, you're the young lady who failed to watch her step," he said.

"I'm fine. Really," Vi assured him. "I don't need all this fuss."

"Even so, madam," one of the suits interrupted. "For legal reasons, we need the doctor to talk to you."

She sighed and addressed the man on the other side of the desk. "Yes, I was on the tracks. My train was stopped, so I was just getting a little air."

With a sniff, the doctor rose from his seat and rounded the desk. He perched on the edge, gazing far too deeply into her eyes for her comfort. "The officer told me you are traveling to New Orleans because your husband recently died."

"Yes," she replied warily.

"And is that why you needed to 'get a little air'?" He leaned into the innuendo.

As his meaning clicked into place, Vi had to swallow her guffaw. "Sir, I did fall onto the tracks," she grimaced, "but I promise, I didn't get there on purpose."

"I see," he said, sounding for all the world as if he did not see at all. He leaned back and resumed stroking his whiskers. "Have you had any dizzy spells before now? Fatigue?"

"She can't sleep," Bonnie cut in helpfully.

Vi shot a glare at the other woman, but she didn't notice. When Vi turned back, the doctor's hands were mere inches from her face. As a reflex, she swatted them away.

"You need to let me examine your head, madam," he insisted.

She pursed her lips, then one side lifted into a smirk. "Trust me, you wouldn't like what you'd find in here. But it's not the problem."

"Are you saying there was foul play?" The cop's growled. "Because when I asked the witnesses, they said you were alone. I can go bring everyone down to the station, I suppose—"

"No," cried the second railwayman. "That would delay the entire train."

"That won't be necessary, officer. I wouldn't want you to go to any trouble," Vi said, panic fluttering at the edge of her voice. The last thing she needed was a trip to the police station.

"No trouble, ma'am," he replied amicably. "That's my job."

Without the adrenaline to hold her up, Vi sagged. Her sluggish mind searched for a plausible half-truth, and to her relief, Bonnie supplied it for her. "She's been feeling rather faint lately, sir. She must have simply swooned in all the excitement. We had stopped because of an emergency, or she wouldn't have been outside at all."

"Yes. That must be it. I am ever so excitable, officer, but I feel much better now," Vi tittered.

The men exchanged looks. None of them particularly wanted the headache or scandal of the police becoming involved, so they forged a silent pact in the space of a few glances.

"I prescribe some fresh air before getting back onto the train, and rest between here and Chicago," the doctor declared, pacing back to his chair. "But within a few weeks, you should be completely healed."

The railway representatives counted out the doctor's fee as Vi and Bonnie rose to leave. George appeared at Vi's side, and she did her best to lean inconspicuously on his shoulder. Her ribs still ached, and her ankle protested—minor nuisances compared to being blasted into ghost-dust by a locomotive.

The two men reluctantly allowed her to take Bonnie's elbow and return to standing. "Thank you all so much for your help. Good day, gentlemen."

She kept her wincing to herself as she and her friends made it down the stairs. When they emerged onto the cobbled street, a few people pointed and whispered as she passed, but their condescension and concern didn't matter as she resumed her compulsive search for the ghost. When her eyes failed, she tried pushing out with her spirit sense. The whiskey-laced chaos of the previous night had depleted her too much to detect anything except her own immediate pains. Based on the tarry stink of cigarette smoke, this included Mr. Arthur Sands, New York Star.

As they approached the next corner, he stepped into their path, his notebook in hand. "Care to make a statement, Mrs. Murphy? Mrs. Sinclair?"

"Certainly not!" Bonnie cried.

"It seems the lady doth protest too much," he said smugly.

Vi painted on a pleasant expression. "I'll make a statement. It's as I told them. You had some sort of fit, and you made them stop the train."

"That is not what happened, and you know it."

"Oh, isn't it?" she said coyly. "Well, perhaps I was seeing things. I have been traveling at high speeds for several days now. I hear that can be detrimental to one's health."

He snorted. "You think that just because they took my camera for 'safe-keeping' that the world isn't going to see that picture? Once I get back to New York, all I have to do is develop it. So, you can give me a statement, or let me tell the story my way. It's your decision."

"And if she decides she'd like to speak with you further, we will inform you," Bonnie huffed.

Sands snickered and shifted his gaze between them. "See that you do." He stepped aside, waving them through with a magnanimous wave of his pompous arm.

With her chin held higher than Vi thought possible, Bonnie stalked past him. When they got far enough away from him, her voice dropped to a hiss. "That was the right thing to do, wasn't it? Lying to the police, to him?"

"You did splendidly," Vi replied. "I'm making a mighty fine criminal out of you."

"So, what really did happen?"

"Somebody pushed me. But I didn't want to get anyone involved."

Bonnie's brow crinkled. "Really? But why would anyone do that?"

"I have no idea," Vi groaned. "But Peter was on the tracks with me, and now I can't seem to find him." The image of his body being smashed by the locomotive played over and over in front of her eyes.

"He must be around here somewhere," the other woman declared, scanning the crowd for a few moments before she remembered she couldn't see the person Vi was searching for.

"I'm doing my best." Peter's voice came first, followed by a shimmer of faintly glowing mist that coalesced into something roughly human-shaped blocking their path. As his re-formed face came into view, it wore a combination of annoyance and chagrin.

Her initial flare of relief dissipated, and Vi settled for simple, straightforward annoyance. "What the hell were you *thinking*?"

Bonnie stopped alongside her and took her hand firmly, evidently done with listening to one-sided conversations. "What happened?"

Shame burrowed deeper into Peter's features. "She was on the tracks, but I couldn't do anything to help."

"Yes, yes," Vi said with a dismissive gesture. "But did you see how I *got* there?"

"No." He shook his head emphatically. "I simply had this feeling you needed me... er... that is to say...." the ghost stuttered, seeking safety in Bonnie's open gaze rather than the worry narrowing of Vi's eyes. "I realized when she followed the wailer outside that might not be the end of it. I just sprang to action."

"Uh-huh," Bonnie replied, shifting a meaningful glance between the other two while suppressing a smile.

Peter coughed, then continued sheepishly. "And though exhilarating, no action I sprang to was terribly effective, mind."

"That's not a bad thing," Vi reminded him. "*Nothing* about what happened last night was a good thing. And if risking your chance to cross over isn't bad enough, your little show of bravery got you blown to pieces."

"It didn't stick," the ghost said with a shrug and a sour face. "Though I certainly wouldn't recommend it."

"How does a ghost get blown to pieces?" Bonnie asked. "Except for, you know, crossing over." Her voice hitched on the last word, and Vi noticed the glisten of tears encroaching on her friend's long, dark lashes.

"He picked a fight with the locomotive and then boom!" Vi slipped her hand free of Bonnie's grasp to clap loudly, followed by a flutter her fingers to illustrate the explosion. "Peter dust." The other woman smiled in spite of herself.

"Peter got blown up?" a small voice whimpered from the periphery.

The adults startled in unison at the unexpected sound. Vi reeled and found George standing close at hand. Their unguarded eyes met for first time since their argument, and they both glared away as if the other had stung them.

Bonnie took Vi's slack grasp in one hand, and placed her free hand on George's shoulder, careful to make contact with bare skin. Happiness washed over the boy as the ghost appeared before him. "Not to worry, see? He ran into trouble while he tried to help Vi during her accident. But they're fine now."

"It wasn't an accident," Vi asserted when she regained her voice. Her pique rendered it a savage whisper as she whirled on the ghost. "And you! You scared me half to death. I wasn't entirely sure you'd be able to put yourself back together again."

"Neither was I, to tell you the truth," he chuckled. "And I'm not even sure I *am* all back together, not entirely. I feel so... thin."

"I know the feeling. Trust me. I thought that taking the edge off my senses would be a good thing, but I should have known there was someone behind me. I could have prevented the whole thing."

"Ugh, I feel so completely useless!" Peter cried, his fully re-formed arms slashing into the air as he paced, every gash to his ephemeral garments that indicated his tortured death visible again. "Maybe it's time I simply stop trying. I can't keep you from going to New Orleans, and I can't do anything to protect you along the way. I'm sure I could pull a repeat performance of the train debacle without the putting myself back together step. One 'poof' and your life would get a whole lot less complicated."

George's earnest words came out before Vi could assemble a response. "Don't say that. I'd be awful sad if you poofed!"

The ghost stopped pacing and smiled at the child in surprise. "Thanks, kid."

Vi took a deep breath, but the pain in her ribs sent it whooshing back out again. She regarded her flesh and blood companion. "I feel the distinct need for a new hat, or three. Care to join me, my dear?"

"I'd love to," Bonnie said cheerily.

"Not me, if you please." The ghost grimaced.

Vi smiled back sweetly. "Why don't you go find a nice cigar lounge or something to haunt for a while?"

"Not a bad idea," he chuckled, then bowed out with a wink. "Ladies."

As he disappeared into the crowd, she sighed with relief. "I knew that's all it would take to be rid of him."

"Oh, that was about Peter?" Her friend's face fell. "So, you don't really want to go hat shopping?"

"Are you kidding? I always want to go hat shopping. Let's walk a spell and see what we find. I'm dying to move around after all those days cooped up."

She felt a tug at her elbow. George gazed up at her. "I'm going back to my seat and wait. I just wanted to make sure you was all right. But I done wrong."

Vi sighed, thinking about the bottle she'd pilfered from Sands a few hours before. "Look kid, I won't say it was the right thing to do, but I forgive you. You don't have to be punished anymore. Come with us."

"That's awful kind of you, Miss Viola," he said. "And I'm glad to hear it. But I said I'd stay behind, and I will. I've got to make my word mean somethin' again, don't I?"

When Vi had trouble finding a response, Bonnie supplied one. "That's very noble, George. You go on, and we'll see you later." He scampered back in the direction of the train platform. "He's a good boy."

"Yes, I don't deserve him," Vi choked. She slipped her hand through Bonnie's elbow. "Now, let's see about those hats."

CHAPTER 35

Nebraska had only joined the United States a few years prior, but it didn't show. Omaha lost the privilege of being the capital, but the convergence of railroad lines kept it a busy place. A lazy brown river flowed to the East, but unlike Sacramento, the streets all around the station were paved with multi-colored stones.

They didn't have to go far before they found shops and bakeries lining the streets, the smell of leather and bread mixing with the damp scent of earth and stone. Even the occasional waft of livestock was a welcome change from the rather ripe smell gathering in the sleeping car.

"So, what was all that about cigars?" Bonnie asked as they strolled.

"A nasty habit he picked up sometime before we met. Ugh, how those things can stink. It became sort of a tradition that he'd go off to his lounge whenever I wanted to shop. And they do put off vapors, so it might even work."

Vi caught a glimpse of her reflection in the next shop window. The pale figure before her had lived longer than the shadow-self she'd watched a few days prior, the sun and inner turmoil both doing their parts to etch lines on her face when she wasn't paying attention. Her ankle complained and entreated that she give up on her silly errand and do as the doctor said. Instead, she wheeled away from her reflection, self-conscious about how she'd changed, and how she still seemed to be changing.

Bonnie's voice broke into her thoughts. "You two spent an awful lot of time together in the old days...." Her friend let her sentence trail off suggestively.

She ignored the innuendo and continued down the street. "When we first became partners, we traveled around. But once we decided to try something a bit more permanent, we told everyone he was my bastard half-brother, the product of a fictional plantation-owning father who took advantage of his slaves. A common enough occurrence that we garnered little attention when we rented rooms together. Of course, that does not mean that we didn't drive each other insane sometimes."

Her friend made a skeptical sound, but didn't press the Peter issue anymore. "This was in New Orleans?"

"Yes. It's a quite a town." Vi motioned to a brightly painted shop across the street and Bonnie acquiesced. They headed toward the rows of hats beckoning from the window. "I'm interested to see how it's changed since I left."

They reached the door, and a passing gentleman stopped to open it for them. The two women bobbed in thanks and went inside the store. The beautiful wares were displayed on shelves and on stands all over the room, and they both stood simply enjoying the view for a few moments. The conversation resumed as the pair moved around the room, making small, appreciative noises over the goods.

"Tell me more about New Orleans," Bonnie entreated.

"What do you want to know? Ask me anything."

"Really?" The other woman peered at Vi from over the top of a stack of straw hats. "That doesn't sound like you."

"Without Peter around, I find myself feeling rather more talkative than usual."

"Then I suppose I should take advantage," her friend said with mock-sincerity and made a show of stroking her chin as if deep in thought. "Why don't you tell me what it is you were doing to earn your keep?"

Vi chuckled. "I don't know if you'd believe me if I told you."

"I think I've proven I'm made of pretty stern stuff." Bonnie dropped her voice to a whisper. "You didn't do anything too terrible, I hope."

"No, it's well, sort of silly." Vi drew out the moment playfully, ducking behind a large red hat to hide her blush. "I posed as a medium and Peter helped me hold séances."

"You *posed* as a medium?" The little brunette hissed, rounding the corner of the display right behind her.

"Yes. Peter ran the pulleys and levers that moved the table, created drafts to make the candles flicker, and the like. And I sold it to the customers with my acting skills." Vi posed dramatically, a frilly pink confection perched on her head.

The other woman opted to be more discreet and held a hat between her face and the shopkeeper as she whispered. "But if you can really speak to the dead, why would you have to go to all that trouble?

"I got the idea from my aunt Prudence, actually." Vi traded the pink hat for a puce bonnet and screwed up her face like she'd eaten a crab apple. "She used to go out and expose the fakes and liars who pretended to speak to the dead, so naturally I learned a lot about how to make people believe they were seeing ghosts." Her eyes fell on a lovely black hat with lace trim, and her face went back to normal as she held it over her coiffure, admiring it in a nearby mirror as she continued. "Peter and I set up shop in New Orleans and held parlor sessions a few times a week. Eventually, real ghosts somehow found out about my claims and showed up."

"I'd assumed you'd always seen ghosts." Her friend's face appeared in the reflection, peering over Vi's shoulder with eyes wide with surprise. "But you mean to say you just suddenly started to see them one day, out of the blue?"

"Yes and no."

"Can it happen to anyone?" The reflection repressed a shudder, but not well. "Because I've been around a lot of ghosts lately—"

"I don't think so, and it didn't come as a complete surprise." Vi grimaced, returning the hat to its place. "There were… glimmers I guess you could call them, that happened when I was a child. Aunt Pru was certain I had 'the gift', but I never believed it. Then that night, everything she told me got confirmed."

The little brunette scanned the immediate area, but they had the corner of the shop to themselves. "What made her so sure you would be able to see them?"

"It's a family trait," Vi said distractedly, moving on to the next display. "My aunt can see them, and as another woman in that family tree, she seemed convinced I was doomed to the same."

"No wonder she researches death. Ooh, I like that one," Bonnie said as she took the dark brown bowler hat from Vi's hands. "Tobias would have looked rather smart in that." Her voice hitched, and she placed the hat back on its stand. "That must have been a relief though, to have someone in your life who would believe you when you came home with a story about seeing a ghost."

"Well... about that," she hedged. "Pru doesn't actually know."

"You never told her?" her friend trilled in astonishment.

"No. I somehow never got around to it...."

Bonnie's eyebrows drew together. "I'm starting to understand why you don't want to face her. When was the last time you spoke?"

Vi thought for a few moments. "Probably ten years ago now?"

"Ten years," she tutted.

"You don't know what it was like. She hosted tea parties for empty rooms, and did all sorts of strange things in the attic for days on end. And she's probably gotten even crazier since I left."

"But you just said it yourself, she wasn't crazy. She was right about being able to see ghosts. And now you're having visions? Pru can probably help!"

Vi's chuckle interrupted. "Don't let her catch you calling her that, by the way. She's painfully proper. I remember once, she—"

"Don't change the subject," Bonnie hissed, giving Vi a gentle nudge in her sore ribs. "It sounds to me like those rooms weren't as empty as you once thought. And I'm starting to agree with Peter."

"Not you, too!" she cried, slipping around the table of menswear and over to a glass display case.

Bonnie followed her to the counter and tapped on the glass to get her attention. "I think we need to go see your aunt. After what happened on the train—"

"What do you think about those ones? With the little green things?"

"Vi—"

"You know, you should probably start calling me Annabelle in public."

This time, Vi's evasion earned her Bonnie's hands on hips and resounding stomp on the floor. "Stop doing that!" she groused.

The reluctant medium gestured at the case full of accessories, taking a spoonful of pleasure from pushing the other woman into a tantrum. "I know what I need to do. I should buy lots and lots of gloves. That way I wouldn't have to touch anyone and—"

"Ever?" Bonnie's voice lashed out harshly, and far too loudly for such a public forum. Vi stood stunned in the face of both her fury and wisdom. The widow continued into the silence. "This thing that you can do, it's not something that you can run away from. It's part of you. Do you really want to go through life afraid to be touched?"

Vi smirked, trying to recapture the levity of a few moments before. She gestured at her battered body. "It's not like I had any particular plans to be touching anyone."

"That didn't stop it from happening. And you scared George half to death."

"This is why I went to California in the first place," Vi groused. "To keep exactly this sort of thing from happening."

Bonnie returned fire. "And now you've decided to leave California, so it's time to face the truth."

"I see. And what 'truth' is that?"

"That we need help!"

The disembodied voice of the shopkeeper rose up behind them. "I'll be right with you!"

"I don't know, I'm starting to feel like I've already got more help than I could ever want," Vi seethed.

"Fine!" Bonnie's palm slapped against the display case. "Buy a thousand pairs of gloves if that makes you happy!"

"Did someone say something about gloves?" the shop girl asked brightly as she turned the corner.

An invisible rope somewhere inside of Vi snapped, and all of the tension of the past three days burst out of her in a torrent of laughter. No matter how her bruised ribs protested, she couldn't stem the tide. She contented herself with placing a steadying hand on the counter as the other people looked on, bewildered by her laughter.

Bonnie tried to keep her mouth in a dour, straight line, but even in the wake of the argument she couldn't help but be swept up in her recalcitrant friend's uncharacteristic giggling. Her stubbornness gave way as she asked, "What on earth has gotten into you?"

Vi struggled to drag in enough air to respond, tears streaming from her eyes. "Can you imagine trying to fit a thousand pairs of gloves into our accommodations?" she cackled and choked. "We'd suffocate around eight hundred."

The last of her anger dissolved, and Bonnie's whole body shook with her own bout laughter. "At least it would muffle all the snoring!"

The dumbfounded shop girl stepped away awkwardly. "I'll be over here if you ladies need anything."

This sent the pair into another fit of giggles. The lack of oxygen eventually forced them to regain some control or collapse into a heap on the floor.

"I'm sorry," Vi sighed, wiping the tears from her eyes. "All of this time bottled up has been getting to me." They moved toward the door and the pleasant afternoon sunshine of the street. She got up the courage to murmur, "You're right, though."

Bonnie smiled and hooked her arm through Vi's elbow. "I know."

"Let's stop by the telegraph office, and I'll tell Aunt Pru we're on our way." She patted her friend's hand as they fell in step together. "Like you say, what's the worst that could happen?"

Chapter 36

October 7, 1871
Illinois

The blue skies of the Midwestern plains had already banished the sunrise and stretched on into eternity outside the train window. Lazy clouds watched the train's sinuous progress across the landscape. Farms with crops ready for harvest flashed by, while hills dotted with cows held steady in the distance.

Whether out of concern or because it helped him re-form after his tango with the train, Peter had stayed glued to Vi's side since pulling out of Omaha the day before. At present, he was perched on the edge of the divan as she performed the last of her toilette.

"Isn't your aunt a tea totaler?" the ghost asked with a chuckle.

"Thanks for reminding me. I'll have to smuggle in some hair of the dog somehow this evening."

"Ah yes, that hallmark maturity of yours."

"I've only just started to like you again. Don't push me," Vi teased. "I must go see to the last of the packing. Will you be joining me for that as well?"

"I think I'll pass," Peter said with a charming smile. "I don't want to miss the view coming into Chicago. You'll wait for me in the station?"

Her breath hitched for a moment, the words so close and yet the circumstances so far from when they'd first been spoken. Vi forced a smile and turned her attention back to the mirror to put the final touches on her face. The big day had arrived; it was time to face Prudence. Now that she stood at the precipice, she found she'd rather simply dive in and get it over with. Anticipating the reunion was far more stressful than avoiding it.

She returned to find her bed banished and seats back in place. Bonnie tidied the last of their belongings into a carpet bag as she approached. "What did you do with George's memento? The one from before Omaha?" Vi asked, her mind returning to the fate of the emerald necklace for the first time since she'd fainted.

"I added it to that little bag of yours, which I stowed in here," Bonnie replied, patting the carpet bag.

"I hope you didn't prick yourself," Vi said, thinking of the naked point of Peter's pin.

Bonnie's eyebrows knit together. "What do you mean? I didn't see anything sharp." They rocked as the train slowed, signaling the approach to the station. Her eyes lit up. "We're here!"

A few minutes later, Vi stepped down the metal stairs and onto the train platform in Chicago, and the view all but slapped her in the face. The interior of the station struck her as both totally new, yet completely familiar at the same time. Her mind reeled, trying to reconcile the inky tones of Peter's memory with the bright colors and heady aromas of the real Central Station.

An impatient group of passengers shouldered past Vi, and she stepped out of their way. Happy reunions and sorrowful partings unfolded, comings and goings punctuated by those precious moments of change. It was good to know the world continued turning no matter what might be happening in her own drama.

George appeared, and she sent him to get a cab. With Cassandra gone, she had a quiet, restful night, but that didn't mean she wanted to hoof it all the way to the family manse. Her ankle was not shy about reminding her of its poor treatment the day before, and had gotten even more swollen and sore after her shopping trip. She leaned against a post to appease it while she waited for Bonnie.

"Mrs. Sinclair, how nice to see you." Sands sidled up beside her, cigarette hanging from his lips. "Have you given any thought to that statement?"

Vi squared herself and saw a bulky container hanging near his knees. "You have your camera back, I see," she said evenly.

"Yes, indeed I do. The plate is safe as houses," he replied, unconsciously patting his vest pocket. "And I've got quite a story to tell my editor, not to mention the wonderful *photographs* of my journey."

She smiled coolly and took a step closer. "And it involves a description of a woman with some sort of magical powers over life and death, is that it?"

His Adam's apple bobbed. "The exact wording isn't set in stone—"

Her grin widened as she plucked the cigarette from his mouth. She leaned toward his ear, resting the hand with the lit cigarette close to his face. "Do you think it's a good idea to aggravate someone with magical powers over life and death, Arthur?" she whispered. When she leaned away, the reporter didn't see she had the tin plate and the notebook in her other hand. She put the cigarette back between his slack lips and patted his cheek. "Something to consider."

Vi pushed away from the pillar. He coughed and spluttered, but did not follow. Bonnie emerged from the Pullman and she waved her over. They weaved their way through the people until George found them.

"I got a hackney waiting like you asked," he said. "And the station has the address, so your trunks'll be sent 'round later."

"Then I say, lead the way," Bonnie chirped, holding out her arm. "You'll lean on me. No arguing." She wagged an index finger before using it help Vi into her grip. With an elbow held firmly in her grasp, they made slow progress along the platform together. Vi would never admit it, but the widow's steady gait kept her from weaving and lurching. The ghost followed, his control over his spirit body so tenuous he left eddies and wafts of aether trailing in his wake.

As they approached the exit archways, Vi's stomach gave a squeeze of guilt. She set her chin at a resolute slant, her eyes trained on the distance to keep from glancing at the spot where she'd watched Peter shiver.

The swelter of late afternoon weighed down the air in the confines of the entryway. When they emerged, a breeze kicked up by Lake Michigan meandered through the busy street and offered some relief.

Peter stepped to her side, the thin mist of his body even less solid in the bright sun. "I'm not going to ride with you. I think I need some more time to pull myself together. I want to make a good impression, after all."

"Are you sure you know where to go?"

He returned a rueful chuckle. "Where do you think I scouted out first when you disappeared?"

Peter didn't mean it as anything other than a fact, but the reminder of her betrayal made Vi wince. She stuttered, torn between avoiding the subject and searching for words that could soothe even a fraction of the pain in his eyes. If those words existed, the ghost didn't give her time to find them.

"I feel like walking. I'm strong enough now. And it isn't as though I will be eating supper with you." Peter laughed at his own meager attempt to break the crackle of embarrassed tension between them.

From a nearby archway, George called, "Over here, Miss Viola!"

She spotted him next to a modest, black cab drawn by a modest, gray horse. Bonnie and Peter followed as she limped to the street, and Vi could make out an even grayer driver wilting in his seat several feet above their heads. He nodded a beleaguered greeting when she came into view.

"You're brave, working in this heat," Vi grimaced, limping closer.

He wiped his face with a grimy, checked handkerchief. "I've got to eat, ma'am."

The two-seater cab would put the passengers in close contact, but the open front would at least offer them a breeze along the way. Vi paused and regarded the high step, then braced herself for the ache in her ankle.

Peter automatically offered a hand to help her up. When she only raised her eyebrow in response, he dropped his hand and mortification washed over his face. "Force of habit. Sorry," he mumbled.

George steadied her as she stepped up into the cab on her sore leg. With a muffled groan, she took her seat, and she spied a newspaper folded neatly around a walking stick. Bonnie followed close behind, and would have sat on them if the Vi hadn't swooped them out of the way.

"Excuse me," Vi said over her shoulder, waving the paper. "But I believe your last passenger has left a few items behind."

"No ma'am," the man replied after a cursory glance over his shoulder. "Your boy put 'em there."

"George?"

She unfolded the newspaper, that morning's edition. Her brain soaked in a few headlines as she set it aside, but she couldn't imagine the lumberyard that caught fire on the Southside would hold her interest long. With the paper gone, she saw the head of the cane for the first time, and she laughed with delight. The smooth, black stone had been carved into strong lines and soft contours of a horse's head.

"It's Smithy, see," the boy bubbled from the curb. "I saw it for sale inside, and I thought it could help."

"It's a lovely gift. How thoughtful," Bonnie said. Her feigned innocence didn't fool the relapsed grifter.

"You encouraged this behavior, I assume?" Her voice held just a hint of recrimination; the cane was ever so pretty, after all.

The little brunette grinned and replied excitedly, "Well, George asked me how to make things right between you, and I told him he could use his wages to show you how much he appreciated his position."

"And I do appreciate it, Miss Viola. I want to be your valet more than anything," the boy pledged. "I made a mistake, but I won't do it again. I promise."

Vi ran her fingers over the satiny jet of the cane's head and chuckled. "All right kid. I know you're sorry, and I believe you when you say it won't happen again. So, the question is, do you want to ride with us, or up there with the driver?"

He beamed at her and climbed to the bench, repeating the address his employer had told him. The carriage lurched into motion, and Vi let all the air out of her body.

"Are you sure you're prepared to see your aunt after what happened?" Bonnie asked. "We could still take you to a hospital, or stay in a hotel if you don't want to go home."

"I want to get this over with," she sighed.

"Who knows? Perhaps your accident will make your aunt forget how long it's been since you came to call, and we'll be spared that lecture."

"Maybe," Peter shouted as they pulled away. "Or you'll be in for a whole new one."

CHAPTER 37

The room was so quiet, even the ticking of the grandfather clock reached their ears. Every tiny scrape of a utensil or creak of a floorboard under the butler's foot echoed all the way to the tall ceilings of the dining room. A golden chandelier encrusted with crystals and dust in equal measure hung over the center of the table.

A huge, Venetian mirror reflected the stoical scene from over an ornate mantel; a tall woman, with gray hair cropped close to her skull, scowled at one end of a long wooden table, while two other women sat in awkward silence staring at the other.

Even though it had been almost a decade since Vi had last seen the room, nothing had changed. The same family portraits kept watch from the bloody red walls, the same servant still served the food, though his age had slowed his movements. She moved the elegant meal around her plate with her fork as she thought about George enjoying what would probably be plain but delicious fare in the cozy surroundings of the kitchen alongside the old cook. She'd never wanted to trade places with a child so much in her life.

Bonnie started to speak, but Vi quieted her with a shake of her head and nervous glance to the woman at the far end of the long table. Her friend looked from the matriarch's stern and quiet visage and back, mouthing, "Why not?"

Vi returned a frustrated but silent, "Just don't."

The other woman rolled her eyes. "Miss Prudence—"

A vehement, short shush interrupted her from the corner. When she searched for the source, Bonnie found the ancient butler bringing a quivering finger to his lips.

The little brunette's face screwed up in defiance and she continued. "Thank you ever so much for welcoming us into your home." Prudence didn't even lift her eyes from her plate, her knife squeaking as she cut off another tiny piece of pork chop and brought it to her lips. Bonnie raised her voice and tried again. "You have a lovely home, Miss Prudence."

The room held its breath as the older woman picked up a linen napkin and dabbed at the corner of her mouth. Prudence gently set down her fork and leveled her razor-sharp, green eyes at her niece. "Viola," she said, voice soft but her tone wrought with iron.

Vi swallowed hard. "Yes, ma'am."

"You know how I feel about talking during mealtimes."

"*I* didn't say anything."

"I'm sorry," Bonnie cried, blood rushing to her cheeks. "I didn't know."

Prudence waved away her concern with a skeletal hand, but continued to glare at Vi. "No. Of course you didn't. Because my wayward niece never thought to inform you."

Vi began to protest, then slumped back in a sulk. "No, ma'am."

"And why do we do that?"

She mumbled, "Because silence is golden."

"Indeed," her aunt replied. The barest hint of a smile crossed her lips, then they returned to a straight line. "I rather thought you'd taken that particular lesson to heart. All I've had from you is silence." She balled up her napkin and threw it onto her half-eaten meal. "That will be all, August. I've lost my concentration completely. Clear the dishes."

The grifter slanted protectively over her plate. "I'm not finished."

"Very well." Prudence let out a long-suffering sigh at the small act of defiance. "Carry on. I suppose we'll all simply have to wait for you."

The butler shuffled over and cleared away his mistress' plate and utensils while she stared at her former ward over steepled fingers. When August went to Bonnie's place, she allowed him to take away her unfinished dinner, her eyes flicking uneasily from one woman to the other. With a saccharine smile, Vi cut a tiny piece of potato and placed it delicately into her mouth with a theatrical 'mmm.'

Prudence clucked her tongue, then turned to her other dinner companion and gestured widely. "You're right. It is a lovely home."

Bonnie let out a squeak, withering under the unexpected turn of the woman's granite gaze. She recovered her aplomb, replying. "Yes, er... has it been in the family long?"

"There's been a Thorne in this house since it was built," Prudence replied proudly. "Though I don't know how much longer that will be true. I thought to leave it to her when I pass, but Viola seems to have made her home... elsewhere."

"You're going to leave me the house?" Vi exclaimed, choking on her half-chewed bite.

"This is why we don't talk and eat," her aunt scolded, then returned her attention to Bonnie. "So, tell me. How do you two know each other?"

Her friend shot Vi another look, uncertain of how to proceed but unwilling to be the one to spill the secret. "It's quite a long story..." she hedged.

"I see," Prudence replied coldly. "And you believe I am somehow unequipped to listen to a long story?"

"Well, I—" Bonnie stuttered.

Vi re-entered the conversation. "Leave her alone. You're angry with me, not her."

"Do I sound angry?" the older woman replied with an infuriating lack of emotion. "I'm not the one raising my voice," she pointed out.

"You never *sound* angry," her niece replied. "But that doesn't mean you aren't. I know you too well to believe you aren't furious with me right now."

"Are you quite finished yet?" Prudence sighed. "We could adjourn to the study like civilized people if you would surrender your plate."

The corner of Vi's eye twitched, but she pushed away the remains of her supper. As August rounded the table, he stopped to whisper something in his mistress' ear.

"Apparently, I already have a visitor waiting for me in the study. If you'll excuse me for a moment, I'll see to what he wants."

The butler assisted Prudence with her chair as she rose, but Vi's next words stopped her halfway through the motion. "He's with me."

Her aunt regarded her skeptically. "I highly doubt we're talking about the same... person." She brushed at non-existent wrinkles and straightened her cuffs before stepping away from the table.

"The ghost?" Vi asked, savoring the moment. Her heavy heart lifted a little as she watched her aunt stop dead, confusion twisting her features. With a smile, Vi continued lightly. "Yes, Peter is my guest, but he preferred to take a nice stroll rather than arrive with us in the carriage."

Prudence lifted her chin and glowered down her aquiline nose at her niece, but she couldn't keep the curiosity, and perhaps even pride, out of the creases of her stately face. She gestured at the study door. "Come along," she said, her eyes momentarily flashing with satisfaction. "And tell me everything."

CHAPTER 38

The two younger women hurried across the hall after their host, Vi's cane adding a quiet drumbeat for their march. Her aunt still hadn't mentioned it, so the relapsed grifter made sure to thump it even louder in the hope of garnering some sympathy.

Most of the rooms were closed against the dust, and more recently, the heat. But as they passed, Vi could clearly picture these interior spaces of the old manse that had dominated her life after her mother died. A ballroom that was never used, a row of bell pulls to call non-existent servants, but most importantly, the room full of books, pipe smoke, and war stories that had served as her father's private office when he was in town.

Prudence's imperious voice carried from the sitting room and snapped her back to the present. Her aunt greeted Peter politely before turning to Vi, saying loftily, "I do apologize for not receiving you directly. No one told me to expect another guest until a moment ago."

Vi entered the room in time to see Peter's graceful bow. "It's no trouble, really." The walk did appear to have done him some good; the pearly fog of his body now completely obscured what lay behind him.

The long, lace curtains wafted in the breeze of the open window, revealing a pair of window seats peeking out through the veil. Vi drifted over to the nearest one and ran her finger over the familiar softness of the worn cushion. Lace may seem delicate, but those curtains had protected her from the imaginary cavalry when she was a child alone at play, and from her aunt basically any time she'd called her name.

"I wasn't expecting your butler to know I was here." Peter straightened and continued sheepishly. "I hope you'll forgive me for simply walking into the foyer."

Her thin brows crept ever so slightly higher. "August is a sensitive, though his family line doesn't possess the gift as strongly as ours. But why ever would you need to apologize?"

"Your niece is the only other 'sensitive,' as you say, whom I've ever met. She isn't too fond of ghosts, so I wasn't sure what sort of a welcome to expect."

"Yes, Viola always did have the worst manners," Prudence tutted. Her primness cracked to reveal a tiny smile and she leaned in conspiratorially. "You should have seen her as a girl. All scraped knees and dirty fingernails. And that mouth!"

"I'm right here," Vi grumped, flicking the curtains wide enough to allow her to take a seat. Bonnie followed and placed a hand on hers, both to offer comfort and to fully enter the conversation.

Prudence continued. "I remember on one occasion, she walked in on a luncheon I was having for some prominent ghosts in the city, and she was simply a horror."

The horsehead cane thunked loudly on the hardwood floor as Vi made a show of propping it against the wall. In case Prudence had missed it, she also put a little groan into her voice as she settled into her seat. "As far as I could tell, you were pouring cups of tea for empty places and talking to no one. How was I supposed to react?"

The hall door opened and George rattled a tea trolley across the threshold. A large, glass pitcher full of ice tea sweated at the center, and Vi licked her lips in anticipation.

"And who's this?" asked Prudence.

The boy put on his grown-up face and bowed. "My name is George, ma'am. I came here with Miss Viola. I'm her valet."

"Indeed. And he knows about... your condition?" her aunt said primly, then walked over to serve the tea. "For someone who professes a bias against the dead, you certainly are telling a lot of people about it."

"It's not like that—"

"Unfortunately, you've got too much of my brother in you to admit when you're wrong."

Peter snickered, and Vi shot him a dagger-laden glare.

"I suppose it's not your fault he raised you to be like him," Prudence sighed as she filled a second glass and started toward the window seat. "But I had hoped that your time traveling would have done something to smooth out those rough edges he left behind."

Vi didn't fight the sardonic pull at her mouth as her aunt handed over her glass. "Sorry to disappoint you."

After another purse of the lips, her aunt replied, "I highly doubt that."

Bonnie snatched the other glass, blurting, "Vi helped my husband!"

Glaciers moved faster and held more warmth than Prudence as she regarded the little brunette. "Excuse me?"

"That's how we met," she stuttered, but gained composure as she spoke. "So, she obviously can't be too biased, or I wouldn't be sitting here. Or Peter for that matter."

"Indeed." Prudence turned back to the ghost. "And how do you know my niece? Is she helping you with your passage?"

"Yes, but we knew each other before," he replied, the old woman's stare turning the seasoned conman into a bowl of jelly. "We were on our way to deal with my unfinished business when the trouble started."

Her neice fell under the weight of her gaze next. With eyes like Pru's, she didn't need to bother with niceties like words to ask questions. Vi took a long draft from her tea, then confessed, "I'm seeing more than merely ghosts. I've had visions, or I think they're memories?"

She expected to get at least some sort of reaction to her 'big news,' but Prudence simply bobbed her head absently. "How long would you say it's been since you've embraced your gifts?"

"I don't know that I'd call it that exactly...."

A long-suffering sigh, followed by, "Very well. How long has it been since you started talking *back* to the dead?"

"Oh. Um, seven years, give or take?"

Another curt nod. "I suppose that explains what you're doing on my doorstep."

"It does?" Bonnie asked.

"Seven is a significant number. You see it in many different religions, even fairy stories. I see it quite often during my research."

The reluctant medium leaned against the wall, her exhaustion turning her question into a whine. "Your work is fascinating, as always, but what does it have to do with me?"

"Simply put, you opened the door a crack seven years ago. Now, it's opening wider."

Vi grimaced. "I don't suppose you've got anything stronger than iced tea, do you?"

"Yes, if you must," her aunt waved vaguely at the other end of the room. "There's some brandy in the cupboard."

"Truly?" Vi burst to her feet, but the protestations of her sore ankle succinctly reminded her that was a very bad idea. After fumbling for a moment with her cane, she limped with exaggerated care to the sideboard. "I'm surprised, but I'm glad to know you've loosened up some in your old age."

The older woman scowled. "My age has nothing to do with it. I keep it in the house for when I'm entertaining incorporeal guests, in fact."

"Speaking of which. I'll take one, too. If you're pouring," Peter said and crossed to Prudence's side. "I've been doing some experimentation with alcohol, and it seems cigars are also still within my reach. In a limited capacity, of course, but it is rather nice to have a *little* joy left to me."

"Any sort of gas, smoke, strong smells, things like that, can have a great effect on ghosts. Fire has so much energy, it can actually act as a barrier," she replied. "The corporeal energies mingle with the spirit energies, and from what I've been told, it's quite an experience."

"Fascinating!" he cried. "Maybe death won't be a complete waste of my time after all. I would love to talk to you more about your research this evening."

If Vi didn't know better, she'd say that her aunt actually preened at the compliment. When she opened the cupboard, a crystal decanter and half-dozen glasses greeted her. She unstoppered the bottle and took an approving sniff.

Before she could pay Prudence another compliment on her selection, Bonnie's nervous voice interrupted. "Could you please explain something to me? I'm sure it all seems rather straightforward to all of you. You've known about all of this for quite some time. But what *are* ghosts precisely? What have I been seeing?"

"Yeah," George interjected. He checked his volume. "I mean, yes please, ma'am. What are ghosts?"

"There are competing theories." With an eager audience, Prudence metamorphosed from a disapproving caterpillar to a butterfly keen on espousing her point of view. "But I will tell you what I have been able to ascertain through my research. Ghosts are the product energies and their interactions with aether."

Disappointment dampened the young widow's voice. "So, they are not souls?"

"What is a soul, if not what lies at the core of a person?" Prudence replied, pooh-poohing thousands of years of tradition with a dismissive flap of her hand. "Anima, ka, spirit, psyche—or you could call it a soul if you wish. But semantics aside, ghosts are composed of the energy that occasionally remains once a person sheds their earthly body. And this energy is strongest when it is unbounded. Sensitives, such as Viola and myself, can detect and sometimes manipulate these energies and their movements."

While Bonnie mulled this over, George's voice filled the gap. "And what's that eee-ther stuff you mentioned?"

"Why, the very fabric of the universe."

Vi snorted and splashed brandy into a pair of squat pieces of utilitarian glassware. "That's putting it rather poetically."

"That's putting it scientifically," her aunt corrected. The reluctant medium snorted again, then glowered at the drinks. Two glasses plus one cane equaled an awkward return trip, yet her hostess remained seated. Prudence's manners were far too developed for it to be a mistake; she was daring her niece to ask for help. She would get no such satisfaction.

Vi struggled to get both glasses into one hand and steadied against her belly before trying to retrieve her cane again. In a flash, her diminutive valet was at her side, taking up her burden. She handed over the glasses with relief.

"...and scientifically speaking," the matriarch continued, "those memories you've seen work in much the same way. Those bursts of psychic energy end up trapped inside a capacitor rather than being strong enough to manipulate the aether itself and manifest. Metal makes an excellent conductor for energy, be it electromagnetic or otherwise. Other materials dissipate the spirit's hold on the aether, and they lose coherency. But when a good conductor comes in contact with another conductor, such as a sensitive's bare skin, some of that energy is transferred. It works through the air to some extent as well, but touch is the most the reliable way to access the memories and death echoes trapped inside."

"I've never heard of a death echo before," Bonnie said.

"They are somewhere between a memory and true spirit. They are harder to detect than ghosts, and memories usually come later as one's powers develop. All ghosts deteriorate over time, but some of them never get much of a start."

"Ah, so like the wailer."

Prudence hardened. "Excuse me?"

"There was a thing, a death echo I suppose, on the train," Bonnie squeaked.

"And you called it a 'wailer'?" Not a single facial tic gave away her state of mind as she continued levelly. "Charming."

Bonnie straightened her face when she realized nothing about Prudence suggested she would, in fact, like charming things. Peter coughed, rescuing the little brunette from the matriarch's granite stare. "So, say there's a gold pin that someone wears habitually, and then that person happens to also spend some time haunting it...."

"Yes, that would make an extremely powerful conductor," she replied, taking a minute sip of her tea. "Though strictly speaking, many things could act as one."

The ghost turned to his friend with a smirk. "I'll take that pin back whenever you've got a chance."

Vi forced a smile at him as she directed George where to set down his glass. As she passed Bonnie, she flashed her a quizzical expression, hoping she'd seen the pin at some point and forgotten to mention it. With their contact broken, the widow had no clue what her friend was trying to ask and offered no aid.

"Was that the only time you saw a memory?" Prudence asked, voice cool and clinical.

"No, there was a necklace that belonged to a... friend of mine. I saw terrible things when I touched it." She reclined on the sofa opposite her aunt. "Do these capacitors usually pick up the worst of the worst? Or am I just lucky?"

"It depends on the object, but strong negative feelings certainly do make an impression." Prudence sniffed pointedly at the cloying smell of brandy and took a sip of her innocuous iced tea. "Still, once you learn to control it, you should be able to excavate whatever sort of memory you want. Provided the object has been present at some sort of psychically or emotionally charged event."

"I'm definitely in favor of controlling it. Which reminds me," Vi said, holding out her glass. "To your health, Aunt Pru."

"That's not going to help you learn control."

"You're wrong there." She smacked her lips after he quaff and sighed. "It's been helping me keep my talents right where they belong for the last seven years."

"Ignoring your gifts isn't the same as controlling them," her aunt scolded. "All *that* will do is help you avoid them. I must assess how you've progressed, and then instruct you in the right course."

The brandy trickled through her and the happy heat settled in her gut. As warmth spread to her aching rib cage, she replied, "You can't deny its value as a palliative, and I need something to take the 'rough edge off' right now."

Prudence's innocent tone didn't do much to mask her gratification at making her niece admit her weakness. "Oh my, something's happened?"

Rather than answering, Vi took a long draught of her brandy. Peter lifted his face out of the trail of alcoholic vapors and responded for her. "When we were at the station earlier, she took a tumble—"

"Viola!"

"—in front of a train."

"What were you thinking?" The older woman scoffed and her pleasure at winning the game disappeared.

"You make it sound as if I was being careless. I didn't *want* to get hit by that train."

"I don't think it was carelessness," Bonnie piped up.

Vi gestured toward the confirmation of her claim. "See?"

"However," her friend pressed. "You didn't tell her how you fainted after touching the necklace. What if you fainted again and fell then onto the tracks?"

The reply came out low and grave. "I. Do not. Swoon." Vi tossed back the last of her drink. "I was pushed."

"Who would want to do a thing like that?" Prudence asked incredulously.

The ghost whispered ominously, "I've got an idea or two…"

Vi slammed her empty glass on the coffee table and cut in before her aunt could ask him to elaborate. "Maybe it was an accident, I don't know. But I can tell you that I did not end up black and blue on purpose."

"Very well," her old mentor crossed to a small table to pluck the miniscule brass bell and ring for the ancient servant. "It sounds as though you've had a taxing journey. August will show you to your rooms now, and you should go get some rest. We'll need you sharp for what lies ahead tomorrow."

"Do not pack me off to bed as if I am still a child," Vi harrumphed, struggling to her feet in order to refresh her drink.

Prudence watched her rickety progress, asking archly, "You are sure you wouldn't rather wait?"

"After one more tipple of that fine brandy, I think I'd be prepared to face just about anything."

"Well, if you believe you are ready, we could begin now." In spite of her words, her aunt's tone of voice made her doubt abundantly clear.

Vi refilled her glass before raising it in her aunt's direction. She polished off her second brandy and gave a small cough. "Bully."

"Ready for what exactly?" Bonnie warbled.

The matriarch shook her tea-totaling head and replied with an imperious sniff. "Pushing her limits."

Chapter 39

"You need to be like a clear, still pool," Prudence said as gently as her habitually disapproving mouth would allow.

Vi fought a snicker. "A pool, you say?"

"Yes." The older woman turned back to stone in the space of a single word. "And most importantly a *still* pool."

"Yes, ma'am." She gave an exaggerated salute and winked at George.

"Vi," Bonnie hissed, half in reproach and half in amusement. Peter leaned against a bookcase on the other side of the sitting room, but no trace of laughter creased his face.

"Stillness requires balance," the old woman continued, taking a few brisk strides toward a side table. Her hands came to rest on the back of an upholstered chair as her eyes returned to her student. "I want you to bring this to the center of the room and stand on it."

"Have it your way," Vi mumbled, laying her cane aside. "But that doesn't sound like something a pool would do."

A nervous giggle escaped from Bonnie's mouth before she could stop it. She slapped her hands over the offending half of her face, her eyes growing nearly large enough to swallow the other half.

The matron regarded the little brunette as her niece fought with the chair. "Mrs. Murphy?"

"Yes, ma'am?" she squeaked through her fingers.

Prudence let her squirm under her hawkish stare for a few moments, then tilted her head to the corner of the room behind her. "Do you happen to be musically inclined?"

Her prey relaxed as she spotted the instrument. "Yes," Bonnie chirped, dropping her hands. "I play the piano a little."

"Then if you'd be so kind, I think some music will help Viola to *focus* on the task at hand. George, dear, you can turn the pages for her."

Vi slammed the chair down between them with a thud and grimace for her friend. "You don't have to do it if you don't want to. I'm the only one who actually has to be here. You and George could go explore the city if you wanted."

Peter spoke up. "Sounds to me as if you're trying to get rid of us."

"It's fine, really. I don't mind," Bonnie assured her, leaving her place on the couch and settling onto the piano bench.

"You see, Viola? She doesn't mind. Now, take off your shoes so you don't ruin anything, and step onto the chair."

"This seems like some sort of trick," Vi said suspiciously, but bent over to slip off her shoes all the same. "Since when do you condone standing on furniture?"

"Desperate times call for desperate measures, I suppose." Another hint of a smile crossed Prudence's face. "And speaking of measures, where is our music, Mrs. Murphy?"

Another squeak and a few bungled notes, and the song began in earnest. Vi tugged at her second shoe. "Why are you torturing my friends like this? I'm sure you can humiliate me all on your own."

"Are you serious?" Peter called. "This is starting to look more and more like a circus act. I wouldn't miss this for the world."

She stabbed her hand at the ghost for emphasis and implored, "If this is about focus, how am I supposed to do that with him here?"

"I see. So, you expect that you will never have to handle a situation when a ghost is present?"

"Well, of course not—"

"This is going to be an exercise in focus, but it is an exercise in *keeping* your focus and *losing* your focus at the same time," her aunt said sternly, then let some scientific distance creep into her tone. "We need to see what you can do before we know where you need to go. I think you can agree, this a logical place to begin."

Vi pointed her shoe accusingly. "You say logic, and I say an opportunity for me to fall on my face."

The matron sighed. "Then, I suppose *logically* you should *focus* on becoming a still, clear pool."

"Fine," she huffed as she dropped the shoes to the floor and stepped onto the seat. "But I am not responsible for the consequences."

"Once you're ready, I want you to close your eyes, take a deep breath, and picture the pool."

The piano music plunked along pleasantly in the corner, and Vi let the rhythm wash over her. She closed her eyes, spreading her arms before her and flexing her feet against springs of the chair for balance. When Prudence's voice sounded again, it was from another part of the room.

"Don't allow any ripples to pass over you or your pool, just breathe." In a few breaths, the voice came from the other side. "Are you seeing the calm water?"

The image sprang to life, the blush of sunrise reflected on the surface of her hot spring. The Northern California scrub extended into the distance. Her soaking pool beckoned to her, the image so strong she could almost smell the sulphur. She counted heartbeats as she breathed, calm and content. "Yes, I see it."

A bright flash of pain seared into the knuckles of one hand and she yelped. The shock cleared away the pleasant calm of the brandy. She opened her eyes, dispelling the image of the calm pool and leaving only the sight of Prudence's disappointed face behind.

"What was that?" Vi spat, rubbing her sore hand and glaring accusingly.

Her aunt stood with her hands behind her back. "That was a ripple," the old woman said simply.

"*That* was a ruler." She swayed precariously on her awkward perch as she tried to peer over the other woman's shoulder for verification.

"For the sake of what I have to teach you, they are one and the same." With the ruler gripped in one hand, Prudence reached out and steadied her student before she toppled. The moment tiptoed on the edge of tenderness, so the old prune couldn't help but take a good swipe at it, adding, "Besides, that was a mere tap to get your attention. No reason to bleat like that."

"How is striking me going to help me be a pool?" Vi asked petulantly. As she straightened, she mumbled, "Maybe I don't want to be a stupid pool."

Her aunt sighed, pinching the bridge of her nose. "This is how my aunt taught me, and it is how I'm going to teach you. I want you to be so in tune with your own energy that nothing can get in the way of you being able to draw from it."

"That sounds like the opposite of what I want to accomplish," she groused. "I just want to be able to turn it off, not muck about with energy and aether and all that."

"Aether is all around you, whether you are inclined to 'muck about' or no," Prudence chided, drawing a white handkerchief from her sleeve. "And the same goes for energy. You can't shut it all out, not forever. It's impossible. So, you should learn to accept it."

"I still don't see what that has to do with my hand. Can I really be sure this isn't all an elaborate hoax?"

If she had been anyone else, Prudence would have rolled her eyes. Somehow, she managed to put the sentiment into action with only her voice. "Whatever that means."

"Admit it. You're trying to trick me into allowing you to break my knuckles."

"Don't be preposterous. This is all for your own good." She held out the handkerchief. "Now. Cover your eyes, put your hands out in front of you, and imagine a clear, still pool."

Vi begrudgingly did as she was told, and in a few moments, the happy image of her pool swam back into focus. She'd started to plant wildflowers along the edges when pain shot through her other hand. Lightning flashed across her vision, momentarily blocking out the pool. "Ouch," she said pointedly.

Prudence's voice shifted, coming from over her shoulder as she circumnavigated the room. "Breathe through the pain, Viola. Take it in, make it a part of you, and let it back out."

The student swallowed her agitation and brought back the pool. While her inner eye hadn't been looking, the morning light had progressed, leaving the pool a delightful shade of cheery blue.

"Where is Peter? Point him out for me."

Vi pushed outward with her extra senses, and the ghost blazed bright and blue over her other shoulder. She pointed with her right hand, just as the ruler smacked her left.

"What was that for?" she cried, ripping off the blindfold. "I was right, wasn't I?"

"Yes, you were, but this has nothing to do with being right," Prudence replied. "It has to do with stopping it from happening again. Put the blindfold back on."

"How can I stop you if I can't see?"

One of her aunt's thin eyebrows crept toward the ceiling. "How indeed?"

She spluttered in frustration for a moment, then yanked the cloth back over her eyes. As she regained control of her breathing, Vi could feel Peter moving from his place in one corner and stepping silently around the edge of the room. With a huff, she brought back the pool and put her hands out before her. One song ended and another began as she strained to locate the real threat of the ruler rather than the obvious presence of the dead man.

"Where's Peter?" Prudence asked quietly, her voice coming from nowhere and everywhere at once.

The ruler started to move even before Vi had a chance to reply, and without realizing she'd acted, she snatched it from her aunt's hand. In one fluid motion, she twisted and threw the ruler, sending it spinning end over end before passing through the ghost and lodging itself between two books. Peter patted himself convulsively, but remembered he couldn't be harmed and turned an astonished gaze to his former partner.

With a smug smile, Vi said, "I think the test is over."

"The test is over when I say it's over," Prudence admonished, bustling over to the place where the ruler still vibrated on the bookshelf. "And believe me when I tell you there is much more to learn than throwing things about my parlor." Her eyes fell on the tattered spine of the book she was touching and let out an uncharacteristic, excited shout. "Take this, for instance."

Curiosity got the better of her pique, and Vi asked, "Take what?"

"Do you believe in providence?"

Vi stepped down from her perch. "I never really gave it much thought."

"There are no coincidences," her aunt said with a hint of conspiracy. "There is only aether and the waves that flow through it; energies that are acting, reacting, and quite often attracting."

Prudence held out the ragged volume for her niece to examine. It had to be among the least remarkable books in all of bookkind. The worn brown cover boasted neither title nor author, but cracks running the length of the spine proved it had been put to good use. As Vi ran her fingertip over the uneven edges, the book seemed to hum with pleasure. "I don't understand. What is it?"

"Think of it like a handbook," her aunt replied, with a crook of her fingers. When her student didn't immediately hand it over, Prudence dragged her customary granite stare from her hand to her niece's face and back again. "But it is something that you will have to *earn*. Give it here, you're not ready for it yet."

Glowering, Vi shoved the book into her mentor's waiting hand. "And I suppose I'll only 'earn' it by doing exactly what you say?"

"Exactly."

"Well, we both know that isn't going to happen."

"Viola."

She demonstrated a theatrical shrug and a dramatic sigh. "Honestly, I'm not sure I am physically capable."

Prudence pursed her lips. "It appears you aren't physically capable of taking anything seriously, either."

"I am being serious," she snapped, the temperature of her anger rising with every syllable. "And if blind faith is what it will take to find out what I need to know, let's stop wasting everyone's time, shall we?"

"You insolent, mercurial girl!" her aunt sputtered.

"Don't forget pig-headed," Peter joked.

Vi flashed him a lopsided grin. "Yes, I am insolent, mercurial, and pig-headed. But most importantly, I am *leaving*." She dipped into a deep curtsy, then she and her horsehead cane stomped out of the room with as much dignity as a woman in her stockings could muster. When she got to the door, she turned back, her face set in a mask of mock sincerity. "Always a pleasure, Aunt Pru. Good evening."

CHAPTER 40

October 8, 1871

According to the cursory glance Vi gave her old room before crawling into the canopy bed, it had remained untouched by the years. She expected this was due to the abundance of available rooms and lack of guests rather than any actual sentiment on her aunt's part. Whatever the reason, she'd been surprised and vexed by the wave of nostalgia when she opened the door, and went straight to sleep after the argument.

Peter tried to wake Vi far too early the next morning, but she banished his annoying cheerfulness and buried her head deep in her stack of pillows. Prudence may lack a general warmth and comfort one might seek in a mother figure. Luckily, the same couldn't be said for her beds.

The next time she woke, the scene in the parlor replayed in her mind. She kicked off the covers, and her furious stomps carried her from one side of the room to the other, her fingers flexing convulsively as she continued the argument in her head. When her eyes fell on the closet, she rushed over and ripped open the doors. The neat rows of dresses mocked her with their orderliness, so she punished them by grabbing an armload and tossing it onto the bed.

A quiet but insistent knock accompanied a voice on the other side of the bedroom door. "Vi? It's me." Bonnie peered around the doorframe, Vi's abandoned footwear from the previous night dangling from her hand. "I wanted to check and see if you were alright."

She dragged another load of clothing out of the closet. "Peachy."

"What do you think you're doing?" her friend asked, an unexpected edge to her tone.

Vi spun around, pointing in the direction of the sitting room. "After the way she was treating me, did you really expect me to stay?"

"I expected you to *try*. And perhaps to try *sober*?" The other woman tossed the shoes onto the pile and perched on the corner of the bed that wasn't covered in lace and frills.

"I *was* trying," she groused, attacking the rest of her unfortunate footwear next. "You were there. I hit my mark perfectly, and aunt Prune couldn't even acknowledge it."

Bonnie scoffed. "And she was trying to tell you there was more to it than that. That's the whole reason we're here, aren't we? Because she knows more about all this than you do? You're getting *hurt*."

As Vi opened her mouth to answer, a glint at the foot of the bed caught her eye. The shoes rained down onto the pile, and she stooped to investigate the metallic glimmer. "Hello? What's this?"

"Are you even listening?"

"Yes, but look what I found." Peter's lucky pin winked at Vi from the shadow of the bed skirt. Before her fingers could make contact, she remembered herself and hunted for something to use as a barrier. "And I've been dealing with ghosts for years now. I can handle them."

"What about the memories?" Bonnie asked. "You may have forgotten already, but I watched you crumple to the floor. It was terrifying."

"Really?" Vi chuckled and crossed to a chest of drawers. "That's good to hear."

"So, you think it's good that I was terrified? Thanks ever so much for your concern."

Her reply was muffled by the bump and scrape of her rifling. "Honestly, I've been worried about you. You're far too accepting of everything that's been going on, in my opinion. This is all completely insane. Aha!" She flapped the handkerchief in triumph as she crossed back to the bed.

"Perhaps it's simply that I know how to bend," Bonnie pointed out, her slight body responding to her rising anger by sending her to her feet. "Unlike some people."

Vi snatched up the gold pin in the cloth. "You think *I'm* unbendable? I'm a wet noodle compared to that woman."

"That doesn't change the fact that you *need* her."

"Ha!"

"And that's the real problem, isn't it?"

The pin disappeared into the safety of the handkerchief and Vi crossed back to the closet. "I'm done talking about this."

"Good, maybe you can try listening for a change," the young widow seethed, then softened. "Look at you. You're afraid of a little piece of metal. The woman I met a few short days ago wouldn't have been." Vi took in her clenched fist, knuckles white from strain as Bonnie pressed on. "If Prudence is right, you'd be able to actually control which memories you get to see. Maybe you can use that to help you find out what happened to Peter. Not to mention, you wouldn't go around fainting. But the only way we know of to make that happen is to listen to her."

The muscles of Vi's jaw worked as she turned the words over in her mind. Bonnie had a point—several in fact—and there was so much at stake. Eventually, she asked with a smirk, "What do you think are the chances I could get her to help me without actually apologizing? Because I can't be certain, but it's possible my heart would give out rather than tell her I was sorry."

Her friend smiled back, all of the anger of the previous moments washed away. "If anyone could manage to die of stubbornness, I'm sure it would be you."

"No more. I already surrendered!" Vi cried, throwing her hands up as if to shield herself from blows. "Once I've been fortified with some coffee, I'll see right to it."

Chapter 41

It took until more like noon, but her feet finally found the courage to bring her to the third floor. The laboratory had always been off-limits when she was a child, and the residual fear of punishment still clung to the staircase like spider silk. Annoyed ancestors glowered at her from their ornate frames as she made her way down the corridor, but despite the long years, not a speck of dust could be found anywhere.

Vi had managed to stretch her morning by drinking enough cups of coffee for three people and scrutinizing every inch of the morning paper. August informed her upon entering the dining room that Prudence didn't wish to be disturbed that day. It had seemed like a perfect excuse to forget the whole apology idea; unfortunately, Bonnie didn't see it that way. The little brunette had marched Vi over to the landing and watched her start to climb the stairs before she took George out to explore the city.

The top stair creaked under her careful tread. Vi let out a squeal, then chided the butterflies in her belly for their acrobatics. She was just going to go speak with one old woman, not a dragon.

A door beckoned from the shadows at the end of the hall. The pain in her ribs had converted to a distant aching rather than the insistent throb of the day before. Her ankle was less obliging—reminding her of its trials and tribulations with each step—but it also clearly benefitted from her long night's rest.

She could have managed without the aid of her cane, but she'd already begun to find comfort in its solidity and weight at her side. She leaned on it as she gave the door a tentative tap.

A haughty response returned almost simultaneously. "Enter."

The knob rattled in her shaking hand as she slipped into the room. Early in the manor's grand history, the attic had housed a number of servants, but later, several walls were knocked down to create a single large room. A twenty-foot work table dominated the space, with a strange collection of machinery seemingly growing right out of the far wall like an inorganic weed. Shelves of books and vials crowded in from the other side, accompanied by a display of statues and religious fetishes from all over the globe. Vi's father had no doubt brought some of them home from his journeys, but it only now occurred to her that Prudence may have done some traveling of her own in her youth.

Her aunt hunched over something on the table, leaving the scratch of her pen and the buzz of some contraption in the corner to fill the tense silence. The pewter head never lifted from her work and her niece shifted awkwardly on the rug.

The seconds ticked by until they were startled into silence by a hushed, "Good afternoon, Viola."

"Hello," she croaked in relief, then coughed nervously and tried again. "So…" The syllable hung in the air, suspended between them on ribbons of unvoiced pain. "This is where the magic happens?"

Her nervous chuckle was cut short by a curt response. "Not magic. Science."

"Right, of course. I didn't mean—"

"I know," Prudence interjected with a sigh and a sidelong glance. "Forgive me, that was rude."

"I seem to bring that out in people." Vi offered a conciliatory smile. "You can add it to the list after pig-headed."

The older woman snorted a short laugh before turning her attention back to whatever lay on the table. "I had a long talk with your friend."

She froze; Pru could only mean Peter, the one person on the planet who knew all of Vi's dirty secrets. Though she mentally flogged herself for leaving the two of them alone together, she kept her tone noncommittal. "That must have been interesting."

"Yes, it was," Prudence replied, her voice just as steady.

Vi flashed between dozens of stories she'd never want her ex-partner to tell. Fleecing the Colonel may have been their biggest job, but he was the last entry in a long list of marks. Not to mention, her aunt had no clue about her ward's fake seances or involvement in the war.

The moment stretched on until Vi finally blurted, "Well? What did he say?"

The older woman turned away from her scribbling and removed the pair of tiny spectacles perched on her nose. "I'm worried about him."

The relief flooding through her colored her response. "Oh!"

Her aunt narrowed her eyes. "Why on earth would that make you happy?"

"It's just that... never mind." She dragged a second stool from under the workbench. "Tell me why you're worried."

"He's losing heart."

"I know he's been a little blue, but he has just *died*—"

"It's more than that," Prudence insisted. "You've got to help him with his passage, or I'm afraid he might get lost."

"Peter wants me to help him. You want me to help him. But what can I even *do* to help?" she cried. "I'm trying to take care of his unfinished business as fast as I can. The only reason we even took this detour was because *he* insisted on it."

"I see," her aunt replied, voice sharp and cold as an icicle.

Vi winced. The slight had been wholly unintentional, but there was no taking it back now, so she pressed on. "Please, tell me. Is there actually anything else I *could* do?"

"His path really isn't that different from your own, actually—"

"Last time I checked, I wasn't dead."

Prudence's tone shifted from aggravated matriarch to expert. "You are both trying to master skills that draw on and manipulate the same energies, which requires a similar state of mind. Neither of you can hope to take control of your situation unless you learn to accept things as they are. It's like breathing." Vi opened her mouth to protest, but her aunt continued. "Think about it. Despite the fact that you should just do it automatically, if you stop to think too hard about breathing, the task somehow becomes more difficult to maintain rather than less."

"If you say so," she replied reluctantly. "It sure doesn't feel like breathing. More like drowning."

"Let me ask you this. The first time you truly saw and communicated with a ghost, what were you doing?"

She chuckled. "You're going to hate this story."

"Oh?" One of Prudence's thin eyebrows crept toward the ceiling.

"Well...." Vi hedged, wishing there was some way to keep tenuous ceasefire intact, but she saw no way around it. She girded her metaphorical loins and let the truth out. "For a short time, I made my living by holding false parlor sessions."

Her aunt somehow managed to sit up even straighter, her voice acidic. "Viola Margaret Thorne. Even with all you've seen of my work? The terrible exploitation of the grieving? That is despicable."

"*That* is supply and demand," she corrected. "The war left a lot of people with questions—"

"And you decided to give them false answers?" Prudence glowered.

"At first? Absolutely. I saw an opportunity." Vi leaned one elbow on the work table. "But then, I was practicing my bit—"

"Bit?" The older woman nearly spat the word.

"Um, yes. My... well, I guess you could say 'performance.'"

With an effort, Vi kept her amusement off her face as her aunt's nose wrinkled at the word. It was no secret; there were few things in the world that Prudence hated more than actors, or what she called 'professional liars.'

She must have been very interested in the rest of the story not to take a moment to make a snide remark about Vi's late mother and her line of work. Instead, Prudence sighed, "Go on."

"I was imitating other mediums I'd seen, making it so I looked like I was in a sort of sleep."

"Could you call it a trance?" Prudence interjected. "Deep breathing, emptying your mind, that sort of thing?"

Vi chewed this over, then turned a chagrined smile to her aunt. "Sort of like being a clear, still pool, perhaps?"

One corner of the older woman's mouth lifted in response to Vi's equivalent of an apology. "Precisely."

"I never thought of it like that. But I suppose that could have been how this all started."

"I assure you. That is definitely how you came to embrace your gifts. I know it probably isn't what you wanted." Prudence raised her hand fractionally and hesitated, as if she might actually reach out and touch her niece.

Vi cleared her throat. "But enough about me. I believe we were talking about Peter?"

Her aunt's hand retreated to her lap. "He's strong and determined to make his death mean something. He is becoming frustrated, angry. But navigating this all requires a gentler approach."

"Says the person who left my knuckles stinging last night."

The old woman chuckled. "I suppose you have a point."

"I do?" Vi asked, struggling to keep her jaw from hanging slack.

"I understand it may be difficult to wrap your head around, dear." Her aunt finally extended her hand to offer a quick pat, the hint of mocking sympathy creeping into her tone. "It must not happen too often."

Blood rushed to Vi's head and pounded at her temples, but she restrained her pique to a flaring of her nostrils before replying. "So, I've got a point. What does that mean for Peter, and for me and my 'gifts'? Especially this fun new trick I picked up."

"As you say, let us leave behind ghosts for now and focus on the memories," Prudence replied. "If you can control how you interact with the energy stored in objects, it will be a step along the path to all of your potential. There are many avenues to explore when you're ready."

"I'm not ready to talk potential, yet. One thing at a time." Vi wiggled her index finger into her cuff and retrieved the bundle containing the tie pin. "I brought this with me, in case it would help."

"This is what Peter haunted?"

Vi held out the pin. "It's hard to believe he could fit himself into such a neat little package."

"I've written a paper on possession. Fascinating subject," the older woman said as she held the sliver of gold before her face. "Not that anyone in these parts will read it, let alone publish it. There has been some interest from a correspondent in New York, but even in that nexus of new beliefs and emerging sects, I am being met with skepticism."

"Can you really blame them? This is all so unbelievable."

"You only think that because your father wouldn't let me tell you about it when you were small. It would have saved everyone a headache."

"I think you might be right." Vi grimaced and rubbed temples. "Why didn't he let you?"

An ironic smile parted her aunt's usually straight line of a mouth. "He didn't believe any of it was true. Thorne men don't see what we do, just the women are affected, so he thought I was lying and making trouble. And he forbade me to speak of it to your mother, though of course, I didn't have much of an opportunity."

"What about your teacher? You had an aunt or someone who knew the truth. She couldn't make him understand?"

Prudence released a sigh tinged with bitterness as she replaced the pin its linen nest. "Some people don't want to believe."

The conversation had inadvertently steered to something that had the potential to turn into feelings, so Vi changed the subject. "Do you sense anything when you touch it?"

"Definitely. It's obvious that this has memories stored inside. There's a sort of tremor you can detect, if you know what you're looking for."

"Like that book you won't tell me about?" Vi asked suspiciously.

"Yes. In fact, there are many memories stored inside, and far more."

Vi arched her brow. "Such as?"

"How are you feeling today?"

"Surprisingly well. That brandy certainly did the trick. I slept like a rock."

Prudence allowed herself a superior smile. "It wasn't the brandy."

"Then what?"

"The tea," she replied, tapping her temple. "It's a special blend I took from the pages of that book."

Vi scoffed. "Why didn't you just tell me? I would have had more."

"Because you were feeling so receptive and open to my teachings last night?" Her aunt sneered.

"Touché. I'm being receptive though, now, aren't I?"

"Indeed. Let's work with the pin for now rather than starting on something new. You have already pulled a memory from it once, so it will likely be easier to do it again."

"You keep saying that it is possible, but how? I wouldn't know what I was even looking for."

"It will take time, and you may never be able to do it with precision."

Prudence gestured to a pair of low, upholstered chairs and they settled into their more comfortable seats before continuing. "It is only one skill among many, but you've already shown some aptitude, so with guidance, you should be able to master it. Over time, the different sorts of energies will speak to you, but the easiest difference to feel is how old or new a memory is. They fade and break down over time as they bounce around the conduit, so fresh memories are stronger."

Vi spread open the handkerchief on her lap but did not dare to touch the pin. "I know what I saw the first time is at least four years old, but it may have been the newest one. It certainly seemed strong."

The old woman frowned. "There's definitely something fresher than that held inside. We shall see if you can find it. Try to sort the strong pull from the weaker ones."

"Last time I did this I fainted." She regarded the pin warily, her heart thundering like a salesman's fist on the front door.

"Which is why we are sitting down," Prudence replied reasonably, then reached out one spidery hand. "And why I'm going to go in with you."

"We don't know what we're going to find in there." Vi gazed at her mentor's outstretched fingers. Anything newer than the memory on the platform couldn't be about her, but she didn't want to see Peter's death, either. "There's a lot you don't know about…"

"One thing at a time."

Vi took a final, deep breath. She took her aunt's hand in a resolute grip. The pin winked up at her as her other hand descended.

"Here goes nothing."

CHAPTER 42

As she quested for the strongest throb of energy below her fingertips, the churning void gave way to a colorless facsimile of Vi's bedroom in the Thorne mansion. She and Prudence stood near the empty fireplace, watching the curtains gently ripple on either side of her open window. The first sounds of a city waking bounced off the buildings outside and into the room. A shadowy Vi murmured in her sleep in the middle of the massive, overstuffed bed.

"This has to be this morning," Vi hissed, then remembered she couldn't actually wake herself and spoke normally. "Last night was the first time I've slept here in years. How can that be?"

"You really shouldn't sleep with your window open," her aunt scolded. "With the stink in this town, you could catch your death."

"It's a thousand degrees."

"Still."

Somehow, Vi kept her eyes from rolling enough to give offense. "So, where's the pin? It has to be in the room somewhere."

Prudence's eyes widened as she pointed at the window. "Look!"

"Yes, the window's open, but can we—"

She grabbed her niece by the shoulders and spun her around. "Do as I say."

As Vi's gaze fell on the windowsill, fingers of mist crept over the top and swirled to the floor. The strange pool of cloud glowed with the same subtle blue as spirit flesh, but coiled its way over the threshold and poured itself into a form at the foot of the bed. The gold pin floated in the fog of the ghost's body, and when her hands coalesced from the mass, it stood pinched between two pearly fingers.

"Do you know who that is?"

Vi took a few steps forward to get a better vantage point. The malevolent sneer of the interloper resolved itself within a riot of curly, once-blond hair. The reluctant medium turned back with a shake of her head. "I've never seen her before in my life! Though... there is *something* familiar about her."

The shade of the unknown woman glared at the shadow-Vi, her face contorted in both anger and satisfaction. She rolled the pin between her fingers and took a step toward the prone figure.

"What do you suppose she was doing with Peter's pin?"

"I think she may have used it to track you."

"What? How?"

"Not you precisely, but Peter."

"Another skill for me to learn?"

"Possibly."

Vi watched helplessly as the ghost took another step, the long shaft of the pin flashing wickedly in the early morning sun. The strange ghost beamed as she took another step, murmuring an old nursery rhyme.

"Needles and pins, needles and pins. When a man marries, his trouble begins...."

Even though Vi couldn't affect what she saw, it was hard to stand by and watch herself lying there so helplessly. If applied to the right places, a pin that size could be deadly. And a ghost with enough control didn't need a weapon, merely the ability to squeeze. Vi almost called out a warning, but the menacing figure glared sharply at the door as if she'd heard something.

"See you tonight," the ghost whispered, and dissolved again into a puddle of mist.

Peter's head slipped across the threshold and through the door just as the pin dropped to the floor. "Rise and shine, Vi!" he called.

The sepia-toned doppelganger mumbled something incomprehensible, and the ghost sighed theatrically and crossed to her bedside. "Hurry up. From the smell of it, there's going to be a feast this morning, and I want to explore this vapor theory some more."

The vision rolled over and blinked at him blearily. "Then you go haunt the bacon for both of us. I'm still sleeping."

As Peter's gentle cajoling continued, the fog at the foot of the bed crept across the floor and over to a vent. It slipped out as noiselessly as it had come, leaving the pin where it lay. As the last wisps of the would-be attacker slithered through the grate, the dark billows of the memory closed in on the scene, and the walls of the lab came rushing back into view.

Prudence snapped to attention at her side and held Vi in a steady, concerned gaze. "You're in danger."

"But at least I didn't faint," she replied weakly.

"This is no joking matter."

"Who's laughing?"

The older woman huffed angrily. "You've brought a malevolent spirit into my house."

"Not on purpose!" Vi cried, sticking the pin into the arm of the chair so it stood at attention at her side. "You make it sound as if I've adopted some mangy stray."

"And my concerns are far bigger than fleas, Viola," her aunt replied, primly removing the pin and pointing to it. "That was a powerful and angry spirit. And she isn't a danger to just you. Mrs. Murphy, that sweet little boy, me—she could strangle anyone under this roof before they knew it was happening. Or perhaps that doesn't concern you!"

Vi crossed her arms and hunkered into her armchair. "Maybe now you all will believe me when I say someone pushed me. She must have been the one who 'helped' me onto the tracks."

Prudence began pacing, her arms clasped behind her iron rod of a spine. "And you're sure you've never seen her before? You didn't do something to make her angry?"

Vi shook her head absently, then bolted upright as things clicked into place. "I've never seen her before, but I think I've *felt* her. There was this time on the train when I felt a presence. At the time, I thought it was that tattered old rag of a ghost I'd seen earlier in the trip, but now I think it must have been her."

"*That* was no tattered rag, that's for certain. And she followed you here?"

"Apparently. Though I have no idea why. No one in California knew anything about me, especially not anything that had to do with ghosts."

"And this *other* business of yours? Whatever it is you and Peter have gotten yourselves into?"

Vi glowered. "I don't see how it could be related. There's no chance a ghost could have gotten out to me so quickly. Those people would have barely received my telegram before I left Sacramento, and it isn't as if ghosts can fly."

Prudence stopped striding back and forth. The look she gave Vi was so heavy, she felt herself sinking even deeper into the chair. Finally, the matron bobbed her head curtly. "It's time for you to go."

"You find out I'm in danger and you're sending me away?" She scoffed, adding sardonically, "Your support is underwhelming."

"Don't be so melodramatic," her aunt tutted. "I think it is time for you to go *because* you are in danger." She marched to the door, only pausing to throw it open and gesture for Vi to follow. "Whatever the reason, I believe that ghost means to do you harm, and as long as you stay here she knows where to find you."

"But I'm not done here." The words came out shrill and desperate as Vi grabbed her cane and scrambled to catch up. When she was beside her aunt, she insisted, "I don't know anything yet."

"I can still assist you with that."

Vi had no choice but to follow. They descended the two flights of stairs in a tense silence and passed into the sitting room. The old woman squinted into the lengthening shadows of late afternoon and went straight for the nondescript volume her recalcitrant student had nearly skewered the night before.

"You may have to leave, but you don't have to leave empty-handed." Prudence slipped the book out of its place and gazed at it reverently. "Take this with you, read some of the passages, and try to do what simple things you can to train on your own. Meditate. Make the tea. And I assume this trouble you are unwilling to talk about, this is something you can handle?"

"Yes," Vi quavered. The matriarch raised one eyebrow a fraction of an inch, and her niece repeated the word with conviction. The book slipped into her waiting hands. "What is it?"

"It is a record, sort of like a diary. Our gifts have a long history, and the women who have borne them have been writing down their experiences as well as leaving behind memories to guide those who come next. It will take you time to unlock all of its secrets, but there is much that you can learn about your abilities and yourself just by reading it."

"I don't know what to say." Vi opened the cover and slid her hand over the loopy slant of the inscription on the first page, which read: *On Seeing the Unseen.*

Her aunt held Peter's pin out to Vi. "My, my. This is a day of 'firsts.'"

"Thank you," Vi said, her voice husky with emotion. She took the sliver of gold and closed the cover of the book on it for safekeeping. "Really. Thank you."

"You can thank me by taking care of... that book. Bring it back in one piece," Prudence replied, painting on a scowl to cover the tightness around her eyes. "And the best way to do that is to go from here. There is sound advice in that journal, as well as a few things that may be able to protect you along the way. Things that harm the dead."

"That sounds an awful lot like magic, wouldn't you say?"

"I can tell you all about the scientific principles, but we both know you'd never sit still long enough. But I can attest to their usefulness. I have had occasion to banish ghosts before."

"Banish? To where?"

Prudence sniffed. "I don't honestly know."

"And you're comfortable with that? Sending someone off to god-knows-where."

"Evidently."

Vi shook her head slowly. "I'm not. I don't kill the living, why would I start killing the dead? Can't I just lose her?"

"We have to assume she's watching the house, waiting for another opportunity. But you don't have to dispel her," her aunt sighed and held her hand out for the diary. Vi reluctantly returned it, but to her relief, Prudence leafed through the pages until she found a particular one and handed it back. "Before one can banish, one must bind. This is a reliable snare, if it comes to that."

"Got any other advice for me in the short run?" she asked, scrutinizing the strange collection of overlapping circles and lines.

"Running water causes lesser spirits some disorientation. I haven't been able to determine the cause, but the reality is clear. So, crossing the river a few times couldn't hurt. Though, this woman who hunts you appears to be exceptionally strong in death. This is all highly unusual, and I do not like deviation. It could point to something much bigger afoot."

A grim expression spread over Vi's face, and she held the book back out to the other woman. "It sounds like I've given you the perfect reason to test those barriers right here."

"I suppose that's true." Prudence made a demure sound, what usually passed for her laughing. "But I've got the portions I copied in the lab, so I don't need the original. It's yours now, truly. I did always mean for you to have it," she said, if not warmly, at least somewhere above freezing. Vi's jaw and eyebrows worked furiously to keep her eyes from leaking. Her aunt gave her a circumspect look. "What's wrong with you?"

"Nothing," she replied with a genuine, lopsided grin. "I'm fine, really."

"Good. Because it sounds like you have trouble ahead."

"That's nothing new," her niece joked, but then her face grew somber. "Actually, there is a favor or two more I need to ask of you."

Without hesitation, the stern woman replied, "Anything."

CHAPTER 43

Vi spent a while drifting from room to room. Her need to say a proper farewell to the family home was impervious to any sense of urgency, and she had some time before darkness fell. Her thirsty gaze drank in the details of her father's study; every hunting trophy and rack of weaponry subject to her cataloging stare. There was no telling when she'd be able to come back to this house again, and she wouldn't make the mistake of letting its outlines grow blurry in her mind's eye.

As she moved on to the next door, her fingers trailed along the edge of the wainscoting. She reached the carved double doors of the ballroom and slowly pulled them open. The tall windows all had dark curtains pulled to keep out the heat, and the twin glowing of candlelight and Peter's aetheric body pulled her attention to a candelabra a few yards inside the room. The brass stand was a head taller than George and boasted at least a dozen branches, but only a single flame illuminated the darkness. The ghost was too absorbed in watching the flame to notice the slice of light spilling in from the hallway. Vi slipped through the doorway and gently closed the heavy door behind her.

When she was a few feet away, she coughed quietly to announce her presence. Peter startled, and as he spun, she said, "What are you doing all alone here in the dark?"

Her former partner regarded her warily for a moment before turning back to the flicker of light. "Prudence and I have been talking about how the energy in fire relates to ghosts. I had August leave this burning for me."

"Really? I thought I was the only one getting an earful of mumbo jumbo from dear auntie Prune." She grimaced and stepped to the other side of the candelabra.

"She's not making it up," he scolded. "When you think about it all in terms of waves moving things around, it makes a lot of sense. For instance, this flame is made of lots of tiny, excited pieces moving around extremely fast. Moving so fast, in fact, that I can...." He extended a finger toward the candle, and when it reached the flame, it came to a stop. A delighted smile spread across his face.

The ghost whispered in awe, "It's so solid. And it even feels warm." When Peter caught her staring, he dropped his hand and coughed to cover his boyish fascination. His voice became distant and aloof once more. "That's probably my second biggest complaint about being dead—the cold."

Vi lifted another taper from its resting place. She touched the wick to the tongue of flame, and the twisted string unfurled as it caught fire. "There," she said with satisfaction. "Now it's even warmer."

His brow furrowed skeptically while she lit the candles one after another. "I didn't think you'd want me messing with Pru, or any of her theories for that matter."

"I guess I don't really think it's all mumbo jumbo," she admitted. "It is all starting to make at least a bit of sense. I may actually find a way to fit inside my own skin, someday."

"Must be nice." His smile took on a bitter tilt. "I'd settle for feeling useful. But I'm starting to think I'm never going to master any of this, with or without your blessing."

"You're a fine conversationalist," Vi teased. She came to the final candle and they stood bathed in a golden pool of light. Peter harrumphed and she continued in a more serious tone. "Truly, there's plenty you can do to be useful—"

"Tell that to the train. How exactly did I help you?" he snapped, the clouds inside his body beginning to swirl menacingly. "All I wanted was for you to stay out of danger, and now you're going on some fool errand. You call that helping? You should be home safe, in California! I never should have gone to you!" He swung his arm at the candelabra, and when his fingers met the taper, it tilted. "I did it! It moved!" he crowed, his form growing darker and more solid with every passing moment. "I told you. I told you both. I needed this... this anger."

Vi made her voice gentle and firm. "Peter, stop it."

"Don't take this from me!" He raged, tiny bolts of lightning jolting across his murky spirit-flesh. "This is what I've been working toward!"

His edges became painfully bright and sharp against the darkness of the shrouded ballroom. The lightning-lit clouds gave way to fissures churning with something thick and hot as magma. It bit into the deep gray clouds of his body, spreading and pulsing across his limbs even as it strove to burrow deeper inside of him.

"Okay, you win!" she shouted in desperation. "I'll help you."

"Is this some kind of trick?" He thundered. The whole ballroom glowed orange in the path of his rage.

"No trick. I was looking for you so I could tell you I'd changed my mind," she assured him. "And I *will* help you, but not like this. Look at yourself."

Peter gazed down the length of his body and gasped. The hot orange glow receded, and the cracks across his body knit shut as they watched. He deflated, the bruise-colored clouds giving way to the misty white of his regular form as he regained control.

"Obviously, I can't stop you from trying," Vi said reasonably. "But I can stop you from tearing yourself apart in the process. What's the point of finding out who killed you if you're just some busted shell of yourself when I do it?"

"All right, professor," he sniffed. "Where do we start?"

"First of all, you've got to stop feeling so sorry for yourself."

The ghost scoffed. "Pardon?"

Vi ticked off the items on her list with her fingers. "Grief over your death, anger at your predicament, at me—these are the things that are going to turn you into nothing more than that poor forgotten soul on the train. Tattered, aimless, and maybe even beyond my reach."

The ghost grimaced, eyes carefully averted. "I see your point," he mumbled. "But I need those things. They make me feel stronger."

"I thought you said I make you feel stronger. Is that because I make you angry?"

Peter sighed, "No." He added with a snicker, "at least, not all of the time."

"So, there must be other ways to feel that way besides giving in to those feelings."

"Okay, I'll bite. What should I do?"

Vi leaned her cane against the candelabra and put her arms out before her as if draped across an invisible partner. "Lead," she replied.

He blinked at her in disbelief. "I can't. You know I can't."

"What I know is that you are the best damn dancer I've ever met. Waltzing used to be like breathing for you."

"That's true," he puffed up with pride, but soon deflated. "But I wouldn't say I'm exactly up to the challenge right now."

She gave the ghost a wink, then closed her eyes. Her body rocked backward and to the side as she took the first steps of the dance.

Peter called after her. "But you're hurt."

"The key is to stop thinking," she said, stepping again. "And let go." Without opening her eyes, she twirled out of the candlelight and across the shadowy floor. "I'm waiting."

A piece of music she'd never be able to name drifted into her mind, helping her to keep the three-point beat of the waltz without a partner. In the cavernous room, she had no worry of colliding with anything, so she let the swoop and step of her feet carry her where they may. A subtle ache crept through her ankle, but she remembered the strike of the ruler and breathed through it. The blue flame of Peter's aura stayed in its corner for several heartbeats, but soon closed the gap between them.

A smile tugged at her lips as she felt the first faint hints of pressure on the small of her back and her fingertips. She dipped and swung again, and the pressure doubled, pulling in her spiral and gently directing her next step. Her heart thudded as they rocked and swayed, remembering the rhythm of its own brand of dancing.

Despite the chill tinging the air as Peter gathered more power, a forgotten heat sent out its tendrils where he touched her. For a few stanzas, the world with all its plots and schemes simply fell away and she was nothing more or less than a dancer in the arms of her partner.

Her eyes drifted open, and she found contentment settling over his face. Peter's whole body glowed silver as if he'd swallowed the moon. Under the weight of her gaze, he opened his shining blue eyes—the eyes of the dead.

She stumbled and spun as the spell they'd been weaving with their feet was broken.

They stood a few feet apart, the moment stretching taut as a bowstring between them.

"Vi, I—"

"I didn't come here to dance," she interrupted. With a sniff, she ran discreet thumb below each eye before turning to face him. "I have to tell you something."

He gazed at her, confident for the first time since they'd left Sacramento. "Yes?" So much hope poured into a single syllable.

She stalled, pacing over to the flickering candles with a sigh. Even if she were to tell him exactly what he wanted to hear, it wouldn't do anyone any good. Not now. They needed to sever his ties to this world, not strengthen them. And inevitably, she would have to let him go.

Vi cupped one of the small, dancing flames with her hand, letting the heat come close to burning before she blew it out. She moved from candle to candle, puffing out a light every few words. "Someone is trying to kill me."

"You...that's...what?" he stuttered. When she brought her eyes to him again, the moonlight sheen had disappeared, but his spirit flesh finally appeared completely recovered from his dalliance with the locomotive, and no worse for the wear after his rage.

"Not to worry, though," she said.

The final candle stood between them, one feeble point of light to ward off the darkness.

"I've got a plan."

CHAPTER 44

The haggard brown nag snorted and tossed her head, but no matter how the omnibus driver urged her on, she refused to pick up her pace. A wind blew from the South, but only a hint reached Vi as she passed through the corridor of buildings. The day shift had all made it home, and no children wanted to play in the oppressive heat, leaving the streets empty and forlorn in this part of town. She watched the city roll by, her hungry eyes taking in the new buildings and raised sidewalks that had been constructed in her absence. No matter how far she'd traveled or how long she stayed away, Vi had always kept up with the news about her beloved Chicago.

The omnibus trundled along the rails, and the steady but weary beat of the horse's hooves echoed off the wooden buildings on either side of her. As she and her ghostly companion approached their destination, a pristine white gateway topped by several pointed archways came into view. It watched over the grounds of the cemetery with a solemn grace, a single wrought iron door left ajar for visitors brave or stupid enough to be out in the heat. Her nervous fingers tapped against the collection of mismatched blooms wilting across her lap. As they came to a stop, Vi held her cane and the bouquet in one hand and swung herself to the cobbled street.

"Are you sure you want to go in there?" Peter leaped noiselessly to the sidewalk.

Vi fanned out the soft jade fabric of her crumpled skirt with her free hand. She turned to give the omnibus driver a polite bob of her head as he left. When she was sure her voice would be lost in the rumble of the wheels, she finally answered. "Why wouldn't I want to go in?"

"I thought, what with there being so much death here. Aren't cemeteries full of ghosts?"

"How long did you hang around your body after you died?" she asked, scowling at the dust already clinging to her scalloped hem. "Even ghosts seem to find cemeteries to be rather depressing places. Or dull, at the very least."

"I still don't see why you had to drag me here," he grumbled.

The hinges of the gate creaked as she widened the opening and slipped through. Dusty iron bars framed her face as she turned. "You didn't have to come."

"Of course, I did," he sulked, passing through the gate unhindered. "Someone has to help keep you alive. You really think I'd let you out of my sight after what you told me?"

"And I appreciate that, really, I do, but—"

The ghost's harsh whisper stopped her. "You also told me there was no reason for you to visit his grave."

Vi swallowed her anger and started down the path. "I know that Patrick's not there, not the part that matters. But that doesn't mean I don't take some solace from visiting his headstone."

"I think you're just trying to get rid of me. Again."

"We're leaving after this," she sighed. "And we're not coming back. Bonnie, Pru, George—they'd all be a lot better off without me in their lives."

The ghost's features twisted with irony. "But you've already ruined mine, so it's okay to drag me along for the ride?"

"I told a moment ago you do not need to come with me to the grave. We could always meet at the station."

"No," he huffed. "I'll go."

Vi made her face and tone as gentle as she could. "Actually. I think I'd rather be alone, Peter."

His spirit flesh swirled and darkened as he glared. "Fine. You want me to leave you alone? I'm gone. I'll just go wait for you at the bus stop, shall I?"

"Yes," she replied quietly. "Thank you."

"You think you'll be able to find the place?" the ghost snarled. "I know how hard it is for you to find your way sometimes."

"Peter—"

"Forget it."

She didn't have to watch him go with her eyes, the blaze of azure ebbed away from her as she traipsed the rest of the way to through cemetery. The area was quiet except for the crunch of her feet along the gravel walkway. The birds had already left for the winter, but now that the unseasonable heat of day finally ebbed, squirrels came out to gather the seeds and stalks of the wizened flowers left by mourners. The setting sun cast deep shadows as it sank behind the city. Where the darkness couldn't reach, the rows of flat gray headstones were painted with cheerful splashes of orange and gold.

As she made slow progress, her hand snaked behind her back and in between the folds of fabric to check on her contingency plan as she walked. The knot held; the emergency pouch remained secure. She squeezed the edges and felt the outlines of everything a lady on the run might need. A box of matches rattled against the coins and shiny baubles she could always sell in a pinch. And the first to go would be Bella Harrison's emeralds.

Vi felt the spirit's malevolence long before she perceived her shape. The same sharp blaze of anger, the intense, unwavering regard from a short distance away; they reeked of the would-be attacker from the memory. Vi continued looking from stone to stone without breaking stride, swallowing a flare of anticipation and picturing her hot spring. A neat row of identical graves stretched out before her, but the widow knew exactly where to stop. Her index finger trailed along the incised letters that spelled her true husband's name as she allowed a single tear to accumulate on her lashes. The blossoms in other hand felt woefully, comically inadequate. She almost threw them to the ground before kneeling and placing them gently before the stone.

The cerulean blaze crept up behind her, and Vi schooled her features before saying, "Hasn't anyone ever told you it is rude not to announce yourself?"

"My apologies Mrs. Sinclair," the ghost cooed, stopping a few yards away. "I see you've decided to wrap yourself like a gift. That was very generous of you."

Vi brushed her hands free of a spare flower petal. "Actually. I brought you out here on purpose."

The assassin snorted. "Oh really? And why is that?"

"I wanted to get you out of my house, for one thing. The people there, they have nothing to do with whatever this is about. Hurting them won't help anything. I'm not going back, so you don't have to either."

"You're probably right," the ghost replied, her expression darkening. "But that's not really up to you, is it?"

"Who *are* you? I don't know you, do I?"

"My name is Mary, but that doesn't really matter, does it? What's important is that I know someone who is exceptionally interested in you." The misty form grew more solid as she took a step forward. "More specifically, he's exceptionally interested in what happens when you are not breathing anymore. He worried I would not be worthy of the task, but here we are."

"But there must be a reason." Vi added a convincing quaver and slouched against her cane for effect. "What did I do?"

"Nothing, really," Mary admitted. "You're in the way. We've got big plans, and they involve putting your inheritance to good use. The son is ours; we just need the widow out of the way. We couldn't do that without finding you. And if it happens before you reach New Orleans, it's all a bit... cleaner. Don't you think?"

"So, this *is* all connected?" Vi snapped her fingers. "Damn, I'll have to tell Peter he was right."

"You won't get the chance." Mary's mouth contorted into a grim impression of a smile. "I admit, I am rather surprised there was enough left of him to make a ghost after I rifled through him. I left things in rather worse shape than I found, I'm afraid."

A wash of red blurred Vi's vision. She breathed it out and managed to keep her voice nonchalant. "You've been up to all sorts of tricks I never knew about. How does that work, if I may ask?"

The ghost sighed. "I suppose I could explain it—you'll be dead in a few moments, so you might even get a chance to try it yourself. But that would be far more tedious than choking the life from you."

"You have not managed to kill me yet," Vi retorted. "You sound awfully sure of yourself for someone who has been failing at her task since Sacramento. I think your master may be right."

Mary's tone stayed level, but she narrowed her eyes until they were thin blue lines. "I didn't know who I was looking for at first. I'd never seen even a picture of you, so that slowed me down. I admit, when I heard that woman on the train call herself Bella, I thought it was short for Annabelle. But when I went through her things, I could tell she wasn't the one I wanted. We knew you were coming, and I spotted your friend, so you had to be on that train. I simply bided my time until I could search all the rooms and figure it out. When you were in the parlor car, I went through your things and recognized the pin we took off your friend. I knew if I took it, I merely had to wait and it would lead me right to you."

"Another good trick."

"You don't know the half of it. I can even ferret out the living for some time after I've had a taste." Mary's mouth twisted with disdain. "It shouldn't have come to that, but your friend also made it nearly impossible for me to act against you. I could tell there was a medium on the train, but I got lucky; I didn't know it was you until after we'd arrived in Chicago. But staying out of *his* path kept me out of your path, too. For a time." An ugly slash of a grin parted her rapidly darkening face. "But he's not here to help you now, is he?"

The ghost took another step forward. Vi fluttered her fingers to her collarbone and painted on an expression of terror, made all the more convincing by the voice in her head telling her to run.

Mary's face contorted with amusement. "What, you thought if you kept me talking, I'd forget that I'm here to kill you?"

"No. But, I thought you might tell me something useful." Vi couldn't resist any longer, and her mouth curled at the edge. "And if I could kept you talking, my partner would be able to sneak up behind you."

Mary gaped as Peter's arms closed around her. She jolted and kicked in a vain attempt to get free. Clouds gathered beneath the surface of her spirit-flesh, and her eyes burned with rage, but Peter's grip held firm.

"But you left," she snarled. "I saw you. How—"

"A show for your benefit, my dear," Peter replied and turned to face his partner. "I don't know how long I can hold her, but I'll do what I can."

"This should help." Vi stepped around and rested her hand on Peter's shoulder. She gave him a push of energy to reinforce his defenses. The angry ghost took advantage of the distraction and lurched one arm free. With a roar, she slashed at Vi's face, but Peter held her tight.

To Vi's surprise, a stinging gash opened in the wake of Mary's hand. When she touched her cheek, there wasn't any blood, but there did seem to be *something* clinging to her hand when she brought it away. The residue she pinched between her fingertips had a subtle, cerulean glow.

As Vi opened her mouth to question the assassin, Mary licked her fingers. A sinister grin spread over her face, and she relaxed back into Peter's grip. "Go ahead and run," she jeered. "I dare you."

"I think it's time to go get yourself good and lost," Peter said. "Don't you?"

Even though the fight had been staged, Vi's guilty conscience pulled at her. "When this is over, I *will* be waiting for you. I promise."

"I know." Her partner grinned, but it was wiped off his face by another powerful jolt from the aspiring murderess in his arms. "Now get out of here!"

CHAPTER 45

Vi took off across the field of headstones as fast as her three-legged gait allowed. Her path led her back to the archway, and she passed through the gate before daring to slow down. She leaned her back against the white blocks of stone, panting. The sun had finally disappeared, but gas lamps brightened the darkness with their haloes of gold. A few pedestrians strolled along the block, eyes carefully averted to allay themselves of the responsibility of helping the distressed stranger.

With a world-weary sigh, she heaved herself away from the wall and made her way toward a busier street. Sweat beaded on her face and she fought to get her stuttering breath under control. Peter had cut it pretty damn close, but she'd gotten about as much information as she was likely to get from Mary. Now, all she had to do was outrun a homicidal spirit. Simple.

She reached North Avenue and found a wide street bursting with anticipation for the night to come. The hot day had given way to a warm evening, and couples walked arm and arm down the sidewalks. A boy not much older than George stood across the street, shouting out the headlines and peddling the evening newspapers. There should be safety in numbers, but Vi suspected Mary would be too angry for subtlety at this point, and panic nipped at her heals as she slipped into the throng.

A hansom cab disgorged itself of its passengers at the corner before her, and Vi rushed over to claim it with a smack of her cane. "Excuse me, sir."

The driver sniffed. "Where to?"

"South," she replied cheerily, resisting the urge to look over her shoulder. "Just feeling like a drive across the river."

"If you go too far, it gets to stink of pigs and suchlike that way, ma'am."

The man took off his flat cap and wiped a brow wrinkled with concern. He jerked his thumb in the direction Vi had just come from. "You sure you don' wan' me justa take you to the park? Or the lake?"

She smirked and tucked the cane beneath her elbow. "Yes, I'm quite sure. And if you're quick about getting me South, there's even a nice tip in it for you."

"Yes, ma'am."

Vi pulled herself into the cab, and off they went. Her ribs protested every bump as they jolted into traffic, and her sore ankle pulsed in protest, but at least she wasn't on foot anymore. First, she needed some distance, then she could work on getting lost among the neighborhoods and packing plants of the south side.

Though her breathing relaxed, caustic tendrils of paranoia began to inch across her skin. Then, the sense of calamity coalesced into a single point. Though she groped for the flicker of other spirits, Mary and her rage burned so brightly, it became the only aura she could feel. Her mind touched on Peter for a moment, but she assured herself her fear was nonsense. There couldn't be any real risk to him; the worst had already come to pass. But the would-be assassin had already displayed several unexpected skills; who knew what kind of damage she was capable of doing to the dead?

Vi shuddered and praised her own foresight in telling Prudence to put up the wards as soon as she'd left the house. Here's to hoping her ancestors knew what they were talking about. The diary would be waiting for her if all her little cogs performed their functions, but she hadn't been able to resist tearing out one page and adding it to her emergency pouch when Prudence was out of the room. It couldn't be considered an "ace" in the strictest sense because she had little faith that anything in the spirit world would be helpful. Still, better safe than sorry.

The Mary-pulse grew stronger, moving faster than Vi and her cab as it clopped across the bridge. The ghostly assassin's claim that she could home in on her quarry was proving itself painfully true. Never much of a hunter herself, she knew very little about how tracking something worked. But from the what she knew of dogs, there would be ways to lay a false trail along the way.

Vi thumped on the ceiling to signal him to stop. She burst out of the carriage before he could open the door for her and immediately pressed double the cost of the fare into his palm. The weight of the coins, and her ability to project confidence she didn't really feel, persuaded him to go to Illinois Central and away from her. Hopefully, some residue of Vi would cling to the carriage and draw Mary in the wrong direction. The cabbie was obviously curious about her strange behavior, but simply tipped his cap and bid her a cheerful good evening as she slipped into the gathering dark.

As the driver had promised, the stench of pig dung rolled through the streets and mingled with the scent of coal smoke and tannins from the industrial part of town. The wind had decided to play a cruel joke on the populace. Rather than bringing in a much-needed cool air from over the lake into the city, it blew the foul stench right at its heart.

Vi turned west to where the river curved around the neighborhood, weaving her way through the streets until she came to one of the tunnels that burrowed beneath the busy waterway. A trio of dirty, ragged men perched near the mouth, hands outstretched when they weren't coughing into them. Chicago may be booming, but it appeared not everyone was booming along with it.

Just as she'd allowed herself to hope she'd gotten away, Mary's familiar, menacing presence throbbed at her, spreading the icy burn of warning across her shoulders. The tunnel opened wide as the mouth of Jonah's whale, with a throat just as deep and foreboding.

Vi took three more breaths to make a decision, then plunged ahead into the belly of the beast. The answer was forward, no matter what her fear said about what lay ahead.

The clack of shod horses and rumble of cartwheels bounced off the masonry walls. One narrow lane was reserved for pedestrians, and she hugged the wall as she made her way down the corridor. The reassuring glow of lamps beckoned from the other end of the tunnel and promised an exit a few hundred feet ahead.

The angry beacon flashed, and she veered left out of the passageway. The area had become a warren of alleys, fences, and industrial buildings during her absence; she was utterly lost. For a moment, Vi considered staying near the thoroughfare and finding shelter among people. But there wouldn't be anything they could do for her, and chances were good she'd get them hurt even if they believed in her invisible pursuer.

Instead, she limped along, searching the wooden fences until she found a loose board. With an apology to the poor horse on the head of her cane, she used the handle to pry at the board until she'd made a gap. Her beleaguered dress caught and tore in several places as she squeezed through, and she added its destruction to the list of sins piling up at Mary's ephemeral feet. Vi reached into her wilted bustle and, despite her rude treatment, found the emergency bag in its place.

The boards creaked as she leaned against the interior of the fence and took a moment to calm her ragged breathing. Even with her panic in check, dragging herself all over the city was taking its toll on more than just her wardrobe. This pace would be impossible to maintain.

If she couldn't beat the ghost by speed, or by stealth, the time had come to try something else. Her fingers fumbled in the bag for the piece of charcoal she'd brought along in case she needed to draw. She couldn't fight the ghost physically, and for the snare she needed time or distance to get ready. With her body in need of a respite, she only had her wits to gamble on.

An angle became clear in her mind. Her heart gave a flutter when her brain shared the plan with the rest of her body, but she gripped her charcoal stub and settled against the fence to wait the handful of seconds. The presence drew nearer from the direction of the street, slowing as Mary realized her quarry no longer fled.

"Caught my scent, I see," Vi called over her shoulder. "My, we are a good little hound, aren't we?"

"Scent? Ha!" The scoff came from her back, the assassin's aura blazing brighter. "I exist beyond petty, earthly things like your five senses." Something rapped on the wood next to the grifter's ear and she winced, but remained with her back against the board. The angry presence was like a hot, predatory breath against the nape of her neck. Mary remained on her side of the fence. "Not that I can't employ them if and when I choose," she hissed.

Vi swallowed around the dry lump in her throat. "You know how to do a lot more than that."

"And so could you, medium, but it's become clear after watching you a few days that despite your advanced years—"

"Well, that was uncalled for."

"—you really are as stupid and naïve as a school girl."

A pair of icy, evanescent fingers passed through the wood and walked their way from Vi's shoulder to her neck. As they slithered around her throat, the grifter replied, "What about that teacher of yours? You must have one. They taking on any new pupils?"

The advancing cold halted, hovering over her larynx. Vi would give anything to wet her arid throat, but she didn't dare move even to swallow.

"Are you saying you want to join us?" The ghost's voice held a hint of bemused interest—a good sign. "The way you were talking about protecting people, getting revenge on the bad people, I'd mistaken you for some kind of hero."

Before Vi could form her reply, the misty hand disappeared, then was replaced a moment later by an arctic chill as Mary passed her entire body through the fence. The blast drew both energy and a gasp, but Vi had her features under control when the ghost re-formed before her.

"All I'm saying that I am obviously out-matched here," Vi said slyly. "And I am thinking about my options. How'd you get mixed up in all this?"

"Murder isn't new for me. At least, not when I had a body. You'd be my first kill since I was hanged for my crimes. My teachers recognized my potential even in life, and they've been training me ever since. Now? I'm deadlier than they ever could have hoped for. Once I'm finished with you, they'll all see that."

"On the other hand, you could bring me in on it all. Think about it, converting a potential enemy to your side could win you a lot of respect with your teachers." Or at minimum, buy Vi some time to formulate a better plan.

In life, the spirit's tousled hair would have bobbed as she laughed, but in death, the curls remained frozen. "My master could certainly find a use or two for someone like you, but I doubt you'd like what he chose," she mocked.

"You'd be surprised the sorts of things I've had my hand in. Illegal jobs don't bother me at all."

"You mistake my meaning. I don't mean you'd have moral qualms. I mean that you'd wished I'd killed you." Mary bore her teeth in cruel imitation of a smile. "Just like I did your friend."

Vi squeezed the head of her cane, nostrils flaring. Through the mist of Mary's body, she could make out a single light in the factory on the other side of the yard. But she'd already gambled on her ability to bargain, and the prospect of getting there didn't seem good.

The ghost continued. "Well, not exactly the same as your friend; I won't get to take my time with you."

Even though Vi knew it would be a futile gesture, her anger sent the shaft of her cane slipping through her loosened fingers. The horsehead grip of the cane streaked through the gathering night like a stone fist. But rather than pass through the ghost ineffectually as it should have, it punched a hole through Mary's chest. All the giddiness drained from the assassin's face as she looked at the sudden gap in her spirit flesh.

Her astonishment mirrored Vi's own feelings, though the grifter didn't bother arguing with the results. She dropped her stub of coal to grip the cane two-handed and slashed an 'x' through the ghost's body, the sections drifting to the ground and puddling like a wet fog. Prudence's professorial voice tried to crowd in with commentary on the materials that inhibit spirit energies, but the 'why' of it would have to wait for another time.

"You know more than I thought." Mary's voice echoed from all around her, thin but full of fury. "Which means you must also know this won't keep me for long."

If Vi took the time to squeeze back through the fence, she'd lose her advantage. With a curl of her lips, she tracked through the center of the mist toward the faint glow of the factory. Eddies swirled in her wake as she swung the cane's head through the Mary puddle one more time for good measure.

The disembodied snarl brought her up short for a moment, but she pressed on toward the dormant factory as it growled. "I underestimated you, Annabelle. So, run while you can, because it won't happen again."

CHAPTER 46

The owners of the factory relied on the high fence to keep out the rabble, so Vi had no trouble finding a door to slip through. Somewhere above the factory floor, a light burned, but most of the room was shrouded in shadow. She fumbled in her emergency bag for a match and struck it against a rough, rust-colored belt leading from one machine wheel to another.

As the flame flared to life, her eyes roamed over everything the meager light could illuminate. Various iron tools lay strewn across work tables. Gray machinery sat at waist height, glinting dully from their rows all across the large room. She followed the path of the belts where they were suspended from contraption to contraption, tying the entire system to a bulky control box on the second floor.

A walkway and its bright, white railing circumnavigated the entire space, broken only by a glass-fronted room behind the belt controls. With her charcoal gone, she would need something else to draw the snare. There was a good chance that room would be the office of the foreman, which could mean a desk full of writing supplies.

A narrow stair to her right led to the second floor, and she trod as quietly as the metal steps would allow. Panic fluttered at her neck and shoulders, urging her to move quickly. Behind her, she could feel the assassin regaining control of her spirit flesh, her attention fixed on the factory.

Vi limped her way to the office door, but the knob wouldn't turn. To her misfortune, someone didn't trust his employees. She gawked at her cane, considering its application as a crowbar once more when an unearthly wind rattled the doors on the first floor. The ghost wouldn't be long now, and Vi was both no closer to her goal and farther from the egress. She couldn't afford to give away her position by breaking the glass. Her eyes flicked around her for a distraction. They fell on the controls for the belt system, and she threw the switch at the same time Mary's angry aura marched through the door without bothering to open it.

The corrosive trickle at her back warned Vi that danger drew nearer, the assassin's energy snuffling around for traces of her own. Vi instinctually pulled back from the threat, a leaden weight forming in her gut as she tried to push the energy into the dark space she always kept reserved for it. It struggled and wriggled against her with a howl only she could hear, but she wrestled it into the blackness.

The whir of the belt system covered any possible sound, and with her abilities repressed, Mary's azure aura disappeared. Now neither could detect the other, or at least, that was what Vi hoped. Her limbs twitched with unspent adrenaline, urging her to take action. Instead, she pressed her back against a wall cloaked in shadows.

A mirthless snort, and the assassin's voice rose up sickeningly sweet with condescension. "You're going to hide from me here in the dark and the noise, is that it? I see you haven't been listening to anything I've said." She cackled, then a hissing whisper tickled Vi's brain, coming from everywhere and nowhere at the same time. "I don't need my eyes to see you any more than you need your ears to hear me. I will find you."

The machines continued their whiny rumble, but a tense stillness descended between predator and prey. The energy inside of Vi clawed away at her resolve, begging to let it pinpoint the source of the danger, but she swallowed it down. It could be a bluff. The ghost had to have limits.

Mary's voice eventually continued conversationally. "I meant what I said before. If you don't come out and face me, soon, I'll be forced to pay a visit to your home again. I don't really believe you'd be stupid enough to go back there. But I would be remiss in my duty if I didn't return to at least... ask around."

Though Vi couldn't detect the ghost distinctly, the air grew colder, signaling she'd started to cross the factory floor. The movement was slow, probing. Mary still didn't know. Vi pressed her cheek against the wall, reveling in the distraction of the soft drag of her flesh against the brickwork.

"The old woman, a relation of yours by what I observed. Never seems to leave that house," Mary said, her voice thick with mock concern. "Which is dangerous, considering how easily those big, old houses burn."

Even as Vi pictured the manor in flames, the air grew a few degrees colder. The assassin gathered the stray energy in the room, seeking whatever quality she knew belonged to her target. The crackling ball in Vi's gut grew denser and larger as she pushed away the image of the house engulfed in fire.

"That sweet young lady, she's there, too." The ghost taunted. "Not to mention that little boy who follows you like a lost puppy. You led me right to them, you know. And now, they're the ones who are going to suffer."

Her anger flared at the taunt, and Vi desperately tried to pull it back in again. The weight became a molten churning of power fed by her rage.

"Don't you want to know what I did to your precious Peter? You'd have thought he already suffered enough at my hands, but you put him in my way again."

Vi barely contained a gasp at the blistering pain that sliced through her. Though she needed to hide, there was no going back to the way things had been. The energy had grown too large to bury, and now it spilled over the edges and burned everywhere it touched.

Satisfied laughter bubbled up from below her as Mary picked up the trail alight with agony and guilt.

Through the tumult, an impulse told Vi to push away from the solidity of the wall to lean onto her good foot unaided, and she timidly raised her injured leg. The pool materialized behind her eyelids, crickets chirping merrily in the prairie twilight. She focused her nervous energy first on keeping herself balanced, then breathed into the roiling mass of rage in her gut. Under her attention, it spread out and dissipated. Her awareness expanded with each exhalation, tendrils probing the aether in every direction.

Mary blazed nearly white-hot in her rage, slinking across the factory floor directly below. When the tide of Vi's power reached her, the ghost stumbled for a moment. She stared around wildly for the source. The ghost stopped, struggling to find her quarry's trail—now a needle in a sea of needles. With a shriek, she plunged through another doorway to the next part of the factory, a wild, desperate dash.

Vi started back across the walkway to leave the way she'd come in. Her steps felt buoyant, as if gravity didn't pull her quite as much as it used to.

Relief fed into the strange energies, and before she knew it, the pulse continued outward. Somewhere along the edges, the reluctant medium could feel the faint comings and goings of the living on the street, and farther on, the tiny blue flames of the dead stretching out for miles. The spirits on the leading edge of the tide became aware of her as she touched them, the weight of their regard small but distinct tugs at her like cheap thread snagging on cotton. It certainly wasn't what she would describe as 'pleasant,' but the distant attention of strangers felt a lot better than the immediate sting of the assassin.

She reached the first floor, the door a few paces away. At the other end of the hall, Vi could hear gusts of aetheric wind accompanied by dull clanks and thuds as the ghost tore apart the next room. The con woman slipped back outside and rushed across the gravel lot to the fence.

Mary's shrill voice bounced around her as the ghost extended herself with a message in all directions. "Even if you don't care about your friends, Annabelle, *you'll* have to sleep sometime. When you do, I will find you. And I've changed my mind. I will definitely be taking my time with you when I do."

CHAPTER 47

The aspiring murderess may have changed her mind, but for the grifter, nothing was different; she still needed to set the trap, and she needed to do it fast.

Vi snaked her way through a tiny alley between the railroad tenements and homes turned smudge gray by the coal smoke shouldering in from the manufacturing hubs. The families of factory and railroad workers had settled in for the evening, their cheerful tableaus framed in the windows.

Through the enveloping calm, an angry throbbing from something claiming to be her ankle took the opportunity to nag about its poor treatment. It felt indistinct, separate from her in the trance, but she stopped for a moment to heed its request.

The smell of wood smoke and cows emanated from this neighborhood to combat the pigs, and no one ended up the winner. There had to be barns somewhere nearby, which could give her some cover. No doubt Mary would discover her prey had left the building before long. If she could keep the ghost away from the unwitting families, she would, but at some point, she'd have to attract the assassin right to her to enact the trap. With any luck, she could find some paint or grease to draw her ancestor's design in one of those barns, and would be able to hold the ghost long enough to truly escape.

When she spotted a wide, low building with gently glowing windows, she headed straight for it. The door stood slightly ajar, and she widened the gap with her cane to peek inside. Three men lay on their bellies, ringed around a space they'd cleared in the hay. Two oil lamps burned low, throwing its golden light onto the craps game. The man holding the dice tossed them into the middle, and the other two let out muffled groans when they totaled seven.

Their hushed tones pointed to a game on the quiet, and she would need a light to draw by. Vi burst through the door to startle them on their way, shouting, "I told you to stay out of my barn!"

The man closest to the door knocked over one of the lamps. The tide of oil extinguished the flame, throwing her face into shadow. The men got to their feet, scrambling to the opposite door between muttered apologies to someone named O'Leary. One of them grabbed at the second lamp, still burning merrily, but Vi dusted off an Irish brogue, snapping at him to leave it and go. The excitement drew a glance from the splotched cow chewing cud in its stall, but it soon returned to its private, bovine thoughts.

As the men tracked their way through the spilled oil, they left behind glistening boot treads anywhere hay didn't cover the wooden floor. Once the opposite door swung closed, Vi stared at the spreading, golden puddle and realized she'd found something just as good as paint. Her fingers went for the pouch at her back, and she pulled out the folded piece of the precious notebook. The emergency kit dropped to the floor, and she kicked it aside rather than have an argument with her bruised ribs by attempting to bend to retrieve it.

The writing at the bottom of the diagram claimed it would hold a spirit for as long as a day, but the trap had to be large to manage it. She didn't really understand anything about the magic, or science, or combination promised by the symbol. If only she hadn't wasted so much of her time with Prudence. She'd just have to gamble on whether she'd executed it correctly.

A rack of modest farm implements stood nearby, ready to be pressed into service as an oversized pen, but her cane hadn't failed her yet that evening. She studied the round design with its geometric intrusions closely for a few more moments, then set it down beside the pool of lamplight for reference. The tip of her cane dipped into the lamp oil, and she started to draw inside the circle left by the dice game, widening the cleared area with her feet as she went.

The streaks and smears of oil barely stood out against the dark grain of the floor. Vi squinted at the marks she made, her energy drawing back to aid her concentration as she shed the stillness of the pool. As lovely as it would be to stay drifting in the calm, she'd need her wits to save her, and puddles weren't known for their brains. The tide of power pulled away from the tiny pinpricks and flames of other souls, but as it gathered once more within her, it did not storm and boil as before. It slipped over Mary, and Vi felt the assassin turn and follow the receding edge in her direction.

When she finished her drawing, she swished her hem against the hay to obscure the distinct edges of the sigil and stepped back. The blaze of rage outside picked up speed as it honed in on its quarry. Vi put the design between herself and the ghost; now all Mary had to do was step inside. It sounded simple enough, but that didn't stop the reluctant medium's viscera from crawling themselves into knots as she waited.

Just before the blue flame reached the barn, the assassin slowed. When she passed through the wall, lightning crackled across the roiling clouds of her body and added their light to the flicker of lamplight. The ghost bared her teeth, glowing blue eyes wide but empty like a shark's.

"You stopped running," Mary said, both a question and a statement at the same time.

A puff of steam escaped Vi's lips, the temperature dropping with every step of the hunter. "Yes," she replied. "I thought about what you said."

"Which part?" The flashes of electricity across the ghost deepened to an orange shimmer as she took a step forward. A couple of paces, and she'd be inside of the trap.

"I will have to rest sometime. It's inevitable; I see that now."

Mary stopped, eying her suspiciously. "You expect me to believe you are surrendering?"

"I know you are better than me. So, I'll go quietly. If you leave the others out of it."

"That simple, huh?"

Vi swallowed. "...and tell me what you did to Peter."

The assassin grinned and stepped closer. Vi took a compulsive stride back, and the cow mooed her misgivings about the proximity. With a sweep of the ghost's hand, she tore the horsehead cane away without touching it. It spiraled toward the far door, and the medium winced as it clattered to the floor.

"Not feeling so brave after all. Did you think death would be easy?" Mary snickered.

"And my people?" Vi struggled not to look at the ghost's feet and give up the game.

The angry spirit rolled her eyes, the fissures in her steely body deepening to a fluid boil. "Yes, yes. I'll leave the city once I finish with you. Gladly, in fact."

"And Peter? What did you do to him?"

"Nothing," she snorted smugly, pacing forward to what had to be the middle of the trap. "The dead can't harm each other. Everyone knows that."

"You lied to me." Vi allowed her gaze to flick to the floor. Her mouth curled into a knowing smirk as she confirmed the assassin's feet passed right through the center of the mark.

"This amuses you?" Mary's cloudy toes reached the outer edge of the trap. Any moment, she'd hit the barrier.

"I wouldn't say that," the medium replied. "Though I can't say I am surprised. We have a lot in common, you and I."

The churning magma of Mary's body glowed with a fierce, crimson light and she stepped again. She passed out of the circle, claw extended only a few feet from Vi's throat. The con woman lurched back in surprise, her sore ribs hitting a crossbeam. The snare didn't work.

Before she could fall, the predator advanced and wrapped her far too solid fingers around her prey's throat, lifting her onto her toes.

Vi scrabbled at her throat, but nothing her corporeal fingers could do would affect the pressure being exerted from beyond the veil. The skin of her neck began to blister under the cold heat of Mary's touch.

"We're about to have one more thing in common, Annabelle," the murderess growled, voice thicker and deeper than it had ever been in life. She tossed Vi to the ground like a rag doll and crossed to the rack of tools. "You're about to die."

Vi sucked in a lungful of air and glared accusingly at the sigil, trying to figure out what she could have done wrong. She'd followed the picture, drawn all the lines. But in the darkness, had all of the lines connected?

Mary selected her weapon of choice, a wicked, rusty pitchfork. As she slid it away from a shovel, the metal threw a spark. It momentarily brightened the dark corner, and gave the con woman a last, desperate idea. She got to her knees, frantically searching for the pouch she'd so carelessly thrown aside.

"By all means, pray," the ghost snarled, misinterpreting her penitent pose.

When Vi brushed away the hay to expose the emergency kit, she ripped open the pouch and pulled out the box of matches. The first stick she tried flared and died immediately.

The assassin narrowed her eyes. "Stop that. Whatever you're doing, it's over. Can't you see that?" She shrieked and advanced, weapon raised.

The second matchstick blazed to life, but a pang of danger told Vi to flatten herself to the ground. The pitchfork soared through where her torso would have been and stuck into the floor behind her. Mary bellowed and stepped into the clearing. Vi tossed the match into the circle of oil and debris, which blazed immediately to an alien, chartreuse ring of fire. It danced and rippled higher as the fire bridged the gaps in the design to create a fully working sigil. The ghost's confused screams continued, the unearthly fire hot enough to cause her pain.

With wide, desperate eyes, Mary pushed outward with her aether wind to blow out the fire. The green flames bent and burned lower, but no matter how hard she blew they would not go out. The wind gentled as her energy waned, the sigil fire leaving tongues of ordinary, yellow flames in its wake. The trails of lamp oil ignited on contact and led the flare to the puddle by the door. Vi scrambled away just in time to keep her eyebrows as it combusted, grabbing the pouch as she bolted for the door. A wall of heat pushed out as the fire spread eagerly across the strewn hay and wooden floor.

The warm evening air soothed Vi's overheated flesh as she emerged on the other side of the barn. Mary's despairing cries rose up above the roar of the conflagration. As much as Vi disliked people who tried to kill her, that sort of pain had never been her intention. Though it would do nothing to keep out the sound, she closed the barn door behind her. When she got back to the street, she finally turned to survey the damage. Fire licked the window sills, and smoke rose into the deep, velvet blue of the night. Time for those fabled Chicago firefighters to prove their mettle, no doubt. Nothing to worry about; simply time for Vi to make herself scarce.

When she turned to leave, she paused at the sight of a mailbox. The name "O'Leary" stood out in the growing firelight, and Vi felt a pang of guilt for the owners. She remembered the pouch clenched in her fist, and fished around inside until she found Bella's string of emeralds. Without hesitation, she plucked it from its resting place; the memories didn't scare her now. The gems made a satisfying clatter as she dropped them into the postbox, and she walked along the street with a spring in her step. After all, that should more than make up for the damage done to one little barn.

When she reached an intersection, she paused again. To the North, the Illinois Central station—to the South, the river, and anywhere the water touched. Her friends would be waiting for her. In theory, all that was left to her was to arrive.

She weighed the rest of the contents of the emergency kit in her hand as she pondered. The cursed necklace wasn't the only shiny bauble in that pouch. Vi had more than enough to make her way alone. She could solve Peter's murder without putting anyone else in danger. It would be safer for everyone if she did.

With a deep breath, she turned South.

CHAPTER 48

The gentle lapping of the waves against the pier should have been soothing, but every splash indicated yet another moment slipping away. The waning crescent of the moon dappled the water with its cocky grin a stone's throw from a lone steamship rocking gently in the currents of the Mississippi. It would shove off any minute, and Vi planned to be on board, but she paced along the dock like an impatient tiger. The wind blew from the South, so the stench of the fire she'd inadvertently started couldn't reach her on the pier. The sickly yellow glow painting the horizon told her it was spreading. Warning bells chimed in the distance, but she tried to assure herself they had it all under control. According to that morning's paper, they'd put out that lumberyard fire next door only a day earlier, after all. Chicago's finest would be up to the task. Wouldn't they?

Two ghostly forms approached, so Vi melted against the side of a shed to let them pass. After the earlier outburst, she could barely feel the depleted power inside her. The spirits registered as dull glows as they walked side by side and spoke with hushed, tense voices, never turning. She caught a snippet of their conversation as they passed.

"I think you are far too cavalier about all of this, old boy," one of them hissed. "You said you felt it, too."

"Of course I did," his companion replied flippantly. "*Everyone* did."

"And you are not the least bit worried by it?"

He shrugged his spectral shoulders. "Not particularly, no."

"But I've never felt anything like it!"

"You haven't been dead all that long."

"It's trouble," the first ghost warned. They were almost too far away to hear, but she caught one final comment and shuddered. "Mark my words. Power like that? It has to be trouble."

A shrill whistle rose from the boat and broke into her thoughts. Vi stepped out from the shelter of the shed and peered up and down the pier wildly. Time was running out.

Amid the creak of the planks, she heard the patter of footsteps approaching, and felt the soft ripple of a living person moving through the aether. Bonnie's unbound hair and flaring skirts flashed for a moment in a pool of light, then she disappeared into the gloom. Vi's loyal valet and an over-stuffed carpetbag appeared a moment later. The pair of ghosts turned to watched the living as they rushed past.

A few paces behind, Peter's azure form loped along. The other spirits shouted questions after him, but he merely gave them a cordial wave and continued. Vi's heart leapt into her throat and she waved to her companions. The fist of terror squeezing her heart loosened its grip; she'd decided to wait for them, and they'd decided to come.

As Bonnie got to her, Vi threw her arms open for an embrace and flashed her a relieved, crooked grin. Her friend wiped the smile off her face with a ringing slap across the cheek.

"It's nice to see you, too," the medium pouted, rubbing the sore spot.

"*That's* for not taking the time to explain your plans yourself," Bonnie trilled. "Really, Vi. Making your aunt tell me you'd gone alone on some sort of suicide mission. After everything we've been through. You don't think I would have gone with you?" She bit her quivering lip.

"That is precisely why I didn't tell you," Vi replied hotly. "I didn't want to put you at risk."

"Stop trying to protect me!"

"Fine."

"I mean it!"

"Fine!"

"Good!" Bonnie's chest heaved in anger for a moment, then she catapulted herself at Vi and wrapped her in an iron embrace. Rather than struggle, the exhausted grifter relaxed gratefully into the support.

Peter caught up and chuckled. "Now that's settled...."

"Oh!" Bonnie squeaked at the unexpected voice and pulled away. She scowled for a moment at the angry blisters on Vi's neck, but laid a finger on a clear patch of skin to remain in contact. "I guess we are all here."

"Ugh," the ghost bent closer to examine his partner's wounds. "You look terrible."

Vi grimaced. "So far, I get one insult and one slap for my trouble. Isn't anyone happy to see me?"

"I am," George said. "We ran real fast to get here."

She glanced at the boy beaming at her before her eyes bounced back to the ominous horizon. "Problems?"

"It was no day at the park," Bonnie said. "And I'm sorry if I lost you back there, Peter. With all the hullabaloo, I didn't think I'd make it."

"Not a problem, my dear," he replied, eyes dancing. "Our girl here was burning so bright earlier, I could have found her anywhere."

"What's that supposed to mean?"

"I'll tell you later," Vi grimaced. "But the fire, how bad is it? Will Pru be all right?"

Bonnie shrugged helplessly.

The whistle blasted two more times. Crewmen assembled along the mooring lines to cast off as Vi's mind worked furiously.

"Shouldn't we go?" George asked.

"Yes. I mean, no." She lowered herself to kneeling so their faces were level. "Kid, I've got a special job for you. It is of the utmost importance. I need you to go back to the house and make sure Pru safe. Can you do that?"

"But what about the boat?" He swung his anguished face between the two women. If Bonnie felt contrary, she kept it to herself. "I want to stay with you," he squawked, pulling himself out of her grip.

"I know Georgie, and in a perfect world, you'd come with me," Vi replied, smiling sadly.

"No!" He turned away so she couldn't see his angry tears, but there was no mistaking the clench of his tiny fists.

"This is more important," Vi continued gently. "She's the only family I have, and I am duty-bound to make certain she is safe. I can't do it without putting her in more danger, so I need someone I trust to look after her. I can't imagine a more trust-worthy person to ask."

"You're leaving me. Just like—"

"No," she crossed to the child and turned him to face her. "I am coming back for you. Understand? I *will* come back for you."

As he mulled this over, the dutiful valet replaced the little boy in his stance. By the time the whistle sounded the third and final time, they'd hugged their farewells, and he'd disappeared back into the night. Bonnie took up the carpet bag, and they hurried to the gangplank.

"I didn't think you'd be so worried about auntie Prune," the young widow teased.

Vi chuckled. "I'm not, not really. She's a tough old bird. No, as much as anything, this past day has shown me that this path is going to be dangerous. I can't order him into the fray. Let us depart, shall we? I have friends all along the river. Someone's bound to help us get to New Orleans."

Peter traipsed up the walkway in front of her, sighing. "You didn't learn anything from this whole experience, did you? Still heading straight for trouble."

The sound of Mary's screams shouldered into Vi's mind, catching her off guard. The power, the pain—the 'trouble' the ghost was worried about seemed an understatement. She schooled her features, then waved her companions toward the gangplank.

"I think it's safe to say I've learned a few things," she replied darkly. "That isn't what concerns me."

Bonnie regarded her apprehensive scowl as she stepped onto the ramp, asking, "What's worrying you?"

Vi smiled wanly, taking one last glance at the golden glow of the cityscape.

"Ripples."

EPILOGUE

October 9, 1871

Mary stood over the prone body of the telegraph operator. Her unexpected blow left him spluttering on the floor, so she gave his face a swift kick to stop his mewling. Usually, making such a solid connection would have made her smile, but her mind would not release her from the all-consuming truth. She had failed.

The ghost's body swirled in agitation as she approached the shiny brass telegraph key and rested a spectral finger on the knob. It would be so easy to disappear and never admit her failure. Perhaps she could simply wander around Chicago, pushing her new powers to their limits far from the watchful eye of her master. Of course, if the plan succeeded, nowhere north of the Mason-Dixon line would be safe.

The clatter of hooves outside brought her out of her daydream. A team of horses galloped along the street, the giant tank of water they towed bouncing along behind. She grimaced as the threat of fire drove any plans of fleeing from her master from her mind, taking solace in the hope that she could trade the new information about Annabelle for forgiveness.

Mary's hand touched the knob, and she poured herself into the mechanism, sliding through the key and into the wires. The ghost pictured her destination in her mind, and in a flash, she poured out of the wire on the other side, nearly one thousand miles away.

"The prodigal daughter returns!" cried a man's voice.

"Yes, I've come home, Master." Mary moved away from the private telegraph line on the side table and approached the desk. Unlike the last time she'd been in this room, they were not alone. A figure draped in a dark cloak stood near the fireplace, gazing into the flames. Mary dipped her head in respect and recognition, and turned back to her teacher.

"I admit, I'm surprised to see you, Mary," he said, his voice tinged with amusement. "Few with the courage to defy me would dare return. I hope you are at least bringing me good news about the Annabelle situation?"

The ghost threw herself to the floor at his feet, unable to meet his eye. "Please, forgive me. I've failed you."

"I see you were right about her," the person at the mantle said, voice chilling and devoid of feeling. "She wasn't ready."

"That's not it!" Mary scrambled to her feet and remembered her place, adding, "Masters."

"So what, pray tell, stood between you and one defenseless woman?"

"She has the sight. You never told me—"

"You think you deserve to know all?" The hushed words from fireplace brought the ghost up short. It never turned its face from the flames, but the figure pulsed with power.

"No. Of course not. Forgive me!" Mary entreated, throwing herself once more to the ornate Persian rug.

"Get up!" her master barked from his place at the desk. He scowled at her thoughtfully, stroking his chin. "I admit, we didn't know that Annabelle has the sight. This is an interesting development."

"And a protector," the ghost said. Mary pounded one ephemeral fist into her other hand. "That low-life we used to flush her out is with her now."

"Surely that wastrel couldn't have been a match for you. He's just died, for heaven's sake."

"I don't know how, but he's already become quite advanced. Still, I got past him without too much trouble," she assured them, her expression darkening. "But the medium? She knew our ways too well. She used a trap of some kind, there was no way I could follow through the flame and smoke."

"Not smoke from *this* fire?" He asked, holding up a newspaper. "This fire that is *still* burning its way across the city?" Though she remained silent, angry gray tendrils swirled across Mary's limbs, confirming his assessment. "My, my. She is a formidable opponent, indeed."

"She's still only one woman," Mary declared with disdain. "She won't elude me again."

He chuckled and threw down the paper. "I wouldn't be too sure. If she really knows what happened to her partner and she still decided to answer our invitation, we are dealing with a very different animal."

The figure at the fireplace murmured. "A very different animal, indeed."

"An animal you'd still like me to put down?" the ghost asked eagerly.

"You've had your chance," the man behind the desk spat. He stroked his chin and smiled. "Besides, not all animals are meant for the slaughter. Some of them can be put to work."

"Master?" the ghost asked.

"Yes," he drew out the syllable as he gathered his resolve. "I believe the best way to break this wild animal's spirit is to put her in a cage."

"I could go back out and find her for you. I'll go back to Chicago and—"

He silenced her with a flip of his hand. "I don't see why that would be necessary. There's no reason to think she isn't headed straight for us as we speak."

"I'll do better this time, I promise. I won't fail you again," the ghost groveled.

The figure at the fireplace finally turned its head, the dancing flames casting flickering shadows across its face and leaving the eyes deep, dark hollows. "No. You won't."

About the Author

Phoebe Darqueling has hung her hat in many places as she and her archaeologist husband have chased their dreams around the world. When she isn't sharing tips for writers on OurWriteSide.com or editing SteampunkJournal.org, she writes curriculum for a creativity competition for kids in Minnesota. You can find more of her writing in the novels *Riftmaker* and *Army of Brass*, and her short stories in *Chasing Magic* and *Queen of Clocks and Other Steampunk Tales*.